THE CORNISH
NUMBER S

The West Wind

CROSBIE GARSTIN

ANTHONY
MOTT
LTD

L O N D O N

Published by Anthony Mott Limited 1983
50 Stile Hall Gardens, London W4 3BU

First published 1926

ISBN 0 907746 18 7

Printed in Great Britain by
Richard Clay (The Chaucer Press) Ltd

The life of Crosbie Alfred Norman Garstin reads like that of Jack London, or one of the characters in his own or John Buchan's novels. He was born on 7 May, 1887, the son of Norman Garstin, who was one of the leading figures in the Newlyn School of painters. The third volume in the *Penhales* trilogy, *The West Wind*, is dedicated 'To Norman Garstin, dearest of fathers, wittiest of companions, best of friends. Died June 22, 1926'.

Crosbie was educated at Brandon House School, Cheltenham, Elstow School in Bedford, and in Germany. He went to the United States and Canada, where he worked successively as a horse breaker on western ranches, in threshing gangs, as a sawyer in the Columbia and North Thompson lumber camps in British Columbia, and as a miner on the Pacific coast. He then travelled to Africa, where he became manager of a cattle ranch and ranger to the Tati Concessions in Matabeleland.

On the outbreak of war in 1914 Garstin returned to Britain and enlisted as a Trooper in the 1st King Edward's Horse. He was commissioned in the field in 1915, served briefly as an Intelligence Officer in Ireland, following the Easter Rising of 1916, and returned to the Western Front in the same year. While at the Front he wrote the popular *Mudlarks* series, and other articles, for *Punch*. Following the Armistice he became horse-master to the XIth Corps and was demobilised in 1919.

His publications include a book of poems, *Vagabond Verses*, *The Sunshine Settlers*, *The Black Knight* (with Mrs Alfred Sidgwick), two volumes of *The Mudlarks*, *The Ballad of the Royal Ann*, *The Coasts of Romance*, and *The Dragon and the Lotus*. *The Owls' House*, the first volume in his masterly trilogy, *The Penhales*, was published in 1923. This was followed by *High Noon* (1925) and *The West Wind* (1926).

Crosbie Garstin listed his recreations as foxhunting, rugby football, and boat-sailing. When not travelling he lived at St. Buryan in West Penwith, which is the 'St. Gwithian' of the *Penhale* novels. He was accidentally drowned in Cornwall, on 20 April, 1930, at the tragically early age of 42.

THE CORNISH LIBRARY

'Well-chosen works from a literary heritage which is as rich as clotted cream.'
The Times

The aim of *The Cornish Library* is to present, in attractive paperback editions, some of the best and most lasting books on Cornwall and the Cornish, both fiction and non-fiction.

Titles in print, or shortly to be published:

Up From the Lizard	*J. C. Trewin*
A Cornish Childhood	*A. L. Rowse*
Freedom of the Parish	*Geoffrey Grigson*
School House in the Wind	*Anne Treneer*
Rambles Beyond Railways	*Wilkie Collins*
A Pair of Blue Eyes	*Thomas Hardy*
The Owls' House	*Crosbie Garstin*
Twenty Years at St. Hilary	*Bernard Walke*
Troy Town	*Arthur Quiller-Couch*
The Ship of Stars	*Arthur Quiller-Couch*
Hands to Dance and Skylark	*Charles Causley*
High Noon	*Crosbie Garstin*
A Cornishman at Oxford	*A. L. Rowse*
China Court	*Rumer Godden*
Wilding Graft	*Jack Clemo*
The West Wind	*Crosbie Garstin*
Love in the Sun	*Leo Walmsley*
Lugworm: Island Hopping	*Ken Duxbury*
The Splendid Spur	*Arthur Quiller-Couch*
Hawker of Morwenstow	*Piers Brendon*
The Cathedral	*Hugh Walpole*
The Stone Peninsula	*James Turner*
Cornish Years	*Anne Treneer*
The Devil and the Floral Dance	*D. M. Thomas*
Deep Down	*R. M. Ballantyne*
Corporal Sam and Other Stories	*Arthur Quiller-Couch*
The Cornish Miner	*A. K. Hamilton-Jenkin*
Happy Button	*Anne Treneer*
A Short History of Cornwall	*E. V. Thompson*

All the books in *The Cornish Library* are numbered to encourage collectors. If you would like more information, or you would care to suggest other books that you think should appear in the series, please write to me at the following address: Anthony Mott, The Cornish Library, 50 Stile Hall Gardens, London W4 3BU.

TO
NORMAN GARSTIN
DEAREST OF FATHERS, WITTIEST
OF COMPANIONS, BEST OF FRIENDS.
DIED JUNE 22, 1926.

BOOK I

CHAPTER I

I

JUNE sunlight poured into the great aviary through its glass roof; through the open wires came the scent of flowering gardens and young green leaf gently blowing. The happy captives piped, whistled, warbled full-throated greetings to the sun, crossbills from North Europe, redpoles, blue-breasts, goldfinches, black Bengalies, yellow canaries and scarlet-crested cardinals. The black-capped Java sparrows sat all in a row like beads on a string; the Paddy birds quarrelled as is their fashion; the green parrakeets made love.

The cripple in the wheeled chair threw them seed, fir-kernels, bread-crumbs—a big-built, freckled man, with a bony face worn by suffering. They swirled about him, a cyclone of painted wings, blue, yellow, vermilion; dipped in the fountain, shook the bright drops from their feathers and whirled again.

A parrakeet perched on his finger. "Kiss," he said, and it took a crumb of sugar from his lips.

A woman came to the wires—tall, high cheek-boned, freckled also, a sister evidently. "Tom," she called. "What a din those parrots make! Tom, do you hear me? I am sending Philip to Falmouth this afternoon; have you any errands?"

The cripple considered. "My compliments to Captain Angwin and I trust his leg is making progress, and—oh! have we any rum in the house?"

"Rum?"

"R-U-M—rhymes with Kingdom Come."

"Don't be profane. No, we haven't."

3

" Then tell Philip to get an anker at Blundstone's. I feel sure Captain Penhale drinks rum and gunpowder mixed. . . ."

Honor Burnadick opened the gate and entered the cage. " Tom, will you have the goodness to tell me who this Captain Penhale is and why I should provide for his thirst? "

Her brother patted her hand. " Tut-tut, didn't I tell you? I forgot ! Since Angwin's accident I have had to look for another master for the *Ghost*, and I think Penhale may serve. He is coming this evening and will stay one night at least. I do not know if he drinks rum, his tastes may be cocoa and back-gammon, like Angwin's mate—but I think not. He is a most romantic person, by all accounts."

Honor sniffed. " Angwin was a most romantic person, by your account, but when he came he did nothing but spill snuff and regale me with church-yard epitaphs. He told me he knew over a hundred by heart. Romance ! "

" I admit for a man who had taken two privateers and a score of lesser prizes in the last war Angwin was somewhat of a disappointment," said Burnadick, sighing. " But this Penhale is a different matter. Seven feet high, knots his mustachios behind his neck after the manner of the lamented Tench, is tattooed all over, eats raw meat and takes his cutlass to bed with him."

" He will not take it into any of my beds," said Honor with decision, " and if he insists on raw meat he must eat it in the yard. Seriously, Tom, who is this creature? "

Burnadick laughed. " Seriously, I know little about him, though we were at school together at Helston, and his brother was a close friend of mine, a sturdy, stolid, dog-honest lad. They are small squires in the Land's End district, but this one, Ortho, has been wandering all his life. I have heard that the mother was a gypsy girl and the father fought a footpad for her out on the road one moonlight night. Curious thing for a sober church-going farmer to do all of a sudden—eh? The yeoman strain seems to have come uppermost in the younger, Eli, the gypsy in the elder. He ran from school in the first place, after half-killing an usher, and was next heard of in Devonshire with a band of Romany horse-copers. He then seems to have got himself into trouble with the Preventive and had to fly the country. His flight took him to Barbary, where, report has it, he landed a slave and left a general. He undoubtedly fought with Rodney at the Saintes. For the last ten years he has commanded a Guinea slaver. What more could you wish for? Product of a gypsy charmer and a moonlight night."

Honor smiled indulgently. " Methinks 'tis you who supply the romance, Tom. How do you know she was charming? I have seen gypsy women a-plenty and never one but was a whining bundle of rags and filth. How do you know?"

Burnadick threw his hands wide. "Why else did old Penhale fight for her? Of course she was handsome. Her son, this fellow who is coming, was the comeliest youngster, a tall, slim, black-eyed, flashing boy. You will not be disappointed, I swear."

"He does not sound like epitaphs and snuff, certainly," said Honor. " But is this ex-smuggler-slaver the type of captain you want for the *Ghost*?"

Burnadick shrugged. " I must trust her to somebody. Roscorla has married a wife, Angwin broken a leg. Reliable men are not to be picked like blackberries. One must take some chances. Penhale is, at least, an experienced master and has seen much action."

Honor nodded. " Very well, we shall see—but be careful of the moonlight yourself, Tom. An anker of rum and some gunpowder to mix with it, Philip shall be told."

She wheeled him into the next cage and went about her business.

The second aviary was stocked with larger birds—sulphur-crested cockatoos and purple-capped lories from the Moluccas; blue and yellow macaws, green parrots and splendid red and blue macaws from Guiana; rose-tinted cockatoos from Australia, rose-ringed parrakeets from Senegal, and great green macaws from Mexico. On the ground strutted a Thibetan peacock, its bronze wings spotted with iridescent purple eyes, and a Chinese pheasant with a white cowl, spurred like a fighting-cock, its back all of yellow feathers tipped with black, giving the appearance of golden scale-armour. The cage was a riot of living colour, filled with piercing uproar. The blue and yellow macaws croaked hoarsely, the cockatoos shrilled. The Senegal parrot cried, " Damn my guts ! " Mexican and Guiana macaws screamed all together, the lory whistled a bar of " The Jolly Companion." " God bless this house ! " said the Amazon parrot.

Burnadick tossed them scraps of biscuit, and again coloured wings whirled about him, flashes of barbaric splendour, hyacinth, scarlet, orange, saffron, emerald and electric blue, plumage fit to deck the cloaks of Incas and the fans of Indian queens. They swooped on the scattered delicacies and fluttered back to their perches, squawking, bubbling, screaming, ruffling their gorgeous crests.

The old grey African perched on the left chair arm and stalked up and down it, swearing abominably. The festive parrot perched on the left and (belying its name) muttered benedictions.

" I represent mankind," said Burnadick, with a smirk. " Between heaven and hell."

He heard voices, the latch clicked and his man-servant showed a stranger into the cage.

Burnadick glanced up. Penhale—he recognised

him immediately, though last time they met it was
in the school yard at Helston, stripped for battle,
twenty odd years before. The scene flickered before
him. The ring of excited boys shouting " Burnadick !
Up, Burnadick !" Penhale wincing under their taunts,
clenching his fists nervously, trying to smile. Now
here was the same boy, twenty-five years older, but
still the same boy—and still smiling. He was dressed
in a black riding coat frogged with silver, somewhat
tarnished, and high riding boots reaching over his
knees. He wore his black-bull curls unpowdered and
tied with ribbon at the back. A tall, dark, raffish
figure, with no smack of his calling about him except
for the little gold rings that twinkled in his ears.
About him the rainbow macaws flapped and screamed.

" More buck than seaman, more highwayman than
either," thought Burnadick, and held out his hand.
"Welcome, Captain . . . it's a score of years since
we met."

Penhale laughed. " And then you flogged me."

" Pshaw ! The odds were all with me. I was
sorry for it after. 'Pon my soul I do not know what
it was about, do you ? "

" My faith I do not . . . but that is nothing. I
have fought bloodier campaigns since at the behest
of sultans, kings and governments, and I give you
my oath I do not know what they were about either."
His lively black eyes travelled round the vast aviary.
" My stars ! you have a feast of colour here, it is like
a flower-bed. You are fond of birds ? "

" I like to watch them. They have what I have
not—flight," said Burnadick. " My horse fell on me
out hunting some years ago and I shall not walk
again. As you say, it is like a flower-bed here—and
better, for these bloom the year round. They thrive
well in our mild west. I can breed golden orioles—
anything almost."

" Humming-birds ? "

" No, unfortunately."

" Those are the fairy lads," said Penhale with enthusiasm. " I've seen 'em in the West Indies, bright golden green with sapphire heads, hanging on the lips of the trumpet flowers, draining the honey. I've seen 'em dart across the glades, all mixed up with lilac butterflies. Bold too. When I was a prisoner on St. Lucia there was one came and robbed the spiders' webs by my window regular every afternoon. No bigger than the tip of my finger he was, with a ruby crest and a chestnut frill. He used to make me laugh. The giant spiders boiling with rage and the little thief darting in and out between 'em, a flying harlequin."

" You were held prisoner on St. Lucia? " Burnadick inquired.

" Twice. Once by the English, lately by the French. First time I deserted from the British fleet and hid in the woods, daren't come out. Second time I lost my ship off the island and walked into the hands of the French all unsuspecting. That isle changes hands so often you don't know how you stand from one hour to another. I was at Castries on parole until it was retaken by Admiral Jervis last year. However, I wasn't treated badly. True Republican principles had not then reached the French colonies."

" They may mend their ways. At least the ' Terror ' is over, Robespierre executed," said Burnadick.

Penhale snorted. " I hear, on good authority, that when he arrived in hell Satan offered to abdicate." He pointed through the bars of the small bird cage. " Heh ! There are some old friends of mine, those little black fellows with the paddle-shaped rudders. ' Whydah finches,' we call 'em on the Slave Coast. And those too, Azulinas, the Portuguese ' blue bird.' The French import 'em in thousands. I passed a Rochelle brig thirty leagues west of Cape Verde and she was full of birds—whydahs, azulinas, Bengalies and crimson weavers. They had 'em in cages on deck to get the air. It was stark calm and we could hear 'em singing plain. Might have been in a wood in spring-time. A queer thing to hear, rolling in open sea."

"Blast your soul!" said the grey parrot.

Penhale whipped about, grinning. "What cheer, shipmate! The same to you! He is from the Coast too—eh? I thought so—from his damned civility. We had an old parrot aboard my schooner the dead spit of him. Came from Sekondee Castle and swore like the deuce, learned it from the Governor. My mate, MacBride, said, 'Hey! this'll never do. This bird is getting old and will die soon. He'll never get into heaven and sit among the birds o' Paradise, swearing like that. Moreover, its very corruptive for the cabin boy.' So he taught him to pray—or tried to, but the bird was set in its sin. We are peddling blacks on the Spanish Main some time after, and are riding at a river mouth under Cape Grace à Dieu. There is a mission there with a Portuguese priest converting the Mosquito Indians, so we invite him aboard to tease him a bit, he being a poor simple soul. We have a prime feed and the parrot gets his share, plenty of biscuit soaked in rum, to which he is very partial. He is clinging to an arms-rack in the cabin, drunk as a prince and blaspheming away hammer and tongs. By'm-by the priest notices him. 'I do not speak your tongue well,' says he, 'but that do appear a vastly pious bird. He does nothing but utter the name of the Lord.'

"'That is so,' says MacBride, winking. 'He cannot speak without bringing the Lord in somehow. As a chick he lived at Sekondee and was a notorious sinner, in truth I could not tell you which was the worst, him or the governor. Up to a year ago he was soaked in evil and then, one day, he took up with a dove.'

" ' A dove? ' says the priest.

" ' A dove—*paloma*,' says MacBride, ' a she-dove with pink eyes. She flew aboard off Gaboon and abode with us seven days. She used to sit beside the parrot on that arms-rack and coo at him sorrowful-like night and day. As for him, he never said a word but just perched there, head sunk on his breast, tears streaming from his eyes. Off Corisco she flew away again, and since then—well, you can hear for yourself. It's my belief she converted him.'

" ' He would be a great example to my poor heathen,' says the priest.

" MacBride brings his fist down on the table. ' Begod, he is mine and I'll give him to you gladly. A pious fowl like that is clean thrown away on a Guinea-man, I am ashamed to meet his eye ! ' So the parrot goes ashore in a canoe.

" Next time we are in those parts we hear great talk of a ' miraculous praying parrot ' and went to the church to see him. Sure enough there was our old friend swinging upside down amid candles and incense, blaspheming away harder than ever; a host of Indians bowed low before him, chanting ' Holy, Holy ! ' "

Penhale guffawed, showing a gleam of exquisite teeth, and then abruptly sobered. " But you didn't get me here to talk poultry. My brother spoke of a ship you have."

Burnadick nodded. " Yes. Wheel me out on to the lawn and I'll explain—these deafening macaws——"

Penhale steered the chair down the gravel walk and halted under a beech. Great silken poppies flaunted their scarlet in the ordered beds; anchusas, royal blue; delicately tinted Canterbury bells, columbines and Spanish flags, marigolds and hollyhocks.

Southwards the park sloped steeply down to the still waters of the Helford river, green hill meeting mirrored hill. Red steers lay ruminating in the shadows of old rounded oaks. A sleek mare licked her foal, bathed in golden light, her long tail swishing lazily. On the hillside a bronze labourer whetted his scythe; it flashed in the sunshine like an arc of white fire. The scrape of the whetstone could be heard distinctly grating to and fro, unhurried. A green, deep-bosomed, sheltered land. Two miles away a south-easterly ground-swell broke in thunder on Rose-mullion Head, dragging at the furrowed rocks, bursting in white explosions of spray—but here no ripple etched the glassy surface of the creek. Six miles away, off Coverack, at dawn that morning a black Malouine lugger had been sighted creeping close inshore to cut off the fishing fleet—but here the white fantails strutted and the ring-doves cooed.

The rover, wind-scarred, burnt with tropic suns, gazed down the placid valley and sighed. "My stars, but you are snug-berthed here! Wind and tide, battle and murder can't touch you—eh?"

"You would be content with this? *You?*"

Ortho considered, then shook his head. "N—o. Not yet. When I'm older, perhaps—and want peace."

"Peace!" Burnadick echoed, bitterly. "Yes, we are peaceful here, God knows! but only because other men bear the brunt. It was not always so, my ancestors fought their own battles. Three Burna-dicks went out in the Fowey fleet to meet the Armada. My grandfather was at Passaro and buried over-side in his hammock. My father died in his bed, but he fought with Hawke at Belleisle. Nancarrow has always paid its shot—till now. And that brings me to the point, captain. We are in the midst of war again and it is like to go hard with us."

"Here's the Dutch gone after the Prussians and they say Spain will follow," growled Ortho.

"Doubtless. England beset on all sides, fighting for bare life, and I—I sit here in my dead haven, lapped in comfort, while other men go out and——"

"Oh, come, come!" Ortho soothed. "It is no fault of yours. Damme, what *can* you do?"

"I can do something," said Burnadick. "Physically I am useless, but I have money. Two months ago, as I was driving through Falmouth, they were selling a prize outside a coffee-house. I could not pass on for the press of people, so was forced to listen. The prize was a French slaver captured off Finisterre by a King's ship. She was nearly new, a prime sailor and pierced for eighteen guns, the auctioneer said, adding that she would make an excellent privateer. The thought came upon me in a flash : 'This much I can do.' I saw an acquaintance of mine in the crowd, a packet-captain, and I signed to him. 'What sort of craft is this he is selling?' I asked. 'She's all he claims and more,' said he, 'a fly-away. But for a chance shot breaking her rudder-head that frigate would be seeking her yet.'"

"You bought her?"

"On the spot."

Ortho strode up and down beside the chair, four paces east, four paces west, plainly excited. "I will warrant you made no bad bargain. They build very sweet models, the French. My last ship was built in Bayonne, and in the ten years I sailed her she was never out-stepped—no, nor challenged. You have ridden good horses—well, she was like the best, docile and eager, leaping to your touch. When I lost her I wept like a child, swore I would sail no other, leave the sea—but now I realize one cannot stop like that, life goes on and you with it, a chip in a tide-race." He made a pass of his ringed hand as though brushing the past aside. "Well, what of your fly-away, sir?"

"Captain Angwin of Flushing was to have commanded her, but last week he fell down a hatchway and broke his leg. Would you be agreeable to take his place?"

The rover's dark eyes sparkled. "By God, I am vastly obliged to you. . . . May I see her?"

"By all means. She lies in the King's Cove. The mate, Pentacost, is aboard. But before we go any further I have this to say. There is a certain prejudice against letters of marque, many holding them to be little better than pirates. But I see no reason why a private ship of war should not be as well conducted as a public ship of war. I cast no reflections on your character, captain, when I say that any ship of mine must be kept clean of stain."

"If I could not fight honourably I would not fight at all," said Ortho. A noble sentiment somewhat marred by an afterthought to the effect that one was "damned liable to swing by the neck if one didn't."

Burnadick repressed a smile. "Good, then we understand each other and there is no more to be said for the moment. To-morrow you shall see the ship and decide. Will you be so good as to wheel me to the house; I see my sister beckoning."

2

The hall clock was chiming midnight when Ortho went to bed. The butler led the way up the panelled staircase, a candle-stick in either hand. Ortho followed, somewhat unsteadily. He was not precisely drunk, but it had been a long sitting. The butler showed him to his room, a dainty chamber done in white and rose, faintly scented with lavender.

The man coughed. "Ahem! Shall I pull your boots off, sir?"

"No, you shall not. I have been able to both dress and undress myself for some years."

"Very good, sir. Good-night, sir."

"Hi!"

"Yes, sir."

"Here's something for yourself."

"Thank you, sir." The butler withdrew. It was the second *douceur* he had received from Penhale in four hours. "Common sort!" he sneered.

Ortho tossed his coat over a chair, wrestled his boots off and padded round the room in his socks, admiring the furniture, stroking the fine French polish, patting the spindle legs approvingly, pawing the deep pile carpet with voluptuous toes. The rose-pattern wall-paper was pretty too, also the flowered chintzes. All very dainty, very elegant. Meeting his reflection in a long mirror he winked at it. "Snug berth for a night—eh, old shipmate? We've met worse in our time, you and I." The smiling reflection winked back. His presence in the room struck him as intensely funny. He gave a hoot of laughter, then, remembering where he was, clapped a hand over his mouth. "My stars! . . . wake somebody . . . careful!"

Pulling on a night-shirt he leapt into bed. The sheets were warm. Somebody had been at them lately with a warming-pan. That brown-eyed little chambermaid probably. Plump, pert little duck. He wondered where she was. . . . Perhaps. . . . He got out of bed and crept stealthily across the room, hand outstretched for the door-handle. Perhaps. . . . The pink roses caught his eye. He glanced round. Inlaid walnut, gilt, chintz . . . the furniture seemed to be stiffening in well-bred reproach.

"Good Lord, what am I doing?" he muttered. "This ain't an inn." He was very stern with himself. "What the dicken do you think you're about? Damme, this is a gentleman's house!"

He returned to the warm sheets, snuffed the candle and was instantly asleep. Ten minutes passed, twenty.

There was a soft rustle of leaves outside. A window curtain stirred; a latch creaked. A sigh; a lifting whimper. The rustle of leaves was no longer soft. A window rattled. Instantly the rover was awake, propped on his elbow, listening. "West wind," he mumbled. "Rising fast . . . veer more cable . . . MacBride!"

Then he laughed. "Oh lor'! I was forgetting" —fell back and was asleep again.

3

Burnadick sat below, at the head of the dining-table, brooding, sucking a dead pipe. How the fellow had talked! And what talk! The East, Barbary, the Guinea Coast, the Antilles; cavalry charges, fleet actions, hurricanes and humming-birds—it reminded him of his own parrot house, a medley of barbaric colour shifting and flashing. There was not much he had missed in his forty odd years, this Ortho Penhale. A queer fish, part gypsy, part squire, earrings and riding boots, the one side uppermost, then the other. Sly yet generous, brutal yet oddly sympathetic, over-dressed, vain as a peacock, a swaggering blade—yet somehow likeable, attractive very. Burnadick smiled when he remembered that his sister had hardly been able to keep her eyes off the fellow throughout dinner—his austere Honor! A queer fish, an eternal contradiction, alternately admirable and disgusting. Was such a person fit to be entrusted with a letter of marque? Burnadick thought so. Mulatto pirates and Rif mountaineers were one thing, Frenchmen another. Civilized war was fought under fast rules. Penhale knew this as well as he did. Anyhow he had offered him the ship now. The chance must be taken.

Horse-coper, smuggler, slave in Barbary, captain of Arab lances, navy seaman, blackbirder—queer company for sleepy old Nancarrow! He glanced at the portraits of his ancestors, bare-shouldered dames with nosegays at their high bosoms, men in scarlet or blue, with glossy curled perukes or neat powdered wigs—what had they thought of this guest at their board, lounging in one chair, his spurred heel on another, cracking nuts with his teeth, this handsome adventurer in tarnished black and silver, with his tales of love and plunder, his scars, his oaths, his gay disarming laugh? What were their thoughts?

The painted faces gave no sign.

A spatter of driven rain tapped the window. A draught piped eerily in the chimney. Ten candle flames in the great silver candelabra bent to the right.

Burnadick cocked his head. The wind rising, the west wind, the sea wind, sharp with brine, laden with spindrift. Again the draught-pipe in the chimney. The wind murmured outside, a multitude of whispering voices.

To the cripple they were the ghosts of his fathers, those stout captains, bidding him up and defend his own, as they had done, calling him out : " Burnadick ! Burnadick ! The fleets are beating seaward. The guns are shotted. Where are you, son of ours? Where are *you* ? "

He grasped the sides of his chair, hove himself erect striving by sheer will-power to drive strength into his withered legs. It was moving, his right foot, he felt it ! By God, the spell was breaking ! A little further—so ! Chalk-white, the veins standing out on his forehead, the sweat beading from his brow, he let his weight drop slowly on his legs. They sagged under him like reeds. He crashed back in his chair a huddled heap. The wind voices rose again, beating on the window.

" No, I cannot come," he groaned ; then, jerking his head upwards, " Your man is yonder."

4

Twenty miles to the westward a sick woman lay abed and listened to the wind rising. She had been born on the bleak Bodmin moors during a tempest, and her youth had been spent in the very farmhouse where she now lay, a house which, perched high on granite cliffs, looked out upon the confluence of the English Channel and Atlantic and took every westerly gale straight in its weathered face. Few strangers came near the lone farmhouse, but always there had been the wind scurrying hither and thither about the place, whispering, crooning, singing rough shanties or bellowing with rage. The voice of the wind ran through her life like a *leit-motif*. She had invested it with personality, maturing as she herself matured. A lonely child she had fancied it a playmate, a mischievous boyish creature who scattered ricks, uprooted trees, blew hats off the dignified, inflated the washing into grotesque human shape and set it dancing on the clothes lines, pants, drawers and shifts, in a comic aerial ballet. As she grew older the wind took fresh shape, it became a lover, a bold, tempestuous, roving fellow who came up from the sea and rapped at her window o' nights. She could never quite visualize him, but, for some unexplained reason, pictured him as tall and dark, bare-footed, wearing a knife in his belt. He would climb the old sycamore tree just under her window and sit swinging his legs in the branches and call to her by name. Then, in imagination, she would creep downstairs through the sleeping house, open the door and go off with him over the seas and far away, to the lands where there are palm trees, elephants and pagodas, to the isles of sunset and the gates of morning.

Then came a big lover of flesh and blood and she put the wind-man out of her mind—or tried to. But he came with a south-westerly gale in the grey dawn of her wedding day. She heard him as she lay abed, raging round the house, buffeting the window with his fists, threatening, imploring. "Go away," she said, putting her head under the bed-clothes. "That foolishness is done with."

But it was not—she had been listening to that voice too long and she could not stop the wind blowing. While she was well her thoughts were her own, but whenever she was ill and no longer had full control of herself, he came to the window and whispered.

Hovering now in and out of consciousness, listening to the sough of the gale, the patter of driven rain-drops on the pane, she knew that he was even then at hand.

She awaited his coming with every over-wrought nerve strung to its fullest. Would she see his face this time? Each time he came he seemed to grow a little clearer, less nebulous. Tall, dark, stripped to his shirt and breeches, the rain dripping from him—or was it salt water? Why should it be salt? A drowned man? A shudder ran through her. No, no, not that! What ghostly thoughts possessed her? It was madness. She must fight it off, must not weaken, must not listen. She strove to compose herself, to fix her mind on stable, mundane things; on her good husband and affectionate children, on household matters. Were the cows being properly milked, the poultry fed? That old braggaty* hen was given to laying out, at the back of the hay-loft usually—she must tell the girl.

She was getting control. Her mind had stopped slipping backwards into the dark. She was herself again—almost. She would defy him, not listen—such foolishness!

Then clearly she heard it; the remembered creak in the sycamore boughs, the soft rap on the window and a low voice calling her name.

* Spotted.

CHAPTER II

I

> " ' Ye gentle gales that fan the air
>   And wanton in the shady grove;
> Oh, whisper to my absent Fair
>   My secret Pain and endless Love.
>
> And in the sultry heat of day,
>   When she doth seek some cool retreat,
> Throw spicy odours in her way
>   And scatter roses at her feet.' "

ORTHO PENHALE rode towards Falmouth town
in high good-humour, giving his robust, melodious
voice full play. The bay mare, full-fed, well-groomed,
stepped briskly, tossing her head, whisking her tail.
He lifted her into a canter, thrilled to feel the smooth
muscles gather and release under him; swerved her
aside to jump a big wind-fall and turned into the
track again. A farm girl, plodding towards Bareppa,
her skirts drawn high out of the mud, revealing
deplorable ankles, backed into the bushes to let him
pass. Ortho swung the mare about and sweeping off
his hat greeted her tunefully.

> " Tell me, tell me, charming creature,
>   Will you never ease my pain?
> Must I die for every feature?
>   Must I always love in vain? "

The girl glanced at him, startled, and backed
farther into the bushes. Ortho swayed towards her,
hand pressed to heart.

> " Are such giddy ways beseeming?
>   Will my love be fickle still?
> Conquest is the joy of women,
>   Let their slaves be what they will."

There was a loud snapping of twigs as the damsel scrambled through the hedge and beat a retreat across the field beyond.

Ortho stood up in his stirrups, flourishing his hat in the air.

> " If your wandering heart is beating
>   For new lovers, let it be.
>   But when you have done coquetting
>   Name a day and fix on me."

He sent a piercing tally-ho! after the fleeting fair and crowed with laughter to see her scuttle. " It is a damn curious thing," said he to the bay mare, " but the uglier the woman the more convinced is she that every Tom, Dick and Harry is threatening her virtue —you may have noticed it yourself ? "

The bay mare flicked her ears at a fly.

" You have? Then that settles it. In my opinion the delusion is sent them in divine compensation. Now step along, my lamb."

The mare stepped on through green tunnels of oak and chestnut, netted in a flickering web of sunlight.

Ortho was in exuberant spirits. Things were looking up. Three months before he had landed in Bristol with the bare clothes he stood up in. Now he was getting a fresh command and, unless things went grievously amiss, a most profitable one. He had no doubt whatever that he would take this ship. He *must*. There were reasons why he could not stop at home, and, moreover, he needed money.

On he rode, past white-washed cottages, swathed, in climber-roses and thatched with reeds. Idyllic dwellings in a bowery land. They reminded Ortho of pictures in moral works for the young in which the industrious labourer is represented returning to the bosom of his rejoicing family at close of day, roses over the porch and the sun setting in the background. He

searched his vocabulary for an apt expression and
pounced on the word ' smug.' " That's it—' *smug*,' "
said he.

Better his own bare, western parish, fronting the
broad Atlantic and the wild sea winds.

A small boy crouched beside a duck-pond sailing a
cork boat to and fro, much to the consternation of the
titular ducks.

" Hello !   Hello ! " shouted the cavalier.

" Hello ! " chirped the boy, undisturbed.

" That's a smart craft you've got there."

The boy sniffed. " I don't think so then. When
my uncle do come home from Halifax he's goin' to
make me a wood one with real sails to h'ist up and down.
He's a gunner he is."

" Good luck to him ! And are you goin' to be a
gunner too ? "

" Ess, surely—an' voyage foreign on the packets
and kill Frenchies."

" Good luck to you as well," said Ortho, laughing.
" Come to me when you're ready and we'll voyage
together and kill 'em all. Here, go buy yourself a
cutlass and a cocked hat, Admiral Drake o' the duck-
pond." He tossed the lad a shilling and rode on
whistling merrily.

The silver in his pocket was getting woeful short,
but he had never allowed his expenditure to be limited
by his income—furthermore, money would be tumbling
in ere long, he told himself, money by the barrel.

Over Pennance hill he went, round the reedy pool
whereon white swans cruised with all the full-blown
majesty of ships of the line, and thence, by leafy
lanes, to Falmouth itself.

The straggling town was all a-bustle. A fleet of
eighty merchantmen were lying in Carrick Roads
waiting convoy to the Thames. They covered the
blue harbour like a flock of riding gulls; brigs, barques,
ketches, pinks, schooners, snows and yawls; grimy

Tyne colliers, Irish pork boats, salt-stained New-foundlanders, sun-bleached West Indian sugar ships. Amongst them the bumboats, water-boats and Press-gang cutters plied. From the town quay Ortho witnessed an exciting race. A ship's boat containing three men pushed suddenly out from under the bows of a chequered brigantine—a fourth man dropping off the dolphin striker as she went by—and headed for the Trefusis shore, her crew rowing desperately. Then from the other side of the brigantine shot a Press cutter in full pursuit. The trader's boat had a good start, but it was a clumsy tub, whereas the cutter was built for speed and pulled three oars of a side. It leapt after the merchant boat like a greyhound after a rabbit, gaining one foot in two.

" They're cot, poor souls," said a longshoreman at Ortho's elbow.

" Not yet, they ain't," his mate replied. " They're pullin' wid the dread of the blasted navy in 'em. They'll pull till they burst."

The two boats neared the shore, the pursued battling nobly on, the pursuer close upon her. A gangster sprang up in the latter's bows, cudgel in hand, ready to leap.

" Cot ! " said the pessimistic longshoreman.

" Wait," said his friend. " Ah ! "

The runaways, recking nothing, had crashed their boat on the rocks at full speed. The gang coxswain, mindful of his cutter, backed water. The minute lost to him was sufficient for the fugitives, who could be seen—about the size of ants—scampering across the fields above Trefusis Point. The gangsters re-embarked and paddled slowly back, greeted by derisive howls from the assembled shipping.

But this did not exhaust the attractions of Falmouth that June morning. Three Post-Office packets lay off Flushing making ready for sea. One was towing out to the Roads preparatory to sailing next day, and

two—one from the West Indies and one from Rio de
Janeiro—had dropped anchor only a few hours before.
Boats were churning to and fro. Seamen staggered
up Market Strand burdened with passengers' luggage,
their wives at their heels, pestering them for money.
One tattooed stalwart, that moment arrived from
Brazil, deposited his load on the kerb, boxed his
spouse's ears and staggered on again. From a tavern
came the noise of husky voices raised in song. A
small Guiana monkey with a chain about its middle
shot out of the door and gambolled down Church
Street, pursued by a negro steward and a host of
excited dogs and boys. It ran up a hatter's sign and
sat there chattering and grimacing at the baffled
crowd below. Down Arwenack came the royal mail
coach, scattering the crowd, its guard very splendid
in a scarlet coat, a blunderbuss strapped beside him,
a long copper horn at his lips—'*Ta-ran-ta!* Ta-
ran-ta-ra!'

This was followed by a huge tilted wagon, drawn
by six horses and accompanied by a squad of soldiers
—bullion, London-bound.

All Falmouth, gentle and simple, was in the narrow
street, drawn by the arrival of the packets; ladies
with high-waisted gowns, puffed sleeves and mob-
caps, gentlemen in buff coats or blue; here and there
a sombre Quaker. But most noticeable of all were
the packet captains, at once conspicuous by their gold
epaulettes and cocked hats as well as the deference
they compelled. Ruddy-faced, prosperous gentlemen
striding full-chested through the town with an air of
owning it—which, as a fact, they very largely did.
Ortho watched their progress enviously. Ah, well!
before very long he would be a man of mark himself,
outshining them all. In imagination he saw the
Ghost swimming in past Black Rock, a train of rich
prizes in her wake, St. Mawes and Pendennis castles
thundering salutes. He pictured himself landing on

Market Strand amid the huzzas of the populace, a Cornish Duguay-Trouin. Delightful dreams! He swaggered in anticipation, edging the mare through the press with chin held high and back well hollowed.

"Lud sakes! There goes a very handsome person," twittered the lovely Miss Sarah Hocken to her friend Mrs. Bown Harris. "Who is he, I wonder?"

Niels Falck, destined to die at Salamanca, shrugged his broad shoulders. "Black Jack of the Bath Road, I should guess—come to rob the mail."

Ortho drew rein at the New Hotel and, handing the mare to an ostler, swaggered within.

The hall was blocked with passengers' luggage and porter-seamen refreshing themselves. Upstairs bells pealed, doors slammed; voices, male and female, shrilled and bellowed. Chambermaids scurried, waiters ran. The barber, followed by his lad bearing powder bag and razors, rushed out of one door and dived into another. A boot boy, grasping two armfuls of boots, tripped on the stairs and fell headlong to the bottom, an avalanche of foot-wear clattering about him.

In the coffee-room, serenely indifferent to the confusion, lounged those great heroes the packet captains, taking their morning tipple. Ortho strutted in and ordered himself a glass of Madeira. The captains raised their eyebrows slightly, turned their backs and went on with their conversation.

"Ned says he spoke the *Lady Pelham* off Cape Frio thirty-four days out," said one. "Smart work—eh?"

There was a general murmur of agreement.

"Meet with any trouble, Ned?" a second inquired.

"Lost his foretop-mast in a tornado three days out."

"I meant in the way of hostiles."

"Not a thing. Kirkness did though, in the Windward Passage. Three small privateers, swarming with men. He lashed a broadside into the foremost and got away, the wind hardening."

Said a third, " I hear there was a Breton armed lugger off Black Head this mornin'. Did you? "

" Yes. Lord bless you, they're everywhere ! "

" What are the underwriters asking for the Jamaica run, d'you know? "

" Twenty-three per cent., I believe."

" Whew ! "

And so on, professional chatter. They took no ostensible notice of Ortho. A sociable soul, he was in a mind to ask them to drink with him, concluded that it would only mean a snub, so emptied his glass and strode out again. They'd be glad enough to know him some day.

A packet captain jerked his head. " Who is that tall buck—just gone out? "

Another sat up. " I'll take me oath I've seen him before—at Rosario's in Kingston, playin' billiards with a set of rake-hell Guinea masters. I have an idea he was one himself."

" He don't look like a seafaring man," said a third.

The first grunted. " He looks up to anything—if you ask me."

" He's a notable-lookin' person. Would make hay with the females, I should say," said a dried-up little fellow, sighing enviously.

" Not with mine," growled a bloated old gentleman in the corner, withdrawing his nose from a glass of grog. " Not with mine. I'd plant a bullet in him."

" Always supposing he didn't plant a couple in you first, Charlie," said a friend. " At the nimble pulling of triggers and corks these Guinea rascals are second to none—they live by it. If fight you *must*, shoot him first and challenge him afterwards. It's your only chance."

Whereat there was a general titter and the scandalous insurance rates came up for discussion again.

Ortho walked down the water-side and asked for the *Ghost* of a longshoreman.

" Privateer fittin' out for Mr. Burnadick of Nancarrow? " The man pointed a calloused finger. " Over there, behind that collier brig."

" Row me out to her, will you? " said Ortho, and the fellow complied.

Like most watermen he was a confirmed gossip and as inquisitive as a flea. He prattled on concerning this craft and that master, apprising his fare the while with a beady, curious eye. It was plain he could not fathom Ortho's business with the *Ghost*, the spurs and riding boots upset him.

" The *Ghost*, brigantine," he remarked, presently. " Handy little craft, there's no denying, but what do Mr. Burnadick want with her? Proper gentleman, none better, but Lord bless you, what do he know of ship-owning? Man needs to be bred up in it."

No reply from Ortho.

The boatman spat on his palms and rowed on. " If ' Oakum ' Angwin could of taken she out 'twould 'a been well enough, I dare say. But he stepped backwards down a hatch. Old ' Parson ' Pentacost is in charge now." A snort of contempt. " Heh ! "

" That's the mate, ain't it? What's amiss with him? "

" Oh, I s'pose he's a smart enough sailor," said the boatman grudgingly. " He was sailing master in the packets for twenty years, so he ought to know some'ot. But all the same he's . . ." The man rapped his forehead and winked. " You understand."

" Mad? "

" As a May-gum."

" What does he do foolish? "

" Thinks he's a prophet."

" A *what* ? "

" A prophet—one that foretells trouble. A notable one for grog and jollification in his youth, so they say, but he heard Mr. Wesley preach one day, fell down in a fit and rose up again converted. He was with the Methodies for a while, but they weren't pious enough for him by this time, so he up and starts a dissent of his own. They hold meetings in an old sail-loft in Penryn, singing and moaning and carrying on."

" What do they call themselves? "

" ' The Trumpets '—' Trumpets of Jehovah.' But Lord save you, they ain't got the breath to blast very loud. Just a parcel of ancient widow women and one old blind shoemaker."

" Is there a second mate aboard? " Ortho inquired, none too enraptured with the description of the first.

" Aye."

" What sort is he? "

" Fowey," said the waterman, with a shrug, as who should say, " You know what Fowey people are." Letting the boat drift for a second he pointed to a trim little barque lying off Flushing. " Now if _I_ was a gentleman wishful to try my fortune—a ' volunteer,' as you might say—that there would be my choice. The _Killigrew_, Captain Nankivel, as fine an officer as ever trod a deck. He'll get the pick of the Falmouth boys, he will. They know _him_. . . . That old Pentacost . . . ! "

A jet of tobacco-juice enriched the harbour waters, expressing the boatman's opinion of the prophet.

Ortho was amused. Took him for a volunteer, did he? A bumpkin seeking to fill depleted pockets by an adventure at sea. He was tempted to let the fellow's rabid curiosity go unsatisfied, but on consideration determined it were better to give him something to bite on. He did not want to have this creature hanging about the water-front warning every likely boy against the ship.

They had rounded the Tyne brig by this time and the _Ghost_ lay in full view. Ortho's critical eye leapt upon her, swept her from bow to stern, from trucks to water-line, and was satisfied. She lay low but buoyantly in the water and was painted dead black all over, except for a single narrow yellow line and the white figure-head—that of a woman rising from the grave, flinging back her shroud. The French name *Revenante* had been painted out and the translation *Ghost* imposed. Ortho did not like the figure-head; the staring eyes, hollow cheeks and streaming hair sent a shudder through him. " By heck, that is a pleasant thing to go sailing with ! " he muttered, knowing, nevertheless, that sail with it he must; ghastly as the figure-head might be, nautical superstition would permit no change. He turned from the sinister image to admire the vessel's lines. Very graceful they were, flowing away from her sharp stem, swelling over her beam to meet again in her exquisitely moulded counter. She would sheer the blue ridges like a knife, ride them under and slip on, clean-heeled. " She'll skim like a flying fish," he said to himself. " Wave 'em all good-bye."

He turned on the boatman. " Suppose Mr. Pentacost is not commanding her at all. Suppose I am."

The man's jaw dropped. " Eh ! " His incredulous eye travelled from spattered riding boots to fashionable cravat. " *You* ? "

" Yes, me," said Ortho. " You must not imagine the supply of masters is confined to your prosperous if relaxing town. I have commanded ships before. Ask 'em in Port o' Spain or Habana if they've ever heard of Captain Ortho Penhale of the *Charming Helen*. Ask 'em anywhere down the surf from Goree to St. Paul Loanda. Ask 'em in Bombay, Fort William, Macao, Foochow, Panama or Callao, Valparaiso, Archangel or . . ." His geographical knowledge failed him for the moment. " Anyhow ask e'm and blast you ! "

" Sir," the man protested, not unreasonably, " how the devil can I ? "

"You can't, I know, but if you could you'd hear enough to fill even your long ears. Your hand—quick!" The command came sharp as a pistol shot.

The fellow, bewildered, put his hand out. Ortho grabbed it in a flash and pressed it slowly backwards. The boatman resisted with all his might. It was useless. Back he went, back, impotent, squirming across the thwart.

"Now forwards, towards me—so."

The boatman strained and wriggled to no avail, the iron wrist was screwing his arm out of its socket. He sagged forwards and flopped on his knees on the bottom boards, cursing foully.

"Hmm!" said Ortho. "If you're a sample of Falmouth manhood Nankivel is welcome to 'em. You will pardon the liberty, I trust. Here's something to wet your throat."

So saying he ran up the *Ghost's* ladder.

The boatman, still on his knees, watched him go. Active as a cat, strong as a lion. Could twist your neck with one hand, devil take the big black bully! What had he given him? A crown, be Japes! A crown for five minutes' pulling! Lavish, be Cripes! A proper gentleman, be Jasus! Most he'd ever had out of the eminent Nankivel was a shilling, from Angwin sixpence. A crown! He could get drunk as an earl on a crown. God bless the princely hero! He swung his punt about and tugged rapidly for the shore, half his mind reducing a crown-piece to terms of gin flip, half engaged with the surprising fellow in black and silver. There was a personality aboard the *Ghost*. Nankivel—pah! Angwin—tush!

2

Ortho sprang to the *Ghost's* deck, grinning broadly. He had never been within a thousand miles of Macao, Valparaiso or Archangel, and that wrist business was a mere trick, giving an impression of prodigious strength but requiring little. He had learnt it from his old mate MacBride, who in turn had learnt it from a Japanese in China seas. MacBride used to practise it on young seamen who showed signs of getting above themselves. That boatman would jabber in his cups that night, Ortho felt sure, and the recital would not be unflattering to himself. So this was the *Ghost*. Let 'em say what they like, nobody could build like the French, anyway not for lines. His eye travelled aloft. Brigantine rigged and well set up. Pentacost might be mad, but he knew his work. That fore-yard must be fifty feet long, if an inch; with stunsails set both sides she'd show a spread like an albatross. He thought he'd cross a square-sail on her main-mast as well. The stick would bear it and it made a ship twice as handy.

With her beam she would stand a power of canvas. Ortho wondered if her top-masts could be increased and moon-rakers carried in light airs. "By heck I'll make her fly," he muttered. "I'll show this Nankivel the way out and home."

"Well?"

He turned about to find an extraordinary old man at his side. He wore sea-boots, a canvas smock smothered in tar and tied in at the waist with lanyard, and a blue knitted nightcap pulled down over his ears. His nose was sharp and commanding; his eyes restless, blinking this way and that as if searching for something; his leathern face entirely without hair, which lack gave him a strangely reptilian appearance.

"Well?"

"Mr. Pentacost aboard?"

"That is my name."

So this was the founder and high-priest of the 'Trumpets'! Ortho had expected something out of the way, but nothing quite as odd as this. However, he concealed his surprise and produced Burnadick's note. The old man read it and glanced up, blinking his lashless eyes.

"Mr. Burnadick says you may be taking command of this ship, Captain . . . er . . ." he referred to the note again, "er . . . Penhale?"

"It is as good as certain. I have taken a strong fancy to her already, if I may say so; her fitting out reflects great credit on yourself, Mr. Pentacost."

"I thank you, sir. I thank you. One does one's poor best. But, a seafaring man yourself, you know what these riggers are, scamp what they can, and the pilfering that goes on—chut, chut! . . . sinful!" He rolled his eyes heavenwards, showing the whites in a ghastly manner. "Demand the most constant vigilance . . . ah!" He pounced upon a chip of wood on the deck and cast it overboard. "Um . . . yes . . . will you be stopping aboard, sir?"

"No, I have business over Penzance way which will take me a day or two," said Ortho, thinking that if the old fellow was disappointed in not getting the command himself he was taking it extremely well.

"Yes, sir, I understand. The Lord willing we should be ready for sea in a week at most. The difficulty will be men."

"Why so? I should have thought there would have been plenty of lusty young fellows anxious to try their fortunes aboard a smart craft like this."

Pentacost shook his wool nightcap. "Not so many. Seamen give Falmouth a wide berth on account of the Press, and now that Captain Angwin has been laid low all the available landsmen will flock to Captain Nankivel."

"What men have you aboard now?" said Ortho.

"Myself, second and third mates, bos'un, carpenter, cook and four boys—ah, yes, there is a surgeon engaged also. He is lodging ashore at Mr. Burnadick's expense. Eleven in all."

"Well, we must see what can be done," said Ortho. "Now, let's have a look below."

"By all means. I think you will find all in order, except, of course, stores. Um—er—you will excuse what may seem an impertinence "—Pentacost turned upon Ortho, humming and hawing, his eyelids fluttering like moth wings—" seem an impertinence, but are you a papist?"

"Me?" said Ortho, astonished. "I belong to the English Church, I believe—I mean I know I do."

"Thank you, sir. You will excuse me," mumbling and muttering; making hen-like rushes at odd ends of rope and planking and hurling them overboard, he led the way below.

3

It was not until evening that Ortho left the *Ghost*. Pentacost accompanied him, a metamorphosed Pentacost. Gone were the clumsy sea-boots and tarred smock, giving place to steel-buckled shoes, black stockings and black broad-cloth coat. The blue nightcap was displaced by a wide-brimmed beaver hat and plain white wig. Pentacost, first mate of the privateer *Ghost*, was laid aside. 'Parson Pentacost,' highpriest of the 'Trumpets,' was going ashore.

A ship's boy rowed them to the Greenbank, and all the way the old man said never a word, but sat bolt upright, staring straight ahead, his lips moving soundlessly.

"He's composing to-night's sermon," said Ortho to himself. "I'll warrant he spits brimstone like a volcano."

As they stepped ashore two old women in long black cloaks rose up off a bench where they had been waiting, and placing themselves on either side of the Prophet marched him off in the direction of Penryn.

The ship's boy told Ortho that the stouter of the two was the mate's wife. "She've got a house of her own at St. Gluvias," he added, " a tan-yard and two farms."

" Then why does the old fool go to sea? " said Ortho.

The boy grinned. " 'Cos he says the French are idolaters and the Lord háve commanded him to destroy 'em."

" Oh ho ! " said Ortho. " So that's how the wind lies. And why do *you* go to sea, my son? "

" For battle and glory, sir," said the boy, glowing.

" Myself, I go for money," said Ortho. " Well, between the three of us we ought to do something."

CHAPTER III

"ALL Gentlemen, Seamen and able-bodied Landmen that have the courage to face Monsieur and make their Fortunes may meet good encouragement by entering aboard the *Ghost*, privateer, Captain Ortho Penhale (late master of the famous Guineaman *Charming Helen*). The *Ghost* carries 18 carriage guns (nine-pounders) besides swivels, and has every convenience for the accommodation of her crew. A brave vessel underfoot that can either speak or leave any Cruizer on the sea.

"N.B.—The ship lies in the King's Cove, Falmouth, and will be ready for sea in seven days, when she will proceed to her station to intercept some rich Frenchmen that are expected from the West Indies.

> "Be Ready, Lads—slip out in quest
> Of riches bound to faithless France,
> And bravely take another chance.
> Revenge and Riches both invite
> A Foe insidious to requite :
> May your attempts, my willing Boys,
> Be crowned with Honour, Wealth and Joys."

The pride of a young mother in her first-born filled Ortho as he gazed on his initial appearance in print. The woodcut at the top represented a frigate, whereas the *Ghost* was a brigantine. The prose was largely copied from stock advertisements and the closing doggerel cribbed wholesale from a Liverpool newssheet. Nevertheless Ortho tasted the sweets of authorship. Albeit he wished he could re-write it. Several improvements had occurred to him, long words for short. 'Adventitious encouragement' instead of

34

'good encouragement,' 'excluding' for 'besides,'
'possesses' for 'has.' He mentioned his regret to
the printer, who, while agreeing that grandiloquence
was style, doubted if it would make the same appeal
to the unlettered classes. Ortho admitted the force
of this, gave instructions that copies should be broad-
cast, and mounting his mare turned her into the
western road. At noon he baited at the Angel,
Helston; hammered the potman for spilling ale on
him; pursued and embraced an unwilling kitchen-
maid, repulsed another who was too willing; promoted a dog-fight in the yard and won a guinea in
bets thereon; nailed one of his advertisements to the
beadle's notice board and rode on again, having in
the short space of one hour made himself deservedly
popular. By late afternoon he was in Penzance, but
he stopped only long enough to place another hand-
bill with the town-crier and pushed on for home.
By eight o'clock the Keigwin valley lay below him,
a green river of tree-tops flowing through bare hills,
a surprising valley, cleft in the high country, as it
were by an axe stroke. The sun was westering in calm
glory. Gwithian church tower stood bold and dark
against a sky of clear amber. The broken tors to the
north-west lay basking like lions in the glow, their
flanks tawny-gold. Eastwards over the sea drifted a
bubble moon. Ortho checked the mare and gazed
on the valley of his boyhood. Two hundred feet
below him, hidden by green billows of oak and ash
was his home, Bosula, the Owls' House. There he
had been born, there grown to man's estate. There,
daunted by misfortune, he had time and again returned
as to a sure haven. But his wounds healed, his spirit
revived and he was away again. He could not help
it. Twenty-five years he had been wandering; the
gypsy itch—legacy from his reprobate old mother—
was in his blood. Not a ship sailed past the valley
mouth but his heart sailed with her. Not a gale

rocked the valley tree-tops but blew a trumpet call in his ears; the echoed boom of surf on the Twelve Apostles reef was the far thunder of guns. When he should have been ploughing he lounged idle against the plough handles dreaming of the Antilles, green jewels set in shining sapphire; or of the minarets of Morocco City coral pink against the Atlas snows. When he should have been sowing he sat on a gate and saw sunset flame over the white corsair port of Sallee with the Bou Regreg running blood and gold; or the surf at Christiansborg, league-long breakers romping shorewards with rainbows glimmering in their manes; and so on, endless flickering pictures. Memory gave him no peace.

At such times he hated the sheltered valley where life fitted its step to the slow trudge of plough oxen and the years rolled through an ordered calendar of sowings and reapings. Now, in the hour of farewell, his heart went out to it. It was his birthplace, his home, and they had had good sport here, he and Eli, as boys. He remembered wonderful spring days bird's-nesting in the upper valley; glimpses of blue sky seen between clouds of hawthorn, the deep purple of bluebells underfoot. Summer days down at Monk's Cove, idling among the rock pools, the sun warm on one's bare skin; diving into delicious cool green deeps where air bubbles streamed like jets of pearls and the bronze weed banners swayed to and fro lazily. Winter days on Polmenna Downs in the wind and rain; a flutter in the gorse, a zigzag streak in the mist, the roar of the old flint-lock and a whoop from Ned Bohenna : " Well shot, zur ! As pretty a cock snipe as ever I see ! " That old flint-lock ! The first time he had fired it he chose an easy mark, the farm cat. The gun knocked him flat, his mother thrashed him for disturbing her nap, Bohenna thrashed him for playing with firearms and the cat went scathless. They had dug foxes out of that hill-side yonder, aye and badgers too. He remembered the first badger he had tailed, swinging it round and round, afraid to let it drop, the dogs leaping and barking, Bohenna waving the lantern, shaken with laughter. That hill-side had seen his first love affair also. A farm girl she was, from Baripper, a sly, sleek, rosy thing. Well he remembered her coming down Rocky Lane between banks of pink campion and tall foxglove, the defiant toss of her chin, the smile that followed. They had sworn eternal fidelity up there amid the campion. Two days later he had come upon her with her blonde head snuggled into the bosom of a fisherman from Monk's Cove, a married man with three children. All that had been a long time ago—twenty years and more. He was in his forties now, getting on. Another twenty and he'd be downright ancient, grey-haired, wrinkled, too stiff to dance, too gruff to sing, too slow for cutlass play. He'd have to wear a top-coat o' nights and ride staid horses. Out in the world without a penny to bless himself with, living desperately from hand to mouth and day to day, he felt as young as ever. But when he came home here he felt as old as Moses. There was Eli with his three growing daughters to remind him, the manifold responsibilities of landed property, and Nicola—above all Nicola. As soon as he was out of it the better.

He kicked spurs into the mare, and working his way down the precipitous hill-side into Bosula yard, put his horse away and entered the house. Supper was in progress. The hay-makers sat on each side of the board stuffing food into their mouths with both hands, sun-bronzed, sweat-stained, grunting with animal voracity. At the foot of the table, in startling contrast to the rough boors about her, sat Ortho's wife, Nicola, dressed in sprigged muslin, with a be-ribboned mobcap on her shining ringlets, Valenciennes lace at her throat and elbows, an exquisite and lovely figure. In a corner, waiting to share the supper leavings with the dogs, crouched her familiar, the half-wit cow-herd Wany, sharp chin sunk on ragged knees, dark mystical eyes glowing behind shocks of brindled hair.

Ortho bowed formally to his wife and took his place at the top of the table. Nicola inclined her trim head, curved her pink lips and beamed upon him. A beautiful woman, a charming expression, yet somehow meaningless, blank. Ortho groaned inwardly. " She'd smile at Satan just the same," and seizing his knife and fork attacked the food, not daring to look up. Twelve years before he had first met her, Miss Nicola Barradale, only daughter of a rich Bristol shipowner, travelling in state with duenna and maid. Half in love with her, half with her state, he had swept her up in a whirlwind courtship and married her. A week later the father was ruined and a suicide and the devoted daughter off her head from shock. There was insanity in the family; it was unlikely she would recover her mind, though physically she bloomed, untouched by time, a slender fragrant creature, tinted like apple blossom. The normal Nicola had been a tart, imperious lady, spoilt daughter of an indulgent parent; insane her mind was that of a child, sweet and infinitely trustful. Had she been otherwise there is no saying what Ortho might not have done to free himself, a devil in her would have raised a devil in him, but before her helplessness he stood impotent. She was his wife, yet no wife. Children there were none and there could be none. She was dead in mind but not in body, and the carnal half of her would see him out. He had a vision of Nicola standing at his grave-side thirty years on, still pink and white, still slender, smiling that sweet, empty smile of hers. It was a life sentence. Fate had trapped him both neatly and completely.

Seated at supper now he stole a covert glance at

her and his heart beat faster. How lovely she was! The poise of her slim body, the perfect moulding of her shoulders, the white throat rising like a lily stem, the proud shapely little head!

All his old passion for her was up in an instant, the blood running in his veins like wild-fire, overmastering him. "By God, I'll break this cursed spell," he thought; "I'll shake her awake! I'll. . . ."

Nicola glanced up from her plate, met his hot, consuming gaze and—smiled.

The tension snapped like thread, the fire in him quenched as though plunged fathoms deep in polar seas.

He threw his knife down with a clatter, scraped his chair back and rose. The housekeeper, Naomi Davy, railed at him. "My dear life! Finished so soon? Eddn my vittles tasty 'nough for 'e—or what?"

"I ate in Penzance," he lied, buttoned his coat up and walked out.

Naomi followed him into the yard. "Goin' up 'long to Roswarva, are 'e?"

"I am."

"Heard the news, s'pose?"

Ortho nodded.

"Eli has poor speed," Naomi commented. "Only boy he's ever had born dead—and no more to come."

Ortho turned upon her. "What's that?"

"That's what doctor says, shan't be no more," said Naomi. "Mrs. Penhale's been in a poor way. Didn't you hear that?"

"No! Good Lord! I must . . ." He stepped forward precipitately, then halted and called back: "Hi! When did you hear last?"

"Yesterday."

"Yesterday! Why the dicken didn't you send to-day?"

"Send!—and who am I to send if you please?" Naomi shrilled, indignant. "Think I'm made of

men? Aren't we busy haying? Go gadding about
the face of the world thyself and then have nought but
complaints for we as stop and mind thy place for
thee! Thou scatterling! Thou skipjack!"

The latter part of the tirade was lost on the evening
air, Ortho was gone, striding up the western hill-side
for his brother's farm. Naomi continued to call him
names for some time after. She had a warm heart
which boiled over easily, and she brooked no criticism
from any man. Her own husband she handled
affectionately but firmly. Nominally he was farm
bailiff, but everybody knew whence the orders issued.
Men to her were simple, transparent creatures, indis-
pensable in matters of brute strength but of a low
order mentally. In her fifty years she had met but
a few men whom she could not fathom, and one of
them was Ortho. Hence her abuse. She eased her
feelings by several more expressions of contempt and
returned indoors to minister to her darling Nicola.
A good woman, but sharp-tongued.

The blue green dusk was down when Ortho reached
Roswarva. The moon hung low, trailing a wake of
light across the summer sea, Venus beside her. Through
the stunted sycamores bats went swooping and beetles
boomed. Cattle, lying out, made dark blots on the
moonlit fields. The air was full of the scents of
new-mown hay and dew-wet hedgerows.

There were lights in the house and somebody moving
in the yard. Ortho heard the scrape of metal on
stone, and a man came from behind a stack, a fork
on his shoulder. Ortho knew him by his bulk.

" Hi! That you, Eli?"

The giant slewed about, the fork-prongs glinting
momentarily in the moonlight.

" Ortho . . . you back?"

" Yes, just come. How's Mary?"

" Better. Doctor says she'll do now."

" Thank God!" Ortho sighed, relaxing suddenly.

The husband said not a word. He had thanked his God already—bent double on his knees—and was not given to repeating himself.

Ortho sat down on the massive water trough that Eli had painfully chiselled out of a single block of granite—they made everything of granite up on that plateau. He had ridden full forty miles that day and realized now that he was tired. Eli remained standing, hands crossed upon the fork, staring across the moonlit sea, a stone colossus.

Presently he broke silence. "Mary will have no more children. Did they tell you?"

"Yes."

Again silence. There was no need for speech. Both brothers knew what was in each other's heart. Both were chewing on the same bitter cud. It was the end of the Penhales. For five centuries men of their family had farmed the Keigwin valley, had carved a holding out of the raw wilderness and clung to it through drought, famine, war, plague and persecution, adding a bit more land here, building a little there and passing it on to lusty sons. Now the end was in sight. Ortho was his mother's son, he had no overpowering love of land, but the idea of a stranger stamping a proprietary foot in his family stronghold cut him on his most tender spot, his pride. The invincible line was beaten at last—and all through him. It was not Eli's fault. If only he, Ortho, had looked before leaping into his disastrous marriage! . . . If only! Too late to count the 'ifs' now. Nicola would outlast him, Eli die sonless. Exit the Penhales of Bosula. Poor Eli! In him was no alien strain, he was yeoman to the marrow, soil of the soil, embodiment of those five centuries of stout farmers. While he had been roaming up and down it was Eli who had stood by the old place, saved it from their mother's extravagances, nursed it through the hard times and slaved early and late to make it what it

was, the best farm in the Penwith Hundred. Poor
Eli! Poor old lad! He had an impulse to throw
an arm about his brother's neck, to blurt some words
of regret, of consolation. He glanced at Eli standing
huge and impassive in the moonlight and kept himself
in check. What use to beat upon this stoic with a wind
of words? Eli had always despised talk.

He changed the subject. " By the way, Burnadick
has given me that ship. I have to thank you for it,
I believe."

Eli stirred, waking out of his trance. " Not me,
Mary. Burnadick told me he was wanting a master
—met him in Truro when I was looking at that school
for Jennifer—but I did not think of you somehow.
When, later, I happened to mention it to Mary, she
said at once, ' Why, that would just suit Ortho;
write to-day.' So I did."

Ortho was amused. There was the whole tale of his
brother's married life—' Mary told me to do it, so I did.'

" Can I see her? " he asked. " I am leaving
to-morrow, or the day after. Might not get another
chance."

Eli said he would ask; took off his boots in the
kitchen and, in a pathetic effort to be quiet—as of
an elephant playing mouse—crept aloft in his stockings, the staircase protesting loudly under his weight.

Ortho grinned and looked about the kitchen.
Queer, Mary getting him this ship! She had always
urged him to stop at home and do his duty by the
farm. Why this abrupt change? Oh, well, whatever
the motive, it was kindly meant, trust her for that.
Nobody like Mary. His mind went back to his fruitless courtship of her—that first day up on the Luddra
Head—in her blue cloak with the brown hair blowing
about her face—big, clean, wholesome as the wind
itself she was. What would have happened if she
had married him instead of Eli? he wondered. She
would have kept him straight, he thought, he might

have done great things. Ah, well, that was dead and
buried. Still, there was nobody like her. This
kitchen, for instance, so orderly in her presence, now
littered with female fripperies. He examined the first
frippery to hand, a fine muslin dress, freshly ironed
and spread over the table. On a chair stood a round
box bearing the name of a Penzance milliner. A roll
of tissue-paper on the dresser contained lace collarets.
What was such finery doing in austere Roswarva?
Mary turned modish all of a sudden? Something in
a corner aroused his curiosity. He stalked it, pounced
on it and opened it gingerly. It was an absurd little
silk parasol, in spread not much larger than his hat
and hinged at the top. "What the devil. . . . !"

There was a patter of light feet on the stairs and
into the kitchen skipped a young lady in a dove-grey
dress caught round her high waist with a single ribbon.
On her head she wore a little chip bonnet with a
bunch of pink roses on one side. She snatched the
parasol from him and minced up and down the room
in imitation of the fashionable walk, wearing an
expression of extreme disdain, skirt held daintily
between finger and thumb. Then down went the
parasol and she was off, dancing round and round
him, in and out among the chairs, brown ringlets
tossing, scarlet slippers a-twinkle, halted under the
grandfather clock and sank to the ground in a sweeping
curtesy.

" Jenny ! "

" Yes, it's me." She was standing now, eyes down-
cast, hands crossed before her, very demure.

" My dear, how pretty ! "

" Really? "

" Of course."

" You're not saying that just to be kind? "

" Kind, rubbish ! You're ravishing, my honey, and
if anybody denies it, you tell your old uncle and I'll
eat him alive."

Jennifer snorted. "'Old uncle,' indeed! You're nothing but a boy—as mother always says."

"I wonder if your mother intended that as a compliment. Howsobe, I am a year older than your father, miss, though you might not believe it—which shows what high thinking and pure living will do for a man. All this prinking and pranking is in honour of school, I suppose?"

"Yes. In less than a week. Oh dear!"

"What is it, Jenny-Wren?"

"M-miserable."

"So gay just now."

Jennifer nodded. "I—I love all the new dresses and things—but when I think of leaving mother and father and Polly and Melinda—and—and the cows, I—I——"

The pink mouth quivered, the long dark lashes quivered ominously.

"Oh, come now, there'll be cows at Truro."

"Yes, but not *our* cows."

Ortho's arm went round her. "Shoo-oo," he soothed, as one might a frightened horse. "Shoo-oo. There's nothing to fret over. What does a year or two of school mean? Why, a mort of fun, that's all. A crowd of you fine young ladies together, up to every sort of mischief; you'll enjoy every minute, I swear. Truro is a brave town, vastly genteel, with oysters very plentiful. And after all it's not to China you're faring. If anything goes amiss your father can be with you in a day. Myself too. I've got a new ship, you know. I shall be constantly in and out of Falmouth. It's no distance. I'll ride over when I'm in port and we'll dine in style at the 'Red Lion'—on oysters."

"I have never tasted oysters and don't like them," Jennifer objected.

"A very sufficient reason," said Ortho. "Then you shall dine on Caraccas chocolate sugar-plums, lollipops, pastries, conserves, manna—anything you choose. Feel better now?"

"Yes," said Jennifer, sniffling.

He turned her wet little face up to his. Mary must have been just like this when young, he thought; the same thick creamy skin, peat-brown eyes and soft sweet mouth.

"Look at me," he commanded. "What am I doing?"

"L-laughing."

"I am bound for the coasts of Spain—and, maybe, further. You for Truro. Can't you laugh too?"

"Yes," said Jennifer, bravely.

"Laugh with me then, and the Lord bless us! You look twice, thrice, ten times as pretty when you laugh. There's a wicked little dimple breaks out on your starboard cheek like a lone star, and your nose turns up the least small bit." He gave an infectious crow of delight. "My soul, it's turning now!"

Jennifer buried her face in his shoulder, bubbling happily. "Dear Ortho!" A violent creaking of the stairs proclaimed the stockinged descent of Eli.

"Nurse says you'd best not go up," he announced. "Mary is very slight yet. She sends you God-speed and her love."

Ortho looked up blankly. "Can't see me—eh? Oh yes—yes, I understand. Her love?—thank you, thank you. Well, I must be going, I suppose, hard day to-morrow."

He caught up his hat, turned away and then suddenly drew Jennifer to him. "Good-bye, my dear," he said, and kissed the soft sweet mouth—but it was not to her he spoke.

CHAPTER IV

IT was 'feasten' eve in Monk's Cove.

St. Peter is the patron of fishermen, St. Piran of the Cornish miners—a full-blooded ecclesiastic who, report has it, died drunk. On March 25th the tinners went on riotous holiday, and on St. Peter's eve tar barrels were lit on the towers of sea-board churches in honour of the fisher saint.

Monk's Cove kept ' feasten ' with spirit and thoroughness. The housewives entertained friends to tea (that, incidentally, had paid no duty), ' heavy ' and saffron cake, while the men held quoit and ninepin matches on the bare patch outside the ' Admiral Anson.' In the evening young couples danced by the light of the stars to the strains of an itinerant fiddler.

But feasten-eve was bonfire night. High on Gwithian church tower the tributary tar-barrel blazed and was seen by sailors pacing through their lonely night watches far at sea.

In Monk's Cove quantities of drift-wood and the remains of an old boat had been stacked up and set alight, and around this the boys and young men danced and shouted. They held hands, forming a large circle, and as they danced around and around, one side tried to drag the other into the roaring red pile. It was a delirious spectacle. The fire-lit ring staggering perilously this way and that, to the brink of the flames, then out again, twirling dizzily. The houses and cliffs glowing ruddy as the fire leapt upwards, ravening the old timbers. Mothers shrieked unheeded warnings to their sons, girls squealed excitedly, small boys cheered, children, long since

46

tucked in bed, flattened their snub noses against window-panes and crowed with rapture. Suddenly a young fellow broke from the circle and with a wild yell leapt at the fire. High into the air he sprang, but the flames leapt higher. For a second he seemed impaled on great orange spear-heads of flame, enveloped by a fountain of blazing sparks. Women shrieked, men whooped, but the boy fell clear and rolled over and over on the far side, brushing the cinders out of his carroty mop.

Others followed on with much noise and parade of daring, but the heart was out of the fire and the redhead's jump was not equalled that night. In the meanwhile the elder men were making merry in an upper room of the 'Admiral Anson.' Every year when feasten approached the landlord, Jacky's George Baragwanath, sent his three unmarried sons to sleep in the sail-loft and turned their bedroom into a dancehall, having first taken the precaution of shoring up the beams from below. He sat on the presidential bench at the end of the room, supported by Uncle Jesse Kneebone and Uncle Billy Kitto, octogenarians all. A little, perky, round-bellied robin of a man was Jacky's George, not five feet three inches in height and of benevolent countenance. Nevertheless he had sailed the world with the admiral to whom his inn was dedicated, sacked cities and plate-ships and, later, been master gunner of a privateer. He ran a bright, bird-like eye round the room. The company was dull, sitting upright on the benches, drinking little and saying less. He battered his pewter mug with the steel hook that served him as a left hand. Obediently two sons came forward, Benbow, an ex-naval gunner, and Boscawen (all the seven Baragwanath sons were named after British admirals), alert, raw-boned, foxy young men who had sailed 'foreign' and seen life.

"Give 'em ale and keep 'em flushed," their

parent commanded, adding *sotto voce*, " 'Tis paid for."

Ale was distributed from big earthenware jugs. The company dipped their noses as one, drank deep and came up to breathe, gasping, after the manner of sea-lions returning to surface after long immersion. Again Jacky's George sounded his pewter. "Crowder,* step forth and favour we with a tune. Come forth, my old worm, and touch the strings."

The fiddler—a tall, emaciated creature in tight breeches out at the knees and a long black coat much frayed at the skirts—bounded from his seat and took the centre of the floor, smirking, bowing, jerking like a thing on wires.

"A tune, eh? At your command, my lords and gentlemen. What'll 'e have? Speak the word. Doleful or gladsome? Eddn no tune made that I can't play."

"Let's have ' Will ye to Cawsand Bay? ' then," said a man who had once visited that place in a smuggling craft.

" 'Cawsand Bay,' " said the fiddler, showing all his yellow teeth in an uncomfortable grin. "Ah, yes! Lemme see, how does it go? Ah, yes." He gave a preliminary scrape of his strings.

"That don't sound like any ' Cawsand Bay ' I ever heard," the proposer objected.

" 'Cawsand Bay ' 'tis for all that," said the fiddler. "I'd know all the songs in the world."

The man was firm. "I do only know one and that ain't it—so now."

The fiddler weakened. "Well, I did know it once. I know 'em all. But seem me I may have forgot it. Teddn once in twenty years I'd get a call for a trashy old-fangled song like that. Any other——"

Boscawen spoke. "Try ' Bold Brittany ' then—that's new enough."

* Old Cornish for ' fiddler.'

The fiddler gave a diabolical smirk. "'Bold Brittany,' saith 'a yes,—ye-es, a-humph!'" Again he drew his bow across the strings, then halted and fixed a painful eye on Boscawen. "Lookee, Brittany's a parish o' France, I believe. Well, playing Frinch songs in war-time do savour powerful o' treason, seem me. I eddn but a poor wandering poet, but I'm a loyal subject by damn! Seem me——"

"Seem me you don't know that song either," said Jacky's George, testily. "For God's sake let the poor fool choose for hisself, something he *do* know!"

The fiddler bowed and broke forthwith into 'The Barley Mow':

"Here's a health to the baarley mow, my braave boys,
　Here's a health to the baarley mow.
We'll drenk et out of the jolly brown bowl,
　Here's a health to the baarley mow."

"That's better," said Jacky's George. "Give tongue, my beauties. Bosy, keep the ale flowing. Now chorus, all of 'e!

'We'll drenk it out of the napperkin, boys;
　Here's a health to the baarley mow,
　The nepperkin and the jolly brown bowl!'"

Uncle Jesse Kneebone wiped his shrunken lips with a hand rendered shapeless by half a century of toil. "Fiddles well enough, the long man, but not so pretty as our old 'Jiggy' Dan to my ear."

Uncle Billy Kitto agreed. "'Ess, sure enough. He were a rare brisk crowder, Dan'l—drunk or sober."

"Died up under the quoit stones on Trewa Hill, I've heard tell," said Uncle Jesse.

"That's the truth," Jacky's George corroborated. "On midsummer night two years back. Played to a passel o' men and maidens merry-making at Zennor till past ten and then went away. A farmer offered

'en a bite of supper and a bed in the cow-linney, but
' Jiggy ' Dan says ' No,' and staggers away southwards
for the hills, drunk as a lord—they thought."

" Most always was," said Uncle Billy.

" 'Ess, I grant you, but not *this* time. Next morning
a boy found en dead, up under the ancient stones, as
you say, his fiddle under him—a red dog fox on
guard."

" 'Tis a braa whist place Trewa of a midsummer
night," said Uncle Jesse. " I heard my mother tell
that all the tribe o' witches do meet there to pay
their respects to the devil."

" No *tell* about it; my grand-da *seed* 'em wid his
own two eyes," said Uncle Billy, " dancing round a
fire they were, dawling and druling—an' by cripes !
one of 'em was his own aunt."

The company inflated their chests for the last
accumulative chorus of ' The Barley Mow ' :

> " We'll drenk et out of the ocean, my braave boys.
>   Here's a health to the baarley mow.
> The ocean, the river, the well, the hoogshead,
> Anker, half-anker, gallon, the pottle, the quaart,
> The pint, the half-pint, quarter-pint, nepperkin,
>   AND THE JOLLY BROWN BOWL ! "

From a seat by the door rose a tottering ancient
with a face like a withered pippin surrounded by a
fringe of silver hair.

" Boys ! " he quavered. " Boys ! "

His thin pipe was drowned in the general clamour.
Jacky's George banged his pot loudly. Silence
reigned instanter.

" What is it, Nehemiah? "

" I'd want for to sing."

" Then sing you shall and welcome, my dear."

Benbow objected. " Oh, see, father, nobody don't
want to hear that old blinkard yawling; just as we
are getting . . ."

" Hold thy clack ! " said Jacky's George. " When

I was young I tarred and feathered Nehemiah's tom-cat and let en loose among the maidens in the prayer meeting. Nehemiah chased me three miles in his best clothes and beat the life half out o' me. I've got a respect for en and you'll have too. Sing up, Nehemiah, my old and bold. What'll 'e have the crowder play?"

"I wean't have en play nothing," said the old and bold Nehemiah. "I got melody sufficient in myself."

"Blow hard, then, my old beauty, and fear nought."

Nehemiah, fearing nothing, blew as hard as he was able.

> "'As it fell on a holy day,
>   And upon a holytide a:
> John Dory brought him an ambling nag
>   To Paris for to ride a.
>
> The first man that John Dory did meet
>   Was good King John of France a;
> John Dory could well of his courtesie,
>   But fell down in a trance a.
>
> A pardon, a pardon, my liege and my king,
>   For my merry men and me a;
> And all the churls in merry England
>   I'll bring them bound to thee a.'"

"Used to sing better when he had teeth; don't fetch the words so clear as he did fifty years back, seem me," said Uncle Jesse to Uncle Billy, under cover of his hand. "Come to think of it, it were up Trewa Hill that 'Jiggy' Dan met with the queen of the Pigsies?"

"That's so," said Jacky's George, "and on mid-summer night too—come to think of it."

"Never heard that droll," said Uncle Billy. "How did it go?" Amid a rising buzz of conversation Nehemiah quavered on:

> "'And Nichol was then a Cornish man
>   A little beside a Bohyde a;
> He manned him forth a goodly bark,
>   With fifty good oars of a side a.'"

Uncle Jesse bent towards Uncle Billy. " Dan'l
had been playing at Towednack and was wishful to
go to Madron to fiddle at a wedding next day. When
he gets up a top of Lady Downs the mist comes in
so thick he couldn't see the tip of his nose before
him, so down he sits behind a rock and waits for it
to blow by. Must 'a fell asleep like that, but he
swore he never remembered coming over drowsy
even. When he wakes up it is a clear night and
starry, and there is some'ot pecking at his sleeve. He
takes a look and behold ! it is a lil' wumman no
taller 'n your fist, and dressed up beaudiful in di'monds
and pearls and she has a crown of gold 'pon her head.
' Good-evenin' to you, your ladyship,' says Dan,
seeing her to be a person of quality. ' The same to
you,' says she. ' I'm told your name is Jiggy Dan
and that you're the smartest crowder in these western
parts. ' Jiggy Dan'l my name, and as for the rest,
well, that eddn for me to say, ma'am,' says he, ' but
'tis gospel truth for all that ! ' ' I got a bit of a merry-
making at my mansion to-night and should be pleased
if you'd step along and play for me,' says she; ' you
shall be well paid.' ' I must be in Madron for sure
by noon to-morrow,' says Dan. ' Time enough for
that,' says she."

Almost inaudible amidst the chatter Nehemiah
droned indefatigably on :

> " ' Run up, my boy, into the main-top,
>   And look what thou can'st spy a;
>   Who, ho ! who ho ! a good ship do I see,
>   I trow it be John Dory a.' "

Uncle Billy took a long swig at his pot. " Well,
what then ? "

" The lady stamped her lil' foot on the ground,
and behold it yawned abroad and there was a flight
of stone steps leading down to the bowels of the earth.
' Come on,' says she, and down they goes, Jiggy
Dan following she like a dog."

" Weren't he 'feared? " Uncle Billy inquired.

" No—he said. Not a didjan of fear in him, only wonderment. Well, down they goes, flight upon flight, and by'm-by they comes to the lady's mansion, and a braa' tidy mansion 'tis, with coloured pictures 'pon the walls—cushions 'pon the chairs, all lit up like day with the best wax candles, the quartz crystals on the ceiling sparkling like glass. There is pigsies there by the thousand, men and wummen, dressed up in red, blue and green, and they sits down to supper, Jiggy Dan amongst 'em at the queen's right hand. After supper they gets to dancing, and Dan'l plays for 'em the best he knows, standing out in the middle of the floor with the little gay people dancing round his ankles. He felt, he said, like a man standing in a field o' flowers, and they blown in the wind. Hour 'pon hour he plays till he thinks it must be getting on for dawn, so he bows to the queen and says he must be going. ' Time enough,' says the queen. ' Time enough,' says all the pigsies, twittering like a flock o' birds. So Dan'l takes up his bow and plays till his head is a maze and his arm nearly falling off. ' Time enough or not enough I can do no more, your ladyship,' says he. ' No more you shall,' says she. ' Thou art a noble crowder, the best I ever heard above ground or under,' says she, ' so here's three golden guineas for thy trouble and a cup o' wine to speed thee,' she says. Dan'l thanks her kindly, drops the gold into his pocket, pays his respects to the company. All the pigsies clapped their hands and shouted, ' Drink hearty, Jiggy Dan, King o' the crowders ! ' and Dan'l swallered the wine at a gulp. Next thing he remembers was waking up among the quoit stones on Trewa Hill and it bright day. When he put hand to pocket he found there nought but three dead leaves, oak, ash and thorn, and when he came to Madron the wedding was two days old. That's the droll he pitched."

" Aye, that's the tale *he* told," said Jacky's George,
" but if I remembers to rights . . ."

The querulous pipe of Nehemiah was heard above
the din. " Jacky's George ! George Matthew Baragwanath ! "

" What's come to 'e now, my old valiant? "

" How can I pitch my music with all this here
hubadullion going on? "

Jacky's George banged his pot. " Respect for the
ancient man's music ! " he thundered. " Attention
all of 'e ! Nehemiah had buried two wives and
courted a third before most of you was weaned. Pay
proper respect to en, dang 'e ! "

Order having been momentarily restored, Nehemiah
resumed :

> " ' The roaring cannon then were plied,
>   And dub-a-dub went the drum a ;
>   The braying trumpets loud they cried
>   To courage both all and some a.' "

" As I was saying, that was the tale Dan'l pitched,"
said Jacky's George, " but there was certain persons
in Towednack reported that it weren't so much
pigsies he visited with that night as pigs."

" Pigs? " Uncle Billy exclaimed.

" Pigs. He left ' The Miners Arms ' drunk as a
lord and fell off the bank clean through the roof of
Meshach Harvey's pig-sty. Meshach left en there a
night and a day to sober off. That's what Towednack
says."

Nehemiah lifted up his voice for the last verse of
his epic :

> " ' The grappling hooks were brought at length,
>   The brown bill and . . .' "

Benbow appeared at the door. " Hey ! Nehemiah ! "

" Eh? "

" Here's somebody looking for 'e."

" Well, let her look—can't a man sing? "

" She says she've been searching the world for 'e. It's two hours past your bed-time."

" I'd cast scorn 'pon she. On feasten eve I we'ant go to bed at all if I've a mind to :

> " ' The grappling hooks were brought at length,
>   The brown bill and the sword a ;
>   John Dory at length, for all his strength,
>   Was clapt . . .' "

But the ballad of John Dory never got finished. A strong round, feminine arm, bared to the elbow, shot through the doorway and a resolute brown hand took Nehemiah by the scruff, withdrawing him backwards into outer obscurity. From the landing came the noise of a short brisk scuffle, a hearty clap as of open palm meeting unguarded ear, followed by the clump of submissive boots descending wooden stairs—then the slam of the street door.

" H-mm ! " said Uncle Jesse. " He won't bury *that* one."

Jacky's George signed to his son, Benbow, who skipped into the middle of the room.

" A man-o'-war hornpipe, crowder," said he, tightening his belt. " Lively, now."

Benbow crossed his arms and held them level with his shoulders hands on elbows. The fiddler took up a position opposite him and began to play. They marched to meet each other, three paces forward, three paces back, and were off. Benbow's steps were a mere timed shuffle at first, punctuated with a clatter of heels. He faced the fiddler, sidled round him, then passed him back to back, holding himself stiff as a ramrod, his face expressionless. Then he introduced conventional sailor exercises into his movements, running aloft, heaving on a capstan bar, hauling, etc., and calling for more speed finished up merrily, heel and toe. A roar of applause followed him to his seat.

"Well done ! Well done !" a fresh voice shouted. "I'll give a pint of rum and a silver dollar to the man who can better that !"

Everybody looked towards the door. "Squire !"

Ortho it was, in his black and lace, filling the doorway with his height, raffish, handsome, showing his white teeth. "Come on !" he shouted. "Who's for the money? Show a leg ! Tom Clemo, I've seen you skip like a pea on a drum-head. Arise and shine !"

Tom Clemo, blushing with pleasure, rose and slouched into position before the fiddler. Ortho passed round the room, addressing everybody by his nickname, shaking old men by the hand, clapping boys familiarly on the shoulder, inquiring tenderly after relatives and ailments, being, in fact, very affable and gracious.

"Hello, Billy Carrots, how's the new boat sailing? I hear she's a witch on a wind—What cheer, Cap'n Nick ! You're looking proud, you old rogue. Rheumatics better? That's good !—'Pon my soul, if it ain't ' Kicky ' John ! Your hand, John, boy. Hear you made a grand show at Gwenap wrestling. Going for the champion's belt next, eh? . . . Oh, pretty work ! pretty work, Tom Clemo ! That's the style —Uncle Jesse, Uncle Jesse, my old shipmate, how goes it? Tell Aunt Susan I'll be stepping in for a bite of her figgy pudding before long. Lizzie Mary has got another, they tell me. A boy, eh? God bless Lizzie Mary ! It's boys we want in war-time.— *Brava !* Tom Clemo, *Brava !* Now the next man."

He greeted Uncle Billy with an eloquent handclasp and found a seat on the bench beside Jacky's George. "How are they going? " he asked quietly.

"Warming up, warming up. I'll have 'em all sweating and swilling in a minute."

" What are they drinking? "

" Ale. They've had four pints a man, so far."

" Then give 'em a dash of rum all round," said Ortho. " I've raised a couple of likely farm boys in Gwithian, half a dozen tinners in St. Just and a few odd ones here and there. They don't come very quick."

" They'll come quicker at the last," said Jacky's George. " When I was in the *Young Elijah*, privateer, we used to get a scat o' men the night before sailing. They'd come off soft-like in shore boats and ax no questions and be axed none."

" Law jumpers? "

" Not always—boys in trouble at home, wanted for little bits of innocent mischief, brawling, poaching, trespass and such-like. There's lads lying up in old tin-workings and cow-bowjies that is counting off the hours till your *Ghost* sails, but you won't hear nothing nor see nothing o' they till she do sail."

" How many will I get from here, d' you think? "

" Couldn't say. Might get six, might get twelve— if we hook 'em on the rise. There's no money about, fishing's been very slight.

" Seth Nicholas might go—he's been crost in love. ' Kicky ' John too, his wife's got too much tongue— aye, and that Treneary over there, there's a mortgage on his farm."

A man with the long sad face of a disillusioned spaniel had taken the floor. He danced without movement of his body above the hips, arms trailing at his sides, but his feet moved like things inspired, possessed—toe and heel, double and treble shuffle, then toe and heel again, across and across.

" Who's that? " Ortho inquired.

" Willie Tregurtha from Pemberth," said Uncle Jesse. " The cleanest dancer in this hundred—or any other."

" Clean a is, there's no gainsaying," said Uncle

Billy. " But to my mind the savage Irish is the prettiest. When I was on my foreign travels over to Ireland after the fish I seen stepping that would beat that. At Kinsale 'twas, at a funeral. They had the corpse strapped up in a corner by his chin and a bar'l o' whiskey wine open on the floor. There was a heathen Irishman danced, and I declare to you— what with the whiskey-wine—it did appear to me he had a hundred legs all dancing different ways."

Ortho chuckled. " Howsoever, for a poor two-legged man this Tregurtha makes no bad showing."

" Nimble as a flea," said Jacky's George, and tapped his forehead, " but——"

" Pattick? "

" 'Ess—a bit wished. All his brains have run to his toes, seemingly. I heard tell that when he was courting a maiden once upon a time, he couldn't think 'pon words to say, so he just marched into her kitchen and skipped his best. He'll win your money easy enough."

" He's welcome to it—but did he win the girl? "

" He did not. She hove a buzza o' slops over him and married a blacksmith."

A prodigious thumping of boots and cries of ' Willie has it ! ' ' Willie gets the dollar ! ' brought Ortho to his feet.

" Tregurtha wins," said he. " Here y'are, neighbour, and well you've earned it. Now, landlord, serve a round of hot rum bumbo and we'll all shake a leg."

Loud cheers greeted his announcement, louder the appearance of the bumbo.

" Pick your partners ! " cried Jacky's George, sounding his improvised gong. Ortho signed to Tom Clemo and went to the head of the room; Tregurtha and another Pemberth man followed. The brazen laid hold of the bashful by the arms and scruffs and dragged them on to the floor. There was some good-humoured horse-play. One couple started sparring

with open hands, another dropped into a hitch, others
played leap-frog. The rum was working.

The fiddler mounted on a chair and struck the
opening bars.

" Partners face and take hands," Jacky's George
commanded. " One—two—three—Go ! "

The linked pairs clumped four paces sideways to
the left, swinging their arms in rhythm; repeated the
movement to the right; then, throwing their arms
high, twisted back to back and round again, facing
each other. For men wadded, seaman-like, with much
clothing, muscle-bound by years of set exercise, this
last was no easy matter—it being a point of honour
not to let go. The younger and slimmer got round
quick enough, but the elder and stouter stuck back to
back and remained there, grunting and tugging, until
one managed to heave the other bodily into the air
and so over into position once more.

In a short time a stranger entering would have
thought he had stumbled on an inter-tribal wrestling
match, heated but good-natured. Three couples
were jammed back to back, apparently for life;
another had wrestled itself to the floor and two more
had collapsed on top of it. They picked themselves up,
drew fresh stimulus from their pint pots and plunged
into the scrimmage anew, whooping and laughing.

" Warming nicely now, Squire," Boscawen whispered.

" Yes. Keep that crowder at it and don't let 'em
go dry."

" Trust me," said Boscawen and winked.

The heavy hobnailed sea-boots scraped and pounded.
Dust rose from the floor, dust fell from the walls, the
rafters creaked, the horn boat-lanterns quivered on
their hooks The fiddler, mounted on a chair, sawed
at his instrument, bowing, swaying, beating out the
unheeded time with his foot, chanting encouragement
to the dancers. " *Wan*—two—three—fower ! Round
you go, my nimble bullies !—*three*—fower—five—six !

Ha ! my sea-dogs ! Ha ! my Neptunes ! Bravely !
Bravely !—two—three—fower—five—six . . . ! ''

The heat was oppressive—a late June night and
four-and-twenty over-dressed stalwarts struggling to
fast music in a close room. Men began to pant and
blink the sweat from their eyes. The red faces glistened
as with varnish.

Jacky's George glanced at Ortho, and meeting his
eye signed to the fiddler, who brought the tune to a
close with a merry flourish and stepped down from
his perch.

The dancers sank gasping upon the benches to find
their pots miraculously replenished. They sniffed.
More bumbo, redolent of rum ! Very generous !
Very handsome indeed ! The Squire, of course.
They held their pots high. '' Good health, Squire ! ''
'' Good speed to 'e, Cap'n ! '' '' Huzza for Squire
Penhale ! ''

'' Drink hearty, boys,'' said Ortho, waving his hand.
'' There's more where that came from.''

The room was hot, they were hot, and their throats
were dry with dust and shouting. The bumbo disappeared like magic, and behold ! there was more
where the first had come from—Bossy and Benny at
hand with great steaming jugs. They cheered Ortho
afresh and drank again. A princely gentleman, the
Squire ; a wonderful night ! The rum soaked into
their warm bodies, the fumes rose to their heads, their
souls expanded with rich, vainglorious imaginings.
Jacky's George watched them sharply. The company
displayed an unnatural excitement of eye, a certain
swagger and recklessness of carriage. Staid men
smacked each other on the knees and shoulders, laughed
inordinately at trifles and talked all together. Boasts
flew about. The moment had come.

A smart rat-a-tat filled the room. All eyes swung
towards the door, and there was Bossy wearing a
scarlet Marine tunic, beating a tattoo on a side-drum,

and his father standing on a bench holding up his hand
for silence.

"Boys!" he thundered. "Neighbours! Leave
me speak a word. Brave news for one and all.·

"Speak up, landlord," they shouted. "Say thy
say, my dear!"

"Silence for Jacky's George!"

"Braa' famous news I got for 'e," said Jacky's
George. "Cap'n Penhale, whom we do all know,
have consented to take command of the *Ghost*, privateer,
of Falmouth, sailing in eight days' time for the Bay of
Biscay to cut off French ships bound in for Rochelle,
Bayonne and the Bordeaux river, loaded deep with
all the riches of the West. The *Ghost* mounts eighteen
carriage guns and can speak or leave anything that
sails, so what she don't fancy she won't fight, as the
saying is. Never was a sweeter craft seen in Carrick
Roads, and Cap'n Penhale could man she three times
over with the pick of Falmouth and Penrhyn. But
Cap'n Penhale eddn one like that. ' I'm a western
man myself,' he says to me, ' and if I do fall upon a
bit of good fortune I'd like for western men to share
it,' says he. ' Men o' my own valley!'"

A rattle on the drum from Bossy; cheers for the
Squire led by Benny; becomingly modest protestations
from Ortho.

"Well, there 'tis, my lads," said Jacky's George.
"A Cornish ship, manned by Cornishmen, with a
Monk's Cove cap'n who's drunk with you and danced
with you and who we've all known from boyhood.
What more d' you want? Them that's for a golden
fortune stand forth. Them that's for hard work and
a pauper's burial stand back. Cap'n Penhale is
leaving for Falmouth to-morrow, so speak now or
speak never. Wealth or want? which'll you have?
The *Primrose* of Padstow put into Plymouth not ten
days back with a couple of prizes worth THREE THOU-
SAND POUND!—the *Primrose* mounts but eight guns.

Her company was driving on the Hoe in hackney coaches, I hear, a keg of gin and a fiddler to each coach, and every man sporting a gold watch. The *Prophet Daniel*, armed lugger of Fowey, sent in a small prize value five hundred pound and ransomed two Biscay whalers at sea for four thousand pounds. FOUR THOUSAND FIVE HUNDRED POUNDS on one voyage, and she not home yet ! "

Somebody growled, " Aye, and the *Friendship's Adventure* of St. Ives, she ain't home yet, either."

There was a general titter. Everybody knew the fate of the luckless privateer.

Jacky's George bit his lip, feeling the popular tide against him, then gathering himself, roared the laughter under.

" Blast you ! I ain't talking of a crank old basket mounted with salvaged guns and manned by doltards ! I'm talking of the best-found fly-away in the Channel, that can leave the *Prophet* and *Primrose* standing and out-fight both together. Now who's going ? "

A man at the back of the room murmured the word ' pelchurs.'

Jacky's George crowed contemptuously. " Pilchards, i' facks ! Who said pilchards ? Where were the pilchards last season—eh ? Not here, not in this Bay. How do 'e know they'll come this season ? You don't know no more'n I do, or any other mortal man. But the French Indiamen will blow home into Biscay sure enough, their holds bursting, and Cap'n Penhale will be there to meet 'em. Pretty fool you'll look, Hezekiah Harvey, come autumn, when our brave boys do roll down the valley in po'-chaises, dressed in velvet and gold and find you sitting on the slip, with your elbows sticking out of your smock and your toes out of your boots, still looking out for the pelchurs. Pelchurs ! my soul ! "

A bellow of laughter greeted this picture of the unpopular Hezekiah. The tide had turned again.

Jacky's George rose on the wave crest shouting, "Who's for the pilchards and who's for the gold? the doubloons, the moidores, the spice and the sugar? Who would wear a coat of velvet and rings on his fingers? Walk up, my true blues, my hearts of oak!"

The crowd about the door was divided as by a projectile. A carrot-haired boy, his round face smothered with freckles, burst head-first into the room, knocking the men aside in his hurry. It was he of the bonfire.

"Hi! If Squire wants a man to fight Frenchies, I'll go," he cried. "I'm with you, Squire!"

Jacky's George turned upon his youngest son. "You've been promised these two days," he said, drily. "You'n Bossy and Benny. Now stand aside and give your betters a chance. Anybody else here with the stomach of a louse?"

A tall, dreamy youth slouched across the room and placed himself beside the youngest Baragwanath. "I'll go wid Rodney."

The unlucky lover emitted a doleful groan. "Here's another."

"Me too," said the hen-pecked wrestler.

Willie Tregurtha, the inarticulate, shuffled wildly with his feet, as though in an agony of indecision—and held his hand up. Tom Clemo came next and after that men followed with a rush.

"Hooked on the jump," Bossy exulted. "Hooked and gaffed, by the holy!"

'Hooked and gaffed!'—the words struck, barbed, into that strange thing which passed in Ortho Penhale for conscience, struck and rankled. Everywhere they would not have offended, anywhere but here. 'Hooked and gaffed'—his own people, and by him; men he had swam and fished with as a boy, their sons and brothers. Drugged with rum, gulled with sounding talk and then—harpooned. Some might profit, but others would inevitably pay. For a blink of time

the packed inn vanished and he saw again the main
deck of the *Duke* in action off the Saintes, a dismounted
gun lying across the ghastly red mess that had been
its crew, smoke rolling in through the shattered port,
the splinters smouldering. But the faces of that crew
were now those of Monk's Cove—Tom Clemo the
good-natured, big 'Kicky' John and that poor
dancing fool—dead, mangled, staring. Horrible! He
had a momentary impulse to call it off, to give these
deluded simpletons a fair chance; to say, 'Come if
you like, but for God's sake think it over! Money
we may make, but war is a rough game and somebody
will get hurt—it may be *you*. Join me and welcome
—but think it over first; to-morrow—when you're
sober.' He raised his hand, was on the point of
speaking, when his eye fell on Jacky's George. The
old adventurer was sitting on his bench, signing men
up as fast as they came forward, a smile of benevolent
triumph on his lips. Benny stood beside him, doling
out advance money and more rum to the signatories,
who appeared highly pleased with themselves.

Ortho let his hand drop, the impulse gone. "He
must have men. It was war-time, damme! The
nation was fighting for dear life. Why should not
these hulking longshoremen do their share? They
were grown men and able-bodied. He took the same
risks himself, greater even. Besides, what would
Jacky's George say if he weakened now? He could not
weaken. "Crowder, give us a tune," he shouted.
"Bossy, the drum! Drink hearty, one and all!
Here's to the flying *Ghost* and the money we'll bring
to Monk's Cove! Now, all together—Roll it out!—

> " ' While our salt water walls so begird us about
> And our cruisers and bruisers keep good looking out,
> What force need Old England to fear can offend her
> From France or from Spain or from Popish Pretender,
> So Huzzah for King George, long long may he reign!
> By right of Old England, the Queen of the main!' "

CHAPTER V

To Thomas Burnadick, Esq., Nancarrow House, Constantine, Cornwall.

DEAR SIR,
    I have the honour to inform you that we are now lying in St. Marys Roads Isles of Scilly. We left the Carrick Roads at two of the morning of July 3rd, and were off Penzance in six hours where I picked up forty-three men (eleven being stout fishermen from my own parish) under the charge of one Baragwanath who I left to beat the country. It being a fine afternoon I tacked the *Ghost* across and across before Penzance under full sail and all flags flying saluting with bow and stern chasers as she went about and had all the landsmen abord with as many wives and sweethearts as they chose to bring and a barl of Ale and a Fidler for theyr entertainment which outlay was not misspent for next day eight more landsmen came off hearing of the good Cheer to be had. The evening of the 5th I sailed for the westward. The Company now musters 83 which is all too few for a Vessel of this metal and tonage especially as not above a score were ever on a ship before. In truth we should do better founding a Colony than fighting the Kings enemys for we have Tradesmen abord of every sort, a Gamekeeper from Trelowarren, 2 Grooms and a post boy (baker-legged) a pot man (blind of an eye) a Barber, a Rat Catcher (deaf) a Stay-maker, an umbrella maker, a Fustian cutter, a calender man, a Schoolmaster, a chimney Sweep (that hath the St Vitus) and the rest are mostly farm boys, tinners and dockside ragamuffins. Beating to the westard theyr

condition with sea sickness was pitiful to see, they lay about like dead men asprawl and cheerless declining nourishment. I crused to the westard of the Bishop Rock for 8 days but speaking nothing but English Traders and Newtrals (tho' had I met with an enemy of force I must needs of run from him having scarce Men enough to work Ship leave alone Guns) I put in here for Water and Beef. Now that the Company have got theyr Sea Legs I have them constantly at work at pike and cutlass exercise and handling the Guns and trust to make a Creditable Showing before long. There is one Matter I must bring to your notice and that is a gentleman Volunteer who came abord last thing before leaving Falmouth. The Topsails were loosed and the Anchor coming home when there was a Hail from overside and over the Rail comes a very fine Fashionable Gentleman with a sword at his side. I asks him who he is and what he wants and he says (speaking outlandish) his name is De Merdrinac and he is wishful to sail with us as a Volunteer. You are a French man, says I. French Emigray, he says. Kings Officer, Republick, bah ! (spitting). Fight like Hell, you see. With that he outs with his sword and makes play with it shouting Ha Ha and stamping his Foot, the Sword darting like a spit of Lightning thro' all the Parrys, Guards and Thrusts faster than my Eye could follow. Just then the water man uplifts his voice after his Fare. The Frenchman takes no heed but continues ha haing and thrusting round the Deck like it was thronged with Enemys. The Waterman comes abord demanding his Fare very blasphemous whereat the Moosoo gives a yell and is after him sword first. The Waterman runs for the Rail and is over it faster than he came, the Frenchman giving him a prick in the Breech to speed him. The Waterman drops into his Boat like a sack of Potatoes pushes off an Oars length and again hollers for his Fare swearing he will have the Law of us. The

Frenchman feels in his Pockets and turns 'em inside out. All gone, says he, laughing, then he tears off his silver Shoe Buckels and pitches them at the Water man. Go to the Devil son of a Pig, he says and the Waterman is gone rowing for his Life. Put that Skewer up for Gods Sake or you will spit Somebody and I am short-handed as it is, I says, hard put to keep from laughing. Have you a Paper to prove yourself? if not I trust you can swim for I shall surely heave you Overbord. The Frenchman pulls a Packet from his coat and hands them to me with a Polite Bow. I had no time to examine them then but I have since and they Appear all in Order. His name is Rene Phillipe Count of Merdrinac in Brittany—he served eight years in the East Indies. Later being weakened with Wounds and Fevers he was sent home to find his Ancestral Mansion burned to the ground by the Revolution and his Family perished by the Gilloutine. He escaped to England by a Smuggler from Roscoff and has been living in Falmouth giving Fencing lessons. On the night of July 2nd he attended a Venison dinner at Blundstones and played Ecarte with some Gentlemen afterwards. By one o'clock he had lost every Penny he possessed, by half past one he had lost his Cravat Solitair, his Watch, his Seals and his Rings. He then came straight off to the *Ghost* as he stood (hoping thereby to restore his Fortunes and go Gambling again) paying his way with his Shoe Buckles. He declares himself well known to Sir Michael Nowell, Mr. Southwell Curtis and Mr. Pidgley, the Banker, and other Gentlemen of Falmouth. For my part I am Well Satisfied but not so Mr. Pentacost who says that the Count being a French-man must also be a Perfidious Character, but I think Mr. Pentacosts complaint is not so much against the Counts nationality as his Religion which Mr. Penta-cost has discovered to be Catholick, he being very Acrimonious against that sect. I would be vastly obliged to you Sir if you would enquire of Mr. Curtis or Mr. Pidgley concerning the Count not that I have any misgivings but in order to quiet Mr. Pentacost whose continual mumblings are tedius to indure. The *Ghost* sails like a witch if with the trifle of a lee helm which I will correct. All hands are healthful and in good spirits now they have got their sea legs. The young man Sawle from your estate is shaping well, he wishes me to convey his respectful obligations to yourself. I shall cruse to the westward of the Bishop returning here in ten days.

> I have the honour to remain
> your most obedient and humble servant
> ORTHO PENHALE (Master)

Ghost. Privateer.
Isles of Scilly
July 13, 1795.

.　　　.　　　.　　　.　　　.　　　.　　　.

To Mrs. Phoebe Sawle, widow. Constantine. Cornwall. by Silly packet.

DEER MA,

Yest a few lines to say I hope you are in good Health as I am but I thort you wood not see me agen the See ran as big as Hills all around and no land in site I thort wee was overwelmed the Ship jumping like a colt nite and day and the See bursting agen her I cud get no rest nor hold no vitels and if a Frinchman had come along he cud of took us for all I cared. Now I am restored and in good healh as I hope you are for which God be Thanked for I never thort to see another Day. Yest a few lines to say wee are in the Isles of Silly in carm water like helford River yesterday I climbed to the Top Gallant Yard and saw the land of Cornwall far away I wish I was there but did not stop long as I was near ded of Frite being so high. These are poor islands but the People make

a grand Trayd smuggling despite the Kings ship that
is heer to stop them. Capn Penhale is very merry
laffing and joking at the men but Mr. Pentacost is
for ever nagging and complaining at them he is
Religus and will have no swaring or blasfeeming the
sailers call him old sour belly the food is teedius beef
and pork and pees I wish I cud have some of your
figgy pudden and Muggitty Pie and fresh eggs I wood
eat for a week. I am training on the Big Guns every
day Mr. Baragwanath the Gunner is a terrible sharp
man who do not think twice to doust you if you are
slow with a Bar or Rammer wee have not met any
Frinch as yet but Capn Penhale says we shall soon
meet Plenty and make our Fortunes which I am sure
I trust wee shall tell lizzie Prowse I am in good health
and will be home come feasten with plenty money
never more to rome I trust your loving Son Richard
Henry Sawle abord Privateer *Ghost*.

Tell Matt Williams my new Breeches and Westcut
must be reddy come Feasten without fail.

·   ·   ·   ·   ·   ·   ·

To George Mathew Baragwanath. Admiral Anson
Inn, Monks Cove. St. Gwithian. Cornwall.

DEAR FATHER,
We are in Scilly and all well Peter Mumford
says he has sum of the *Rite Stuff* hid on the Island of
Rosevean in the *Old Spot* you will know where He
Says. He card it a sennight since from Gernsay but
cant move it as the Preventive has him watched close
as a Kat. He says will you send a Boat to fish on the
Powll she can cum in by nite and take it and you can
credit him with the moneys which is *twenty two pound*.
I have a crew to train to the Guns as never you saw
Townsmen and Farmers and such-like lousey swipes
yore son Benny.

·   ·   ·   ·   ·

Thomas Burnadick Esq., Nancarrow House.

DEAR SIR,
          I am obliged to you for your letter receeved
this day and for your information concerning the
count of Merdrinac, which is greatly to my satisfaction and which I will convey to Mr. Pentacost tho'
I have small hope to convince him for if a man were
a Heavenly Angel and yet a Catholic Mr. Pentacost
would hang him out of hand, feathers, halo and all.
The Count has already proved himself very servicable
in the exercise of small arms and Borders. He has
also selected a party of marksmen for the Tops and
trained them to shoot at old bottles and casks, thrown
overbord. The Trelowarren Game keeper displays
great murderousness of aim likewise two mine boys
from Camborne whose aptitude gives me to think
they have handled Muskets before and that by the
light of the Moon gathering cock peasants in Tehidy
woods. We are this day in from crusing to the westard.
I have spoke many ships but they were all English
or else plaguey Newtrals. On July 15th at Meridian
we spied a suspicious Lugger and gave chase but
the Wind being light and the Sea overcast she out
sweeps and sweeped from us and escaped in a fog bank.
On July 17th we spied a sail hull down to the westard
so gave chase. He hauled his wind and went away
northerly under a press of Sail. In four glasses I
was up with him and he appeared a Frenchman. I
therefore fired a gun for him to heave to and ran up
the Tri-colour. He also showed the Tricolour but
held his way. I therefore sheered alongside hoisted
English colours and gave him a Broadside. At the
same time he let fly his broadside and hoisted English
colours too. I got my Speaking Trumpet and axed
him what the Devil he was after. He replied in very
opprobrious Scotch axing me the same. It turned
out the brig was a Rochelle vessel prize to H.M.

Frigate *Garland* bound for Plymouth under a Prize Crew. Both ships being French built led to a very natural and laughable Mistake in which there was little damage done the *Ghost* taking a bruse or two in her topsides and the Prize having one man killed and one wounded. The Prize Master who came abord for a glass of grog says he thinks the French Martiniquemen have sailed and will make Landfall on the Coasts of Spain. He says they are reported to be under strong Escort but that does not affright me for I never knew a convoy yet that was not mostly stragglers. As soon as I have taken water I will sail for the Bay of Biscay. Your tenant Richard Sawle has been suffering from the toothache in consequence of learning to chaw terbacca sailor fashion but is otherwise well though somewhat timid aloft. I have rid myself of one Tippet a printer of Truro a sulking argufying chap overweighted with jaw, I passed him to the Captain of a King's Sloop here with two bottels of porter and my compliments and he will get his back well scratched with the Cat if he tries any of his argufying tricks there. In his stead I have picked up a Swede seaman (deserter) and a free Negro who was put ashore here with the itch (but is now cured) and can play the drum.

I am sir your humble and obt. servant.
ORTHO PENHALE (Master)

Ghost, Privateer.
Isles of Scilly,
July 19. 1795.

·   ·   ·   ·   ·   ·   ·

Thomas Burnadick Esq., Nancarrow House.

DEAR SIR,

I have the pleasure to inform you that Success has at last crowned our Efforts. After crusing fruitless for near two months the prizes tumbled in so fast

as to be an embarrassment. On Aug. 27 while crusing between Belle Isle and Isle Dieu I fell in with the
French dogger, *Premier Jugement de Solomon*, bound
from Nantes to the Mississipi with port, lead shot,
Spanish bar iron, knives, Velvet wine, Brandy, beaver
hats, silk stockings, candels, linen Handkerchiefs,
ruffled shirts, shifts and black pepper. She tried to
put back behind the Isle de Ré but I got between her
and the shore and fired a Gun whereupon she surrendered. I had no sooner put a Prize Crew abord
than a fresh sail was spied bearing W by S. Bidding
the Prize follow I stood after her. She proved to be
the *St. Jean de Bayonne* from Newfoundland with fish
and she also hauled her Flag upon my firing one gun.
Her Master informed me he fully thought I was a
French privateer and was never more surprised in his
life when he saw English Colours fly to the peak.
It being then evening I stood to the westard all night
when as Dawn breaks behold there is a big Merchant
Bark right upon us! I showed the Tricolour (to
which she replied with the same) and passed along her
lee unmolested, her Master bawling at me thro' a
Trumpet from the Mizzen Shrouds and all her people
with theyr heads over the hammock nettings looking
for News of France. I jumped to the rail myself and
put my hand to my Ear like I was hard of hearing
shouting Kwar? Kwar? (which is french for what?
what?) by which stratagem I had good observation
of the ship and perceived her to be well manned.
Nevertheless I was determined to attempt her being
all unsuspected and in an Advantageous position and
she having the Appearance of a Rich Vessel so as
soon as we had passed clear I hoisted English Colours
at the same time wearing under her Quarter and
pouring my starbord Broadside into her stern windows.
She was so astonished I slashed three Broadsides into
her before she could make reply. She then veered
giving me a taste of her port guns as she came round.

I put my Helm over and crossed her stern again,
raking her. She then went away southerly, lasking
and I after her playing continuous with my chasers
and Yawing from time to time to bring my Bow
guns into play while she could make no reply her
Stern being nigh battered in and her Stern Chasers
dismounted. We continued this way for a glass she
driving South out of control and us after her goring
her heels like a Dog with a Bullock. At length there
was a loud explosion and part of her topside blew
out and her stern took fire whereupon she surrendered.
She is *L'Amiable Coralie* of Bordeaux, Martinique to
Nantes with coffee, Indigo, St. Domingo cotton,
Muscovado sugar and some bags of Ginger. She
carried eight guns (9 pounders) and four Quakers
(as we call wooden guns) and forty men five of whom
was killed and seven wounded. The *Ghost* has but
one Man wounded from a splinter and that not bad
and one Boy burnt from a powder flask and that not
bad either. I send this by Mr. Rosewarne prize
Master who has orders to proceed to Falmouth with
the *Solomon* and the *St. Jean*. Myself I am following
as escort to the *Coralie* who sails but crank with her
Stern being beat in and a jury rudder.

Your humbl and obt Servant.

ORTHO PENHALE (Master)

Ghost, Privateer,
Off Ushant.
Aug. 29. 1795.

P.S. Shortly after the *Coralie* struck we heard a
great screeching from the water and espied an old
Dame clad only in her Night robe floating on a bale
of cotton and so pulled her abord. It appears she
(a person of consequence) being disturbed by one of
my nine pounder shot entering her cabin sprang from
bed and took refuge in the tween decks among the
cotton Bales. When the powder barl exploded she
was blown out thro' the Hole. All her clothes being

destroyed we had nothing to dress her in but the stuff taken from the *Solomon* which however she took in good part and is now in the Main cabin of the *Ghost* playing piquet with the Count and Mr. Sheringham the surgeon, dressed in a silk Night Gown, some fine waistcoats, a pair of my breeches and a cambric Night-Cap (having lost her wig) which seeing she is very tall and bony gives her a comical appearance. Her maid however (a small delicate girl, not bad looking) is greatly offended at the mishap and was very sharp with the Count when he was for consoling her (some Women look upon War as so much Nonsense and hold the loss of a 40 Gun Ship as nothing against the loss of a Bonnett) Your tenant, Richard Sawle was much upset at the first discharge and cast himself on deck declaring he was Slain. The Gunner took means to restore him and for the rest of the Action (if so it may be called, though indeed a more one sided affair‘I was never in) he conducted himself dutiful but pale.

.   .   .   .   .   ~

To Mrs. Pheobe Sawle. Widow. Constantine. Cornwall.

DEER MA.

Yest a few lines hoping you are in good health as I am tho' I have been in as great Peril as ever a Man saw and was near Slain a Hundred times by canon balls flying round my hed thick as Bes but Thank God I am escaped in good healh wee have been in the Bay of Biscay and have took 3 prizes the first 2 did not shoot but the 3d was roguish I thort I was ded a Hundred times over but did not show Fear and continued Manful thro' out tho' often I wood have given all the Fortunes in the wurld to be safe in constantine plowing or sitting at my dinner I wish Jes Trevellow or Paul Maggs or some other of them Big Mouth Fellows up to Church Town cud of been with us they will not talk so brave before me again I will say yes any Cock can crow on his own Dung heap (meaning constantine) but it takes a Game cock to crow on Anothers (meaning the Bay of Biscay) I will not let any of them Stay Homes speak before me now I have been in Bludy Battels and seen the wurld. Capn Penhale has give each man a Beever hat and a ruffld shirt from a Prize a sailer told me we may get 70 pound a man prize Money beside wages so tel Lizzie prowse she had best make up her Mind for when I come home in my Ruffld Shirt and Beever hat with gold in my pocket there will be every Maiden after me and I can pick and chuse. I am sending these few lines by Sol Jackett who is going to Falmouth ahead of wee in a prize your luving son Richard Henry Sawle.

Tell Matt Williams to cut that wescut so as to show my Ruffld Shirt.

.   .   .

To Doctor Benjamin Starbuck. Bread Street. Bristol. England.

Dear Benjamin,
The armed snow *John* of Chepstow sailing to-morrow for the Avon I take this Opportunity of writing to you. We are in the Port of Bilbao having put in here to replenish water barrels. We have now been out six weeks from Falmouth on this our second cruise and have, so far, been successful in taking two vessels, one of which was of considerable value. A week since, however, we were near taken ourselves being chaced four hours by two powerful French Frigates which approached close upon us on either quarter. To haul to either hand was to fall aboard one of the pursuers, to continue was to crash upon a rock-bound Coast. When night fell a French Prison

appeared the sole alternitive to a Watery Tomb and it was with melancholy reflections that I contemplated the firey descent of Phoebus. The Captain, however, conceived the Ingenious Stratagem of quickly stripping our Vessel to her Bare Poles (whereby rendering her the less visible) and setting the Long Boat adrift under a square sail with a Lantern lashed to her Mast Head. The enemy thinking it to be our Binnacle Light continued the Pursuit, passing us by in the Darkness so close it seemed impossible we should not be discovered. I confess that for myself the Suspense was well-nigh intolerable.

A more admirable Commander in time of Peril than this same Captain (Penhale, by name) I have never met with in my sea experience, resourceful, bold and of a cheerfulness which would seem to encrease in proportion to the Danger in hand and which is a source of the highest Inspiration to all around, yet now is he gone ashore figged out like a Vauxhall Bully-Beau to ogle the Ladies on the gilt balconies or swagger like a common Horse Guard on the Promenade of Los Canos. Human Nature is indeed composed of the strangest Contradictions. Here we have a French *emigré* Nobleman who kills his countrymen first and weeps upon them afterwards. Who resigns his position as Captain of Marines after every action, yet on being again confronted with the detested Tricolour boards with such ferocity as to appal all beholders. Again there is Mr. Pentacost, the first mate. Yesterday walking on the *Arenal* we met with a procession of singing children (headed by Clergy) dressed in white and bearing among them the Images of Saints. What should my companion do but remove his Hat and in stentorian tones demand of Almighty God that He should shower down Blazing Brimstone and instantly consume these pretty innocents as *Idolaters !* Fortunately the crowd mistook his attitude, thinking he was invoking Blessings rather than

Thunderbolts. On the other hand this same Pentacost is possessed of an ancient black Dog, much afflicted with Fleas and Mange, on which he lavishes the tenderest affection. This Port of Bilboa is indeed charming and singular. The verdant Hills are embellished with a variety of Plantations, Vineyards and Groves of chestnut trees, interspersed with the Gardens of Country Houses. On the quay of Olavijaja (close to which we lie) a party of young men and Women are dancing the *Romeria* to the music of Tambourines, illumed by blazing barrels of Whale Oil. The bells of a Nunnery chime sweetly on the night air. All is Peace and harmless Gaiety. To-morrow (alack!) we put to Sea again into the midst of Peril and Sanguinary Strife. Please convey to your sister, Miss Hannah, my Respectful Addresses. Tell her I have her amiable Pursuit in mind and I have culled numerous Blossoms in this vicinity that (to my dire ignorance) appeared rare and I am pressing them, according to her Directions, between the leaves of my *Materia Medica*.

Believe me always, my dear Benjamin
Your assured Friend
GILES SHERINGHAM (Surgeon).

Ghost privateer
Bilboa. Spain
6th Oct., 1796.

Note. I have found in the case of Amputations cauteries to be less tragical than Astringents tho' confessedly more severe. *Pul Vitriol, Roman* is the readiest.

.　　.　　.　　.　　.　　.　　.

To Mrs. Phebe Sawle, Widow. Constantine. Cornwall. by the John of Chepstow.

DEER MA

Yest a few Lines hoping you are in good healh as I am. Wee are in bilbore in Spain it is a fine

Town bigger nor Falmouth the Men wear hair nets and the Wimmen veils but they have Bright Eyes and walk very proud the Monks are thick as crows. Wee have took 2 more Prizes one of them behaved roguish but wee gave him a rare drubbing for his Pains the new Landsmen wee took abord last time at Falmouth was in a grate Fright thinking they was Slain and pale as Death I cud not help but laff Robt Pascoe of Manaccan was a week overcast with Sea-Sickness I had grate Sport with him he is poor Lubber as wee sailors call Landsmen. I cud not come Home last time wee was in Falmouth no man was let ashore wee was only there one night and day I saw Mawnan Church and Saint Keverne as we sailed by and up helford River to calamansack but cud not see constantine no matter I will be Home a month from now with near 200 pound in my pockett and a Beever Hat tell Lizzie prowse I have bought a spanish veil for she to wear come feasten your luving son Richard Henry Sawle abord privateer *Ghost*. Tell Matt Williams I don't want that westcut as I have bought a spanish westcut a red one.

.   .   .   .   .   .

To Thomas Burnadick Esq., Nancarrow House. By the prize *Jong Vrow Maria* Mr. Curnow, prize master.

DEAR SIR,

I am sending this by a Dutch prize taken in the early hours of this morning after a sharp Action costing us 3 killed and 8 wounded. She is from Archangel Russia with Wood Ash, Potash, hemp, Salt Fish, 90 bundels Skins and 25 bales Horsehair. I was three days in Bilboa to fill my barrels hardly escaping before War was declared with Spain. We will have the whole World leagued agen us soon. The Biscayners gave us no hindrance, they lament the War being Friendly to us and having a great Detestation of the French. I can say no more now as there is a Sail reported, bearing down. I will be Home to refit at the end of this Month, all being well.

Your obt. Servant
ORTHO PENHALE (Master)

Ghost privateer.
Off Ferrol
Oct., 11th, 1796.

P.S. I regret to state that your tenant Richard Sawle is among the killed, being struck in the Temple by a Musket Ball. I also regret that his Effects (a few odds and ends of cheap Finery) have been plundered by his Shipmates.

CHAPTER VI

MR. CARCLEW dropped the reins on the roan's
withers and fumbled for his flask. A neighbouring conversation attracted him. "What's that?"
he asked. "Yes, he's home. Saw him myself in
Penzance, dressed up in more gold lace than the
whole Admiralty."

"Seem me he's entitled to it—if what I hears is true?"
growled an elderly yeoman, enthroned on an enormous
grey mare.

"What did you hear?" Mr. Teage inquired,
munching his belated lunch.

"I heerd as how he and another privateer creeped
up Bordeaux river in a fog and cut out six prizes."

Carclew whistled. "My soul! how the story
grows! Two it was, two only."

Said the yeoman, "Well, seem me that weren't so
bad, neyther—under the nose of the guard ship."

Mr. Borlase, idly flipping his whip at a thistle,
agreed: "Bold work."

"Bold! Who the devil said he wasn't bold?" Carclew
snapped. "He's too damned bold, if you ask me."

The yeoman lumbered to the defence. "So it do
appear—for the Frinch."

Barclay Johns laughed in his noisy manner. "Got
you there, Carclew, my son! 'Pon my oath you're sour
enough to turn new milk! Liver, I suppose. Wish we
had you with us for a week. We'd shake the . . ." He
jerked erect in his stirrups. "What's that? Over
yonder, on the green. See it? By cripes it's a fox!
There he goes, over the wall. Away! Away!" He
thrust his brown filly forward, hallooing with excitement.

Carclew was disdainful. " One would think he had not seen a fox before ! "

" He has not—for some time," said Anthony Trevaskis, drily. " They are scarce off Ushant."

" Ha ha ! " the yeoman guffawed—he had been a tenant of Carclew's.

Teage laughed, blowing a mouthful of crumbs over the Reverend Samuel Rogers. Apologies ensued.

The smocked figure of a yokel, standing on a bank a quarter of a mile away, became animated. It danced a species of war dance, brandishing a manure fork.

" Jim's seed 'en ! The old Trevelloe varmint for a hundred poun' ! " cried a tattered moor-man with the fine generosity of the impecunious. " Big as a sheep he is, the rogue ! Gone over ! " He drummed his shaggy pony's ribs with an ash-plant and plunged into the gorse bushes, followed by an urchin on a reluctant black donkey.

" Hold hard ! Hold hard and gi' master and the dogs a chance," the yeoman implored, wrestling with his colossal mare. " Mr. Rose-Price, sir ! Fox gone ovver, t'ards Boskennel ! Ah ha ! Ruby's on to 'en ! Roust 'en, good bitch ! "

Rose-Price came over the moor at a gallop, calling the hounds up; his dapple-grey leaping the furze clumps, its bob tail quivering. After him cantered the whipper-in, cursing the laggards, his whip thong popping like a pistol. " Yah-ha, get forrard there ! Scholar ! Gypsy ! Venus ! Yah ha-ar ! "

The Reverend Rogers pulled his hat over his ears. Carclew took a last swig at the brandy flask. Teage hummed happily :

> " ' So John he went up onto a hill,
> And blew on his horn both loud and shrill;
> Says the fox, ' That's very pretty music, still
> I'd rather be home in my den, O ! '

Please God keep him off the cliffs ! ''

" Please God turn him into the grass country ! " said the yeoman.

" Amen ! " said the Reverend Samuel.

Across the moor they went, splashing through pools, kicking up the bog mud in black fountains. A crumbling bank of earth and stones confronted them. The great mare hooked her fore-legs over it, tore off the crust and wallowed over the gap on her stomach. The rest followed through. Rose-Price showed for a second against the sky-line—a scarlet spot against an immensity of windy blue—then dipped from sight. Came three grass fields, separated by rough granite blocks set upright. The company charged the walls in line. Teage's canny chestnut swung forward with its nose out, looking for gaps; skimmed them with a minimum of margin. Carclew's tall roan took them as they came, exulting in her powers; hovered over them like a bird in flight, tucked her hind-legs neatly under her and sped on again. The grey farm mare crouched, bunched her vast muscles and hurtled into the air like a clumsy projectile. Anthony Trevaskis' dun hireling got over with a wriggle and a peck. He was in for a fall, he knew, but he didn't care, the going was good while it lasted. They were racing over turf on the hill-top now. Gwithian church tower showed on the left hand backed by bronze ridges of moorland. Before them a rolling patchwork of green fields and brown, criss-crossed by grey stone walls. Rooks exploded out of a coppice and circled overhead, cawing hysterically. A few sea-gulls drifted high in the blue, like stray snow-flakes. All this his eye took in at a glance and came to earth again as the grey mare pounded alongside, roaring like an organ, shouldered him into a ditch and knocked a loose wall down with her iron knees. The yeoman called a blasphemous apology over his shoulder and charged on, dragging at the reins. Trevaskis got his cob out of the ditch and pursued as best he could, but he was at the tail of the hunt now. He saw the scarlet blob that was Rose-Price top a bank on the sky-line, the silver twinkle of shoes as his horse kicked off. A score more spots—black, brown, green, blue—bobbed up and under and he was left alone. Nevertheless he kept on. As he had said, foxes were scarce off Ushant and the hireling though slow and precarious was, as yet, unblown. Let hounds check for but a minute or two and they would be on terms again. He pounded down a mirey lane, an arm up-thrown to fend the clutching brambles; floundered through a shallow bottom, of sedge and tussock, and pressed up-hill once more, following the grey mare's elephantine tracks. A bank barred the way, a solid affair, six feet high, topped with blackthorn and gorse. Trevaskis glanced to left and right. There were no gaps and no gates. It was either get over or go back. Lumps of sod torn from the face, stones dislodged here and there, broken bushes, testified that the hunt had passed that way. Trevaskis clamped his knees to the saddle and drove the cob at the bank, fully conscious that he was begging disaster. Miraculously the cob got over, how its rider could not say. He had the sickening impression that his mount was falling backwards on him; then that it had changed ends and was falling forwards; then, as a ploughed field rose to smite him in the face, something came up under him, lifting him clear, and he found it was his steed's neck—they were over. Gasping with relief he worked back to where the saddle should have been, to find there was no saddle there. At that moment the cob stumbled in a furrow and Trevaskis slid to the ground. He rose, caught his mount (which indeed evinced no desire to escape but fell to rolling) and trudged back to find the saddle. It lay under the bank, the last effort having proved too much for its solitary girth strap. Well, that was definite. Remained to get the strap repaired and jog home.

Where was he? Those woods over there were
Treverven, surely?—or else Boskenna. He had been
away thirteen years—forgotten. Gwithian tower stood
clear of Carn Brea, Boskenna back to the right. He
must be—then, with a queer cold contraction of the
heart he knew. He was on that bit of high ground
they called ' The Hayle.' Just over the crest, within
a stone's throw almost, was Joppa—Joppa ! He turned
sharply right-handed along the hill-top, leading the
cob, the saddle under his arm. In the very next
field he met with luck, a ploughman, chirping to his
team.

Had he means to repair the broken strap? The
ploughman had the very thing, needle and twine;
he had brought them afield to mend a halter during
the dinner-hour. There and then he squatted in the
hedge and began to stitch the broken ends together;
a hairy, middle-aged person, barely five feet high, but
broad as he was long; hands like shovels, legs absurdly
bowed, wrapped with strips of old sacking. His two
red oxen stood motionless, except for the movement
of their lower jaws, statues in terra-cotta. Rooks and
sea-gulls stalked the furrows, contesting for worms.
The smell of new-turned earth rose up, moist and rich.
Trevaskis, sea-weary, snuffled it as a novice snuffles
incense. The ploughman chattered, glad of company.
A fine day for the gentry to be out sporting. He had
seen the hunt go by. A sheep-dog had turned the fox
up valley. It must be at Noongallas by now. If it
got among that honeycomb of old earths the gentry
might as well ride home. The gentleman was from
Penzance, he supposed? Lived there? Ah ! only
visiting friends. A fine town, Penzance, full of gaiety
and fashion. He tightened the last stitch and bit the
twine off. If the gentleman was returning to Penzance
he'd best go back two fields, where he'd find a lane
leading past a cottage. From thence a cow-path
crossed the valley and—minute directions followed.

Trevaskis pressed a shilling into the earthy palm. " Anyone in the cottage? " he asked, casually.

The man shook his head. " No, nobody these years." It had been a freehold farm once, but the family was no good and had gone to America after the war. How they found the passage money was a mystery. Hadn't boots for their feet one day and the next were gliding out of Mounts' Bay on an emigrant brig, a suit of new clothes to each member, proud as kings. The farm belonged to Bosula now—Bosula was the manor. " Two fields back and down the lane. Goo-day, sir."

Trevaskis rode back, as directed, till out of sight, then halted. He knew the road to Penzance well enough. The lane lay before him, it was the quickest way, yet he hesitated, debating alternatives. He might go north, crossing the bogs above Bosullow—but that was a long detour. He might go south and cross at Bosula —but that involved passing through the manor yard, and he had reasons for avoiding the manor. He looked at the overgrown lane, scowling, biting his lip, an uneasy glint in his blue eyes, one would almost have said that he was afraid of it. Then he sat up, bracing his shoulders. " P'ff ! Bogies ! Get up, you ! " He pricked the cob with his spurs. " On ! " Down the lane he rode, sitting stiffly erect, beating the brambles back with his crop, staring straight before him, came into daylight again before a tumble-down cottage.

Trevaskis did not turn his head. " Tcluc ! Go on ! " he ordered, a queer tremor in his voice. " Step on, curse you ! "

The cob stepped on obediently, passed the cot by and then was brought up by gathering pressure on the bit. Its rider was slowly turning to stare at the cottage. A poor place at best, it was a ruin now. The ridge beam had fallen, carrying the thatch with it. The windows had been taken out, leaving empty black holes, like eye-sockets in a skull. Moss grew on the window-ledges, the door hung by one hinge, its latch broken, and over the north end ivy poured in a green devouring wave. In the tiny garden nettles and young saplings sprouted; the lone apple tree bowed earthwards, overborne by a strangling weight of ivy. A few years more and there would be nothing left, the wind, the rain and the weeds would see to that. A few years more and there would be nothing left to show that man had been; tits would build and chirrup in the ivy clumps, adders slide among the tumbled stones. Trevaskis, darkly brooding, was glad of it. Let it all go, be wiped out, forgotten utterly. For he had been born here, twenty-three years before, nameless, unwanted, a child of sorrow. Of the circumstances of his birth he knew nothing, wished to know nothing. He remembered his mother, but with little kindness, a shrill, worn slattern. Looking back he knew she must have been overdriven—four young children and a man to tend. Still, no word or sign of tenderness had she ever given him, that he recollected, not one. He tried to think gently of her, but could not. His step-father too, a shambling, sly, ineffectual man. How he had hated him ! The door creaked. Trevaskis started. The door was opening ! He saw the face of his step-father in the crack as he had seen it thirteen years before, a thin cruel face peering round the door—there was a stick in his hand !

The door swayed back again, it was only the draught that moved it. Trevaskis shook himself angrily. That his childish terrors should possess him still ! Him—twenty-three, twelve stone of bone and muscle, a fighting man ! He kicked his spurs fiercely into the cob, urging it away—but memory rode with him, a ghostly magician conjuring pictures in a dark glass, drab, ugly pictures best forgotten. Ten years had he suffered at Joppa Farm. Then, of a sudden, it was all over. He remembered standing, ragged and distrustful, in a lawyer's office in Penzance, his step-father

cringing and whining; old Trebilcock very short with
him. Money passed between them, he believed.
Within a week he was at the Helston Grammar School,
well fed, well clothed.

Three years of that and the invisible force snatched
him up once more and he found himself, a forlorn brat
of thirteen, aboard a King's frigate in Falmouth
Harbour. He was hauled up on the quarter-deck
before the captain and there and then forced to fight
a midshipman years his senior. The midshipman
promptly knocked him flat, and when he got up
knocked him down again. Seeing he could not rise,
the young Trevaskis, bleeding like a pig, bewildered
to tears, made a dive for his tormentor's knees and
pulling him to the deck did his best to kill him. He
was hauled off by a laughing lieutenant and sent
below to the purser's drunken wife to have his nose
swabbed. He was merely being tested for pluck.

Three hours later little Trevaskis lay asprawl in the
'tween-decks, battered, woebegone, sea-sick, wishing
he might die, as the frigate raced out-bound for the
West Indies, night and a half-gale whistling on her
heels. Such was his introduction to the King's navy.
He had now ten years' service to his credit. On the
day he was gazetted lieutenant he wrote to old Trebilcock saying he would no longer require or accept the
allowance that had been paid him with passable
regularity throughout his midshipman days, whereby
cutting (he thought) the last string that bound him
to the unhappy past. But there are strings no knife
will cut.

Clear of the dank lane, halted in plain sunlight on the
rim of the Keigwin valley, Anthony Trevaskis realised,
with a poignant stirring of heart, why he had returned
to the place he thought he hated. They had sprung
a lower mast in the ceaseless buffeting off Ushant and
had put into Plymouth to step a new one. Nine
days' leave was the consequence. Barclay Johns was

his shipmate and fast friend and lived near Penzance.
" Come home with me for a week and hunt," said
Barclay Johns. " My mother is dying to see you."

" Penzance is not Joppa," said Trevaskis to himself.
" I'd like to see Mrs. Johns again." Now he knew
that what he wanted to see again was this valley, his
childhood's sanctuary. The Keigwin stream came
down from Bartinny Downs and ran four miles under
a thicket of trees, gurgling round gnarled willow roots,
plunging through tunnels of fern. Here it rippled
crystal clear, over yellow sand beds, sleek as a snake
skin; there sprayed over a boulder in a silver fan-tail
or boiled in a rock-pit a froth of pearly bubbles. The
trees leaned over it, thorns furred with grey lichen,
elders twisted like old witches and hung with ropes of
wild vine. Nobody ever came there. No voice was
heard but the liquid song of the stream and the coo of
wood-pigeons. Birds nested there by the thousand
in season, trout darted from shadow to shadow in the
pools. In the great barrow at Buccas' Hole badgers
and foxes lodged side by side. Trevaskis, lying covert
in the bluebells, had watched the tawny cubs frisking
like kittens at the earth mouths. A paradise for a lone
boy, this valley had been his one young happiness.
His heart went out to it again, lying at his feet, the bare
trees bronzed with November sunshine. He was no
keen seaman, like Barclay Johns. He was a sailor
because the mysterious agency that had controlled
his youth made him one. He remained in the navy
because he knew no other trade. But his heart was
not in it. It was here, deep-rooted in the land that
had bred him, in the rolling hills, the little patchwork
fields and the secret, song-haunted valley. He saw
himself, as he was always seeing himself in his fondest
dreams, come home for ever, farming these same fields,
ploughing them, seeding them, reaping them, husband-
ing them through good years and bad. Spring would
be spring to him then, the valley white with hawthorn,

the elms pointed with green flame and bird song all
about. Summer nights with the moon coming up over
the hill-top and the scent of dew-wet honeysuckle.
Autumn—his valley hung with gold, with ochre and
scarlet. Winter—long nights before a red log fire,
dogs drowsing on the hearth, a pipe, a book on fishing,
dreams.

Dreams indeed !—for a nameless, homeless man.
A week more and he would be at sea again, threshing
up and down between Isle Vierge and Pointe du Raz,
straining his eyes through the snow squalls and rain
squalls for the enemy that threatened always but came
never.

The bay cob, who had been quietly cropping the
bank-side, lifted its head and cocked its blunt ears.
Trevaskis woke out of his reverie with a start. Somebody was approaching along the hedge, a young girl
picking sloes. So intent on her work was she that she
did not notice the sailor till she was close upon him.
Then she emitted a confused squeak and jumped
backwards, tearing her dress on a bramble.

Trevaskis lifted his hat. " Your pardon. I fear
I startled you."

The girl blushed prettily, the colour coming to her
face like the flush on an October peach, a warm madder.
A charmingly pretty face it was, round, gentle, with
glossy brown ringlets clustered close about it.

" Oh, I—I didn't expect to see anybody here."

" Your dress ? "

" An old one—of no consequence, thank you."
She smiled, one lone dimple making a delicious tuck
in her left cheek, bobbed him a curtsy and walked on.

Trevaskis dragged the phlegmatic cob about.
" Pardon me."

The girl turned, a flicker of alarm in her soft brown
eyes—she had been warned against this kind of
encounter—but it was merely a flicker. The lieutenant
was not of the type that pesters unprotected women,

nor did he look it. His eyes were a blue blaze of admiration, colour flooded the tanned face, but his manner was all deference.

" You called, sir? "

" I—er——" Why had he called? To ask her who she was and where she lived and might he see her again, of course. To say, ' My darling dear, I have never loved anybody before, but I love you now, you dimpling, sweet-faced little brown thing ! Come here to my arms, where you belong. This is sudden, I know, but all the best things come suddenly.' The words rose hot to his lips, he gulped them back. Absurd ! Ridiculous ! This was no dairy-maid. She'd be frightened out of her life, take him for some ogling buck and fly. Nor could he see her again. He was in the navy and it was war-time. To-morrow he must take the Plymouth coach and beat through the rain and snow from Isle Vierge to Pointe du Raz, up and down till the rocks or the round-shot released him. " I—er——"

Curse the navy ! curse the war ! Then, presto ! he was blessing the day he entered the navy. He stood between the French invaders and this girl—this girl he had never seen three minutes before ! His dreary patrolling appeared glorified, a knight-errantry. As long as he had eyes to watch them and limbs to fight, the armies of Bonaparte should molest neither this valley nor this girl. The dumb land would never thank him, the girl never know, but that mattered as nothing.

" I—er—I——"

But he could not sit here yammering like a fool. What the deuce could he say to hold her for another thrice-precious minute?

" I—er—oh, could you direct me to Penzance? I have been hunting—fell out—stranger."

The girl pointed a juice-stained finger. " Straight through that gap and you'll see a cow-path that leads to a ford. Then keep straight up the hill and you'll find a lane joining the road."

"Thank you. Er—is it far?"

She pursed her pink mouth thoughtfully. Trevaskis longed to leap off his horse and kiss it. "About five—six miles."

"Thank you. Er—is it a good road?"

"Fair. The main pack-track from Monk's Cove."

"Thank you." What more could he say? Invention failed him. "Er—good-afternoon—and—er—thank you again, vastly."

"No trouble to me, sir." She smiled that heart-melting smile of hers, bobbed a second curtsy and vanished up the tangled lane.

For some moments Trevaskis watched the spot where he had last seen her, then sighed and turned the dun cob down-hill. Good-bye, little sweet-faced brown girl! Good-bye, valley of dreams! . . . Isle Vierge to Pointe du Raz, Pointe du Raz to Isle Vierge, in the wind and rain.

He passed through the gap, zigzagged down a grass slope bossed with granite boulders, passed a second gap and was aware of a man standing under the hawthorns, a cocked fowling-piece in his hands. Farmer shooting rabbits, doubtless; a tall dark fellow with coarse wool stockings tied above his knees and, in odd contrast, a stylish black coat frogged down the front with triple gilt braid.

"Dressed in more gold lace than the whole Admiralty." Instantly Trevaskis knew of whom the hunt followers had been talking earlier on. This was the man. Ortho Penhale, squire of Bosula, no less; his old enemy. Thirteen years previously, not a mile from the spot on which they now stood, Penhale had thrashed him for trespassing. To be just, Penhale had been bitten half through the hand before he struck, but Trevaskis did not know that (it was his step-brother who did it; they were all mixed up together).

He remembered the episode as a piece of needless brutality to a friendless ten-year-old boy, and his was a nature that, if it forgot no friends, forgave no enemies. Well, here he was, trespassing again. Would the bully attempt to repeat the thrashing? He thought not. Trevaskis, frigate lieutenant, was a different proposition to the poor little nobody's child.

And Penhale recognized him well enough. A sharp upwards jerk of the swart, handsome head, a tilt of the raven brows, betrayed as much. For they had met since that day in the wood, in Kingston Harbour, Jamaica, and not so long ago. Penhale was a ' black-birder ' then, running a stinking Guinea-man. Master of a cut-throat privateer now. A dainty customer ! Would there be another thrashing? Trevaskis only wished he would try it; but the dark, gold-laced figure made no motion. Challenging blue eye met smouldering black—no word, no sign.

Trevaskis passed on, stiff, supercilious, his broad shoulders squared, passed in among the hazels and was gone.

Penhale did not move.

A rabbit popped out of the bank, capered full across the line of fire, sat down, listened and hopped on again, an easy shot. But no shot woke the hill echoes.

A ferret peeped out of the hole, sniffed the evening air with a quivering pink nose and crept into another hole.

Penhale took no notice.

CHAPTER VII

THE *Brave Blakeney* see-sawed over the white ridges, her main-yard backed, butting the cross seas with a clumsy shoulder. An apple-cheeked, high-sided old ship with chequered ports and for figurehead the battered effigy of a scarlet soldier.

The *Ghost*, with her consort *La Belle Poule*, had come up with her not an hour before, wallowing north on the heels of a Dutch convoy. Ortho Penhale seated in the stern-sheets of his pinnace eyed the *Brave Blakeney* with amused disdain.

"I have cattle troughs at home that would sail faster," he remarked to his coxswain.

The man agreed, with qualifications. "Aye, sir—but she's stiff as a church, she'd bear a power o' maulin'; them Cashes too."

Ortho grinned. "Yes, I've heard of them. 'Gog and Magog' they were called on the Coast. Tow astern as soon as you've put me aboard. Now's your chance. Way enough ! Port oars in ! "

The pinnace soared up on the crest of a breaking wave. Ortho leapt to the thwart and from thence, across four feet of bubbling froth, for the ladder, gained it and went hand over hand up the chequered side, water swirling about his sea-boots.

A tall man with a short fat body balanced on long spindle legs met him at the gangway, blinking at him through immense brass spectacles lashed to his ears with string loops.

"Captain Blampied? " he inquired.

"No," said Ortho, "he's coming. I'm from the brigantine."

"Ah, the *famous* Captain Penhale ! We are honoured, sir, honoured ! " said the other, showing his lower teeth in what was intended for a pleasing smile. " I regret putting you to this trouble, sir, but my brother is not very active."

"No trouble at all. I take it you are one of the Cashes ? "

" I am, sir. Maximilian Cash, mate of this ship. My brother, Cæsar, is aft. If you will be so good——"

" I heard of you two often enough on the Slave Coast, though we never met," said Ortho. " If I remember right you had the *Olive Branch* brig."

"Yes, sir, that is so." He hesitated. " An unlucky vessel, captain."

Ortho was amused. " ' Unlucky ' you call it ? "

Maximilian blinked uncomfortably. " The slaves *were* dead when we—we—er—put 'em overboard, sir. The case was shamefully misrepresented by the underwriters. I give you my——"

Ortho cut him short. " My stars, Mr. Cash, who am I to sit in judgment on you ? Where's this brother of yours ? "

Maximilian turned and shambled aft, toes turned out, knees rubbing as he walked, looking for all the world like an egg on straws. It seemed impossible that the immense sloping shoulders and the pitiable legs could belong to the same man, or that the least roll of the ship would not send him staggering. But Maximilian pursued his shambling course without a deviation.

Ortho followed, taking stock of the *Brave Blakeney*. A beamy, short-backed old hog she was, an oblong box with the corners bevelled off. From one thing and another he guessed she could not be less than fifty years old and there seemed no natural reason why she should not sail on for ever. The entire carcase was of oak and of twice the customary thickness, beams, bent-timbers, wales, planking. Her spars were heavy enough for a two-decker, and though she

was carrying full topsails and courses hauled to a
half-gale she wallowed on almost upright. A blundering, blustering, bull-headed old ship, an ex-whaler
doubtless (the smell of blubber hung about her yet
and her cut-water was shod with iron), built to butt her
way through the drift ice of Davis Strait and withstand
the nip of Greenland floes. There was, in fact, a crude
picture of a whale hunt carved on the break of the poop
and her iron bell hung between two walrus tusks.

A queer craft to go privateering in, Ortho thought,
but then the Cashes were a queer pair, by all reports,
and they had probably bought her cheap. The old
whaler was well manned, at all events; that is to say,
she was heavily manned. The waist was packed with
men, men of every nationality and hue. Tow-headed
Germans, Scandinavians and Finns, swart Maltese,
Turks and Portuguese, some yellow Algerine half-
castes, a Chinaman and numerous blacks and Lascars.
Of the Englishmen the majority appeared ex-felons.
Ortho knew the cut well enough, the sly, oblique
glance, the wide-legged shuffle of feet accustomed to
shackles. A scurvy, surly, evil rabble. Footpads
and cutpurses hiding from the law, or else the scum
of ports dragged dead drunk from brothels and taverns
and sold by the crimps and doxies at so much a head.
In all his experience Ortho had never seen so many
obvious rogues collected in one ship, not even in a
French fighting galley, where all the rowers were
convicts. He wondered that the Cash brothers would
sail with such a crew. It then occurred to him that
perhaps the boot was on the other leg and only such
a crew would sail with the Cash brothers. Two
negroes sat huddled together like mournful apes,
wailing a plantation dirge. A mulatto boy with a
bandaged jaw drummed monotonously on an old
powder keg with two beef-bones for sticks. The rest
lay listless along the deck in shelter of the weather
bulwarks, sleeping, spitting, playing at dice or cards.

Not a head was turned as Ortho went by, but he knew every crafty eye was on him. "Trip and they'd be on top of you," he thought. "The after-guard must be indeed redoubtable to control such a crowd."

He followed Maximilian up the ladder to the high quarter-deck. Two hard-bitten down-east Americans lolled over the lee-rail staring at the Dutch convoy, second and third mates, Ortho guessed. A slender young man with a humorous dissolute face sat on the skylight paring his nails. He greeted Ortho with a wink. "G'day, Captain Penhale. Come to help us pluck the golden goose? How fares the ' Mitre ' at Exeter? "

" Have we met before? " said Ortho, puzzled.

"We have—at the said 'Mitre.' You got to wind'ard of me with the landlord's fair daughter, the yielding Patsy. Howso I bear no malice, the chamber-maid consoled me."

" I don't . . ."

" You don't recognize me in this guise? That is comprehensible. I was the Reverend Humphrey Blaine then, a clerk in holy orders. Now I am Blain-God-blast-you and lead the eminent Cæsar's boarders. I scent a couplet there, orders—boarders.

Time was I led a model life, a clerk in holy orders.
The Vicar caught me trespassing and now I order boarders.' "

He tittered. " I must read you my celebrated ode to the Bishop of Bath and Wells. I have a pretty gift in odes. The Bishop died of that one—apoplexy. Step along now and talk to the exalted Cæsar, he wants that goose for supper."

He resumed his nail-paring, whistling.

Cæsar Cash, owner and master of the *Brave Blakeney*, sat on a common wooden chair just forward of the binnacle, a battered spy-glass across his knees. Physically he was Maximilian all over again, only in an exaggerated form. Where Maximilian shambled pain-fully Cæsar appeared immobile. His body was vast and bloated, his legs immensely long and quite inadequate to his weight. He had no neck at all. The great jowled head seemed to be set directly upon the enormous shoulders. But there was force in the head, stubborn, brute determination. The heavy-lipped mouth would eat no leeks. The deep jaw, under its drapings of mottled fat, was cast-iron. The irascible little eyes were unflinching. There was no shock or terror in the world that would cause those eyes to waver. Ortho knew then what kept the fo'castle in hand. It was not Maximilian with his legendary powers of braining men with his bare fist. It was not the hard-case American mates with slung-shot at their wrists and pistols in their pockets. Nor was it the swivels trained into the waist, slaver-fashion. It was the terrible, asthmatic old mastiff on the wooden chair, who never moved, hardly spoke, and yet, somehow, threatened unmentionable things.

Maximilian, the man-brainer, cringed before him, the look in his eyes of a dog who expects a kick in the ribs.

This was Captain Penhale of the *Ghost*. Captain Blampied of the Jersey lugger *Belle Poule* was coming alongside.

Cæsar made acknowledgments with a slight roll of his head, and laid his spy-glass on the Dutch convoy, leaving brother Maximilian to do the talking.

Maximilian indicated the convoy with a knotty forefinger. (His knuckles were raw. Ortho wondered if the mulatto's broken jaw had anything to do with it.)

" Met with them due north of the Salvages. We've been following them eight days in hopes something would scatter them, but," he waggled his neckless head, " we've been unlucky, Captain Penhale, most unfortunate."

Ortho smiled to himself, picturing the stout old *Blakeney* bundling hopefully on day after day (Brother Cæsar rocking on his chair), waiting for something to drop into her jaws. A lame wolf on the heels of a flock.

" The sheep-dog has been too vigilant—eh? " he said, carrying on his simile.

" The sheep-dog? Ah ! you mean the man-o'-war. Yes, she has kept them well in hand. We tried to get amongst them after dark, but the nights have been regrettably clear. She spied us." Maximilian sighed the sigh of one whose best intentions are misunderstood.

" And how do you propose to scatter them now? "

" Scatter them? We don't, sir. We——"

Blampied ran up the ladder and joined the group, a smirking, swarthy little Channel Islander whose natural caution had been overcome by chronic avarice, calculating to a degree but dependable as long as there was money in it. Ortho had cruised with him on and off for two years. He knew every reef and hole of the Breton coast, could pose as a Frenchman and was invaluable for inshore work. The cutting-out foray into the Gironde had been of his conception.

He doffed his hair cap and bowed to Cæsar and Maximilian in turn, his bright black eyes darting from side to side, taking in every detail of the ship and her company.

" Mr. Cash has a plan for splitting that convoy, Pierre," said Ortho. " For the life of me I do not know how."

" *Moi non plus*," said Blampied, " nod in zis vezzer. Zat var-sheep she got 'em all under her ving like fowl vit chicken. Bud led us hear."

" By all means." Ortho turned on Maximilian. " What do you propose? "

Maximilian looked to Cæsar. Cæsar was at his spy-glass. Maximilian wiped his glasses carefully with the corner of a vast red handkerchief. " We—ahem !— propose that the brigantine and ourselves engage the man-o'-war, which will give the lugger a free hand with the merchantmen. Spoils to be divided in proportion to men and guns."

Ortho stared at him amazed. " Engage the man-o'-war—us? "

" Yes, sir."

" My stars! are you crazed! That's a seventy-four,
that is. She fires twice as heavy a broadside as the
three of us together. She'd blow us out of the water
before we could range her. Are you jesting, Mr. Cash?"

Maximilian waggled his great head. " I never jest,
sir. She fires no more than fifty guns and fires them
right unhandily. Three times we have been in full
range, and you can see for youself we came to small
harm thereby. She has twice as many guns, it is
true, but we can fire ours twice as fast, and you, with
your cannonades, four times. That leaves us a considerable advantage, sir."

" My oath! do you expect me to fight thirty-two
pounders with twelves?"

" With our assistance, captain. If she should prove
too strong we can always sheer off."

" Supposing she follows us?"

Again Maximilian shook his head. " She can but
follow one of us, and that would expose her convoy
to the other two."

" Zere is truth in zat," Blampied admitted. " She
vill nod follow."

Maximilian blinked at him gratefully.

" For all that it is ridiculous," said Ortho. " Two
eighteen-gun privateers against a naval fifty—absurd!"

" The *Carnatic* was bigger than that Dutchman yet
the *Mentor* took her single-handed," said Maximilian,
naming a classic action. " And Ryan took the
Salvador single-handed."

" True," chirped Blampied, his black eyes sparkling.
" By Gar zat is true! Zat *Carnatic* she vorth one
half-million."

" Oh, have done!" Ortho exclaimed. " That was
a different case altogether. The *Carnatic* was not
prepared."

Maximilian shook his gnarled forefinger at him. " No
more is this Dutchman prepared, Captain Penhale."

" Not prepared! Why, damme, you've just told

me yourself that she's already beaten you off three times ! " Ortho exclaimed.

" No, sir. We sheered off of our own accord and she did not press it. Why did she not press it? Eight days we have been on her heels and she has not even threatened us once. Why not? Because there is something wrong in that ship."

" What can be wrong? "

Maximilian hunched his thick shoulders. " I do not know—yet. I think she is a sick ship. They have been burying men overboard every day. And, at all events, the Dutch——! " He snapped his fingers. " The French have a saying that a Dutchman chased is a Dutchman taken."

" Oh, pshaw ! " said Ortho. " The French talk in puffs. The Dutch fought stout enough at Camperdown."

" Aye, but not since, sir. Duncan beat the heart out of them. All we ask of you, sir, is to try."

" And if I refuse? "

Came a gasping hiss from behind them, a wheeze as of air squeezed out of broken bellows. " Engage alone."

They turned about. Cæsar was staring through his spyglass, puffing, purple, but they all knew who had spoken and that he meant what he said.

" Engage alone ! " The stubborn old lunatic ! Had his jaws into something too big for him yet couldn't let go. The brainless old fool mastiff !

" Here, what do *you* say to this madness? " Ortho demanded of Blampied.

Blampied fingered his unshorn chin and looked upon the deck. " I tink, per'aps, id is nod so mad. I tink the two of you tak' 'er, per'aps. No 'arm to *try*. Ver' rich prize."

Ortho flared at him. " Oh, that's what you think. My stars ! and so you would, with nothing to do yourself but play the stand and deliver to a lot of unarmed merchantmen. Well, I wish you gentlemen well of this enterprise, but you may count me out.

D'you hear me? I'll take no part in this folly. Back your main-yard, mister, I want my boat."

The boat was a long time coming. Ortho strode up and down the waist, impatient, fuming. Engage a ' fifty ' begad ! Did you ever hear the like? She would brush them off like flies. Ridiculous ! Yet it had been done. There was the quoted *Mentor*, for instance. John Lambert of Liverpool cruising in his father-in-law's lop-sided privateer meets the tall French East Indiaman *Carnatic* rolling up from the south. John Lambert, a desperate man, goes for her head down, and behold ! the tall *Carnatic* fires a few wild broadsides and surrenders. She had sailed before war was declared. Half her guns were wooden ! She, as Blampied said, sold for half a million sterling. There was a box of diamonds aboard her alone worth one hundred and thirty-five thousand pounds. One hundred and thirty-five thousand pounds ! The sum ran in Ortho's head like a haunting melody, a line of exquisite verse. Again, there was Ryan of Dublin and the little *Rebecca*. The little *Rebecca* meets the forty-gun *Salvador del Mundo* eleven weeks out of Lima. Ryan being very drunk in celebration of some saint's day (he was a pious body), squares up to her and bangs off his ten little ten-pounders, and behold ! the gold and crimson banner flutters down ! The *Salvador del Mundo* was out of water, her men were dying of thirst. Her hold was stuffed with worked silver, bar silver, bar pewter, bar copper, wool, Guayaquil cocoa, together with forty serons of sea-wolf skins. Ryan retires to a mansion in Wicklow. You never knew what was going on behind those towering oak walls till you tried—Maximilian was right there. Disease, indiscipline, want or superstition could reduce the proudest three-decker more completely than hurricanes of double shot. Suppose that big Dutchman over yonder had, as Maximilian suspected, something wrong with her? She'd make a splendid prize, and, moreover, once she was taken, the convoy could be had for the picking. Sixteen ships homebound from the West Indies—rum, sugar, tobacco, indigo! A pretty fool he, Ortho, would look if the *Blakeney* and the *Belle Poule* made the haul and he stood out! He was badly in need of a prize. Three months he had been at sea and not a thing had fallen to him, barring a small polacca laden with dye woods and olive oil, which foundered half an hour after being taken—her captain had wrecked the pumps and then scuppered her. Neither had his two previous cruises been successful. One big Spaniard had surrendered after a battle lasting two days on and off and then been blown ashore at Rosscarberry and plundered down to her ground-futtocks by the Irish. A French brig he had taken also after a long running fight, but she was recaptured on the passage home. His first cruise had been his best. Since then matters had been gradually deteriorating. It is a mistake to start too well. People were saying that his luck had gone. Men were increasingly difficult to find. Seamen follow luck. They were deserting him for his rival, Nankivel of the *Killigrew*. The *Killigrew* made no sensational captures, but she paid regular dividends. Nankivel was not the man to try conclusions with a 'fifty.' Not he! Knew better. Ortho decided that he knew better also.

It was all very well to talk of sheering off, they would be dismasted at the first broadside and battered to pieces later. Even supposing they weren't, one had no right to risk one's men against such odds. A master had his responsibilities, damme! His men's lives were a sacred trust—widows wailing, orphans howling. Pierre Blampied had gone money mad. The Cashes were savages. He would leave them to fry in their own fat.

His boat was the devil of a long time coming! He strode to the gangway and demanded where the devil it was. He was answered that it had fouled Blampied's boat in the wash astern, but was even then hauling up.

Ortho resumed his pacing. A negro inadvertently

obstructed him. He thrust the man headlong against a belaying rack. The black rose, looking murder. Ortho bashed him in the face, kicked him over to leeward and paced on.

But supposing Blampied and the insane brothers did make their haul? Suddenly he saw that if they failed he would be very awkwardly placed—even more awkwardly than if they succeeded. " Bark and lugger attack a Dutch convoy. The *Ghost*, Captain Penhale, stands by ! " He could hear the news shouted through the .Falmouth tap-rooms, Blundstone's, the ' King's Head,' the ' Barley Sheaf '; spreading over the county. He heard incredulous squires discussing it in Truro's ' Red Lion,' the ' Angel ' at Helston; Teage and Carclew sneering over their port in the ' Ship and Castle ' in Penzance. " Ortho Penhale afraid ! " For he had no doubt that the wheezing old mastiff would engage alone, no doubt whatever. Blampied would handle the merchantmen, naturally, since it entailed no risk. Very fiercely he cursed Captain Cæsar Cash for placing him in this predicament.

What would Nankivel do under like circumstances? Tell the crazy fools to go to hell, wear ship and get out, never looking back. And so would he, by God !

" Captain Ortho Penhale runs away—the *famous* Penhale ! "

" Boat alongside, sir," said the *Blakeney's* bosun. " Fend her off George, lively ! "

" As she lifts," shouted Ortho's coxswain. " Now, sir—jump ! "

But Ortho did not jump. He turned on his heel and marching back ran up the steps, till his head was above the deck level.

" Hey you, Captain Cash ! I've re-considered. I'll support you in a glass from now, on her lee quarter, and—listen to me—damn the lot of you ! "

He fancied Cæsar's fleshy lips twitched into the semblance of a smile.

CHAPTER VIII

THE wind had backed almost dead astern and was rising fast. The sea, blown first this way, then that, was lumpish and irregular, there was no gauging it. An hour more daylight at the most, then night black and driving. Pretty conditions in which to attack a superior enemy ! Ortho, pacing his quarter-deck like a caged tiger, cursed Cæsar Cash afresh. Oh, well, if the Mijnheer kicked too hard he'd back out at once. Steadying his spy-glass he took a good look at the Dutch man-o'-war. An old ship by her appearance, built high in the stern with a prodigious amount of gingerbread work, giant tritons blowing conches, sea beasts, scrolls and such-like. Two rows of windows blazed in the glare of sunset as though illuminated from within. A pair of copper lanterns were mounted on her taffrail, and between them the great flag of the new Batavian Republic stood out stiff in the wind.

As Ortho watched she fired a signal gun to leeward and clewed up her fore-course. The merchantmen obediently took sail in.

"That man-o'-war captain has put the fear of God into his convoy at any rate," Ortho thought. "Blampied 'll never start 'em running. They'll stay and wait till it's over." He groaned. "I wish I were out of this ! "

Pentacost, standing beside him, the blue wool cap pulled down to his hairless brows, shook his head with a suggestion of reproof. "I have no fears myself, sir. The Lord will preserve His people."

Ortho could not forbear to laugh. "It is the first

time I have heard myself described under that heading. But you are aware, of course, that Hollanders are Protestants also."

Pentacost was not disturbed. " Allied with Papists and Idolators, sir, France and Spain. There is no health in them. 'Their vine is the vine of Sodom and of the fields of Gomorrah; their grapes are the grapes of gall.' "

" My stars, Mr. Pentacost, you will tell me next that Heaven is an English colony ! I wish I had your faith, but I have not. My good friend was an infidel Turk. He died of plague in Morocco City tending the sick, when everybody else had fled, and if he is not in Paradise now it is no place for a true man. The best I have ever known was a Jew, a poor slaver surgeon, whom I verily believe to have been own brother to Jesus Christ. It is inconceivable that the Lord should abase so-called 'infidels' in favour of a person like myself, for instance, who am a Protestant, it is true, but for no better reason than that my father was."

" I wonder you are not afraid to die, sir," said the old man solemnly, " uttering such blasphemy."

" Afraid to die," said Ortho. " I am perishing afraid. I would haul off now and never fight another battle if I were not still more afraid of something worse."

" And that, sir, is ? "

" Poverty, Pentacost, poverty. The shabby coat, the worn boot, the faded ribbon; small beer in the tap-room, stint food at the ordinary. I fear that more than all hell, Pentacost. I dream of it sometimes when matters are going awry. I see myself shuffling through Penzance in an old coat that lets the rain in, the lights of the 'Ship and Castle' over the way and myself too poor to enter. Women who sighed for me once looking askance. I wake up sweating. I had an Irish mate when I was slaving. O'Keefe was his name. It was his custom to make a round voyage in a Guinea-man

and then spend all his wages in a week at Bath or Tun-
bridge Wells, calling himself a rich planter of St.
Kitts. 'I am but a poor Guinea mate,' he said to
me, ' but in my day I have drunk the rarest and kissed
the fairest.' He is at Ambrize now, spliced to a mulatto
woman who, I'll warrant, is as big as a barrel and reeks
of palm-oil, which is less than he deserves, for he was a
rogue in grain. But I have always remembered what
he said and I could wish no better epitaph for myself—
' Here lies Ortho Penhale, dust—but in his day he
drank the rarest and kissed the fairest.' "

Ortho clapped his hand to the rail. " Up goes
Mijnheer's main course. Beat to quarters, Mister,
and serve the rum out—drench 'em plentiful ! "

The *Blakeneys* had also been lavishly enspirited, it
appeared. The old whaler was surging along on the
Ghost's port quarter under a press of dingy canvas,
and up from her waist babel arose, snatches of broken
song, derisive yells, cheers, all mingled with the whine
of fifes struggling with ' Britons strike home ' and the
rub-a-dub of a big drum thumped out of time. The
Brave Blakeney burst a comber with her blunt nose,
sending the spray flying over her fo'castle, emerged
streaming and surged on again.

" *Ma foi*, he goes lak a wild bull ! " said de Merdrinac,
and pointed to starboard, smiling, tears in his eyes.
" Ah ! ça c'est bien jolie ! " It was the squeal of
Breton pipes and the singing of the Vendée *émigrés*
aboard Blampied's lugger that attracted him. They
were singing ' Vive Henri Quatre,' the old royalist
battle song. The *Belle Poule* was drawing ahead, a long,
low-lying vicious craft, leaping like a hound under her
three-reefed lug-sails.

" Here speaks man Dutch," said Ortho. " She
yaws, she yaws."

The Dutchman ahead swung to port. Puffs of
smoke, round and plump like burst cotton-pods,
blossomed silently along her side, followed by a series

of detonations. Fountains of spray spouted in the *Blakeney's* path, most jetted far to the westward.

"Ducks and drakes," said Ortho contemptuously. "She's rolling like a sow. She'll yaw for the lugger next and give us a salute as she rounds. Here they come!"

Two puffs of smoke obscured the sunset glitter of the stern windows. Two spent balls dashed the wave crests a cable's length astern of the *Ghost*.

"Wide and too high," said Ortho, and turned to the helmsman. "Steer straight on her stern and yaw when she yaws, only t'other way. I'll give the word. She'll not hull Blampied now." He spoke too soon. One of the Dutchman's shot dropped so close it sent a cloud of white water hurtling over the lugger and ricochetting smote her hard on the sheer strakes. Aboard the *Ghost* they heard the crash distinctly. Another tore a hole in the fore-sail peak. A second broadside the Hollander buried deep, rolling drunkenly as she fired.

Pentacost was of the opinion that her main-deck gunners must be nearly washed out of the ports. De Merdrinac hoped they would be. He had visited Holland in the days of his prosperity and did not love the Dutch. A dour grasping people with the ugliest women on earth. Men who persistently bred ugly daughters deserved all they got. The surgeon Sheringham, a meditative soul, *en route* for the hold with a roll of anticipatory bandages, paused to comment on the wild beauty of the sunset, which he described as 'the descent of Phœbus.'

Ortho described it as the foulest he had ever seen and curtly ordered him below. "We'll be at it hammer and tongs in a minute," he snapped. "Look, the *Blakeney's* taken a duster!"

The *Blakeney* had indeed. Over the water came the thud of round-shot meeting her stout oaken sides. The reefed foretop-gallant-sail, cut loose at the lee clew, flogged like washing on a line, flogged itself to ribbons. A rent opened in her foretop-sail, a split right down to the bolt-rope. She seemed to reel for a moment, and then, gathering herself, rushed on again, mouthing the foam at her bruised bows. Ortho pictured old Cæsar on his kitchen chair, staring straight in front of him; the great jaw set like rock under its jowls of fat.

He put up his speaking trumpet. "Mr. Veal! The bow-chasers. Fire on your own judgment. Aim at her rudder!"

"Aye, aye, sir!"

Almost simultaneously the long eighteen barked. A gilded dolphin on the Hollander's stern galleries dissolved in splinters; a sun-stained window turned black as the glass fell. The second eighteen spoke and a triton dropped his conch shell.

"Too high!" Ortho yelled. "Fire as she pitches!"

Blampied, away to starboard, was tossing shot in among the merchantmen to make them heave to.

The *Brave Blakeney* shook the reefs out of her main top-gallant-sail and ranged up on the man-o'-war, banging into the seas and blazing with every available gun.

"If the Mijnheer don't dismast him, he'll dismast himself, that Cæsar," Ortho groaned. "Ah, there he goes! right into the trap!"

The Hollander, biding her time, put her helm over and came round on the port tack, loosing her whole broadside on the old whaler. She was, as Pentacost had pointed out, rolling too heavily to be effective. Nevertheless, weak as her broadside was, it tore the *Blakeney* cruelly. Down came her foretopmast bringing the foretop-sail-yard with it and carrying away a mass of running gear. Forward she was a litter of tangled cordage and shredded canvas all writhing and beating in the wind.

Ortho clicked his tongue in his cheek. "Tcluc!— I told him so! and what does brother Cæsar do now?"

He brought the *Ghost* round on the starboard tack,
fired three broadsides, more in the hope of drawing
the Dutchman's attention than of doing any damage,
and wore again. Away to the eastward Blampied was
still firing; the traders were proving intractable
seemingly.

The sun was going, squeezed down into the sea by
the weight of smouldering purple cloud. The eastern
sky was all aglow for a moment. Swollen masses of
cloud, islands and continents, glowing like paper
lanterns—orange, rose, coral pink—drifted and piled
upon each other, changing colour as they drifted.
For a moment the heaving waters showed a bloody
stain; flying spray beads sparkled like precious stones.
A moment's glow, a moment's glitter, then dusk falling
like a shadow, sudden and chill. The chill fell on Ortho's
heart. The wind was still rising, the sea also. Inside of
an hour it would be pitch dark and they would be tumbling about, stunned and swamped, firing at each other's
gun flashes, incapable of distinguishing friend from foe.
And under cover of dark the traders would escape.
A mad game from the first, it was hopeless now. He
must signal Cæsar to break off, that he would no longer
support him.

He made the recognized signal, twice he made it.
The *Blakeney* took no notice. She was within pistol
range of the Dutchman by this time, hulled repeatedly,
her foremast a wreck, the shot singing about her, but
still blundering on.

Even Pentacost was uneasy. " Let her come
round," he growled, " getting raked like that ! . . .
no sense ! "

Ortho sneered. " The Protestant God will be hard
put to pull His good servant Captain Cash out of that
mess—eh, mister? "

Pentacost bit his lip.

The *Blakeney's* maintop-mast tottered and came
down on the run. Her jib-boom snapped, shot through

at the bowsprit cap. What sails still stood were mere lace. She rolled in the trough, trailing a ravel of wreckage over her port side, stunned, crippled, helpless. One gun fired and then was silent.

"Finish," said Veal. "They can sink her or take her at their leisure now."

Ortho nodded. "It is just as I said. The old fool has only himself to blame. Well, we'd best be off out of this—while we can."

"She's hauling her flag," said Veal. "Surrender."

The red ensign on the *Blakeney's* spanker gaff jerked downwards, hung at half-mast for a moment or two and then jerked to the deck. The Dutchman's fire ceased in response.

"Stand by to haul on the port tack, Mr. Pentacost," said Ortho, then put up his spy-glass. "The *Blakeney* 'll be in to that man-o'-war in a minute if she don't put her helm up. What's Cæsar doing? Can't be out of control! What? . . . Hold hard a moment!" In his excitement he sprang on the hammock nettings the better to see. "He's in to her bows on! My God, he's throwing his hooks! His flag's up again! *He's boarding!*"

It was so. Cæsar had crashed his iron stem full into the Hollander's side. The next sea swung the *Blakeney* round and the two ships lay grinding side by side. The red flag was at the peak again, and, irrespective of the fact that he was pitching three hundred men against a probable five hundred, Cæsar had cast his grapples and was throwing his boarders in. From under the litter of broken spars, tangled cordage and split canvas they rose, raving; Irish rebels, runaway slaves, thieves, murderers, pickpockets, tavern scum; jumped for the Hollander's chains and went up hand over hand; probed into the gun ports with their long pikes and crawled in after; swung aboard from the *Blakeney's* main-yard and fought, knife and knife, in the rigging with the Dutch top-men. Some were thrust back to be crushed between the pounding hulls, but most gained foothold. The thunder of gun-fire died out completely, giving place to cheers, shrieks, curses and the popping of small arms. A cunning, desperate manœuvre so audacious it took the Hollanders entirely unawares. But Ortho, staring wide-eyed through the dusk, had no doubt of the outcome—five hundred trained men-o'-war's men versus three hundred dock-sweepings. The Dutch were taken by surprise, for the moment, but once they recovered the *Blakeney's* would be brushed off like crumbs, and then no amount of flag-hauling would save Cæsar Cash, he would be pounded till he sank—and justifiably. But what was he, Ortho, to do? To fire would be to destroy friend and foe alike. To stand by was to be disgraced. There was only one thing possible and that was to board as well. Cæsar had forced his hand again! In a paroxysm of impotent rage he lifted up his voice and called Cæsar every foul epithet he could lay his tongue to, cursed him alive and dead, in his goings out and his comings in, eating and drinking, sleeping and waking, and raging swung the *Ghost* under the Hollander's towering stern, blazing with his entire port battery. She bore the arms of Haarlem over the name ' *Stadenland* ' embossed in letters of gold, and she sent two chaser balls screaming through his rigging as he came round. The *Ghost* spun on her heel, goring into the *Stadenland* abaft the fore-chains with a crash that sent sprawling every man on both ships. The *Ghost's* boarders, headed by de Merdrinac, leapt, cheering, for the Dutchman's ports, too drunk to count the odds. Ortho followed, leaving the *Ghost* to Pentacost. His place was with his ship, but he was too furious to care. The upshot of this would be a Netherlands prison (to say the least) and he wanted blood first. Since it could not be Cæsar's it must be Dutch. He sprang from the *Ghost's* rail straight into a gun-port. A gunner swung at him with a rammer, but a lurch of the ship sent them both flying and 'Kicky' John, coming up behind, put the assailant beyond further mischief. Chaos ran mad on the *Stadenland's* main-deck. It was pitchy dark down there except for the feeble glimmer of battle lanterns, swinging on their hooks. Smoke hung yet under the deck beams, yellow and choking. Water burst in at the weather ports and washed about the deck, knee-deep. The ships bumped and pounded, slogging together as though to stave each other's ribs in, throwing the men over in struggling heaps. From the upper deck came the crash of falling spars, cheers and screams. The Dutch gunners gave back and back, defending themselves as best they might with bars and rammers. Ortho drove at them like a maniac, whooping to his men. Speed! Speed!—that was the only hope. Harry them! hustle them! Give them no time to recover and reorganize. Attack! Attack! A Dutch midshipman stepped coolly forward and aimed a pistol straight in Ortho's face. The trigger clicked harmlessly, misfire. The boy made a grimace, as who should say ' Tut-tut ! ' and hurled the pistol. Ortho stunned him with the flat of his cutlass. " Too young to kill," he said. " A good boy "—and plunged on. Attack! Speed! Fury!

He floundered over a pile of bodies, two dead men and one still writhing. The ex-curate was one of the dead. He lay with his pale eyes upturned to a lantern. His chest was a blot of blood, his mouth twisted into an ironical smile.

There was a flare of powder straight ahead, and by its momentary glow Ortho saw de Merdrinac—stripped to his ruffled shirt, his rapier darting like a snake—hemmed in by Dutchmen; heard his undaunted " Ah-has ! " as he stamped and shifted, " Gare à vous, mes gars ! Gare à vous ! " A glimpse of inferno, fire-lit, demoniacal—then darkness again. He sprang to the Frenchman's aid, and lost himself, blinded in a

rolling cloud of smoke. He fumbled forward; beating
at the smoke with his arm. It rolled over and behold
de Merdrinac had gone and he was in his place,
surrounded by Dutchmen, cut off. A hurled gun
quoin grazed his cheek. A bar, swung by a burly
quarter-gunner, came sideways for his head. He
parried that blow, but his cutlass snapped off six
inches below the hilt. With a shout they closed on
him. He saw them in a ring about him, half-naked,
grimed with sweat and powder, hairy arms uplifted,
Caught! " What shall I do? " he flashed to his brain.
" Nothing," his brain flashed back. " There is
nothing to be done." " This is the end then? " he asked.
" What else? " said his brain. The man directly
opposite had a naked woman tattooed on his chest.
" How fat she is," Ortho thought.

The bars swung for his unguarded head—there was
a crash; the deck hove up under him and they were
all down in a heap, slithering to leeward, clutching
and kicking, the water pouring over them. Ortho
fell with the tattooed man on top of him. They rolled
over and over, clawing like a pair of locked wild-cats.
Then Ortho remembered the broken splinter of cutlass
he still held and drove it home. After that all went
blank, for the ships clouted again and he hit his head
against something.

When he came round it was to find his second mate,
Veal, tugging at his arm. He propped himself up
against a gun breech, sick and throbbing. The
lantern appeared to be revolving in circles, the mate's
voice coming from an immeasurable distance. Shadow
shifted between him and the light, like figures in a fog.

" What's happened? " he asked.

" Burble-burble-blurr——" went the mate. " You
for dead—blurr-urr."

" I can't hear. Who's dead? What is it? "

The lantern revolved slower and slower and settled
down to its habitual swing. The shadow shapes

turned into men, his own men, a sadly battered crowd.
Veal suddenly became coherent. "Burble-burble-
blurr—took you for dead, sir. Better be casting off,
sir. The *Ghost* 'll clout to pieces."

"Casting off?" Ortho queried. "What's
happened?"

"Why, we've got her, sir, she's ours."

"Ours? What is?"

"This ship, sir, the Dutchman."

"My stars !" said Ortho, and again, "My stars !"

.   .   .   .   .   .

Twenty-three dead and thirty-eight wounded. De
Merdrinac shot through the hip and groin, Benbow
Baragwanath minus a leg. The *Ghost* badly torn
aloft and badly strained below. Men at the pumps.
A heavy toll to pay ! This spelt an end of cruising
for the time. This meant Falmouth and a thorough
overhaul.

Nevertheless Ortho, peering into the dark from his
quarter-deck, was far from dissatisfied. He had scant
hopes of catching many merchantmen in this gale,
but the *Stadenland* alone would richly repay them.
An East Indiaman, she would be carrying cinnamon,
Nankin silks, mother-o'-pearl, coffee and tortoiseshell
—possibly diamonds. A second *Carnatic*, perhaps.
Added to that was the glory of it. Glory was very
dear to Ortho Penhale. 'Fifty-gun man-o'-war taken
by two eighteen-gun privateers !' He heard the news
being shouted through the coffee-houses and inn
parlours, at Blundstones, the 'Red Lion' and the
'Ship and Castle.' That would give friends Carclew
and Teage something to chew on. There would be
cheers for him again on Market Strand, and bright
eyes sparkling 'Ortho Penhale, the Cornish Duguay-
Trouin !'

Twenty-three dead and thirty-eight wounded
weighed as little against that. One must pay for
glory. He still did not understand how it had

happened. Seeing Veal at the binnacle he called him. Veal appeared to have been everywhere and seen everything. "Some of the *Blakeneys* had entered through the ports as well," he said. "The Dutch gunners were caught between two boarding parties. They were very short-handed, having lost scores from scurvy in the voyage home—or so the survivors reported. As for the upper deck, there had been hard doings up there. The Hollanders fought very stubborn and the *Blakeneys* could make no headway. Then at a critical moment Mr. Pentacost sent up every man, boy and cook's shifter left on the *Ghost*, and that turned the scale. Mr. Pentacost had led them himself. Came over the nettings waving a tomahawk and chanting the Old Hundredth, blue cap standing on end, enough to freeze anyone's guts," Veal said. "The *Blakeneys* had behaved very ugly once they got the upper hand." Veal reported. "Knifed the wounded and stripped the dead. No stopping them. Turn on you as soon as not. A murderous crowd. He had protested to the chief mate, Maximilian Cash, but Maximilian only shrugged his shoulders. Told him, Veal, to mind his own business and get after the merchantmen. A hard case, that Maximilian, for all his knock-knees and spectacles. Cæsar too. That hanky-panky with his flag, giving the Dutch the notion he'd surrendered in order to get closer. Veal considered that a very questionable bit of work. Lucky for Cæsar he won the day, else he'd have been hung at the yard-arm, nor considered himself aggrieved. Very hard cases, the Cash brothers at sea. Ashore, at Runcorn where they lived, the soul of respectability, churchwardens in fact."

This was news to Ortho. Veal gave his sacred oath on it. Churchwardens they were, both of them. He had seen them, dressed in black, pompous as Justices, bellowing the responses louder than the clerk. Their father had been rector of Runcorn, he understood.

Ortho asked if the *Blakeneys* could handle the prize.
Veal had no doubt of it. The after-guard had closed
the ports and got her away before the wind with the
old whaler still lashed alongside. Furthermore, the
rabble were sobering up. Maximilian and his down-
east man-handlers would get to work on them ere
long.

Ortho turned away to watch for Blampied's gun
flashes. Then a thought struck him and he called
Veal again.

" By the way, did you see the Dutch captain? "
he asked.

Veal shook his head. " No, sir. He was on the
poop encouraging his men up to the moment Mr.
Pentacost's party broke aboard, but after that he was
not seen. It was thought he was killed and thrown
overboard in the confusion. The third officer formally
surrendered the ship."

" H-mm," said Ortho. " Well, no matter. That'll
do, Mr. Veal. Tell 'em to keep a sharp look-out
forrard. From the way Blampied is firing I take it
those damned traders are on the run. Send a couple
of men to the fore-top."

" Aye, sir."

The night was black as ink. The wind came booming out of the south, tearing the tops off the combers,
driving the spindrift like hail. The *Ghost* went tearing
before the gale under reefed topsails, burying her sharp
nose, kicking her heels up. Her backstays hummed
like harp-strings in the blast, her scuppers streamed.
Seas leapt upon her out of the dark, spouted high above
her rail in ghostly grey columns and fell back staining
the black with milky patches. Ortho's only hope
was to get ahead of the merchantmen and round them
up at dawn—given any were in sight. Board them he
could not with that sea running. Came a frantic hail
from aloft. An indefinite shape loomed vast in the
flying murk to starboard and they drove past a labour-

ing trader, missing destruction by the barest margin.
An escape so narrow it made one's backbone tingle.
Ortho hailed the fore-top. " Watch out, curse you ! "
well knowing that the men aloft could see nothing.
He was running blindfold among the blind, only
chance could save a collision. The convoy would be
scattered half across the Bay of Biscay before dawn,
unless Blampied had managed to lame a few. He had
small hopes of the merchantmen; not that they
mattered in comparison with the *Stadenland*, the
Stadenland with her East Indies freight, Nankin silks,
tortoiseshell, diamonds (he had convinced himself
that she carried diamonds). Nevertheless at the back
of his mind a grain of uneasiness rankled. That
captain ! He wished they had found that captain,
dead or alive. He was dead, of course, wrapped in
seaweed, sixty fathoms deep. Of course he was dead.
Even supposing he wasn't, what could he do? one
man against Cæsar and Maximilian and that mob?
Nothing, less than nothing. All was well. The
Stadenland was theirs, definitely. Ortho was on the
point of turning to speak to the helmsman when the
whole night was illumined by a blinding flash. For a
second the *Ghost* was lit up redly from stem to stern.
He saw old Pentacost—a long wet nose poked out
between collar and cap—bent over the rail, a hand
cupped to his mouth as if frozen there; the tall masts
leaning at an angle of thirty; the arched topsails with
a glitter of rain dribbling out; a man flattened spider
like, in the web of the foremast ratlines. Followed a
deafening boom of thunder and the glare died down.
His first impression was that they had been struck by
lightning. His second that one of the stern chasers
had exploded. He spun about, saw a leaping blaze
upon the sea far astern and immediately knew what had
happened.

Somebody, thrown off his balance by a lurch of the
ship, fell against him. It was the second mate.

" My God ! " he screamed. " They've blown her up ! The bloody drunken swine ! The careless——! "

" Not them—*he*," said Ortho quietly. " Now we know where that captain got to. We have no luck, Mr. Veal."

.   .   .   .   .   .

One man only they saved. Maximilian Cash clinging to a spar, burnt raw all up one side yet miraculously retaining his spectacles. Ortho did his best for him, but he was out of his mind and past hope. He babbled unceasingly. The *Blakeney* had been out four months and had taken nothing, he said. The men were mutinous and wanted to turn home, they could not hold them much longer. If they went home the *Blakeney* would be seized and he and Cæsar thrown into a debtor's prison and lose their respectability. They *must* take something. It was the Cash brothers' passion for respectability that had dragged them all into this *débâcle*, it appeared.

Later he imagined he was in the midst of the battle and bawled and cursed in an appalling manner.

" My stars ! he can't die saying the things he's saying," Ortho whispered to the surgeon ; " stop him, can't you ? "

" How can I ? " said Sheringham.

However, Maximilian stopped of his own account. He sat up abruptly, saying he had an idea that his brother was in trouble somewhere and he must go to him at once, as Cæsar was not very active.

They buried him at dawn, tilting him off a grating at the gangway.

.   .   .   .   .   .

Of the merchantmen Blampied managed to capture one small schooner—in ballast.

CHAPTER IX

EIGHTEEN hundred and war-time. England fighting half across the world from the East Indies to the West, alone confronting France and her dupes, Spain and Holland—three nations at once. The Northern League of Russia, Sweden and Denmark forming against her into the bargain; Portugal in the balance. Bonaparte—by way of supporting the usual British pacifists who declared there was no real harm in him—had ravished Egypt, massacred four thousand prisoners in Palestine, attacked Acre under a flag of truce, and was now back in France, First Consul for life, and shaking his fist across the English Channel. Frederick Augustus, 'the good old Duke of York,' trounced in the Netherlands, was home again licking his inglorious bruises in the arms of Mrs. Clarke. A gloomy outlook—but, on the other hand, the Irish rebellion broken (at the cost of one hundred and seventy thousand English and Irish lives); Tippoo Sahib killed in the breach of Seringapatam, and Wellesley, for the moment, master of India; Pitt in power.

Eighteen hundred and war-time; black days in England. Press-gangs combing the seaports, recruiters scraping the country towns, seizing the hale and the halt, dragging the breadwinner from his children, the bridegroom from his bride, the widower from his dead. Famine prices, heavy taxes and tight belts.

Eighteen hundred and war-time—but the eighth of May and high holiday in Helston town, in the Duchy of Cornwall.

On the first of May long, long ago, so historians relate, the Archangel Michael, riding forth with a daffodilly stuck in his golden helm, met with the devil on Goonhilly Downs. St. Michael, a good man of his hands, incontinently charged. The devil, no less willing, met him at full tilt. They fought for hours. They broke their lances to splinters and went on with their battle-axes. They blunted their battle-axes and hacked their shields to shreds. They tossed them aside and went on with their swords. The hooves of their war-horses tore great holes in Goonhilly Downs that may be seen to this day. The steam of their horses hung over them in a fog. Sparks as big as shooting stars flew from their armour as they slashed and cut. The ringing of their armour could be heard in the Scilly Isles and as far north as the Four Burrows—some say Launceston. They fought for days. They snapped their swords and went on with daggers. They turned their daggers and went on with their fists, and when their fists were broken grappled on the ground. On the eighth day, as the sun rose, the devil turned his forked tail to the dawn and legged it for his life. Through Burnoon, Tregoose, Bowjyhere and Culdrose he sped, St. Michael after him, and popped into a hole in the courtyard of an inn. The Arch-angel, coming up a moment later and seeing a granite 'hepping block' close at hand, hastily wedged the stone into the hole, thus sealing the road to hell. That done he presented his daffodilly to a little girl as a memento of the occasion and walked back to Goon-hilly to find his horse. A very gallant gentleman. From that day the spot has been known as Helston—Hell-stone—and the inn the 'Angel,' and the towns-people have celebrated the eighth of May with appro-priate ceremony.

Eighteen hundred and war-time. The shadow of death on every household, the threat of invasion over the land; tight belts, tightened heart-strings, yet Helston keeping its 'Furry' day.

Of the young men present not many would survive

the fifteen years that were to see Waterloo and peace.
Some would die in Egypt under the walls of Aboukir
and Rosetta; some in the Peninsula, on Moore's
retreat to Corunna, in the ditches of Ciudad Rodrigo
and Badajoz; in India in the Mahratta wars; in
America at Longwood, Fort Erie and New Orleans.
Others be buried in bloody hammocks off Copenhagen, Cadiz and Trafalgar, or their broken bodies
scattered over the wide seas from the Celebes to the
Gulf of St. Lawrence, victims of innumerable frigate
actions. Few would dance at the 'Furry' again.
They stood straight and proud in the spring sunshine, but the ghostly drummer was beating the roll
and they heard it plain enough.

"Come, let us dance as never before," they said in
their hearts. "We may not dance another."

Few girls there would know old age with their first
sweethearts. "Dear God, make us pretty and witty
to-day," they prayed in their souls. "We may not
see *them* again."

Dawn had been rung in with gay peals of the church
bells, and the apprentices and servant-girls had arisen
and gone forth into the country for breakfast. At
eight o'clock they returned to town laden with green
boughs, singing the old Hal-an-tow song.

> " Robin Hood and Little John,
>   They both are gone to the fair, O !
>   And we will to the merry greenwood
>   To see what they do there, O !

Refrain :   With Hal-an-tow ! Rumbelow !
>   For we are up as soon as any, O !
>   And for to fetch the summer home,
>   The summer and the May, O !
>   For summer is a-come, O !
>   And winter is a-gone, O !

>   As for St. George, O !
>   St. George he was a knight, O !
>   Of all the knights in Christendom
>   St. Georgy is the right, O !

God bless Aunt Mary Moses,
And all her powers and might, O !
And send us peace in merry England
Both day and night, O ! "

It was now after eleven of the clock and the country
was rolling up. Those of the gentry who could find
lodgings in the town had driven in over-night. Others
were arriving every minute. Young squires a-horse
or in high-wheeled gigs, family parties in coaches,
berlins or post-chaises. They forged through the
crowd in Coinage Hall Street with a great cracking
of whips and shouts of "Way! Way!" Apple-
cheeked farmers there were, forcing their cobs against
the press, bawling greetings to friends, their good wives
clinging to the pillions, bidding them be careful,
clucking like hens. Miners there were, hundreds of
them, from the tin-streaming districts of Crowan and
Townshend, rough-looking fellows with oak-leaves in
their caps, already half-drunk, their wives resplendent
in tawdry silks. Fishermen also, dark, square-built
men from Cadgwith, Porthleven and Bessy's Cove;
farm hands from the parishes round about, dragging
their feet as though weighed with plough mould—all
West Cornwall, in fact. Booths lined each side of the
street, selling ginger-bread, sweets and fairings. Orange
women shrilled, cheap jacks barked, old soldiers sat
on the kerb displaying their stumps, street singers
wailed doleful ballads at tavern doors. A gypsy, his
waistcoat armoured with brass buttons, paraded a
pony for sale. His spouse rattled a tambourine under
windows while his children picked pockets—an industrious family. A Jew, perched on an empty barrel,
advertised pure gold watches at ten shillings each,
chain included. Opposite was a man with a per-
forming bullfinch which fired off a tiny brass cannon
at a penny a time. Down by the Bowling Green a
contortionist in dingy salmon tights tied himself into
knots. The bullfinch fired its gun in the face of the

gypsy's pony, which lashed out with both heels, knocking the Jew off his pedestal. The barrel bounded down the steep street like a small juggernaut and, up-ending, eclipsed the writhing contortionist as a snuffer eclipses a candle. Loud cheers from the delighted spectators.

On the Bowling Green a fisherman and a farm hand were wrestling, Cornish style, for a pot of beer and a fat goose. In the yard of the 'Rodney Inn' some Relubbas tinners were fighting a main of cocks. In the yard of the aristocratic 'Angel' some young gentlemen were baiting a badger. More cheers and down Wendron came a mob of apprentices bearing a chalk-faced man upon a pole. He had been caught working, they declared, working on 'Furry' day! The time-honoured penalty was that he must jump the Cober stream. The man appealed to the crowd. He was only putting a couple of slates on his roof, he whimpered, two slates only, where it leaked. His wife had ordered him to. If anybody was sacrificed it should be his wife. They were welcome to her. The crowd dismissed the appeal and he was carred off to his ducking.

Mr. Teage of Carhilly came up the hill in his new black and yellow curricle, his two bright chestnuts stretched at full gallop. Mr. Teage standing erect with his whip out, coat-tails flying. The crowd gave him passage, the women squeaking, the men huzzaing. Opposite the 'Blue Anchor' he rolled an orange-woman over. The oranges went down the flowing gutter in a golden spate to be absorbed by the mob. The woman sat up in the gutter and cursed Mr. Teage alive and dead, red-hot curses. Mr. Teage grinned and jerked her a guinea. Imperceptibly her curses changed into blessings, no less warm. He could do it again at the same price, she crowed, and kissed a mottled hand to him.

The wind blew gently out of the south, the sun shone

its brightest and best. A gay Flora day, for all it was eighteen hundred and war-time. Barclay Johns sauntering up-street from his lodgings regarded the cascade of oranges with a wistful eye.

"Oranges!" he sighed. "I remember on my first cruise, standing in for Gibraltar, when we passed a Tangiers felucca in-bound too. She was loaded with oranges, full to the gunnels with 'em. A dirty old green boat, piled high with oranges, rolling in a blue sea. I pushed my dirty little snout over the hammock nettings and sniffed with all my might. 'This is the South!' I said to myself. 'Palm trees, pagodas and cannibals—hallelujah!' Myself being twelve years old at the time and half the length of my own dirk. Oranges!" he sighed again. "I wish we were bound for the Mediterranean, don't you?"

Anthony Trevaskis was not so sure. There was this to be said for the Channel station, that one got one's leave in England—given there was any leave.

Johns did not find England so perishin' attractive. Good old land, of course, best in the world—but the perishin' climate! He'd like to see the sun again, the unstinting southern sun.

"Well, you have nothing to complain of to-day?" said Trevakis, "you'll be melted down to your spare ribs before you've pranced half the length of this town."

Johns laughed. "That's so. By the way, have you got a partner?"

Trevaskis shook his head. "No, not yet; have you?"

"That I have. I'm going to shake a leg with little Theo Carlyon, she of the golden locks. She's light in the head, but she's also light in the hand. If you want a partner you'd best look lively. I'll introduce you to Mother Gage if you like. She's got a fleet of daughters and there's sure to be one going spare. They ain't much to look at, but they carry their own weight. Shall I dip a flag to Ma Gage?"

"No—no, thank you. Not yet."

" Any nymph in view? "

" Yes," said Trevaskis; " that is, no, nobody."

Johns nodded. " Very interestin'. Would it be impertinent to ask her name? "

Trevaskis flushed. " You heard me say there was nobody, didn't you? Who should there be? "

" That is what I am asking you."

" You are a hopeless fool, Barclay," said Trevaskis. " There is nobody, nobody at all." Then he gripped his friend by the arm

A party of gentry were coming out of a house, a middle-aged woman, two girls and a gawkish boy fumbling with a pair of white gloves. It was the second girl that caught Trevaskis' eye. He could not see her face, but there was something in the carriage of her head, in the moulding of her shoulders, in her general bearing, that set his heart pounding. It was *she!* For two years the image of a girl, every curve and manner and movement of her, had been in his mind day and night. He could not be mistaken. His grip on Johns' arm contracted.

The party moved up-hill towards the Market House, but as they did so the second girl turned to glance at a cheap-jack and Trevaskis saw her face. By all the merciful gods, it *was* she !

Said Barclay Johns, wincing, " That's my arm, when you've finished with it. Thank you." He rubbed the released member. " You're devilish free with other people's property. What's the matter? "

" Who's that girl? " Trevaskis demanded.

" Which girl? Place is full of girls."

" That girl—in front—dressed in sprigged stuff ! "

" Fair ringlets—big ankles? "

" No, you ass ! *Brown* ringlets, small ankles."

" Blest if I know. Never saw her before."

" Find out who she is at once. Find somebody to introduce me. Quick ! "

Barclay Johns stared at his friend, delighted.

" My perishin' oath !   Old Dash-the-women hulled at last !   Old curse-the-petticoats hit 'tween wind and water.   God bless my perishin' soul ! "

" Barclay," said Trevaskis very earnestly, " do as I ask you—please."

In an instant the good-natured Johns had sobered. " Certainly, old son.   I'll find somebody.   I'll dodge ahead up to the Market House, and do you keep close behind 'em."   He plunged into the crowd, upsetting a small boy in his haste.

Trevaskis followed the party as close as he dared. Had the girl recognized him?   Of course not; why should she?   A muddy fox-hunter met with for five minutes two years before and forgotten immediately. And even if she had, what of it?   What could he do? What had he to offer?—frigate lieutenant without name, family or influence, living on his meagre pay. The young squires around her had estates behind them, fine houses, shipping shares, tin mines—he one battered sea-chest.   He fell back, despondent.   She wore the simple muslin bonnet then fashionable, and her glossy brown hair escaped from under it and lay curling lovingly on the nape of her round neck.   Adorable little white neck !   Trevaskis pushed on again.

He had come to the ' Furry ' in the hopes that she would be there, and now that she was there he was holding back.   Faint heart !   Poltroon !   Coward ! He stemmed the mob with his broad chest, closing in behind.   Penniless salt-horse he might be, he was a man.   Though he hated his unknown father with all his force he believed him to have been a gentleman. He, Trevaskis, had as good blood in his veins as any-one there, possibly better.   Not a bumpkin squire in the place that he could not break to pieces with his bare hands.   He earned his living without anybody's help, could navigate ships anywhere, in any weather. No reason to give any man best.   He pressed on till he was almost treading on the girl's heels.

Supposing she turned and saw him, what should he say? He couldn't say anything—without an introduction. He would stand there yammering like a fool, blushing and writhing. In sudden terror lest the girl should turn and recognize him before he had been properly introduced, he fell back again. She was probably engaged for the ' Furry ' a dozen times over, anyhow. It was no use. Thus, impelled and withdrawn by alternate waves of audacity and timidity, Trevaskis followed the party up Coinage Hall.

It was on the stroke of noon. The band was assembling in front of the Market House in preparation for the dance of the day.

Gentlemen were squeezing into white gloves, settling neck ruffles, regarding their shapely legs with satisfaction. Each wore a spray of lilies of the valley pinned to his coat. The ladies, in their flowered muslins, stood with hands demurely crossed before them, covertly eyed each other's toilettes, blushed prettily, whispered.

" What complexions ! " Trevaskis thought; " only the soft West Country could give such lovely blooming pinks and whites. These girls of ours are like roses," he thought, " God bless 'em ! "

The party halted, Trevaskis behind them, on tenterhooks. A man came forward, bowed, joked with the chaperon, bowed to the two girls and, to the watcher's unspeakable relief, passed on. Where the blazes was Barclay Johns?

The two beadles waddled down the steps of the Market Place, their wands festooned with flowers. A bassoon player blew a mournful trial note on his instrument. The big drummer drained the last drops of his beer, handed the empty pot to his wife and picked up his sticks. Barclay Johns ! Oh, Barclay Johns !

The gentleman in question burst through the throng as a dolphin bursts through a wave crest. " Its all right," he hissed. "I've found a man. People by the name of Killick, retired corn-dealers from Truro, plenty of money. Man 'll be here in a minute."

"They'll be off in a second," Trevaskis groaned. "Too late ! "

"I'll fetch him by the scruff," said Johns. "Keep your heart up."

He plunged whence he had come.

The band formed up. The beadles took station before it, very portly and dignified. The chattering gentry began to pair off.

Said a strange voice over Trevaskis' shoulder : "Hey ! but there's a sweet little filly, Tom. See her? In front. Cherry ribbons. Know who she is? "

A second voice replied that its owner did not, but that he would precious soon find out. The first complained that he had seen her first. The second proposed that they toss for it.

With difficulty Trevaskis restrained himself from turning and slaying the pair of them.

Three men approached the Killick party, an elderly buck with wattles like a turkey, a young squire in a lavender coat who would have been good-looking but for protruding teeth, and a tall boy, nervous but determined. They bowed to Mrs. Killick, who bobbed and waved her fan towards the two girls. Bows, bobs and both the younger men turned as one on the second girl, she of the brown ringlets. Trevaskis' heart fell to his boot soles.

The boy bent forward : "Er—may I—er—have the honour of . . ."

The squire cut in in front of him. "Your pardon, Mr. Julian ! Will you honour me with . . . agh ! curse it, sir ! look where you're thrusting ! "

"Ouch ! " yelled the boy. "Damme, sir, that's my foot ! "

"May I have this dance, please? " said Trevaskis, surprised at the steadiness of his voice, amazed at the suddenness of his action. At one moment he was standing wavering, determined that all was lost and that he had best bolt home out of it, back to his lodgings; at the next he had stepped hard upon the boy's foot, shouldered the squire sideways and was, quite steadily, asking the girl to dance. He didn't recognize himself in the matter at all, but nevertheless blessed the exotic impulse.

"You may not remember, but we have met before," he went on. "In a field above the Keigwin valley, on November the fourteenth, two years ago."

"Your memory serves you very well, sir," said the girl.

"It is infallible—in some cases," Trevaskis replied. "You may not recollect, but I had lost myself out hunting and you very kindly put me on my way."

"Indeed I recollect perfectly," said the girl, and smiled, the remembered dimple dinting her left cheek in a manner that made Trevaskis feel he must either kiss it or die. "You had a most comical spot of mud on the end of your nose."

Trevaskis laughed, a deep-chested, pleasant laugh. Better to be remembered by a muddy nose than not at all. He was dimly conscious that the squire was demanding an apology on one side of him, the boy lamenting his injured foot on the other, but he took no notice whatever. The girl that had inspired his hopes and sweetened his dreams for the last two years was actually before him in the flesh and he was actually talking to her. The growls of the frustrated suitors were no more than the remote buzzing of infinitesimal flies. He was aware that the drum was banging in earnest and the dance was on. The two suitors, abandoning their complaints, closed in on the bewildered girl with fresh solicitations.

"May I have—er—the honour . . ." "Sweet lady, be kind and . . ." Trevaskis pressed them back with a sweep of his arms. "You will give me the dance, won't you? Please."

He saw the affirmative forming on her lips—then she hesitated, remembering herself, blushing deliciously. " But I don't know your name, sir. We—we haven't been introduced."

" Introduced, my oath ! What do such formalities matter when . . ." Trevaskis bit the sentence off short. " I crave your pardon. There is a man— somebody coming to introduce us in a minute. Give me one minute's grace. Promise not to accept any- body else for one minute. It is my only chance. I join Hyde-Parker's fleet to-morrow. *Please !* "

Turning, he snarled into the boy's ear, " Off, or I'll snap your neck !—You too," he hissed at the squire.

The latter glared at him, blood mounting to his forehead. " By God, you . . ." he stuttered.

" I mean it," said Trevaskis, through his teeth. " One step forward and I'll half murder you."

The squire chewed his lip, then muttering some- thing about " Answer for this," stepped back.

Trevaskis, the diffident, was coming on.

A hand fell upon his shoulder, Barclay's.

" Dragged him here bodily," his friend panted ; " it's all right."

Trevaskis heard a murmur to his left, was aware that a perplexed stranger was introducing them, and that Johns had promoted him for the occasion. He heard himself described as *Captain* Trevaskis.

" Captain Trevaskis of the Royal Navy—Miss Jennifer Penhale."

Miss Jennifer Penhale ! *Penhale !* Met within a mile of Bosula ! Name and place connected in Trevaskis' mind in a flash. She was a daughter of Ortho Penhale, his old enemy. Trevaskis went white under his tan, swayed momentarily on his feet. Daughter of the bully who had thrashed him out of his beloved Keigwin woods. Ortho Penhale, ex- smuggler, blackbirder and general disreputable ! His

daughter ! Of all the ironical jests of Fate, of all the
sorry tricks to play a hapless man !

The band was in full blast, brass, wood and drums,
marching up street, the beadles with their flowered
wands leading the way. The couples were joining in
behind, tripping merrily—one, two, three and a skip;
one, two, three and a skip, then round about.

> " As John the beau was walking home
> He met with Sally Dover——"

" Come on you two, show a leg ! " said Barclay
Johns, prancing past with the feather-headed but
nimble Miss Carlyon.

Trevaskis pulled himself together. The girl was
smiling at him, the dimple adorning her cheek like a
lone star, an angelic beauty spot. Her hand was
upheld to his. She pointed one toe, then the other,
eager to be off.

Trevaskis mentally consigned Ortho Penhale to hell.
The sins of the father were no affair of the daughter.
He loved her, loved her utterly, and that was enough.
He would be with the fleet again in forty-eight hours
and to-day was 'Furry' day. *Carpe diem*.

He laughed back at her, took her hand in his and
they skipped after Barclay Johns.

The band swerved up Meneage playing its one
recurring verse.

The rattle and blare of the band suddenly died down
to crash forth again at the back of the houses. It had

passed through a shop and out the other side. The couples tripped after, missing never a step.

In and out of Meneage Street they wound their serpentine course, up Wandron, down Church Street and up the slope to Cross Street, disappearing through decorated doorways, reappearing through others, jangling the bells as they passed, clashing the knockers. Spectators in upper windows fluttered handkerchiefs, the rougher elements in the streets cheered and danced among themselves. Trevaskis had consigned Ortho Penhale whence he belonged, but he could not dismiss him from his mind. If this was Penhale's daughter she did not look it. There was nothing here of that swart and raffish desperado. Romany blood, of course. His mother was a gypsy. Trevaskis remembered her vaguely. A vast, full-blooded virago, riding the country on a roan horse, getting drunk with anybody. Penhale was her own son, but there was no visible Rom in this girl, with her creamy skin and brown dove eyes.

His daughter! Trevaskis had never associated Penhale, the most finished seducer in West Cornwall, with anything so permanent as matrimony. That was quite outside his line of country. Then boyish memories stirred and he remembered something, somebody. A woman roaming the Keigwin woods with that mad slammerkin Wany at her heels. Once only had he seen her, peeping through a break in the willows. Beautiful she was with a sort of delicate, porcelain beauty, hardly real. Beautifully dressed too. He remembered the shimmer of her satins as she walked through a pool of sunlight, the froth of lace at her bosom and elbows, the rich many-hooded cloak that trailed from her shoulders. A fairy princess she had seemed to the ragged ten-year-old crouched in pussy willows—till he saw her face. Then he knew she was mad, as mad as the shock-headed cow-girl that followed like a shadow behind her. Penhale's wife. He remembered the story now. ' Buck Penhale aimed at an heiress and brought down a lunatic.'

And this was the daughter, child of a rogue and a mad woman ! His mind reeled, but his devotion did not swerve by one hair's breadth, hardened rather. " What a home ! Poor little thing ! Poor little darling thing ! "

The band played them into a garden and halted, draining the moisture from their instruments. The owner of the garden requited the band with ale, the ladies with Madeira wine.

The ladies sank gasping to rest on rustic seats, on the rim of the fish basin, fanning themselves busily. Gentlemen adjusted their wilting stocks, wiped sticky hatbands.

" La, sir, I vow I am quite overcome." " Never so devilish hot in me life. I am like those little gold fish there, surrounded by water." " La, sir, how indelicate ! " " I beg your pardon, I'm sure—true nevertheless." . . . " That woman over there, Mrs. Bickford of Caerthillian, wears a wig. I have suspected it ever since the Tehidy ball, but now I know. It has slipped over her ear." " Well, the ear is equal to the burden." " Fie, sir, you are cruel ! " " I protest I am as mild as a lamb." . . . " Hot, eh ? " " Boilin' over." . . . " A glass of wine for Mrs. Tyack ! " " Coming, sir ! " . . . " Very warm for May." " It was warmer in '76. I recollect the late Sir Bevill Godolphin telling me that——" . . . " Miss Carkeek has fainted ! " " Fainted, fudge ! A stratagem to be taken in a gentleman's arms. I know her, she does it every year." . . . " Hey ! where's that glass o' wine for Mrs. Tyack ? " " Coming, sir, coming ! " . . . " Hot, eh ? " " Melting." . . .

Barclay Johns approached, sponging his cheerful countenance with a monstrous spotted handkerchief. " Phew ! That gal will gallop me to a standstill. She bounds like a—like a—what are those active little

Alpine creatures? Edelweiss. Bounds like an edelweiss. Weaker sex, forsooth! I say——" He dragged Trevaskis aside. "Razzy Truscott was talkin' of callin' you out for chokin' his luff with the charmer. I said it would be very entertaining if he did, as you were the most notorious duellist in the Western Squadron, had been twice up before the Admiral about it."

"Me!" said Trevaskis.

"Yes, you," said Barclay Johns. "My soul! you should have seen him! Turned green from the hair down. If you see him, just stamp your foot at him, will you? He'll run up a tree. I say——" He dragged Trevaskis still further. "My felicitations on the charmer—charmin'. Well, I must to my Theodosia. Good luck!"

Trevaskis returned to Jennifer's side. Lovely she was indeed, standing under a pink may bush, the sunspots hovering like gold butterflies on her sprigged muslin. Ortho Penhale! He could see nothing of Ortho Penhale in the sweet face turned up to his, with its frame of lustrous curls and cherry ribbons. Cherry ribbons and cherry lips and that love dimple coming and going. Ortho Penhale be damned! yet Ortho Penhale would have to be reckoned with sooner or later!—if all went well.

Then, in a sentence, Jennifer set him at ease. "My uncle is a sea-captain too," she said. "Only he's not in the King's Navy. He commands a fine privateer, which is almost the same, isn't it?"

"Hmm—ye-s," said Trevaskis, "almost. But, you'll pardon me, did you say your uncle or your father?"

"My uncle, my uncle Ortho."

Trevaskis drew himself up to his full height and breathed a long, deep-chested sigh of glorious relief. "A—a—ah!"

"What is the matter?" Jennifer queried.

"Nothing," said Trevaskis, hastily. "Er—the heat, the heat."

" But I thought you sailors were accustomed to all weathers."

" All weathers but hot weathers. At sea the calorific influence of the diurnal luminary is counteracted by the—er—by its vaporizing effect upon aqueous expanses."

" Dear me ! " said Jennifer.

" Exactly," said Trevaskis. " I got that out of a book, and if you understand its meaning I'm sure I don't. So your father is not a sailor—ah—ha—a ! "

" No, he's a farmer," said Jennifer. " We live at Roswarva in Gwithian. I came here with the Killicks. I was at school with Amy Killick in Truro."

" Marvellous ! "

" What do you mean, ' marvellous '? "

" Everything is," said the radiant Trevaskis. " The weather, the ' Furry,' you, me, life in general—ah—ha—a ! "

" I'm glad you're enjoying yourself," said Jennifer.

Trevaskis' memory, overlaid by absence, was reviving rapidly. Of course there was a brother; a steady-going decent fellow called by some Biblical name, Enoch, Elijah, or something. Of course there was ! Ortho stood so much in the forefront of his vision as to obscure all else. He had forgotten there was a second Penhale. And this was his daughter. All was well, all was very well indeed. Ortho Penhale need not cost him another thought. Exit Ortho.

But Jennifer began about her infernal uncle again. Had Trevaskis met him, cruising up and down? Trevaskis had, once, on the deck of a stinking slave ship in Kingston harbour, Jamaica, but he thought it prudent to say he had not.

Jennifer thought it a pity, as she was sure they would like each other. Her uncle commanded a pretty little ship called the *Ghost* and had a chief mate called Mr. Pentacost, who was a prophet ashore. He had also with him a French nobleman who wrote poetry

and gambled all his prize-money. He, the Frenchman, was on his back in Falmouth at the moment,
wounded. Jennifer had sent him a jar of clotted
cream and received a poem by return, ' Villanelle à
Jennifer ' it was called, sweetly pretty. Trevaskis,
scenting a rival, declared that that was all Frenchmen
were fit for, scribbling sweetly pretty verse. Ought to
be deported. How old was this rhyming frog-eater?

Jennifer defended the poet with spirit. The Count
de Merdrinac was as brave as a lion and a perfect
dear, so there ! As for his age. Oh, quite old. Forty
or so.

Trevaskis, feeling that there was nothing to be
feared from a man of so advanced an age, admitted
merit might be discovered even among the French.

Thereupon Jennifer enlarged upon René Philippe,
Count of Merdrinac. He said the wittiest things in
the oddest broken English and was very handsome
into the bargain—though not so handsome as her
uncle Ortho (Trevaskis groaned inwardly). Her uncle
Ortho used to ride over to Truro to take her out to
dinner at the ' Red Lion.' All the girls in the school
were violently smitten and would have eloped with
him had he asked them.

" And did he ? " Trevaskis inquired, slipping.

Jennifer looked shocked. " My uncle Ortho !—
why, he's married."

Trevaskis bit his lip. " I meant, would they?
Would they have eloped with him ? "

" Readily," said Jennifer; " mistresses too."

" Must be very fascinating," said Trevaskis, drily.

" He is," Jennifer glowed. " He's a duck."

Ortho Penhale as a duck was a new aspect. Trevaskis smiled a wry smile. It was evident the little
niece knew nothing of her precious uncle's way of life.
He imagined she did not know he had been engaged
in the black-ivory traffic. Before her time probably,
and her decent parents would hardly enlighten her.

Commanded the *Ghost* now, did he? In naval circles there were numerous rumours afloat concerning a corsair of that name. She, along with another of like kidney, had engaged a Dutch man-o'-war and eventually captured her. A gallant affair, marred by certain ugly incidents—Penhale running true to form. He might find himself in for a court of inquiry when he came home.

" Cruising still—your uncle? " he inquired.

" Yes, we haven't heard from him for a long time."

" If he's wise he'll continue to cruise," thought Trevaskis, and changed the subject. The drummer wiped the beer froth from his lips and dealt the drum three resounding wallops. Gentlemen bowed to their ladies, ladies curtsied low to their gentlemen. The beadles waddled forward, the band blared forth again, and the procession went tripping and twirling through the garden gate and up the abrupt slope of Lady Street.

> " As John the beau was walking home
>   He met with Sally Dover,
>   He kissed her once, he kissed her twice,
>   He kissed her three times over."

Cherry lips and cherry ribbons, the brown eyes upturned, sparkling happily, her hand in his. Anthony Trevaskis forgot that he was both nameless and penniless, forgot Hyde-Parker and the shadow of Bonaparte, even forgot Ortho Penhale. He only knew he was with Jennifer, the sun shining and summer coming in. Cherry lips and cherry ribbons !

.   .   .   .

Four, five, six, seven—seven houses below the ' Angel.' This was it. Happy house to shelter her, if only for one night. It should have a marble tablet placed above the door, ' Jennifer slept here,' and be closed for evermore lest unworthy guests profane it. ' Jennifer slept here.' Trevaskis stood bare-headed in the middle of Coinage Hall looking up at Jennifer's window. It was blank, the light out, the curtains drawn. She was asleep, curled up like a little dormouse in the white bed, her face pillowed on her burnished hair. 'Furry' day was over, sublime and rapturous day!

An hour since he had seen her home from the Assembly. For an hour he had been wandering on the hills. Now he was back again under her window. Another few hours and he must take the Plymouth stage. Rapturous day! Glorious night! The men had been tumbling over each other to dance with her at the Assembly, she was the toast and the rage. But with whom had she danced the first, the second, the fourth, the sixth, the tenth, the thirteenth, the sixteenth and—best of all—the last dance? Why, with him, Anthony Trevaskis. The bucks had scowled and growled, but his fabulous reputation as a duellist stood him in good stead and the faithful Johns attended to the chaperon. The lilt of the fiddles ran still in his head. He saw the musicians nodding in their gallery, the long lines of dancers swaying and circling, the men in their bright hunting coats, the women like flowers— and Jennifer, Jennifer beside him, sweetest and fairest and dearest of all, Jennifer, Jennifer!

Radiant and wonderful day! Day to be written in letters of flaming gold, to be carved in imperishable bronze, to be sung by poets till the end of time—the eighth of May, eighteen hundred.

A rooster bugled on the church hill and was answered by another up Meneage. The cocks of Helston broke the silence with their crowing.

The tap of a staff was heard approaching down Coinage Hall and the voice of the watchman crying in the dawn.

"Good-morning, my sweet," Trevaskis whispered to the blank window. "Good-morning and good-bye!" Then with his hat still under his arm slipped home to his lodgings.

CHAPTER X

MARY PENHALE lifted the Bosula latch, called twice "Naomi!" and getting no answer walked into the big kitchen which served as a general living-room. A fire of ash sticks burnt in the hearth, the copper pans on the opposite wall reflecting the flames. The black stock-pot bubbled lazily to itself. Over the hearth hung Ortho's powder-horn and long fowling-piece, its barrel burnished, also the flag of a captured privateer, shot to rags. In the dim light Mary could discern white chalk marks on the doorsteps, a sign that the floor had been scrubbed that day. Fresh sea-sand gritted under her feet. She passed into the dairy and from thence upstairs to her sister-in-law's room. All was in order, the bed made without a crease, Nicola's hair-brushes, backed with tortoise-shell and silver, laid out tidily on the table, Nicola's array of dresses hung in the oak wardrobe. The house was, as Mary antici-pated, spotless. Naomi was a reliable housekeeper, but servants were servants. An occasional inspection had a salutary effect, Mary considered, and in Ortho's continual absence she kept an eye on his property. She examined the dresses with admiration and no envy. Pretty, flimsy, colourful things. Almost the only sense that had been left to Nicola when the crash came was her instinct for dress, and Ortho indulged it to the full. "See that she gets all she wants to wear," he had said. "Dress her like a queen. It's her only pleasure, poor little soul. I'll pay the piper somehow." And pay this particular piper he always had—a scrupulous-ness not invariably extended to his other creditors.

Poor Nicola! Poor Ortho! Fate had played a

tricksy game with both of them.   Nicola—fortune's
darling, so vivid, so lovely—come to this; a sawdust
doll, without memory or hope.   Poor Ortho clutching
always at the moon and grasping—dust.

Pausing on the twilit stairs, Mary gave herself up
to wondering what the effect would have been on Ortho
if his wife had not broken down.   She fancied Nicola
could have held him.   She had had brains by report,
and considerable character.   Children might have come,
home interests.   This was no home for a man, this sad,
echoing, empty house.   Small wonder he ranged the
country, playing fast and loose.   She did not condone
his wild amours, but she understood.   Properly
directed he might have done great things.   Could
Nicola, sane, have controlled him?   It was not difficult.
All that was needed was a little patience and sympathy.
Ortho was a boy really, with a boy's faults and virtues.
Cruel, vainglorious, hasty, yet once his affection or
pity was aroused capable of heart-rending generosity.
Play on his affection or his pity and he was yours.   A
story of misfortune would bring tears to his eyes—she
had seen it, often—accompanied by an immediate
emptying of his pockets.   Her children adored him,
he was to them a merry and bountiful prince, his
home-coming a red-letter day.   They would hear his
tuneful voice outside singing his own, time-honoured,
version of Spanish Ladies :

> " Fare-well and adieu to you, fair Spanish ladies,
>   Fare-well and adieu to you, ladies of Spain,
>   For I'm going home for to see my own sweethearts,
>   My Polly, Melinda and dear Jenny Wren ! "

Her three little daughters would arise squealing
" Uncle Ortho ! " fling open the door and there he
would be, laughing, straddled across the step, his arms
full of gifts for all of them.

Once when she was taken suddenly ill he had ridden
into Penzance for a doctor.   Attempting a short cut

he threw his mare down, dislocating her shoulder. He cut the mare's throat and ran on, four miles, with three ribs broken. Often, when Ortho was proving most trying, she remembered those four miles with the broken bones pressing on his labouring lungs.

A man capable of that was capable of anything— properly directed. Musing there in the dusk of the stairway she put back the clock, imagined herself and Ortho both young again, at the start of the road. What could they not do? he with his dash and virility, she with her plain sense? Her mind took wing, soared forth over continent and ocean, over deserts tawny as a lion's skin, ranges glittering ice-clad under frosty stars, seas blue as a kingfisher's wing. She saw the world as a bauble beneath her, a coloured ball spinning in illimitable star-dust, and Ortho stooped and caught it in his hand and held it while she moulded it to her fancy. She traced new river beds with her finger-tip so that the deserts bloomed, kneaded the mountains aside so that new roads flowed through the gorges and warring peoples met in friendly commerce. She gauged safe harbours with her thumbnail and smoothed away dangerous reefs. She blew gently, steadily and the tiny windmills twirled their sails and the ships sped rejoicing from shore to shore. Ortho, the slaver-captain, handing her the world to shape, she the farm-bred farmer's wife. Splendid and preposterous fantasy! Mary caught herself up sharply. She had been slipping. No more dreams, no more looking back, it was dangerous. The little world of family and farm was in her hand already, more than enough for her to cope with.

She descended the creaking stairs, crossed the passage and came out into the twilight, a big, full-breasted woman holding herself erect as a young pine, with serene brown eyes set below level brows, and a firm-lipped, generous mouth. She was not handsome, but her skin and eyes were beautiful and she had, above

all, presence. The Dean of Gwithian, visiting his
flock for the first time in five years, and being com-
plimented by his clerk on the large congregation,
replied, " Was there? I only noticed that Mrs. Eli
Penhale."

Mary bobbed her tall head under the carved doorway
and stood waiting. A tortoise-shell cat squatted on the
stone drinking trough, watching its kitten frisking
after gnats. In the midden a vast pig slumbered
noisily. Over the way in the stable Tom Davy could
be heard singing as he wisped the horses down. The
cows emerged from the linney and processed leisurely
through the gate, *en route* for the valley pastures for the
night. Wany followed them, making curious music on
a sycamore pipe.

At last Naomi appeared, carrying a pail of milk,
red arms bared to the elbow.

She bobbed to Mary, " Evenin', Mrs. Penhale," and
kicked her miry patterns off on the doorstep.

" Cows doing well? " Mary inquired.

"None so bad. That old braggaty 'Blossom' is
coughing again. I've kept she in to-night. 'Ave 'e
got a bottle of syrup up to Roswarva that you could
spare, please. Oh, an' look, if we was to kill a pig
come Saturday could you take half of 'en ? "

Mary would send the cough mixture first thing next
morning, but declined the half-pig.

" Then we'll eat half and smoke half," said Naomi.
" Any word from the Captain? "

There was no news of Ortho. Mary thought it
probable he had gone across to the West Indies. He
said he might if his Biscay hunting-grounds proved
unfruitful.

Naomi clicked " Tchuc ! How the man doth range
about the world ! Biscay one day, West Indies the
next. Here and there, hither and thither, and him
with a good home too. 'Twould almost appear like
he was ridden."

" Perhaps he is," said Mary.

Naomi stared. " How do 'e mean, ma'am? I've often heard tell as how this old place was walked, but I never seen nothing. Though mark you I have heard bra'e whist sounds in the night."

" It is not ghosts I was thinking of," said Mary.

" How do 'e mean? Is there——"

" Hist ! "

Nicola was approaching, coming in from the twilit woods, dainty stepping, delicately clad. Roam she the tangle-woods from end to end no mire appeared to soil her shoes, no bramble clutched her skirts or twig whipped her cheek. It was as though the very wilds sensed her helplessness and chivalrously guarded her. She was not fair game for their hooks and barbs. " Let her pass, the poor thing," said the wild vines to the blackthorns. " Hands off ! " said the brambles to the nettles. She saw Mary, smiled and held her charming face up to be kissed. She was over forty now, but she did not look a day older than when Ortho had first brought her home, seventeen years before. Her figure was still as slender, her colour as bright, her hair as luxuriant. Time, like the tangle-woods, seemed to stand aside when Nicola passed by.

" She'll be blooming like a rose when we're all gone," Mary thought, and kissed the uplifted mouth. " She'll be a millstone round Ortho's neck to the end."

" Get thee within before the fire, my lambling, my dear worm," Naomi ordered, with a wealth of zoological endearments. " I'll skat Wany's chacks for keeping thee out in this night air. Get thee in to once, my liddle pigeon ! "

" Been up valley looking for the gate to Pigsie-land," Naomi explained, *sotto voce*. " Wany do fill the poor dear up with a lot of fabulous old stuff. Says there's a pigsie prince fell in love with Nicola. He's down in his dad's palace waiting for she to come and marry him. A lot of old widdles—but there, it do keep the dear darling occupied. Miss Jennifer up to Helston dancing with all the grand notables—eh?"

Mary smiled. "Not so very grand. Mr. Killick kept a shop once. I don't want Jennifer to get grand. She can dance with a lord to-night, if she likes, but she shall milk our cows as usual when she comes back."

"A great one for sense you always were, ma'am," said Naomi admiringly. "But seem me there eddn many too grand for Miss Jennifer. She'll have Roswarva one day, I 'spose, yes, and Bosula as well, two bra'e strong great farms—and she as pretty as a picture into the bargain."

"Bosula is the Captain's to do as he likes with," said Mary.

Naomi nodded. "Maybe, but who else can he leave it to but Miss Jenny, she the apple of his eye and him childless?"

"It is no affair of mine," said Mary.

Naomi looked at her curiously, then set down her bucket and shuffled a step nearer. "Begging your pardon, ma'am, but is there any more Penhales left anywhere—any men?"

"No," said Mary, surprised. "How could there be? What do you mean?"

"You mind old Bohenna—worked on this place, man and boy, sixty years?"

"Of course I do."

"Well, he talked very curious at the end."

"What did he say?"

"Didn't come to work for two days. Says Tom, 'That old man is took slight, I blow.' 'If he is he'll come here to be tended,' says I. 'That he won't,' says Tom; 'he've lived like a wild animal all his life, and when he's took slight he'll hide like a wild animal,' says he. 'I go forth and seek for 'en,' he says. By'm-by he's back again. ''Tis as I said,' he says, 'man's struck deathly, and he's crawled up into his holt like an old badger. Do you fit some broth and come along

to once,' says he, and I went. Sure enough Bohenna
was in his liddle crib among the rocks, lying on a bed
of bracken, his face to the wall. Broth, he wouldn't
look at it, nor cordial neither, very near bit me he did
when I tried to coax it into him. 'Can't 'e leave a
man in his own company for once?' he says. 'Go to
bloody hell the both of 'e!' 'Come away,' says Tom.
'We're only plaguing him.' So we stepped outside
and sat on the rocks in the dark, not liking to leave
him altogether. Getting on for midnight he rouses up
and begins to talk to hisself, thinking hisself alone.
Thought he was in the wrestling ring, he did, and
starts to jest and jibe at his old opponents, men dead
these twenty years. 'Ha!' he says. 'Thought
thee'st had me that time, eh, Jan boy? Thee's not
smart enough. Mind that hug I gi'ed 'e at Gwennap?
Scat a rib, did it? Well, I'll scat two on 'e this day.
Come close, come close, let me grip thee, Jan my
beauty.' Whist it was, sitting there listening to 'en
calling to the old wrestlers. He's quiet for a bit after
that, then he starts druling and rambling again, and
I hears 'en cursing old Mrs. Penhale and the Captain.
'Gypsy trash,' he calls 'em, saving your presence."

"He never liked Ortho," said Mary. "His heart
was in Bosula and he thought Ortho neglected it.
What else?"

Naomi resumed. "He said it would all be right in
the end, that the gypsy strain would perish and John
Penhale come back to his own."

"The father's name was John," said Mary. "He
died just after Eli was born. There is no John Penhale
now."

"Bohenna said there was, ma'am. 'Little John
Penhale' he called 'en. 'Thee shall come back to thy
own place in God's good time,' he said."

"Rambling," said Mary.

"So 'twould appear. But——"

"But—what?"

" The dying have long sight, 'tis said."

" They look backwards," said Mary, " look back into their young days. Bohenna was calling to old John Penhale, whom he dearly loved, so I've heard. Rambling."

" Well, that's what he said," said Naomi, picking up the pail. " Must be getting on, s'pose. Must drive they fowls in or the foxes 'll have 'em. Wany do belong to do it, but the Lord knows when she'll be back. She do go siller 'n ever under the moon and stop up valley half the night. What with she and my poor little lamb this is a bra'e whist old place, ma'am. I wake up sometimes of a night and hear the stream chuckling among the rocks and the wind moaning in the trees and wonder if I eddn turning pattick myself."

" Nonsense," said Mary; " you've got Tom with you."

Naomi was contemptuous. " Tom ! what's a man I ask you ? Why, little better 'n a bullock for higher feelings ! If Tregeagle and Wild Harris and all the bucca-boos and spectres from here to Plymouth was to fill the room moaning and gnashing, Tom would do norra thing but turn over on the pillow mumbling about mouse-traps ! Tom ! "

" Well, I must be getting home along," said Mary, laughing. " Eli 'll be back from Penzance. I'll send that syrup first thing to-morrow. Good-night, Naomi."

She wrapped her blue cloak about her and turned up the hill path. Birds twittered drowsily in the bushes, settling to sleep. The gentle wind, blowing up valley, was heavy with the scent of mingled gorse and hawthorn blossom. Eerily came the hoot of owls in the woods below, the little brown owls from which the old place got its name. " To-who—To-whee-whoo-hoo ! "

Mary reached the hill-top and saw the young moon low in the west, the solemn clouds drawn back, like curtains, to reveal her. A slim, nacreous thing, chaste and shining.

"Hush!" the night winds whispered. "You'll wake her, the sleeping beauty." All creation seemed to stand a tip-toe, a finger to its lips. "Hush! Tread lightly!"

Mary curtsied to the slim moon and walked westwards over the still uplands. She passed the Pipers, giant men who piped on a Sunday and were changed to granite; passed the Merry Maidens, that great ring of stones that once were dancing girls; crossed Polmenna Downs and saw the lights of Roswarva before her, twinking among the stunted sycamores.

As she neared the door she heard the stamp of metal on stone and saw a horse tied to the mounting block. It whinnied softly to her and she recognized it as Eli's brown mare 'Prince.' The name was characteristic of her husband. His first horse had been called 'Prince,' hence all its successors, irrespective of sex, had inherited the name.

Eli had returned from town, but why was 'Prince' not stabled? Such was not characteristic of its master. He invariably tended to his beasts before himself. Mary entered the kitchen, wondering what the reason was for this small, but significant, lapse. Eli was standing before the hearth, still in his best coat, his hands crushed deep into his pockets, his square chin sunk upon his breast. Mary, who read the simple yeoman quicker than she read print, knew instantly that something was amiss.

"What's the matter?" she asked.

He started at her voice, then sighed with relief, "Ah, you've come at last."

"What is it? Jennifer?"

Eli shook his head. "No, Ortho."

"Is he . .? Is he . . .?"

"He's wounded and taken."

"Ah!"

" You sound as if you were pleased, almost."

" I thought you were going to say he was killed."

" This is bad enough, seem me," Eli grumbled. " Ship taken and him wounded and a prisoner. Me sitting here with the best of food and comfort, and him cast away in a Spanish dungeon suffering and starved, maybe.   All the way out from Penzance it's been haunting me."

" Has he written? "

" No.   Written, no.   I don't know where he is or if he's alive even.   Veal has written.   Veal, the second mate.   He wrote to his uncle in Fowey, and the uncle sent the letter on to me.   It's all over the place that the *Ghost* is taken.   I was the last to know, living out here."

He pulled a crumpled letter out of his pocket and placed it on the table.   " There you are.   Read it for yourself."

Veal wrote at length, entrusting the letter to a Swiss merchant who had befriended him.   He said that they were homeward bound with two prizes when they fell into a dense fog off Cape Finisterre.   Hearing the creaking of blocks close at hand and thinking it to be one of the prizes, Veal shouted to the invisible ship to keep clear or the two vessels would fall foul of each other.   There was no answer, and the next thing he saw was a three-masted ship close aboard of him flying Spanish royal colours at her spanker gaff—a sloop of war.   She then hailed him, asking who he was.   Veal knowing no language but his own, could not reply. Ortho, hurrying on deck, shouted out that his craft was the *Revenante*, letter of marque, out of St. Malo, home bound from the Mediterranean.   Whereupon the Spaniard inquired why the first hail had been in English and why he himself spoke such curious French ; to which Ortho replied that his mate was an Irish rebel and himself a Breton.   The ready answer seemed to satisfy the Dons and there was a long pause, during which they were apparently consulting. Then the Spaniard hailed again, saying he was sending a boat. That would never do, so Ortho hoisted himself to the rail and shouted that before they sent a boat he thought it only fair to warn them that his ship had cleared from Oran.

This news was greeted with a loud exclamation of " *que el diablo* ! " followed by shouts of " Plaga ! Plaga ! "

The plague was raging in Barbary, and if there was one thing the Spanish dreaded more than another it was the plague.

The *Ghost's* company, crouching behind the bulwarks, grinned broadly, and were congratulating themselves that the bluff had worked, when the persistent Spaniard hailed again, saying that they must send a boat instead and hand up the ship's papers at the end of a boat-hook. The bluff had played out. Ortho replied that he would send his boat as soon as he could clear it of hamper and quietly motioned his people to quarters.

" Cap'n Penhale had no doubt of the outcome." Veal reported. " ' I carry as many guns as she and can fire 'em twice as fast,' he said to me. ' Three or four broadsides will sicken her. She will be sorry she spoke.' Nor was any member of our company less certain than the Cap'n, all hands standing to their posts with steadfast, cheerful countenances."

The Spaniard hailed, asking why the boat was so long in coming. Ortho, standing on the quarter-deck rail, took off his hat and bowed low. He deeply regretted, but his boat had been built in King George's own loyal duchy of Cornwall and positively refused to go visiting with a treacherous dog of a Spaniard. That being the case he must needs send his credentials by another agency. So saying he jumped from the rail, hoisted the red ensign and incontinently opened fire. Veal said that they fired three broadsides before the

Spaniard got off his first. They fired four more before he loosed his second. After that they hammered her as they liked. The fifth broadside brought her mainmast by the board, masking her midship guns. An ammunition tank on her quarter-deck blew up, killing everybody near it and setting her afire. Only one forward gun replied, and that fitfully.

"She was completely at our mercy and Cap'n Penhale dancing like a boy," Veal wrote, "when judge of our mortification on being swept by a storm of heavy shot from *t'other side*, and perceived an enemy *second-rate* right atop of us and plenty more looming up in support ! "

It was not a solitary sloop they had blundered against in the fog but a fleet !

Little remained to tell. " Cap'n Penhale said he would fight as long as he floated; Mr. Pentacost supporting him, declaring that Jehovah would haul us out of it yet. The second-rate closed with us and served us unmerciful, sweeping our decks and holing us through and through like a rabbit warren. There were many men there I have had cause to think shirkers and King's Benchers in the past, but on that day when they were in great hardships and stood no prospect but to be drowned or beat to pieces they made no complaint whatever, but continued manful by their duty to the end.

"Presently a double shot comes through, dismounting a gun served by men from Monk's Cove in the Cap'n's own parish, killing three (their names are Thomas Clemo, John Boase (called ' Kicky ') and William Tregurtha). Cap'n Penhale turns as white as if he had seen a ghost. ' Enough of this murder,' he says. ' Haul down the flag, Mr. Veal.' But Mr. Pentacost threatens me with his cutlass. ' Keep your hands off those halliards,' he says. ' Will ye bow down before popish idolaters ? Shame on ye ! Everlasting shame ! ' ' You do as you're bid, Mr. Veal,' says the

Cap'n, very quiet, ' and if Mr. Pentacost so far forgets his duty as to interfere with you he will have me to deal with.' ' You may deal with me now,' says the mate, ' for I will be no party to this evading of the Lord's battle—guard yourself!' But the matter went no further, for the pair of them were shot down by a discharge of grape. I surrendered as I was bid, considering that we had well maintained our honour as British seamen."

The *Ghost* sank that night, plunging suddenly and taking half the prize crew with her. "An unlucky ship to the end," Veal remarked, "which is not to be wondered at, seeing the figure-head she carried." The prisoners were landed at Corunna. Both Ortho and the mate were carried ashore, very weak, "but Mr. Pentacost contrived to raise enough strength to spit at a Romish shrine as he was borne past, for which he received a blow on the head from a soldier's musket." Those prisoners that could limp or crawl were marched into the interior two days later. Veal wrote from Leon, but he was expecting to be marched south any day. Followed a request to the uncle (a linen-draper) that he would use his utmost influence to get the captive exchanged, also a list of the killed and wounded, compiled to the best of the writer's knowledge.

Mary read the letter through to the end. "We must get Ortho exchanged too—if he's alive," she said.

Eli stirred uncomfortably.

Mary repeated herself. "I say we must get Ortho exchanged on—what do they call it?—on cartel?"

"I'll do all I can, but——"

"But! Why can't we?"

Again Eli shuffled. "Appears Ortho did something wrong in that fight with that Dutch ship, the *Stadenland*. I'll apply, but it ain't thought likely that the Government will forward it."

" What wrong did he do? "

" I don't know properly. Some hanky-panky with his flag, they say—and killing Dutchmen after they'd surrendered."

" I don't believe a word of it," said Mary. " That is not Ortho at all. God knows he has faults enough, but foul fighting isn't one of them, he's too vain. Do you believe it? "

" Of course I don't," said Ortho's brother stoutly; " but the point is that the Government does—and so does Mr. Burnadick."

" Then is he to stop in prison for ever—Ortho? "

" Till the end of the war."

" And when will that be, pray?—fifty, a hundred years hence? "

" My God, I don't know," said Eli, miserably, turning towards the door.

" Where are you going? " Mary asked.

" Down to Monk's Cove to tell the news."

" You'd best have your supper first—you'll need it, my dear."

Eli shook his head. " No. Those poor souls have a right to hear at once."

Mary heard the misnamed mare grunt as she felt the master's weight descend on her back, the clip-clop of her shoes diminishing down the lane.

Eli had gone down to Monk's Cove to tell the women that they were widows, sonless, fatherless, to be spat at, screamed at, cursed at as the brother of the ill-starred captain who had led their men away. Eli would see horrors that night, women tearing their hair, wailing like kelpies, out of their minds, old men bowed down. And Eli knew perfectly well what awaited him.

Mary felt a tingle of pride for her husband. He had courage. Obvious, somewhat dull, he was a rock to hold to. Never in the years she had known him had he caused her one moment's doubt, one instant's pain —the very antithesis of Ortho.

Ortho !—a prisoner in a foreign land, suffering and alone.

She moved to the open door, paused there, looking out to sea, then, almost without knowing what she was doing, began to walk towards the cliffs.

It was she who had found him the ship that led him into this strait. He was eating his heart out in idleness at home, and in that state he was dangerous, for who could foretell down what paths of disgrace his hasty feet might stray? His slaving period had been one long nightmare to Eli and herself. Privateering was at least an honourable occupation. She had done it for the best, not only for Ortho, but for all of them.

Jennifer dancing at the Helston Assembly, Ortho lying wounded amid the vermin and filth of a Spanish gaol. Life was a mixed affair. Ortho in prison ! The caged sea-hawk.

" He'll break his wings against the bars," she thought, " break his gay heart."

Mary halted on the cliff edge. Far below great stripes of foam writhed and twisted like ghostly serpents, dimly glimmering. The rumble of the ground-swell along miles of iron coast was as the rolling of a million wheels, the marching of armies; the breakers on the reefs boomed like muffled guns. The moon, that silver witch, had gone her ways, night, sombrous and muttering, wrapped land and sea. Mary stood still as a statue, staring south-east into the dark.

BOOK II

CHAPTER XI

" ' THE Lord is my Shepherd; He maketh me to
lie down in green pastures ! ' . . . ' If I ascend
up into heaven, Thou art there : if I make my bed in
hell, behold, Thou art there ! ' Vast heaving ! Vast
heaving ! Anchor's a-peak, sir. Overhaul your cat
and fish."

" Sh-oo ! Quiet, man."

" Serve it 'em hot and fast, my lads. Aim low, into
their ports. Ha ha ! smartly, smartly ! ' Be of good
heart, be cheerful. Big they are and many, but the
Lord is with us. He shall break them with a rod of
iron, He shall dash them in pieces like a potter's
vessel.' . . . Serve 'em with double shot, my hearties.
Huzza ! "

" Easy ! If you strain like that you'll open your
wound again."

" I think we're in for a heavy swell from the west'ard,
Mr. Veal. Fog, they say, is the mother of big seas . . .
Call upon Brother Menhenick to unfold the holy
revelation that came upon him between Flushing and
Mylor last Friday night . . . Breakers ! Hard down
your helm ! Let go and haul ! "

" Easy, man ! You're ashore, all's well."

" In Georgetown, Barbadoes when I was young . . .
sinner unredeemed . . . Quadroon girl . . . played
the guitar . . . a coral necklace . . . before I met
you, Betsy. . . . ' He hath seen the abominations they
have set up, their idols of wood, stone, silver and gold.
His anger is kindled against them, His day is at hand.
His arrow shall go forth as the lightning, and the Lord
God shall blow His trumpet and shall go with the

157

whirlwinds of the south. Instead of a sweet smell there shall be a stink, and burning instead of beauty. Hell hath enlarged herself and opened her mouth without measure, and their glory and their pomp and their multitude shall descend into it. He will avenge the blood of His servants and bring them——' " There was a long pause, then the last word came sighing, almost inaudible—" ' home.' "

Ortho sat for some time with the wasted head on his knees. Pentacost was dead; he was alone. Pentacost had been shot the day before in an attempt to escape. Just when he appeared to have won free a chance bullet ricochetted, striking him in the kidneys. To do the Spaniards justice they had tried to ease the wounded man. Two sisters of mercy came, under guard, with the object of ministering to him, but he would have none of them, tearing off their bandages and spitting out their medicines. ' Popish Jezebels ' he called the two good women.

As a matter of fact he was beyond help, the flattened bullet had done its work too well. He had been in a heavy stupor most of the day. Ortho hoped he would never wake from it, but night and its fever had roused him up and he had been raving for an hour, off and on. He would rant long Biblical passages, imagining no doubt that he was in his sail-loft at Penryn, admonishing the faithful. Again he was in the midst of the *Ghost's* last fight, encouraging the gunners to further efforts. Then he would grow quieter for a while and maunder of the summer lanes about Devoran, where he was born.

Three attempts he had made to escape. He was free now, had fought his good fight and gone home. Now that Pentacost was dead, Ortho realized how much he had been to him in the last twenty months. Common interests they had none. Pentacost's conversation was negligible, his outlook rigid, not a trace of humour or sympathy did he possess, but it was he who had kept them going. Not for one instant had the old fanatic lost hope. No sooner was one avenue of escape blocked than he was looking for another. Hope shone from him as from some fixed star, constant and inspiring. Now he was gone and Ortho was left to work out his own salvation. He doubted if he could. Animal courage was his in abundance, but that is not enough when the pinch comes. Long confinement, vermin, prison fever and miserable food had sapped his vitality, and with his strength his spirit. He had no inner fire of faith to keep him going. But keep going he must—or rot. Easier to rot, to lie down and give in. Mouldering was a slow, easeful death, one did not feel it. The rot ate you imperceptibly, bit by bit, layer by layer, till one day there was no more of you. That was all.

If he behaved himself for a time and did not again try to escape they might throw him back to moulder in the common jail, in among the army deserters, bandits, thieves and chancery debtors. That would mean company of a sort, but there would be no chance of escape there—too many eyes watching, too many people anxious to betray the solitary Inglés and gain the warders' favour. Not that it was any use trying to get out, the luck was always against one. At Segovia they got in touch with an escape agent, who engaged to find mules and guide them over the mountains into Portugal. They broke prison to find the smuggler's hovel hung with black and the man himself lying in an open coffin at the door, between rows of burning tapers. He had been knifed only that morning. They were recaptured and confined in a cell in the Alcazar. It took them three months to scratch a hole through those walls, to be moved suddenly to Valladolid the day before their preparations were complete. And now it was a chance bullet that had killed Pentacost, a misaimed ricochet.

One could not contend with luck as well as

murderous guards and stone walls. He must moulder. Some day, perhaps, there would be peace. Then he would go home, white-haired, rheumy, old, to sit in the chimney corner opposite Nicola and listen to the rain and the stream, two broken things together. He lifted the heavy head from his lap and tried to cross Pentacost's hands. But he had delayed too long, the body had stiffened, the hands would not remain in position. He gave up. It did not matter, anyhow. Then he felt his way along the wall to the corner where his bed lay, pulled the sparse and filthy straw round him and tried to sleep, worn out body and soul.

He could not sleep at once; the cold ate into the small of his back, the lice ate at him all over. He scratched himself violently, made a wad of straw and jammed it between his back and the wall and lay down again, twitching and shivering.

Down in the common jail they all lay packed together and kept passably warm; they also searched each other for vermin. He must go back there and moulder. By comparison the common jail appeared a heaven of warmth and good-fellowship—even if there always was a free fight over the food.

He dozed off, wondering if the governor would take his parole and let him go back at once—woke to hear the straw rustling where Pentacost lay. Those damned rats! He propped himself on his elbow and shouted; heard them scutter, squeaking, down their hole in the far corner. As soon as he fell asleep they would be back again, gnawing at the body. Oh, well, what matter? worms or rats, what did it matter? Pentacost would not mind. He was free and far away in the green pastures and beside the still waters of which he had babbled. The rats were welcome to his leavings.

His stomach was cold now, also his feet. He drew his knees up to warm his stomach, curled himself up into as small a compass as possible and redistributed the straw, it went further that way. Again he dozed.

Night lay black and heavy on Valladolid, *la muy noble y bel ciudad*, that once-royal city of Castille where Torquemada was a monk, Columbus died and the second Philip was born. The Rio Esgueva, swollen with winter rains, clotted with snow and filth, went brawling through the town like a drunken muleteer, shouting to its comrade the Rio Pisuerga, growling to the westwards. The bell of the Benedictine monastery boomed morosely and was answered by the bell of San Pablo. Their chiming pierced Ortho's sleep. He was in the Carrick Roads and the ships' watchmen were striking the hour. On the morrow he would ride to Truro and take Jennifer to dine at the ' Lion.' He was never tired of looking at Jennifer, she was so like . . . Then he remembered. No, he was not in Falmouth, he was in Valladolid, and to-morrow he was going back to the common jail, giving in.

" Curse those rats ! Hi ! Shoo ! A-ha ! Gone again, down that hole in the corner." Rats seemed to get through the stoutest wall. Nothing but tiny teeth and claws to do it with, either. Found the weak spot and just scratched away. Got through all right—in time. Problem was to find that weak spot; then— patience. Pentacost had that, illimitable, terrifying patience. The hole he had made at Segovia, worked the stones out one by one, a week a stone, sometimes two weeks, niggling at the mortar with horseshoe nails picked up on the road. At the end he was lying up a hole half his length, wedged so tight he could not move his elbows, wrist-work all of it. After a night's work he would replace all the stones, sealing up the last with a paste of dust and spittle. Ortho wondered if any future prisoner would find that hole. If so he could be a free man in a couple of hours. He wished they would return him to Segovia and that cell. But what was the use of wishing? He was in Valladolid, worn out, finished.

He scratched his shoulder-blades against the rough

wall to ease the itching, rearranged the straw and dozed off again into a sleep troubled by uncomfortable dreams. He was pinned under the spare spars, the ship's waist flooded, icy water sluicing over him. He was up in the Atlas mountains in a blizzard, the tent blown down. He was on the Grand Banks in spring, icebergs all about and the wind off them, biting him to the marrow of his bones. He was everywhere where he had been chilled and miserable. He twitched and shuddered as he slept.

He mumbled and groaned, cursing his cabin boy for not keeping in the cabin stove, called to his steward for his Magellan jacket. Then his dreams changed. There was a sound of rushing air in his ears, the beat of myriad wings and a deep throbbing, as of drums, very far away.

Well he knew that sound, that peculiar, pulsating rumble. It was surf on the Twelve Apostles. He was born during a gale (' came in on the wind,' they said); it was the first sound he heard, the voice of the Twelve Apostles, echoing up the Keigwin valley.

" Growlin' for 'en like a g'eat dog, eddn a ? " said the Gwithian midwife. " There ! there ! don't 'e cry, my liddle beauty. Teddn farmers a do eat, 'tis sailors."

The Twelve Apostles ! In a flash he was there, sitting on Pedn Boar, looking out to sea to where the great reef spouted and creamed, snow-white upon dragon green. He heard it all, saw it all; the maned combers thundering on the ledges below, the caves bellowing back, bull-throated; the scream of gulls as the air eddies sucked them hither and thither. He saw the long arm of the Lizard away to the eastward, bathed in sunlight; cloud shadows fleeting, purple-winged, over meadows of jade and emerald; rainbows flickering in the spindrift; the diamond glitter of spray.

A stab of exquisite pain stabbed Ortho's heart. Oh, to be home again ! To smell the salt ! To feel the wind ! To feast on all that living beauty ! To be free, free, free !

He opened his eyes, half awake, met nothing but darkness black as the pit, felt nothing but the itch of the lice and the gnaw of the cold, but he could hear something, a whimper, a whispering at the high grating, nothing more, but he knew its voice. It was the west wind come to him over the plains of Leon, the mountains of Portugal bringing a smell of the heather and imagined echoes of the sea.

"Go on. Try again ! "

Pentacost's voice, imperative, imploring. Ortho heard it distinctly. He sat up in the inky darkness, startled, prickling.

"Joe ! My God, Joe, is that you? "

No answer.

Ortho scrambled across the floor on all-fours, fell on the body, picked it up in his arms, hugging it.

"Joe, answer me. I thought you were dead. Did you speak just now? Joe ! "

The body was as stiff as wood, heavy as lead.

"Who called? Wasn't it you, Joe? Did I . . ? My Lord, has it come already? Did I. . . . Am I *mad*? "

No answer.

"I could have sworn . . ." Ortho pumped at the rigid arms, pressed the cold head to his cheek, thrust his hand under the coarse shirt to feel for heartbeats.

The heart was still, but his fingers met something they had not expected, four horse-nails hung round the dead man's neck by a bit of string. Four horse-nails ! The keys to that freedom of which the wind had sung. Pentacost had called to him across eternity. It was a sign and a portent. He was not mad, Pentacost had called to save him from madness. He would not moulder, he would go on. He would dig another hole, and if that failed, another and another. Freedom !

he would worship her as the one and only god, on his
knees would he worship her—digging.

Carefully, almost religiously, he took the string from
Pentacost's neck and hung it about his own. He
stripped the body of its one shirt and pulled it on.
If he did not take it the guard would, and Pentacost
did not need it any more. It would be dawn soon.
He would hear the bells break out again and the market
people coming in; women shrilling to each other in the
street outside, mules slipping on the cobbles. Then the
guard would arrive, stare at him through the peep-hole
in the door and carry Pentacost away, slung across a
scavenger's donkey. As soon as they had gone he
would look for the weak place. Every cell had one,
they said. Jack Sheppard had broken through the
Newgate condemned hold and three outer rooms in a
single night, weighted with leg shackles. He wondered
if any previous captive had found the weak spot in this
cell, delved at it night after night to be taken away
when the hour of success was at hand, as had happened
to them at Segovia. In the three centuries that this
old pile had been a prison surely somebody must have
tried, some desperate, patient man who would not give
in. Supposing there had been such, where would he
try first? On the west wall naturally, since it faced the
street, and in the south corner, being nearest the door
and invisible from the peep-hole.

Creeping into that corner Ortho felt the edges of the
stones with his fingers, testing the mortar here and
there with a horse-nail. The upper stones were scored
with prisoners' names, expressions pious and obscene,
signs of the cross, etc. The lower were greasy from the
rubbing of generations of verminous human bodies.
Here were scars where the masons' chisels had slipped
there small cracks where the grain had flawed, but there
was no chink deep enough to provide a grip. Ortho
swept his hand along the face of the bottom stone and
encountered some curious scratchings, like writing,

low down, almost on the floor. Carefully he traced the marks with a finger-tip. Writing it was. He spelt it out letter by letter, ' Gil Lerma y Mateo Nunez. Ora pro nobis,' with, underneath, an oblique stroke.

Who were Gil Lerma and Mateo Nunez who had left this request that they might be prayed for? Captives of the Holy Office doomed to appalling, lingering agonies? Or more fortunate civil prisoners, awaiting comparatively merciful strangulation. Whoever they were their mundane troubles were over and their trembling souls surely at rest—having experienced a sufficiency of hell on earth.

A curious place to scratch one's name, Ortho thought, right down there, out of sight. His finger, rubbing along the oblique stroke, discovered that it was nicked on each side at the lower end. It was, in fact, an arrow, pointing into the corner angle.

Trembling he swept his hand along the wall in the direction given, and behold it plunged in, up to the wrist.

The rat-hole in the corner !

But why all this trouble to point out a rat-hole? Instantly it occurred to him that it was not the rats that had made the breach in the first place, but Gil Lerma and Mateo Nunez, Gil Lerma and Mateo Nunez, the unknown, who, not being able to save themselves, would save others.

He turned his wrist so as to get a purchase and felt a trickle of dust fall on his arm. The mortar, if mortar, it was, was crumbling away ! Working his right hand under the stone also, he placed his forehead against the wall, drew his knees up under him, took a full breath and wrenched with all his might.

The stone stirred.

CHAPTER XII

AT the first blink of daylight old Ester Pradilla awoke, dressed herself and lit the fire. She was alone on the little *granja*, her remaining unmarried daughter, Enriqueta, having gone into Valladolid and was not expected back until the morrow—if then, Enriqueta being prone to dally. Not that Ester minded, she had not lived forty odd years in the Torozos hills for nothing. Solitude did not trouble her, moreover, it being midwinter there was little work to do.

The fire lit, the breakfast pot hung, she opened the door and sniffed the morning air.

A notable old person was Ester Pradilla, with bright black eyes set in cavernous sockets and wisps of cotton-white hair dangling on either cheek in strong contrast to the saddle-tan of her skin. Since her husband's death she had done the man's work on the farm— Enriqueta being too dainty—handling the *álama negro*, the back-breaking wooden plough of Castile, and time and toil had warped her somewhat, but she moved with surprising decision and speed, and when she bit it was with all her teeth—for all her sixty-eight years there was not a gap in her jaw.

Forty odd years before, Enrique Pradilla had brought her, a bride, from Villanueva, twenty miles away over the Leon border, but she still wore the costume of her country, the scarlet *jabon* and square-cut, cloth mantilla and, moreover, dressed Enriqueta in the same fashion—a conservative old party.

The air she sniffed that morning had an edge to it. Fresh snow lay upon the Torozos; over the low-lying Tierra de Campos, towards Valladolid, a frost mist

still hung. Presently *Sol criador*, the all-conquering
Castilian sun, would clear it all up; but at that moment
there was nothing to be seen beyond the immediate
surroundings. A bleak, steeply-rising hillside culti-
vated in erratic patches; a few woe-begone vines on the
sunward slope; the *adobé* farm buildings appearing
like some ordered excrescence of the earth, which in a
manner they were, being built of mud dug on the spot.
Not a tree, not a shrub in sight, yet out of this arid slope
Enrique and Ester, working early and late, had
scratched sufficient to raise five healthy children,
satisfy the demands of Church and State and even save
a little money, an achievement as miraculous as anything any wonder-working saint ever accomplished—
though the Pradillas themselves would have scouted
the idea. Ester released four yellow goats and two
dun plough oxen from the stable, watered them at the
well from leathern buckets and turned them loose on
the hill-side to pick what they could. That done she
went to the granary to fetch the fowls some grain.

Stable and farmhouse were under a common roof, but
the granary stood apart, on the far side of the corral.

Ester inserted two fingers through a hole in the door,
jerked the bobbin, opened the door, paused—and
carefully shut it again.

There was someone in the granary, someone who
groaned and muttered. Ester laid a crinkled ear to
the bobbin hole. The intruder maundered on, now
barely articulate, now almost shouting. She could
not understand a single word he said. It was plain
that he was asleep and in the grip of bad dreams.

Ester drew back. What did the man want? No
good evidently. Had he been honest he would have
knocked at the farm door instead of skulking in the
granary. Why had he come to the farm at all? The
answer was obvious, because it was the only cover
within miles. The man was a fugitive, probably a
prison-breaker from Valladolid, hungry and desperate.

Enriqueta would not be back until the following day
—if then. The nearest neighbour was four miles
distant. By the time Ester had hobbled the four miles,
summoned Mariano Vasco and returned, the rogue
would have rifled her house and gone.

She must deal with the matter herself. That the
whole of her stealable possessions were worth only a few
piastres did not affect the situation. She had spent
most of her lifetime in collecting them and was prepared to risk the remainder of it in their defence.
Stealthily she recrossed the corral and, taking Enrique's
aged blunderbuss from its hooks, loaded it with a full
charge—powder, wad, a handful of slugs and a second
wad, all rammed home with care. It was by no means
the first time Ester had handled that flint-lock. The
household defence was part of the man's work she had
assumed on Enrique's demise. Driven by hard winters
wolves had, from time to time, appeared in the Torozos.
Four grey pelts on the earth floor of Ester's bedroom
testified to her marksmanship. The human wolf
who lay muttering in her granary daunted her not at
all. Asleep he was at her mercy. At ten yards with
a charge of slugs she could, and would, riddle him like
a sieve. The only disturbing thought was that he
would make such a mess on the grain. However, that
could not be helped and Enriqueta could wash it
later. Also there would be a reward paid, much
money. Ester had heard public criers in the streets
of Valladolid offering unheard of sums for the capture,
dead or alive, of escaped prisoners. As much as a
hundred piastres sometimes. A hundred piastres in
a lump sum was a fortune to Ester, who had collected
her scant hoard real by real, quarto by quarto. With
one hundred piastres as dowry she could get Enriqueta
well married. She would have shot fifty men without
a wink for one hundred piastres.

One hundred piastres! She cocked the hammer
and stalked towards the granary, sunken eyes a-gleam.

Carefully she twitched the bobbin, slowly she swung the door, like lightning she whipped the heavy gun to her shoulder, finger closing on the trigger.

The man was lying in the corner, his face full to the open door, the maize cobs scraped over him for warmth. Only his head was visible, that and one arm in a tattered shirt-sleeve ripped off at the elbow. He did not move, he had ceased to mumble, but slept like the dead, tired out.

Ester brought the gun muzzle to bear on his head. A handsome head covered with thick black curls greying slightly over the ringed ears. Ester examined the rings. Gold! She would cut them out before delivering the body to the *alguacils*, that would mean an extra piastre or two.

Best not shoot him in the head, it might damage the precious rings. In the heart—he would never know what struck him.

The man slumbered peacefully on, his dreams had changed for the better, apparently; a smile played about his mouth.

The gun muzzle dropped an inch or two. Aiming at the pit of the exposed arm a slug should reach his heart at once.

Ester steadied the gun, holding her breath; her finger closed on the trigger, the hammer rose slowly.

Under the arm-pit. Her eye travelled up the outstretched arm, halted at a little blue device tattooed above the wrist.

The hammer dropped back. Ester stepped a pace nearer, two paces, her eyes glued to the blue mark.

Slowly she lowered the gun, quietly she tip-toed out of the granary, gently she closed the door.

The man slept on. Smiling to himself.

"Hola! Señor! Wake up! You have slept long enough!"

Ortho woke with a start. What were those overhead?

Deck beams? He was in the cabin of the *Ghost* off Cape Torinana. No, they were rafters. He was in Spain still, in that farm in the hills—and discovered. He sprang to his feet prepared to do battle, let his hands drop to his sides again, sighing. Only a bent old peasant woman, nodding at him.

It was evening, he noticed, the sky seen through the open door was a blood-red smear. He must have slept some fourteen hours. The old creature said he had slept long enough. How did she know how long he had slept? Obviously she had discovered him earlier in the day. He thought he had hidden himself completely in the maize—must have shifted in his sleep. Why had she not given him away? There could be two reasons, either her pity was roused or there was nobody to whom she could give him. He resolved to trust to the first and work still further on her pity.

" Good-evening to you, Señora," said he cheerfully, loosing his most ingratiating smile.

" Good-evening, Señor."

" You will pardon this intrusion, I trust, but I am travelling—er—lost my way. Came upon your farm late last night—er—did not like to wake you up."

" The Señor is very considerate." There was a touch of irony in the old creature's voice, a twinkle of sour amusement in her deep eyes.

Ortho wondered how much she guessed.

He grinned. " As well make a clean breast of it. Madam, to tell you the whole truth I am fleeing from the law, nevertheless I am no criminal, there is no harm in me."

The woman shrugged her cramped shoulders, she seemed completely indifferent as to his morals.

" No criminal," Ortho repeated. " The victim of gross injustice. I will tell you how it was——"

" The matter is of no importance to me, Señor."

" Nevertheless I insist on your knowing," said Ortho. " I am a horse-dealer from the province of Guipuzcoa.

A month or two back while I was in Segovia about my affairs the officers impressed me into the army, which they have no right to do as I am a free Basque and protected by my Fueros. I trust you understand me? As a Basque, *El Vascuence* comes more readily to my tongue than your Castilian."

The old woman nodded solemnly. "I thought I detected a foreign flavour in your speech. So it is *El Vascuence* is it? Yes, I understand."

"Good! Well then, finding the officers deaf to my protests and entreaties, I very naturally deserted and have been hunted like a dog ever since. Were I a single man I would ask nothing more honourable than to serve *El Rey* against the detestable English, but I have a sick wife at home dependent on my exertions, also five little children. I crave your pity, Señora, not for myself but for my innocent mites criminally deprived of a father's love and protection."

"My heart bleeds for them," said Ester.

"As soon as I saw you I knew I had found a friend, and determined to tell you the whole truth and throw myself upon your mercy," Ortho exclaimed. "All I ask of your charity is silence and a handful of dry bread to stay the pangs of hunger which devour me."

Ester pointed to the door. "I will stay your pangs with something more palatable than that. Pass into my house, Señor."

"Serenissima, I kiss your hands."

"Tchut! You will find the ham more appetizing. Come, stranger!"

Ortho stepped out into the corral, wondering. Why this hospitality? Was she walking him into a trap? Unlikely, he thought. She had him securely trapped in the granary; why risk moving him to another? For all her grim looks he did not think she meant him any harm. His story of the sick wife and children may have touched her heart. Not a bad yarn for the spur of the moment, it accounted at once for his foreign accent, his rags and his furtiveness. He mentally awarded himself a palm or two. He was a very clever fellow.

He strolled up to the door of the house, prepared to enter, then halted and walked across to the gate. The snow there bore the hoof-marks of shod horses. Dung droppings not yet frozen over proved them but recently gone. He found the old woman in the kitchen ladling soup out of a black pot.

" So you knew all the time ? " he said.

She nodded.

" That I am no Basque horse-coper, but an English prisoner of war ? "

" An English sailor, yes."

" How long have you known ? "

" I suspected as much at dawn."

" How ? "

" Your gabble and that mark on your arm."

Ortho examined his wrist. " This anchor you mean ? "

" I do not know what you call it, but it is the emblem of sailors, is it not ? There is an image of St. Peter in Valladolid holding one of those."

" When did the *alguacils* come ? "

" About an hour ago."

" And they said——? "

" They said there was an English sea captain escaped from the Carcel. Had I seen him ? "

" And you said you had not ? "

" I said I had not."

" Why ? "

" Eat your soup, *hombre*. You must be famished."

Ortho drew the basin to him, hunger conquering curiosity. Famished he was. He had eaten nothing since mid-day the day before, and in the interval broken prison, scaled the city walls and made twenty miles, steering north-west by the stars. He ate wolfishly

and noisily; four bowls of soup thickened with chick-
peas and cubes of bread, a huge egg tortilla, the best
part of a *jamon en dulce*, a cooked ham covered with sugar.
A meal for three men, washed down by plenty of
passable local wine. The crone hung over him supplying his every need. He knew well enough that she did
not furnish meals of this sort every day, had he been the
King of Spain she could not have feasted him more
royally; him, a man she had never seen before and
would never see again, an escaped convict with a price
on his head, an alien heretic to boot. His wonder
grew.

Replete he scraped his stool back, wiping his mouth
with the blue anchor.

"Tia," * said he, "leave those dishes be. I will
wash them for you later. For the moment let us
take our ease like Christians. I have not seen a fire
or full meal for two years and I feel as gorged as an
alderman." He toasted his broken shoes before the
blaze, snuggling luxuriously into his rags, "Sit down
I prithee."

Ester drew up a second stool as bidden.

Ortho patted her wrinkled hand. "Ah—ha ! Now
here we are as sociable as a brace of tabbies on a farm
hearth. Upon my soul I feel extremely well ! After
two years enforced sobriety this wine of yours is mounting to my head. I should not be surprised if I burst
into song."

"Sing if you will, Señor."

"I see a guitar hanging up there. I wonder if——"

"Take it by all means. But it belonged to my
husband and is very old."

"So it appears," said Ortho. "There is one string
snapped already. However, what is a string more or
less? By rights I should chant a Te Deum for my
escape, but I am not yet out of the wood, and moreover
do not know one. In my present exalted state I yearn

* *Tia*—aunt.

to sing a love song, but what the devil's the use if there's nobody to love? After two years in the grave the thought of seeing a pretty woman again sets me a-burning. Do you know that were I to see a pretty woman now, be she swineherd or duchess, I believe I should eat the little pet alive."

"In that case it is as well my daughter, Enriqueta, is spending the night in Valladolid," said Ester.

"Pretty?"

"Passable."

Ortho sighed. "Then perhaps it is as well. Poor little Enriqueta! What she is missing, though! The chance of a life-time. Give her my love when she returns. Pop! goes another string. If I do not sing soon I shall have nothing to sing to. What shall it be?"

"A sea song."

Ortho shook his head. "When I tread a deck again I will sing a sea-song by way of a Te Deum, and I hope the good Lord will not examine the words too closely, but take it in the spirit in which it is meant. But I'll tell you what I will do, I'll sing you a song that has a smack of the sea in it and also of my own country, which is very dear to me at this moment. We have only four strings left, but are we hangmen to depend on strings? 'Islands' is the name of this song, and the man that made it fell overboard off Cachacron Head, Dominica, and was taken by a shark—which is neither here nor there. *Adelante!*—

> The Isles of the Indies have shining blue havens,
>   With three-deckers riding secure as can be,
> The fair Creole ladies they sit at their windows
>   To welcome bold captains that sweep in from sea.
>
> The Isles of the Indies have cloudy blue mountains,
>   And forests as high as a top-gallant truck;
> There green parrots perch in a blaze of red blossom
>   And golden fruit hangs for the monkeys to pluck.

The Isles of the Indies they sparkle with sunshine,
  And glitter with stars and with fire-flies by night;
A man may have yams there and rum and molasses,
  And lovely mulattoes to be his delight.

The Isles of the Indies are rare isles and fair isles,
  With sweet odours blowing from garden and tree;
The Islands of Scilly are poor isles and bare isles,
  But there, where my home is, ah ! there would I be !

I would I were far from Port Royal, Jamaica.
  I would I were stepping ashore at Hugh Town.
My true love should have a gold ring for her finger,
  A red coral brooch and a taffeta gown.

My love on my arm I would walk on Peninis
  And watch the gulls flying like tatters of spume.
On Sallakee Downs I would walk with my pretty,
  On Sallakee Downs when the gorse is in bloom.

The Isles of the Indies are islands of wonder,
  The Islands of Scilly are poor isles and drear,
But fain would I give all the spice and the blossom
  For the sea pinks that bloom in the cheeks of my dear !

" I think I have sung very creditably, seeing that for
the last three verses I have had no strings at all," said
Ortho. "You will excuse this outburst, but a man
does not break prison every day." He tossed the
mute guitar aside. "Would it be an impertinence if
I were to ask you a question or two? "

" I can judge of that when I hear them."

" Then, do you know you are entertaining a
desperate character who might well rob you of all you
possess? "

Ester shook her head. " You cannot rob me of what
I would willingly give you."

Ortho whistled softly. " So? Again, do you know
that for befriending me you might be thrown into
prison yourself, whereas had you given me up you
would have gotten considerable money? "

" I do."

"The deuce! Without flattering myself I have reason to know that I am not an impersonable man— still, at your age, it can hardly have been a case of love at first sight. It would therefore seem that you are a damned fool or a holy angel, and I mean it as a compliment when I say that you have not the slightest appearance of either."

Ester emitted a dry sound which might have been meant for a chuckle. "Neither am I. At dawn this morning I was on the point of shooting you as you slept, and I would have too, had I not seen that mark on your arm."

"The mystery deepens," said Ortho. "What have you, living here, to do with anchors?"

"It is the emblem of sailors, is it not?"

"It is—but what of it? Are you a sailor's daughter by any chance?—from the sea-coasts?"

"I have never seen the sea, or a ship, or, to my knowledge, a sailor before. In all my life I have not been fifty miles from this place."

"Never seen the sea! The Lord preserve us! But I suppose it is possible. Nevertheless it sounds very peculiar to these ears of mine, which, until lately, had scarce been out of the sound of it."

"What is it like, the sea?" Ester asked.

"Like? Like? That is a tall order, lady! Ask me something easier, the order of the stars in their courses, the mysteries of birth and death, the workings of a woman's mind. Like? It is like a sheet of glass, or molten diamonds, or liquid sapphires. It is cloth of gold, or rainbow silk, or a peacock's breast—or black as the shadow of Doom. It is studded with lazy islets where palm trees grow and bright birds flutter. It hath weed gardens more splendid than Seville's Alcazar —and coral grottos most wonderful that rip your keel off while you wonder. It is cold as steel and blocked with glittering ice mountains that crack ships between them as you would a nut. Sea-lions herd on the floes as thick as sheep on your Jarales, and giant sperm bulls battle in the channels blowing fountains of blood and spray. At one moment it is as flat as the Plain of Castile; at another spewing up endless foamy mountain chains and tumbling them together. At one moment it is as hushed as the grave; at another howling like a million furies. It is as trackless as the Sahara, yet laced as thick with currents as a common with foot-paths. It is as lonely as death, yet packed and swarming with marvellous life. It has winds that blow straight all the year round, winds that blow forwards for half the year and backwards for the other half, winds that spin like tops, sucking pillars of water up to heaven. It belts the world from top to bottom and side to side. It hears the temple gongs of China and the hunting chant of the Esquimo; the South Sea savages blowing on their conch shells, and the Grimbsy fish-hags cursing one another. Wealth may be got quickly upon it, disaster more quickly and surely. Men voyage it from end to end yet understand little of it, and the oldest sailor lies the most. It is the great mystery, the supreme gamble. Old woman, I could sit here for a thousand nights telling you what the sea is like and you would be no wiser in the end. Since I have not a thousand nights to spare, but only one, I will compress the description into three words— it is hell—a hell of privation, brutality, hardships, anxiety and shattered hopes."

"Yet you will sing a Te Deum when you return to it."

"Yes, and another when I quit it. For my part I believe a man goes to sea for the joy of getting ashore again."

"I do not understand."

"Will you understand if I say that it takes a sinner from Purgatory to appreciate Heaven? Your hardened saint will not appreciate the advantage of golden pavements over red-hot tiles, seeing that he never went hop-skipping over the latter. After a twelve-week

thrash to wind'ard in a crank ship I have landed in
lousy little ports that stank sky-high and thought them
paradise; quaffed vinegar dregs and deemed it nectar,
clasped blowsy slatterns to my bosom and called
them queens. A week and I should have recognized
them for what they were, but there was seldom
a week. A day, a night and it was up anchor and
fare-ye-well, the illusion intact. In a world of bitter
realities a little hellery is a small price to pay for one's
illusions."

" But where do these illusions lead you? "

" To the same port that you are bound for—and the
Pope of Rome and the King of Spain, all of us, everybody, Don and *peon*, landlubber and sea-dog. On
the Day of Judgment you will see sailors enough, Tia.
Bosun Gabriel's pipe will pierce the deep seas as clearly
as the vaults of Escorial. You will see us come rolling
up, shaking the water from our pigtails. The seamen
of Vasco da Gama, Columbus, Cabot, Hudson and
Drake. Morgan's buccaneers and the Dutch ' Sea-
Beggars,' navy men and harpooners, slaves and
merchantmen—all of us, a tarry, salty, ear-ringed crew.
But perhaps you won't after all. Perhaps, as the
legend has it, we have a heaven of our own where
our language will not shock the little cherubims and the
spitting is free. They say there is a still lagoon set in the
midst of an eternal sea where all the lost ships ride, the
high-flying clippers that sailed to glory, the ships of discovery that pushed beyond the charts, the fighting
ships that sank with colours flying. No wind comes
there, but the trade blowing gentle and steady over the
spice islands; there is no sound but the drone of the
surf outside and the thunder of the saluting guns as
some new-comer limps into port. The old, bold
tarpaulins take their ease in hammocks under deck
awnings, or lay out on the jib-boom ends and dangle
for fish. By night they dance to fiddles, swill their flip
and tell enormous lies, and each man has for his

dear a golden sea-maid who never grows old, or
faithless, or picks your pockets. It is a sweet picture.
I hope it is true."

He stretched his hand towards the wine *bota*. "May
I? My throat is parched with talking so much
nonsense."

"Help yourself," said Ester. "When that *bota*
is finished there are others."

Ortho bowed. "This will be quite sufficient,
thank you. I am more than half drunk already. But
we have not yet heard the mystery of the anchor.
Tell me?"

Ester shifted on her stool. "Have you ever sailed
the South Sea, which is beyond Panama?"

"I have sailed the Caribbean, the Mediterranean,
the Indian Ocean, and the South Atlantic, including
innumerable gulfs, bays, channels and estuaries appertaining to them. The North Atlantic is as familiar to
me as the crown of my hat, but what you Spaniards
call the South Sea I do not know."

"Oh-oh!" Her tone was a wail of disappointment, shot with pain.

Ortho threw an arm about the bowed shoulders.
He had a feeling that in some way he had failed her
terribly. "I am sorry," he said. "I have not
voyaged upon that one sea it is true, but I have been
very close to it, just across the isthmus, peddling slaves
in San Juan del Norte, Limon and Puerto Bello. I
have been shipmates with men who knew it well. I
can tell you much. Why are you concerned with that
ocean?"

Ester blinked the tears back into her sunken eyes.
"I have a son there, an only son."

"A sailor?"

"He was."

"What is he now?"

"A king." The words came stoutly and proudly.

"A king!" Ortho stared. This peasant woman's

son a king! Was she mad? She did not look it, not
by any manner of means.

He whistled "Whew! He has done well for himself,
your son. A *conquistador*, eh?"

Ester nodded. "Yes, a conqueror. From a little
boy, always he dominated the other children. If they
disobeyed him he beat them. If they were good he
stole fruit and sweetmeats to give them as a mark
of his royal favour. A very bold and lordly boy. At
twelve he called himself King of the Torozos and stole
his father's gun to go and shoot wolves, which he said
were infidel Moors in disguise—a Cid among boys. At
seventeen he was the bravest *Novicio* in the Valladolid
bull-ring. He had sweethearts in every village. When
Enrique, his father, remonstrated with him, bidding
him confine his affections respectably to one, he
declared no one woman was worthy of him. 'I shall
be a king some day,' he said quite solemnly; 'pretty
fool I should look with some village cow for consort!'
Enrique laughed very loud. 'The puppy foams at
the mouth,' said he.

"'I am not mad,' said Jaime. 'Santiago has
appeared to me several times in my dreams and placed
a flaming sword in my hand and bade me go forth and
conquer.'

"'I know nothing of Santiago's intentions,' says his
father, ' but San Enrique will place a wooden plough in
your hands to-morrow and bid you go forth and conquer
the lower barley-field—or take the thrashing of your
life. That I do surely know.'

"Enrique had his way for a time and Jaime walked
behind the *álama negro* till he was nineteen. Then one
evening he returned from a *fiesta* in the city and told
us he was starting for Cadiz and America next day—
Santiago had appeared to him again, pointing towards
the setting sun. There had been officers drumming
for recruits for the west, telling great tales of riches
and making huge promises, and Jaime was going also,

two of his associates whom he had persuaded. There was a fearful scene. Enrique raved and cursed, his sisters wept and implored."

" Which did you do, Tia? Rave or pray? "

" Me? Neither. I knew by the look in his eyes that he would go, so I got his things ready."

Ortho nodded. " I guessed it. Go on, mother."

" Jaime went next morning, his bundle on his back. Enrique cursing him all down the hill-side. That was twenty years ago. I have not seen him since."

" Then how do you know about this kingdom? "

" A priest wrote from Buenaventura at the dictation of Andrés Luís, one of Jaime's companions, who was dying of a fever. Andrés said they sailed to Puerto Bello in the Cadiz fleet as common seamen, Domenicio Ribalta, the other companion, being killed by a fall from aloft on the way. From Puerto Bello they were marched overland to the South Sea and placed aboard the plate ships that sail between Lima and Panama. They were thus employed for several years. Then one night, when they were lying off Guayaquil, Jaime comes to where Andrés is lying asleep in his hammock and wakes him up. ' It is time for me to go,' says he. ' I did not come out here to carry other people's silver up and down, like a pack mule, all my life. I have risen to the rank of pilot, which is as high as I can get, not being of noble birth, and the downiest-lipped *alferez major* is better than I. I had begun to fear that Santiago had deserted me, but this night as I slept he has come again, pointing eastwards to the mountains with his fiery sword. My kingdom is waiting for me up there and I am going.'

" ' When?' says Andrés.

" ' Now,' says Jaime. ' If you come with me I will make you my chancellor, and you prove worthy.'

" But Andrés heart failed him and Jaime went alone, swimming for the shore, his sword strapped across his back."

" That is all? " Ortho asked.

" All that was in the letter."

" Yet you believe——? "

" Certainly. I know my Jaime, a bold and lordly soul from his birth, born to a crown. I believe it with all my heart, but I would like details. Plain belief is sufficient for the soul—but sometimes one yearns for a little more. I would like to hear how he won his way, my proud boy, all alone. Tell me, heard you anything from your shipmates or along the coast? "

Ortho drew a deep breath. " What Spaniard has done, Spaniard may do. Pizarro was a bastard swineherd, Cortes little better. Both rose to be kings in all but name. Given faith and a quick wrist all things are possible. Of your son what shall I say? Shall I tell you that the Isthmus ports hummed with rumours of a Christian king among the fabled white Indians of the Cordilleras, an ex-sailor sitting in majesty in the lost cities of the Incas, with the Incas' crown on his brow and on his shoulders a cloak of humming-birds' breasts. Shall I tell you that? "

" Tell me the truth."

Ortho let his hands fall. " I could lie to you, but I dare not. I heard nothing."

Silence fell between them. The old woman bowed over her lap and seemed to grow smaller and smaller as though shrivelling into herself.

Then slowly she drew erect again. " It does not matter," she said. " I know in my heart he is there, I have my sure belief. When I saw that little mark on your arm this morning I said, ' Here is a sailor sent by God Almighty to this inland place to tell me all I long to know—the details. How my little boy Jaime won his kingdom and how he rules in peace and justice in the name of Christ and the Blessed Virgin '—but it was not to be. Of all the seas you have sailed you have not sailed the South Sea and can tell me nothing.

I have spared your life and lost the hundred piastres in vain—and must still wait."

She rose unsteadily. " I am tired now and will go to bed. There is my daughter's room. You may sleep there. Good-night ! "

.   .   .   .

Next morning when she arose to water the oxen the stranger had gone, and so also had the remnant of ham—but the dishes were washed.

CHAPTER XIII

EL TIGRÉ DE CALAHORRA opened first one eye, then the other, listened, drew La Virgen de Rayos to him and sat up, taking extreme care to keep himself under cover of the boulders.

There was no living thing in sight. To the north the wintry plains of Leon flowed away to meet the Cantabrian mountains, empty as the sea. At his back rose the spurs of the Peña Negra, upheavals of bleak rock, their summits capped with snow.

Immediately before him, not fifteen yards distant, lay a morass of wheel-tracks and mud-holes dignified by the title of Camino real, or royal road. It switch-backed into sight over a ridge, wallowed across a shallow gully, disappearing over another ridge. By the track-side stood a tall stone Calvary on which Christ was crudely portrayed, hanging crucified, with comic little faces representing the sun and moon on either hand. Opposite lay the remains of a donkey, picked to the bare bones.

A desolate scene; even El Tigré was impressed by it, and he was inured to desolation, his profession necessitating much solitary retirement in waste places. Having, perforce, to see a good deal of himself he had got used to his own company, but on this particular evening he felt socially inclined. He had prospered that morning, lunched well and rounded it off with a most comfortable siesta wrapped in his *zamarra*, the boulders sheltering him from the wind. Delightful dreams, induced by the excellent lunch, had been his, dreams of luxury and bliss. He was home again, in his native province of Granada, in a Moorish palace hung with sweet

Alpujarras hams, skins of full-bodied Valdepeñas and
garlands of Alcalá rusks, which is the bread of angels.
Droves of luscious houris appeared and ministered to
him with their own fair hands and afterwards sat at
his feet while he twanged La Dulzura and sang the
self-composed epic of his deeds, " La Balada del
Tigré," which commenced somewhat in this style :

> " The clouds have their eagles
> The plains have their lions
> The floods their behemoths
> Flesh-eating, enormous.
> But La Calahorra
> Has Estéban Rúiz
> The fiercest of any,
> The terrible tiger."

Woman, wine and song, all that the manly heart could
wish for—and to wake to this ! Cold night descending
on the desolate plains and not a living thing in sight,
not even a crow !

The heart of Estéban Rúiz yearned for companionship, for the crowded fireside of a *venta*, with the *bota*
passing round, songs and dancing. What was the use
of being a hero if no one acclaimed you? Of being a
poet if one never had a public? *Qué estima !*

However, inns were not for him—not in this part of
the world, anyhow. He must return to his cave in the
hills, cook his solitary meal and waste the sweetness of
his voice, the dulcet thrummings of La Dulzura, upon
desert air—*el Diablo !* It was disgusting that a gallant
such as he should have to do his own menial tasks, his
own cooking. Properly there should be a seraglio of
worshipful women to welcome him home and wait on
him hand and foot while he rested from the ardours
and perils of the day. But he had no woman and must
fry his own bacon—*caspita !*

He examined the morning's takings. A skin of Toro
wine, half a loaf, four red sausages, a couple of eggs, a
piece of bacon, a cow's horn of oil and six onions, added

to which was the hare he had shot early in the morning. Bacon, sausages, the hare, the onions, materials for a *puchero*, that savoury stew beloved of all true Spaniards. He would sup well at all events. It had been a good day. The bag, apart from food, amounting to one gold *onza*, four *duros*, a fistful of piastres, reals and quartos, one watch, three razors, a pair of blue spectacles, two silver rings, an image of the Virgin of Grief of Cordova (silver) and scapularies of St. Michael de Sanctis and St. Benedict which, though of no intrinsic value, provided immunity from tumours and venomous bites, respectively.

Estéban Rúiz was a thief of the genus *salteador*, which Spanish etiquette ranks midway between the *ladron*, the dashing mounted highwayman, and the *raterillo*, the common city snatch-purse. Estéban took small risks for small profits. He did not hold up gentlemen's equipages, or specie trains that were likely to resist, he ambushed travelling barbers, pedlars, solitary peasants and muleteers, and scattered their brains for what few pence they possessed. Since he destroyed people of no consequence the police did not trouble about him over-much.

His title was self-conferred. Calahorra was not proud of the association. She remembered him only as the most worthless of her sons, a long, lazy, sulking, skulking ragged ne'er-do-well who snoozed by the fountain all day, annoying the women, and prowled all night robbing the vineyards. Early one morning a local grower was found lying in the *vina* with a knife wound between his shoulder-blades. He could not say who had struck him, but Estéban Rúiz was seen no more in those parts.

Estéban had the common Spanish weakness for high-sounding titles. 'The Virgin of Thunderbolts' was merely an old blunderbuss worm-eaten as to the butt. La Dulzura (so charmingly named 'the sweetness') a cracked guitar, lacking a D string; 'La Balada del

Tigré' a vaunting, interminable catawaul, a chain of preposterous heroics entirely imaginary. Not once in his life had Estéban faced an armed man eye to eye, he stabbed in the dark or shot from cover. Some men rob from necessity, some for the excitement. Estéban could plead neither of these motives. He had had good parents and a fair start. He took to his mode of life because he was bone lazy and cruel as sin. He was now, in the forty-sixth year of his life, a little mad into the bargain.

Ah, well! time to go. The light was getting bad and nobody further was likely to appear. Estéban stuffed the money and trinkets into his sash, crushed the oddities of food into his wallet, slung the wine-skin over his shoulder and stood up, a tall, narrow, shambling creature with unshorn, bluish cheeks and close-set, gimlet eyes divided by a drooping nose; he looked more like a lean and grizzled wolf than a tiger, a wolf in a sheepskin *zamarra*. He would lie up on the morrow, he decided, and move camp altogether in a day or two. Three people he had shot that morning, and though he had dragged their bodies well in among the rocks he was not taking any risks. He did not worry about the police, but there were such things as shepherds, and shepherds had dogs, ferocious brutes used to wolf-hunting. The dogs might wind those bodies and then, possibly, their masters would form a posse among themselves and beat the hills for him with those same dogs as an advance guard. Estéban loathed and feared dogs. Fortunately everything moved slowly in Spain, retribution slowest of all. He decided that he had at least two days of grace before him, two days loafing up in his cave, composing fresh verses for the great ballad. Wine he had in the *bota*, song in his soul, only the third ingredient for manly happiness lacked—woman.

He picked up the Virgin, sent a quick glance up and down the road, and folding up in the middle, merged into the boulders again, the Virgin at full cock.

Somebody was coming along the road from the south !

First of all he saw a head lift above the rise of ground, then the shoulders, then the whole pedestrian.

Estéban, squinting along the barrel of the Virgin, emitted a low snarl of disgust. A priest, a parish *cura* with nothing on him but a wooden rosary and a Book of Hours—Peugh ! Or a monk perhaps, he could not distinguish in the failing light. A Capuchin or a Carmelite for a certainty. You would not catch a respectable Benedictine or Bernardine afoot, ten miles from anywhere, at this time of night. A Capuchin or a Carmelite, a miserable mendicant with a bag of bones, teeth and hair, spurious holy relics, and a whine like a door-hinge—Peugh !

Estéban had a good mind to shoot the fellow for the fun of watching him writhe. There was something very piquant in the idea of a Carmelite (or Capuchin) beating the air with agonized hairy legs, scattering holy relics.

He covered the traveller, foot by foot, as he approached, the Virgin steadied in a crevice between the boulders. Ten yards nearer and he'd pull the trigger.

Eight yards—six yards—four yards—three yards—Estéban's trigger finger slowly contracted—two yards—one.

Estéban's finger relaxed. What he had mistaken for a cassock was a skirt, the hood a cloth mantilla, the traveller was a woman, a woman !

He jerked to his full height, the Virgin at his shoulder, presented. " Halt ! "

The woman jumped with astonishment, glanced this way and that as if looking for a way of escape, saw the Virgin's bell mouth gaping at her not twelve yards distant, and stood still, petrified, muffling the mantilla about her face.

" Are you alone? " Estéban inquired.

The woman did not reply.

Estéban sniggered. "*Malcontento.* eh? Sulky? *Poco importa*, we will find means to make you sufficiently talkative later on. We have our little persuasions. For the moment, if the Señora will excuse me, I will retire myself behind these rocks in case the Señora is not alone. If you move or cry out I give you my word as a *caballero* it is the last word you will utter."

He sank again among the boulders, leaving only the muzzle of the Virgin visible.

Five minutes passed. No second wayfarer showed on the road.

Estéban chuckled and smirked. This was astonishing luck, a lone woman and a handsome one at that. He could see nothing of her face for the mantilla, but her figure was fine, a straight-standing, tall wench, nearly as tall as himself. She was young too from her lithe step, he would have great sport with her. His diseased mind planned every detail of that sport, his lustful eyes gloated over his prey. Sullen now was she? A twist or two of the arm, a prick or two of the knife would alter that. He would have her grovelling for mercy before the night was out. She should be his slave to cook his food and suffer his will till his days of grace were up, and after that she would be easily disposed of—one twisting thrust under the breast.

Ten minutes passed and nobody else had appeared. Estéban stepped out of cover. "Ah, ha, my little nugget, my little pearl, come to the arms of thy true love, thy bridegroom, the Tiger of Calahorra. Come to my bosom, star of my existence."

The woman stood her ground.

"Coy, my treasure?" Estéban sneered. "Art fearful of the immense joy that is in store for thee? The fondlings and caresses of the brave? Art gripped in a trance of love? *Vamos!*" he roared.

Still the woman did not stir; except for her left hand clutching convulsively at the wrap there was not a movement in her, she might have been frozen stiff, a rabbit fascinated by a snake.

Estéban noted this with satisfaction, he liked to make helpless creatures wince and scream and go cold with terror.

" Your Highness will not come to me? *Bien esta*, I will come to you—this once." Carefully he rested the Virgin against a boulder and advanced across the road, capering grotesquely, sweeping off his hat in extravagant obeisance, purring like a cat.

Nearer and nearer he came, his grizzled head thrust forward, his small eyes squinting horribly.

" Queen of my heart ! Moon of my——" He thrust his right hand out, wrenching the mantilla away and simultaneously realized that he had made the crowning mistake of a mistaken life.

It was not a woman's head that the tearing wrap revealed, but that of a man, a well-shaped, very masculine head covered with close-cropped bull curls. He saw the blaze of amused black eyes, the flash of strong white teeth clenched in effort, and then an iron fist smote him on the jaw and he fell through immeasurable depths of oblivion amid a coruscation of shooting stars.

When Estéban came to himself next morning he was bound hand and foot to the base of the stone crucifix. The Virgin was gone, his money, his wine, his titbits —also his clothes. But in compensation for these last the unknown deceiver had left a peasant woman's costume, brown basquina, red bodice and all, neatly piled beside him.

Estéban Rúiz, the Tiger of Calahorra, cursed and shivered and raved and trembled, until a party of *ladrones* cantering down the road (fresh from rifling the Duke of Osuna's baggage) put him out of his misery by putting a bullet through him.

He was, they said, a blot on an honourable calling.

CHAPTER XIV

NIGHT in the valley of the Neira, in the Galician mountains; supper-time in the Venta del Sol.

Despite its title, suggesting warmth and golden brilliance, the 'Inn of the Sun' was a poor affair, a mere road-house, a single-storied barn divided by a partition of rough planking into two compartments, the one for beasts, the other for their masters.

The stable was a gloomy cave unlighted save by a tiny window at the far end. The accommodation for human beings was also the simplest. In the middle of the long room stood a ring of flat stones with a fire of oak boughs blazing in the centre, the whole overhung by a conical chimney. Grids, pipkins, pots and iron ladles decorated the walls; bunches of maize cobs and wine-*borrachas*—made of the whole pig-skin and having the appearance of so many bloated carcases—hung from the rafters. On the rafters also a bevy of meagre hens roosted undisturbed. Of furniture there was little; one plank table stained with wine drippings, a rickety bench and a few blocks of wood which served as tables for those who sat on the ground and stools for those who sat at table.

Fastidious travellers did not patronize the 'Inn of the Sun,' but it did brisk business with humbler wayfarers who made it the half-way house between Lugo and Puebla.

On this particular evening it was crowded and supper in full swing.

A crone, twisted double with age and rheumatism, was in attendance on the *ollas*, hobbling round the circle, giving them an occasional sniff and a stir. Fire-lit, smoke-clouded, with her ring of black pots, she looked like some old sorceress engaged in the brewing of unholy potions. As each stew came to perfection she signalled the event by a piercing howl, whereupon the owner arose, emptied the *olla* into an earthenware dish and gobbled for dear life.

The muleteers ate out of party dishes, squatting on the floor, baling up the juice with horn spoons, prodding for bits of meat with their long Albacete knives. Those single travellers who could afford it had pots to themselves; those who could not ate maize bread and black sausage.

"They tell me that the bridge at Otero has fallen," grunted a one-eyed *arriero*, tearing the flesh off a rabbit's leg with his teeth.

"It has been cracked these many years," said a Castilian. "Never have I crossed it of late without first promising St. Isidro a wax candle for my safe passage."

"St. Isidro is well enough in Castile, but here in Galicia I consider it wise to appeal to Santiago," said a Andalucian horse-dealer.

"You speak as though a saint were an alcalde whose authority halts at his town gate," One-eye scoffed. "Moreover, this flitting about from one *santo* to another is bad business, to my mind. Place yourself in the saint's position, 'Here is this Miguel offering me candles to-day,' he says to himself, 'but it was San Jerome yesterday and may well be San Thelmo or Santa Teresa or San Ovidio to-morrow,' and he does not bestir himself in your case. It is reasonable to suppose that in heaven, as on earth, a regular customer is preferred."

A Toledan nodded his head. "I am in agreement with you, Nufro. Select a patron of the first rank and stick to him and he will stick to you, I say. San Ildefonso for me. He is a good Spaniard."

"San Ildefonso worked a miracle on my 'godmother' mule in Puerta de Santa Cruz last year," a Murcian observed.

" How so? "

" She was taken sick in the morning, would not eat and groaned dismally, biting at her flanks. I washed her in hot wine, gave her a physic and applied a plaster, all to no avail. It was plain she was bewitched. I hung a medal of the Holy Countenance of Jaen about her neck, placed her head towards the church, and an old woman who was reputed to have great skill in the exorcizing of spells said several Ave Marias over her. The *madrina* became, if anything, worse. I therefore went to the *cura* and besought him to bring forth the holy water and a relic of San Ildefonso they have there —a lock of the sainted beard. He did so and the beast was on the road next day."

" There you are ! " the Toledan exclaimed in triumph. " Marvellous ! " said an old Catalan who was sitting close by, eating noisily from a private stew. " Your Grace will pardon me, but I take it that on the occasion of the miraculous resuscitation of your *madrina* holy water was plentifully employed? "

" Your Grace is correct. She was drenched from head to foot."

The Catalan nodded. " Then I am of the opinion that your animal suffered from common strangury and that the holy water or, for that matter, river water would have been sufficient without the sainted beard."

The Toledan was aghast. " Eh ! What have we here, may I ask? A sceptic? An atheist? An anti-christ? A disbeliever in miracles ? "

" By no means," said the Catalan. " You have here one who professes some small knowledge of therapeutics, and, being of an ambulant nature, of mules also."

A chubby youth, sitting by the fire, cocked his ears at this. He sprang up, and placing himself before the old man swept off his hat in a low bow.

" Your Grace will pardon my presumption, but have

I the honour of addressing a disciple of the Greek Hippocrates, of Æsculapius, of the divine Luke, in short a sapient Medico? Am I so honoured?"

"You are, sir," said the Catalan.

"Permit me to salute you, Señor," said the youth, with another, deeper bow. "Of the learned professions there is, to my mind, none nobler than that which you adorn. What indeed could be more sublime than a life dedicated to the alleviation of suffering?"

"You are very kind, Señor," said the quack. "Am I to understand that you are in pain yourself? If so I can do you an excellent soothing physic at four reals, purges three."

"Thank you, but I have no need of physics or purges," said the youth. "I merely spoke the homage of a generous heart."

"Heart!" said the Catalan. "Heart is it? I have a sovereign tonic at one piastre the flask. Broth brewed from the fat of snakes, guaranteed Barossa."

"Thank you, but I enjoy robust health," said the youth. "I merely——"

"In that case pray excuse me if I continue my repast."

"Certainly, sir. I only——"

The Catalan bent again to his stew; a savoury mess, rich brown, steaming hot, full of meat, redolent of pimento and garlic. To the youth the smell thereof was sweeter than all the spices of Arabia. His nostrils quivered like a rabbit's.

He cleared his throat. "Allow me to present myself—Don Guzman Maria Rodrigo Blasco Concha, student of philosophy and the arts of the University of Salamanca."

"Eh?" the Catalan grunted, fishing up a succulent morsel of pig's cheek. The youth's eyes yearned for it.

"Ahem!—Permit me to express my delight in discovering, among this rabble of mule-whackers and

horse-thieves, a *caballero* of your culture and address—
another educated man, in fact."

"Ummp!" mumbled the quack, curdling up his
stew so that the drum-sticks of a chicken floated into
view. The youth went moist at the lips—chicken!

"Señor medico, may I have the honour of sitting
beside you?"

"The floor is free."

The student squatted in the maize litter, gnawing
noisily at his lump of bread, and sighed.

The quack gobbled at his savoury stew, unheeding.

From the stable came the melancholy clank of bells
as the mules shifted to and fro, the squeal of two ponies
fighting over fodder, kicks and grunts. A man rose
and cursed the ponies through a crack in the partition,
a Navarro farmer bound to Compostela on a pilgrim-
age, sombre in black velvet with silver buttons all down
the sleeves.

The *venturo*, a pasty, perturbed creature, his shirt
open to display a chest of hair, shuffled round the room,
replenishing wine-cups and getting sorely mixed in his
reckoning.

"Before this precious 'War of Oranges' we could
smuggle English fabrics through Lisbon," said a Madrid
bagman to a compeer of Valentia.

"Ourselves we still slip in a few bales by way of
Oran," said the easterner. "But bribes to the authorities consume the profits. It is impossible to earn one's
living nowadays with so much dishonesty about. Hey!
what have we here?"

A tall ragged man was kneeling before them, making
signs towards his mouth, cringing and grimacing.

"What is it?"

The man made some incoherent noises in his throat,
he appeared to have no palate.

The landlady explained. "A poor idiot, Señores.
He came at sunset and I gave him lodging for the love
of God. There is no harm in him. He has been sitting

in the corner all the evening playing with his fingers quite quietly. He begs food, I think. Here ! " she called, and fishing a lump of meat from a pot handed it to the fool, who clucked his gratitude and swallowed it ravenously.

" There are hospitals maintained at great public expense for the reception of these dementeds," said the Madrileno. " Nevertheless, one must be charitable I suppose. I have a crust here I cannot eat. Catch ! " He flung the crust.

" You are right. Charity is a celestial investment," said the Valentian.

" Hey ! " He tossed a second crust.

The idiot played round it on all-fours like a cat with a mouse, pouncing on it, springing away, pouncing again.

The muleteers laughed uproariously. They would make him drunk later on, they declared; he would be very humorous drunk, *el loco*.

" A droll, eh? " said the Madrid bagman to his friend. " Were you in Seville of late? No? They had the wife of a captain-general in the hospital there. For a small gratification the keeper would show her. Chained to the wall she was, raging and tearing herself like a wild beast. A great lady once; very comical, believe me."

" Ouch ! " the student exclaimed.

The quack glanced up. " What is amiss? "

" I think I have broken a tooth on this hard crust."

" I will extract the stump for two piastres."

" No—no, I was mistaken."

" Probably it is cracked, which is just as bad. Let me look."

" No, it is intact, I find."

" You had better let me see."

" I thank you, *no !* "

" What news of Madrid is there? " the farmer asked the bagman.

" Little of importance. A baby girl is lost from the

Strada de la Conception, and is thought to have been sacrificed by the Jews. A man dressed only in a night-shirt was discovered by the guard at two of the morning climbing into the house of the Duke of Valverde. When arrested he proved to be the Duke himself."

"But why was he in that attire?" the farmer inquired.

"It is presumed he was forced to go home in a hurry," said the Madrileno. "The Prince of Peace is said to be interested in La Coreza of the Opera and the Queen in tantrums in consequence."

The Valentian spat. "Paugh! Him! Godoy! 'El Choricero,' the Badajoz sausage man! Since he has been Minister we have had nothing but wars and wars. Prince of Peace i' faith!"

The one-eyed *arriero* became reminiscent. "When I was serving in the Guard, the same Godoy came first to Court. I remember him well, a plump ensign of no more account than my thumb, and look at him now! He climbed on his guitar strings, that one, step by step. A lady's-maid to her lady, the lady to a *condesa*, the *condesa* to a *marquesa*, and thus to Maria Luisa herself."

"Patience, he will fall," said the Madrid bagman. "*Auncue sea vestida de seda, mona mona queda*—'a monkey in silk is still a monkey.'"

"It will be little consolation if he drags Spain with him, your monkey," said the Valentian.

The student gazed desperately at the Catalan's fast emptying dish.

"Ahem! Señor doctor. Having, in my avidity for knowledge, expended my fortune in the purchase of erudite works I am reduced to this crust, which a God-fearing man would blush to offer a bear. May I appeal to you—as one educated man to another—to permit me to soak it one moment in your stew and thereby preserve my jaw from compound fracture."

"Yes," said the Catalan, "you may—for one moment."

" Sir, how can I thank you? "

" Pray do not try."

" I hear there is an English prisoner of war escaped from Valladolid," the one-eyed muleteer remarked. " Ate a hole clean through the wall of the old carcel and was gone."

" Pouf! They are always escaping—and being brought back," said the horse-dealer, adroitly tilting the *bota* so that a thin stream of wine jetted directly into his mouth.

" True," said the *arriero*. " But this is a particularly cunning devil. Having escaped he goes to a little farm in the Torozos where there is only an old woman, her daughter having gone into the city. He remains with her all day, very civil, washing the dishes. Next morning, when she came to look for him, he is gone. The daughter returned that day, but only next Sunday, when she wanted her *fiesta* dress to go to Mass, did she discover it was missing."

" The fugitive had dressed himself up in it? " the Toledan inquired.

One-eye nodded. " Exactly. And while the *alguacils* were scouring the country for a man, he passed lightly on disguised as a woman, the mantilla hiding his face. A sly one ! "

" He may be as sly as Satan, but for all that he will not go far," said the Andalucian, lighting a cigar. " Spain is too wide and his speech will betray him. He is doubtless behind lock and key by now."

" On the contrary, they say that this *hombre* speaks good Spanish, having been some years in our prisons," said One-eye. " And as for lock and key, he was not behind them four days ago. Four days ago he was near Astorga and free as air—so now ! "

There was an excited chorus of " Astorga ! Near here? Coming this way ! "

" Certainly," said One-eye, pleased at the fluster he had caused. " A cunning, ruthless devil. Four days

ago a party of respectable *ladrones* discovered one
Estéban Rúiz, tied, stark naked, to the Calvary of the
Sun and Moon. Before they shot him for a miserable
thief, he informed them, with many curses, that his
unseemly condition was due to a man who had come
from the south disguised as a woman, and deprived him
of his clothes."

"Four days ago," said the Valentian, making a
mental calculation. "Then he may be close at hand
at this moment."

One-eye wagged his head. "Precisely, and who can
tell in what disguise?—a sly one and desperate. For
myself I do not fear, I was a soldier once and have my
blunderbuss, but you gentle *caballeros*, travelling singly,
beware, I say." He puffed at his cigar, his single eye
twinkling with enjoyment at the consternation on the
faces of the bagmen.

"Compose yourselves, Señores," said the horse-
dealer. "This Nufro here is having a joke with you.
These English always make for the sea as to a mother.
Therefore, if the prisoner were near Astorga, he has
gone north through Asturias, which is leagues shorter."

"Señor student," said the Catalan, "when I gave
you leave to dip your bread in my stew it did not include
permission to extract the most succulent morsels. That
is the drum-stick of a chicken you have in your hand, I
perceive."

"Señor doctor, I crave a thousand pardons. My
mind was occupied with problems of philosophy, my
fingers strayed uncontrolled."

"Well, since they are once more under control, have
the goodness to replace the drum-stick."

"I cannot believe that your Grace means that,
seeing that I have already licked it ! "

"*Venturo !* " a muleteer shouted. "There is someone beating on the door."

The innkeeper shuffled to the summons. There were
sounds of an animal being led into the stable and a

new-comer entered. He was a tall dark fellow, dressed in a short black sheepskin jacket fastened with filigree buttons, a vivid yellow sash, tight breeches of blue velvet with silk tassels and more filigree buttons at the knee, and gaiters brightly embroidered with flowers and birds, unbuttoned at the ankle to display his gaudy stockings. A flaming kerchief was bound about the lower half of his face to protect it from the night winds. On his curly head was a stiff-brimmed Andalucian sombrero, tilted slightly to the right. A brilliant, dandified creature, smacking of horse-flesh and hazard.

His entrance caused a stir.

"A smuggler," whispered the muleteers.

"An *espada*, I warrant; a master matador."

"No, he wears no pigtail. He is a *ladron en grande* for sure. Hoi! *Venturo*, who is the gentleman?"

"He bears the royal arms on his wallets. A courier I think. He is for Coruña," the landlord hissed. "In a vile temper—hey!"

"So would I be night-riding in this weather. Enrique, pass me thy tinder."

The courier strode towards the fire, his spurs jingling on his heels, turned an unsociable back on the company, and drawing the inn *olla* to him began to eat.

The one-eyed muleteer sighed with full-fed content. "Heh! I have fed my belly very creditably and now would refresh my soul. Is there a musician amongst us, by God's providence?"

"Comrade," said the student, "I have a guitar by Pajez of Cadiz and, if I may be pardoned for telling the truth, some small talent thereon."

Quoth the muleteer, "Señor student, I love you like my eyes. Bring forth your instrument and strike up. You shall sing first and then I will give you a song myself. It concerns a beautiful girl, and I learned it when I was at *El Corte* in the Guard. Strike up, sir."

"With much gusto. But not so fast. '*Bien canta*

Marta, Despues de harta.' A good song for a good supper."

" But you have already supped."

" Supped I have, as a dog would on the grudged pot-scourings of that opulent but despicable old saltin-banco yonder. Eaten I have—after a fashion—but drunk I have not, and dry throats and dry axles make harsh music, *amigo*."

" The devil !—if it's only wine you want ! Hey, Gregorio, pass the *bota* to the gentleman."

" I drink to your prosperity, comrade," said the student, " to the prosperity of all the comrades. Permit me to express the delight I feel in entering your unconventional and generous circle after the company of that bloated but parsimonious old medicaster over there. I drink to your honourable calling." He tilted the bottle, sniffing. " Hmn ! Tostada by the smell. Myself I prefer Valdeorrass, but, as the saw has it, '*Mas vale vino maldito, que no agua bendita*,' ' Damned bad wine is better than holy water.' 'Twill serve. I drink to you ! "

" Doña Amalia persuaded her husband to go to the window, whereupon Don Silvestre stabbed him through the curtains, as was pre-arranged," the Valentian was saying. " He then made his escape and reached the Toledo Gate, when, recollecting that he had no money, he returned to his lodgings to get some and was there arrested. That is the story I heard."

" That was the way of it," said the Madrileno. " Don Silvestre confessed everything before receiving the sacrament. I could not get to the execution for the press of people, but I saw the bodies exposed later in the Plaza Mayor. Sitting up they were, and twelve candles of wax burned near them on black stands. I was told by friends of mine who had a balcony that Don Silvestre fainted when the cord was put round his throat, but Doña Amalia sat with great tranquillity, casting her eyes upon her lover."

"Women are incorrigible," said the Valentian. "There was a case in my province, at Villarreal——"

"Hola! What is that *loco* doing with my baggage rope?" the Toledan shouted.

"Leave him be," a friend laughed. "We have given him wine and he is amusing us greatly. He will not harm your rope. He thinks it is alive—ha! ha!"

It was as he said, the fool was playing with the rope as if it were a snake, the end its head. He bounced round the end on all-fours, snapping his jaws, springing forward, recoiling in terror. The muleteers encouraged him with loud shouts, hand-claps and snaky hisses. He pounced on the rope-end, snatched it in his teeth and worried it like a dog, growling and whining. Still biting he rolled on the ground, over and over, so that the rope slipped from its peg and coiled all round him. The *arrieros* thought it excellent fun. They told the fool he was a very good dog, and offered him more wine in hopes of further antics, but he would not touch it. He kept his teeth fixed in the rope as if he feared to let go lest it strike him, and lay writhing and twisting in the maize litter, wrapped in hempen coils.

A tinkle of strings drew the muleteers' attention to the student, who had propped himself against the table and was screwing up the guitar pegs.

"A-ha-a——

'La capa de Estudiante
Parece un jardin de flores,
Toda llena de remiendos
De diferentes colores,'"

he hummed, trying his voice. "Ahem! A-hurrumph! My throat—still a trifle rusty. The *bota* once more, comrades. Just a mouthful. I thank you."

The company closed in a ring about him—everybody but the tall courier, who had finished his meal and sat warming his hands by the fire, and the fool who still played, unheeded, with the rope.

" Señores, caballeros," said the Catalan, thrusting into the circle. " I take this opportunity of bringing to your distinguished notice a powder made from the stones found in the cave of Manresa, where the blessed Loyola, founder of the Society of Jesus, meditated for one year. It is an infallible aperient."

" Pest ! There is an infernal draught," the Madrileno complained. " Has anyone opened the door."

" Probably the *Venturo* has gone to saddle the courier's horse," said the Valentian.

" No, he is yonder."

" Well, somebody else then. What does it matter? It is shut now."

" This flask contains the famous ' *Bebida de cien herbas*,' the drink of a hundred herbs," the Catalan continued, " warranted a cure for every internal ailment. You may enjoy robust health to-day, but who can foretell what the morrow will bring forth? What stomachic disorders, what agonizing cramps, gripes, spasms, convulsive throes and drenching sweats; what——"

" Oh, let us talk about drenching sweats when they come," the horse-dealer protested. " The song, Señor student."

" Sir," said the quack severely, " your unmannerly interruption is beneath my contempt. I shall take no notice of it. In Madrid, where I number the most illustrious members of the Court among my patrons, my charge for this astonishing panacea is ten piastres, but here, among friends, we will call it two, though it ruin me." He pointed a bony finger at the Navarro farmer. " You, sir, I perceive, bear a scar upon your cheek, honourable doubtless, but, if you will pardon me, unsightly. In this pot I have the very thing you are looking for, a balm of cats' grease which will remove the detested cicatrice and restore to your cheek its pristine purity. Price one piastre, one little piastre only."

"Begging your pardon, Señor doctor, but that scratch is not so detested as you think. The two of us have travelled together very comfortably for twenty years and I declare I am grown quite attached to it. Furthermore, if I lost it now neither my wife nor my dog would know me."

The Catalan shrugged his bent shoulders. "Very well; it is your disfigurement, not mine. I do not press you. This pot I hold in my hand contains an unguent prepared from the resin of the storax tree after a secret method known only to the ancient Pharaohs and myself. One application——"

"*Vaya al demonio!*" a muleteer shouted. "To hell with you and the ancient Pharaohs! Push the old croaker out of the ring, Miguel! Push, Cristobal! Push, everybody! Sing up, Señor student! Sing loud and drown his chatter!"

The student, who had been taking advantage of the diversion to drain the *bota* in peace, picked up his guitar and burst into song.

1

"No pæan mine in praise of kings,
    No cardinals with ruby rings
    Who prop the flimsy scaffoldings
Of thrones can fill my lowly muse with eulogistic fire.
        Nor hath the unholy trinity—
        Law, Medicine, Divinity—
        The power to wake my lyre.

2

    I raise no chant of dames and lords,
    With silken fans and jewelled swords,
    Who dance to lutes and clavichords,
In painted chambers, candle-lit; or stray beneath the stars,
        By lily-basins lingering,
        Love-lorn, despondent—fingering
        Mellifluous guitars.

3

I do not lift a battle hymn
To soldiers muscular and grim,
Who hack each other limb from limb.
The tall armadas spread their sails for continents remote,
    I wish them, in sincerity,
    Fair winds and all prosperity,
    But cannot raise a note.

4

No rustic madrigal is mine
Of gambollings beneath the vine
By hinds less graceful than their kine.
The shepherdesses that I meet are sillier than their sheep.
    I have no close affinity
    With pastoral virginity,
    In fact it makes me weep.

5

What is the song I sing you?   An
Ode-royal to the roving man,
The open road, the caravan
That braves the dread Sierra snows and Murcia's blazing drouth.
    My music is the tingling bells,
    The bridle-shaken, jingling bells
    That chime from north to south.

6

The Doñas of Madrid are fair
And elegant—but would go bare
Did not *muleros* bring them their
Flower-garlanded Manilla shawls, their gay Valencia silk.
    And Manuelo would go dry—
    Ha' mercy if he *should* go dry !—
    Without his asses' milk.

7

The Deans of Salamanca sit
And argue, giving tat for tit,
With perspicacity and wit,
But would their tongues so freely wag did not the *mulos* come
    From Toro with the bursting skins
    To fill the pundits' thirsting skins?
    Believe me they'd be dumb.

8

The pinched Toledan friar and nun
Eat Arcos hams when fasts are done,
And Yeste, wilting in the sun,
May taste of Lorca orange trees and cool its fevered veins.
If high-roads are the arteries,
The mule, that long-eared martyr, is
The life-blood of the Spains.

9

So ho ! I sing the jingling files
That thread Trujillo's leafy aisles,
And see Valencia's gilded tiles
Aglow against the burning blue that laps her laughing coves,
And roam in happy vagrancy
Amid the blossomed fragrancy
Of Ronda's almond groves.

10

They know the tang of Biscay pines,
And Ulla's many-terraced vines
That autumn's breath incarnadines.
They see spring kiss austere Castile and set it all a-flower ;
The violet dusk come glooming down
On Seville—deep bells booming down
From the Giralda tower.

11

El Rey he issues his command
And courtiers kneel and kiss his hand
But landless men possess the land
Wherever sheep tracks scale the crags, or stately highways flow.
And so I sing the dusty lads,
The roving, sunburnt-rusty lads ;
God's blessing on the lusty lads
Who make the donkeys go ! "

" Viva ! " the muleteers shouted. " Bravely sung !
qué vico ! Muy bien ! Es admirable ! "

" You sing like a nightingale in the moonlight at
Granada, Señor student," said One-eye. " Your
prowess has set me afire. I burst with music. I will

therefore give you the song about the beautiful girl I learnt in Madrid when I was in the Guard."

" You will not, Nufro *mio*," said the Toledan firmly. " You have done nothing but sing that same song all the way from Cordoba. I am nearly mad with it. If you sing it again I shall go mad entirely and stick my knife in you. The gentleman's tune has set my feet itching. Let us have a dance, I say. Gregorio has a tambourine and the *chalan* castanets. Play us a *Habas verdes*, Señor student, a dance of the country."

" My throat—ahem !—somewhat strained," the student complained.

" Life of the devil ! already. But you do not play with your throat."

" My fingers then."

" For the love of God give him another *bota*, *ventura !* " said the Toledan, " so that he play."

The courier rose to his feet, readjusted the kerchief over his face and strode to the door.

" Go with God, Señor caballero," the company murmured politely ; " go without novelty, Señor Don."

The horseman nodded his head in response, but did not speak. Outside the landlord was awaiting him with a fresh horse saddled. The courier paid his shot, picked up his reins and swung across the sheepskin.

In the ' Inn of the Sun' the dance was already under way. He heard the guitar buzzing like a melodious bee, the jingle of the tambourine, the drumming of heels. The open door revealed the dancers bobbing and twirling in a haze of fire-lit smoke ; the student of philosophy and the arts astride the table, a cigar in his teeth, wine at his elbow. A warm and cheerful picture.

The courier sighed into his muffler, and shaking his reins jingled off up the road to Lugo.

There was a full moon riding the broken surf of clouds like a silver galleon. Mountains loomed on either hand wrapped in streaming scarves of mist, their frosty heads now sparkling, now in gloom. The Neira river followed the track bend by bend, unseen but audible, rumbling and muttering to itself like a poor mad fellow. Dolefully sighed the wind in the live-oak groves, and flying gleams of moonlight and patches of shadow flickered across the road in a ghostly chase.

The courier rode carefully, for the track was execrable, littered with loose stones, pitted with holes, seamed with cart tracks. The wind came down the valley as down a funnel, bending the trees below, whipping the cloud pack on high; the gleams and shadows swept and whirled. Forcing his reluctant horse he passed a balconied farm with its vine trellis and row of maize stores, like small Noah's arks, and entered a straight avenue of chestnuts. It was dark under the trees, but the going appeared to have improved for the moment, his horse's hooves rang on solid metal. He must make the best of it, being in a hurry. Striking spurs into his beast he swung down the avenue at a canter, bent forward, peering for the exit. A cold drop splashed his face, then another. " Rain," he thought. " Storm coming. Best stop under the trees till it had passed? No, get drenched anyhow; must push on."

He lifted a hand to raise his coat collar and was plucked backwards out of the saddle as if grabbed round the middle by a giant hand. Instinctively his own hand flashed to his waist—a rope !

He grabbed it as he fell and it broke his fall. He hit the road shaken, but unhurt, sat up, blinking, collecting his wits. That did not take long, two seconds at the most. Not for nothing had he been pardoned for earlier indiscretions on the highway and entrusted with the King's mails.

A rope—slung pommel-high across the road to strip a man from his saddle. Whoever had done it must be close ahead waiting to catch the horse. The courier knew how the trick was worked; he had worked it himself in his time.

He sprang to his feet and dashed forward. A flying

gleam of moonlight revealed his horse twisting round and round at the end of the avenue, a man scrambling on to its back.

He rushed towards him and saw the man's face distinctly. It was the idiot, the fool of the inn who had tied himself up in the muleteers' baggage rope.

He grabbed for the man's leg, missed and was sent reeling backwards from a kick on the chest.

"Good-night," said the idiot, in English, and vanished into the whirling shadows.

The courier tugged his knife from his sash and hurled it after him, heard it ring harmlessly on the road.

From the darkness came a chuckle of laughter and the tattoo of galloping hooves diminishing in the distance.

CHAPTER XV

DOÑA BIANCA CANTERO issued from the confessional, inclined her head to Doña Constantia Berniejo, who took her place, and passed up the nave of Santiago Cathedral towards the Capilla Mayor.

Her elderly maid and confidante Marta came from behind a pillar and followed, bearing stool and cushion.

Vespers were being sung in the Coro. Choir boys in white surplices over red cassocks lifted their shrill trebles. Comfortable, blue-jowled priests, bearing on their black satin vestments the scarlet cross of Santiago, replied from the stalls in raucous basses. In the gallery a string orchestra wailed and droned, controlled by the beats of an ivory baton. Light from the many hanging candelabra glowed on the twin bronze pulpits, on the gilt relievos, carved with mermaids and battle scenes, on the bald heads of the priests. Many worshippers knelt in the crucero—devout townsfolk, Gallego peasant women with queues of dark hair hanging below their striped head scarves, men in short yellow coats trimmed with black velvet, and here and there a pilgrim. The huge censer, which is one of the glories of the cathedral, swung to and fro above them, diffusing clouds of aromatic smoke which rose, drifted and were lost in upper gloom.

Marta placed the cushion on the flags and her mistress knelt thereon, passing rosary beads through her fingers, murmuring prayers, one Paternoster for ten Aves.

A slim woman was the Doña Bianca, dressed from head to foot in severe black which brought her pale

hands and face into startling contrast. Her face was
bloodless and might have been carved from ivory, her
hands also. She had exquisite hands, long-fingered,
pointed; Vandyke would have worshipped them.
Her eyes were dark, almond-shaped, set somewhat
slantwise and crowned by brows like two neat pen
flourishes. A pen sketch would have portrayed her
adequately, there was no touch of colour about
her.

A gallant, spying out the land from behind one of
the transept pillars, noted her slim figure bent before
the glow of lights in the Coro, and stepping softly
through the crowd of worshippers, knelt beside her,
glancing covertly sideways. Marta, kneeling in the
rear watched his manœuvres with amusement.

The white fingers slipping over the ebon beads
fascinated the gallant, in some way they put him in
mind of running water, cool and swift, slipping over
polished stones. Beautiful hands ! Was her face as
charming? He could not see for the folds of the
cursed mantilla. He uttered a discreet cough and
sighed deeply. The lady would not glance his way.
He began to murmur a Paternoster out loud, loud
enough for her to hear, weaving a supplication into his
chant. " Dear lady of the lily hands, please let me see
your face ! . . . Serenissima of the foam-white fingers,
do look up ! . . ." The lady did not move. Inch
by inch he shuffled forward, stopped and glanced back.
At the same moment Bianca raised her face, rapt with
adoration, to the Coro lights.

One glance was sufficient for the gentleman.
" Whew ! " he thought, " a snow-virgin ! One of
those stone angels would be warmer." He continued
on his knees towards a rosy peasant girl who knelt by
the choir rails. Marta grinned outright.

Doña Bianca came to the last bead, the hundred and
fiftieth, rose and turning her back on the Coro bowed
low before the Capilla Mayor, where, above an altar

of beaten silver, lit by a blaze of silver lamps,* sat the holy image of Spain's patron saint, St. James the Apostle, pilgrim's staff and gourd in hand, his golden cape adorned with scallop shells.

Ecclesiastical Spain has it that his body is buried directly underneath, and thus relate the story of its coming. The Apostle, they say, was beheaded in Judea in A.D. 42. The body then embarked, unaided, in a boat which by miraculous guidance was led first to Barcelona and thence to Padron in Galicia, accomplishing the voyage of some three thousand, two hundred miles in seven days. The corpse then remained forgotten in a cave for nearly eight centuries, when a pious hermit observed clusters of stars nightly forming into the shape of a cross and hovering over a certain spot. He discussed this phenomenon with Theodomir, Bishop of Iria, who had the cave opened, and declared the body therein found to be none other than that of the Apostle, a pronouncement later confirmed by Popes Clement VIII and Urban VIII.

St. James—or Santiago—became the tutelar of Christian Spain and ghostly Captain-general of the forces, and is reputed to have appeared in shining armour at the battle of Clavijo, slaying sixty thousand Moors with his own hand. In return for his military services his church was granted a perpetual tithe of one bushel of corn for every acre in the country; riches and pilgrims poured into ' Santiago of the Field of Stars.'

In the tenth century the great Caliph, Al Mansur, feeling that in Santiago he had a dangerous Christian rival to Mahometan Cordoba, marched north in force. The Spaniards ran away and the arm of the Captain-general must have lost its cunning since the heroic days of Clavijo, for the Moors entered his sanctuary

* These temporal treasures are in Santiago no longer, having been looted, seven years later by the French under the ' irreproachable ' Ney.

unopposed, to find it deserted save for one faithful old
monk sitting on the tomb of the saint. Al Mansur
watered his horse at the porphyry font, razed the city
and returned home, carrying with him the cathedral
bells, which were forged into lamps for the great mosque
of Cordoba.

But out of the ruins of the old a mightier Compostela
arose, and during mediæval times devotees from all
over Europe streamed into the city in such numbers
that the Milky Way received the nickname of ' The
Road to Compostela.' "The damned doctrines
of the accursed Luther" (Molina) checked the influx
of pilgrims from such countries as subscribed to his
teachings, but Catholic Spain remained fiercely constant to the little granite city in the Galician hills, its
Holy of Holies.

Having made her obeisance Doña Bianca went
round to the back of the Capilla Mayor, climbed the
steps and kissed the edge of the golden hood. That
done she left the cathedral by the Door of the Silver-
smiths, turned the corner of the Payo convent, looming
huge and grim in the dusk, and passed under the narrow
arcades of the Rua Nueva. Lights burnt in cave-like
shops where the *plateros* sat bent over their work of
graving little images and medallions of the patron
saint. Women seated beside small braziers cried hot
chestnuts; beggars implored alms in the name of
Santiago; boys flitted like bats in and around the
arches, playing hide and seek; from a tavern came
the squeal of Gallego bagpipes.

Doña Bianca went on, looking neither to the right
hand nor the left, Marta at her heels. The urchins
scuttled out of her way, the beggars' supplications
dried up in their throats. "La Señora Cantero—
nothing to be got there."

A priest went by, a lean, preoccupied man with
horn spectacles and an unshorn, silvered jowl. Doña
Bianca bowed to his cloth. He made acknowledgment

with two uplifted fingers, recognized her, blinking, and passed on. The Señora Cantero, wife of the attorney, an estimable woman, punctiliously devout, would have made a better nun than wife, he thought—too cold. However, Don Jeronimo could hardly demand much at his age. Better mate two frigid things than one frozen and one ardent. He had seen much trouble come of the latter union. He wandered on up-hill towards his lodgings in the Pregun, meditating on the domestic trouble he had seen in his time.

Doña Bianca rapped at a door opposite the church of Santa Maria Salome and was admitted into the presence of her sisters-in-law. Doña Ines was fifty-nine and two years younger than her sister Isabella, but, by virtue of having once been married for nearly a year, took precedence. Their brother, Jeronimo, was youngest by three years. They were short, squat, easy-going women, inclined to fat and superfluous hair. Both had pronounced moustaches, Isabella the foundations of a beard. At the moment of Bianca's entrance they were seated before a brazier their skirts drawn to an undignified height, comfortably warming their shins. When they saw who their visitor was they hastily lowered their skirts and sat up, murmuring expressions of welcome more polite than fervent, for which they were rewarded each by a chill peck on the cheek.

" Sit down, Bianca, my little pebble, and warm thyself," said Ines. " It is raining outside—not? "

" On the contrary, it is quite dry," said Bianca settling stiffly into a leather-backed chair. " You have not been out then? "

Ines shook her head. " No—not this evening. Isabella, give the child some chestnuts, they will warm her."

Isabella fumbled with a pair of brass tongs and produced from the coals a plump chestnut, its charred jacket split across the middle to display its golden heart.

" There, my dear, roasted to a turn."

Bianca declined it. " Thank you, I am sufficiently warm. I have been to confession and vespers at the cathedral. You were not there either of you? "

" No, not this evening," Ines admitted. " I was afraid it would rain and I am not very well. A slight cold—atisshoo ! "

" And you? "

" I also am not very well," said Isabella; " ahur-rumph ! "

Both ladies sniffled and grated for some seconds and then became quiet again, feeling their efforts unconvincing.

" You were at Señora Bercerra's *tertulla* yesterday, I am told."

" Yesterday is not to-day," said Ines, sensing the implied reproof. " My cold did not manifest itself till this afternoon—nor did Isabella's. Will you take coffee? "

Bianca declined coffee.

" Have you any word from Jeronimo? " Isabella inquired, breaking the silence.

" Yes. A letter came to-day by a Maragato muleteer who demanded two piastres. I gave him one, the thief ! "

" Myself I have always found the Maragatos honest," said Ines. " When I was married they took my trousseau to Bilbao and not a handkerchief missing. I remember them leaving the old house in the Instituto, all their bridle *campanillas* ringing, and one of them pointed with his whip and said, ' Wedding-bells, Señorita.' How my heart bounded ! "

She loitered a moment among sentimental memories and then looked up.

" Well, what does Jeronimo say? "

" He is in Toledo at last, having been fifteen days on the road."

" His mule, Urraca, is old," said Isabella.

" Then why can he not buy a young one? "

" Tchut ! Jeronimo is a man of position and dignity. It is not befitting that he should strive with young mules in public," said Isabella, with a touch of asperity. " He very wisely prefers to go safely but slowly, with the good Urraca, who has carried him these twenty years."

" You who have not been married would not comprehend, but the little one's impatience is well understood by me," said Ines. " When my poor Gaspar had to leave me to visit Bayonne on business, I counted not only the days but the hours to his return. Our dear Bianca wishes that Urraca might be endowed with the wings of an eagle the quicker to return Jeronimo to her side."

Bianca, whose sentiments were nothing of the kind, studied her hands.

" Did Jeronimo say how long he would be in Toledo? " Isabella inquired.

" He does not know," said Jeronimo's wife. " He says there is as yet no notice of the case coming up before the Cardinal-Archbishop's court, and he is under the impression that they will delay it as long as possible in the hopes that he will grow tired of waiting and compromise."

Isabella grunted. " That he will never do. Fifty-six years I have known my brother and I have never yet seen the end of his patience. It is they who will tire. He will sit them all out."

" Hist ! " said Ines. " Do not distress the little wife. It will not be as bad as that, *mia*. After all, Toledo is Christian. They must recognize that our Chapter is but maintaining its sacred rights. The tithes are ours by edict of Ramiro and there is no denying it."

" But always they have denied it," Isabella protested. " For years they even denied the authenticity of the sainted body ! "

Ines nodded her head regretfully. " Alas ! yes.

Toledo was always jealous. I remember in our father's day—continual squabbles. Very sad among churchmen."

Isabella waxed hot. "Sad ! It's criminal ! To grudge the blessed Apostle his tithes after all he has done for Spain. Is Clavijo to go for nothing? I ask."

"That was a long time ago, of course," said Ines. "A thousand years or so."

"Such base ingratitude ! " said Isabella. "And it is not only Clavijo. The *cura* of Arzua, who was with the army as almoner in the late war, told me he frequently saw the saint in the shape of a small cloud leading our soldiers on."

"Yet we did not win that war," Bianca asked in some doubt, "or did we? "

"No, I believe not," said Isabella, "but that was because Santiago retired, disgusted at the sins of the Queen."

"Ah, yes," Ines murmured, completely satisfied.

"Yes," said Bianca, nodding, "I see."

Ines picked up the despised chestnut and bit into its mealy heart with well-preserved teeth. Subconsciously Isabella began to hoist her skirt again, presenting stout, wool-encased legs to the blaze. Ines flashed her a danger signal and the curtain fell precipitately. The three ladies sat in stiff silence, their faces red in the glow of the brazier. Some singing students passed down the Rua Nueva. Ines' black cat, Fofo, sprang to her lap and curled there, purring.

"Sugar has gone up again," Isabella observed, apropos of nothing, "and coffee, a quarto."

"It is the war, I suppose," said Bianca, without interest. Jeronimo gave her ample housekeeping money, a quarto here and there did not matter to her.

Isabella nodded. "Yes, the war. Father Sebastian called yesterday on his way to Tuy, and he says English war-ships are so thick off Coruña that nothing can leave

or enter, and it is the same at Vigo and elsewhere.
Soon we shall get no sugar at all, *ay de mi !* "

"There is sugar in Andalucia," said Bianca. "I
have seen it. In sticks it grows."

"Yes, but Madrid takes that. All Spain may starve
so that the Court lacks nothing."

"Do not speak disloyally, Isabella," Ines reproved.
"These little trials are sent for our good and must be
accepted with Christianly resignation."

"It is easy for you to speak of resignation who use
very little sugar," her sister retorted.

"Marta came from market yesterday with a rumour
that the war may soon be over," Bianca remarked.

"Father Sebastian had it too," said Isabella.
"Everybody in Coruña is talking of peace."

"Have we beaten the English then?"

"No—their ships are everywhere."

"Then have they beaten us?"

"My dear child, no! Those heretics! Heaven
would never permit it. It is the French who have
had reverses, Father Sebastian says."

"But I thought the French were Catholics as well."

Isabella hesitated. "Hm-m, yes. I was under
that impression too. Probably they have erred in
some way and are being chastened. I do not know.
These things are in the hands of God and inscrutable—
but I shall be very glad when coffee and sugar are
again at a reasonable price."

Bianca remained for some minutes exchanging gossip
of the cathedral city. A nun at the convent of the
Ensenanza had been vouchsafed a vision of Santa
Teresa and threw a fit. A Capuchin brother was
accused of stealing pastry from a cook-shop in the Rua
del Villar. The bleeding image of the Carmen had
broken out in a fresh place. Monseñor was confined
to his quarters with gout; Señorita Elena Gomez to
hers—for another reason—and so forth. Then Bianca
subjected the old ladies once more to the perfunctory

peck and took her leave. The sisters elevated their
skirts, crossed their hands over their stomachs and
settled back in their chairs. They were never quite
comfortable in Bianca's presence. Her virtue was
above suspicion, her piety proverbial, but privately
they thought her a little severe.

Doña Bianca went her way through the narrow
streets, turned up by the Huerfanas into the Plaza del
Instituto, rapped at her own nail-studded door and was
admitted by Bartolomé, the *muzo*. The Casa Cantero
was a narrow, four-storied house presenting a sienna-
yellow front to the cobbles of the Plaza. Its east side
closed with another house of similar pattern, but from
its western side sprang an arch which crossed the
flanking roadway and joined with a third building on
the far side. The arch was Jeronimo's property and
he had made its flat top into a little garden, adorned
with rose and camellia bushes in tubs, and covered
with a wistaria trellis. It made a pleasant place to
sit, unobserved, of a summer night. One could hear
the fountain splashing musically in the Plaza below,
and at the same time look away southerly over the
roof of the Convent de las Madres and see the Estrada
ranges rising naked and august amid a glimmer of
stars.

Two years Bianca had been in Santiago, coming, a
bride, from Seville. Her father and husband had
studied together at the famous School of Jurisprudence
in Valladolid, playing the parts, respectively, of master
and dog. Damian Tavera was the handsomest
student in the city, also the gayest. He had a tongue
of honey, played the guitar to perfection, and composed
the wittiest *copleros* and *seguidillas*. Women adored
him, he spent his evenings either strumming under
balconies or climbing into them. The doctors winked
at his shortcomings, though he seldom attended their
lectures. The tradesmen gave him credit without
hope of seeing his cash. His fellow-students worshipped

him though he led them into trouble. But most
devoted of all his followers was Jeronimo Carlos
Cantero of Santiago de Compostela. To the ugly,
timid little Gallego, Damian Tavera was romance
personified. He fetched and carried for Damian,
delivered his *billets-doux*, assisted him over the more
difficult balconies and stood guard outside; hailed him
out of the lock-up and lent him money, considering
himself amply rewarded in the company of the golden
youth. Time went on; Jeronimo took his degree with
honours, Damian by the skin of his teeth. His knowledge of law was infinitesimal, but the examiners hadn't
the heart to ' down ' him, he smiled so trustfully at
them. He rode south for home and Seville one fine
morning, accompanied by two servants. Half Valladolid saw him off, neglected lecturers, unpaid creditors,
flouted constables, cast off lady-loves. " Good speed,
Don Damian ! " they cried. " We shall hear of you
again. You will come back to Valladolid a King's
Justice. Have mercy on us then, O boy of our hearts !
Go in felicity ! "

Damian kissed his hand to the city towers and was
gone, his guitar tinkling.

An hour later Jeronimo Cantero crept over the
Puente Mayor on a slovenly mule and headed north
for his native hills, all romance behind him. Repeatedly
he wrote to Damian, long devoted letters, but got no
reply. For Damian was extremely busy—not at the
law, his father's sudden death put him beyond the
necessity of working for his living—but at amusing
himself.

Seville is a delightful, languid, laughing town, full of
shady courtyards, sunshine, palms and roses. Its
women are the most beautiful in the Peninsula (Valentia,
Cadiz, Madrid, Zaragoza, Pamplona, Burgos, Barcelona, Tarragona, in short every self-respecting city in
Spain, will contest this to the knife hilt, but it remains
the truth for all that). Lustrous eyes beamed on our

Adonis over fan-tips on the *paseos*, in the bull-ring and the theatres. Beauty, dark and smouldering, beckoned from left and right, from front and behind, from upstairs and downstairs. Having a soft heart he tried to love them all. It kept him busy. He had bare time for meals, leave alone for writing to that tedious little Gallego—some day, perhaps. His intentions were good. In the meanwhile Jeronimo sitting tight in his grey northern fastness rose to be chief legal adviser to the see, and Damian danced on his happy way amid a whirl of hearts and roses. Time went on again and then, within a single eventful year Damian found himself a bridegroom, a father, a widower and ruined. The loss of his wife was regretted by nobody, least of all Damian; she was a most unsuitable person. Where he had picked her up was uncertain, but there were rumours that it was in a dancing place, frequented by sailors, in Cadiz, and the Seville world concluded that he had married her in a moment of mad passion only because he could not obtain possession by other means. Damian was not used to being denied and the slut was undeniably handsome. The baby did not bother him either, he simply packed her across the river to Triana, where dwelt an ex-maid of his who had an infant of her own. Nor can it be said that the evaporation of his patrimony troubled him unduly.

"I knew it could not last for ever," he said, "patrimonies seldom do. It is regrettable, of course, but I have a second string to my bow, a law degree."

Damian was nineteen when he took gay leave of Valladolid, he was thirty-four when the crash came; for fifteen years he had not opened a law book. Nevertheless he hung up a sign and hoped for the best; his multitudinous friends would employ him, he said. His friends did nothing of the sort, they knew him too well. Damian sold pieces of furniture here and there and hoped on. His heart, though soft, was buoyant.

The first person to employ him was a murderer who could get nobody else. The man was condemned and duly hung in the Plaza San Francisco, but before sentence was carried out he addressed the crowd, saying that though he had been convicted he wished no reflection to be cast on his lawyer, Don Damian Tavera, whose speech for the defence had been so eloquent as almost to convince him (the speaker) that he was innocent—which, as a matter of fact, he was not. He trusted that Don Damian would accept this genuine advertisement in lieu of payment, the only form, of which he was in a position to make him.

After this clients began to trickle in, but they were not of a desirable class; ladies of easy virtue with original ideas as to *meum* and *tuum*, thieves who promised to pay for their defence out of the proceeds of their next robbery, providing they were proved innocent of the first—and so on. There was little money in it. Nevertheless Damian contrived to exist himself and keep Bianca at the convent school of Santa Maria Jesus.

Time went on again, and in his fifty-fourth year death came and tapped Damian on the shoulder. He recognized the summons and became suddenly perturbed as to Bianca's future. She was twenty-two, without a penny of dowry and consequently suitorless. What on earth was she to do? A priest whom he consulted suggested the veil; the girl was suitable and willing and he would use his influence. But Tavera became more perturbed than ever, he had a horror of convents, it appeared. Calling Bianca to him he made her swear that she would not enter a convent if there was any possible alternative. Seeing no possible alternative Bianca swore. Tavera then racked his wits; turned all his multitudinous friends over in his mind discarded them one by one and remembered the ' tedious little Gallego ' he had never written to—it was some time before he could even recollect his name. The long-deferred letter went at last, a fervent letter imploring Jeronimo in the name of their old friendship to come, and come quickly.

Jeronimo came from Madrid, spurring the aggrieved Urraca.

Within four days he had married Bianca. It was a dismal ceremony. Bianca did not want it, she had thought herself as good as back in her beloved Santa Maria Jesus for life, but she could not resist her father's pleading, he had been kind to her always and he was dying.

Jeronimo did not want it. He was quite comfortable living with his old sisters. The thought of being landed at his age with a wife of twenty-two appalled him. But he went through with it out of fidelity to a young ideal, and the smile that came on Damian's lips when the deed was done made it worth while—it was so heartrendingly like the old times, the old romantic times of guitars and balconies.

Damian died next day. Jeronimo paid for his funeral, which was largely attended by the dead man's clients, pickpockets, mule-clippers and riff-raff from Triana, and a host of undesirable ladies who lamented without restraint. The good Señor Don Tavera had always been most sympathetic in their little troubles, they said, and bought Masses for the repose of his soul with their disreputable earnings. Altogether a distressing experience for the Archbishop's attorney.

Two days later he took Bianca north, a frigid bride, riding, white and silent, on an Andalucian jennet. Tavera's housekeeper, Marta, followed; a brown woman with black roving eyes, joking with the *muzos*.

For two years Bianca had been mistress of the Casa Cantero, and none of the disasters that Jeronimo dreaded had come to pass. If the meals were not as good as they had been during his sisters' reign, the deficiency was more than balanced by the absence of chatter. Bianca hardly uttered an unnecessary word, which suited Jeronimo, who was a busy, preoccupied man. He gave her a good housekeeping allowance and supposed she was happy. There were in Santiago at that time more than fifty ecclesiastical edifices, dividing some three hundred altars between them, so that there was always a service of some kind going on. Had she become a nun she could scarcely have had fuller scope for her religionism.

Bianca entered the *sala*, doffed her cloak and mantilla and sat down to the supper which Bartolomé had cooked. Bartolomé could do anything. With the assistance of a small, neat-footed donkey he kept the house supplied with wood and water and thrice a week made excursions to Jeronimo's farm on the Tambre valley for eggs and vegetables. Between-whiles he did house-work for Marta, whose slave he was.

The meal was frugal, a stew of meat and potatoes and olives, followed by some dried figs, the whole washed down by a small bottle of local wine.

Bianca finished quickly and sat before the brazier staring into the hot coals. She heard the big bell of the cathedral boom in the still night and carillon peals hammer out from the Torre de la Trinidad. As at a signal bells broke silence all over the town, from San Roque away up the hill to little El Pilar down in the valley. The great bells bombilated heavily, smaller bells clashed and rollicked in between. The very air trembled with the clamour of their metal tongues. Then the last echoes died away and all was silent again. The holy city was composing itself for the night.

Marta entered to clear away the dishes, flung out some items of gossip, but, meeting with no response, did not linger.

Bianca drew the candles near, opened her Book of Hours, read a page or two and then dropped the book on her lap and sat staring at the coals. Minute after minute passed, she did not move. The Nuremberg clock ticked on and on, two little metal cavaliers caracoling across its brass face in an eternal tilt. A string of belated donkeys crossed the Plaza, their little feet pattering on the cobbles. A mouse came out of the corner, pounced on a bread-crumb under the table and retired at its leisure. The minutes ran into a quarter of an hour, from a quarter to a half still Bianca did not move. At first glance one would have said that she dozed, at a second that she was very wide awake indeed and in the grip of some strong emotion; her eyes were glowing with unusual light, there was a faint flush of colour in her cheeks, her chest was working.

She shut the book with a snap that sent the mouse flying, and picking up the two heavy candlesticks, made her way to her room on the third floor. There she lit other candles, ten in all, all round the room till it was a blaze of light, and stripped herself of her uncompromising blacks, stripped herself down to her most intimate underclothes with fingers that stumbled in their haste. That done she dragged a small chest from under the bed and opened it. The chest was covered with leather, painted a bright scarlet and studded with brass nails, its contents a saffron-coloured dress, the skirt slashed with crimson, the bodice covered with wide black net; orange stockings and high-heeled red shoes; a Chinese shawl embroidered with flowers and pagodas; a black and gilt fan and two combs of fretted horn—her mother's.

She dressed herself in the flaunting saffron dress, in the stockings and shoes; shook her blue-black hair loose of its prim coils, plaited it in double ropes, looped them over her ears and fixed them with the combs. She took off her plain ear-rings and substituted long coral drops, and hung a coral necklace about her slim neck. Then, producing a rouge-pot from the back of a drawer, she dabbed her cheeks with colour, drew a thin line of rouge across her lower lip with a finger-tip, and posed before the long mirror, fan uplifted, one foot pointed forward.

Doña Bianca Cantero, wife of the Archbishop's attorney, was gone; the dead Cadiz dancing girl, white-shouldered, bare-armed, ravishing, had come to life again.

She hung for a moment coquetting with her own reflection, then crossing to the glazed door that led to the arch-top, flung it open. The candles made the room too stuffy, she would need fresh air before long.

Excited shouts came from the Plaza below and the clatter of many feet running under the arch towards Las Madres. Students chasing a cat probably. One was rather over-run with students in the Plaza del Instituto—tumultuous young men. They had gone now; Bianca could hear the noise of the hunt diminishing down the Calle de Sar.

She moved to the north side of the room, tapped out the time with a red heel and began to dance.

Never in her life had she seen the Cadiz *bolero*, but she knew it instinctively, as a partridge its mating dance.

A slim-ankled, willowy ancestress charmed Augustus Cæsar, lying full-fed and rose-wreathed at a Gades banquet. Two sisters of this houri were exported to Rome, along with a consignment of Tharsis copper and pickled tunny. Another stirred Martial and Juvenal to poetry; another was immortalized in bronze and may be seen in Naples to this day as the Venere Callipige. For untold generations men and women of the mother's family had danced the *bolero*. It ran in Bianca's blood as surely as drink or insanity will run. No amount of penance, masses or candles would get it out. She had tried hard enough, but it was useless. She must dance or die. She danced.

The *Bolero Gaditano* is a couple dance. Bianca had no material partner, so she imagined one, a tall Andaluc *Majo*—darted from the north wall of her room towards him. The ghost, springing from the opposite wall, opened his arms to receive her, closed them to embrace her, but she was not there. She had whirled about and presented her satin-white back to him, fooled him. Affronted he whirled too, folded his arms and cross-stepped sideways to the east wall, expressing his temper with brisk *zapateo* work—tip-tap-patter with his toes, punctuated with a double clatter of heels. Bianca followed his gyrations and his beats, pouting, arms akimbo, hips swaying jauntily. Three times the dancers real and imaginary, passed across the room, circling round each other at the corners, shrugging their shoulders, chins held high—young love a-sulk. They broke away and danced at opposite ends of the room, still back to back, throwing quick glances over their shoulders, half-hopeful, half-defiant; drew together again, spun face to face and stopped dead as though frozen solid. The first phrase was over.

In the second phrase the lady sets out to win back the flouted swain. He dances a *pas seul*, stiff and proud, in the centre of the stage and she sidles round him, employing all her wiles. She hovers before him on her toes, light as gossamer, bends her head this way and that way so that he may see how shapely her neck is, ripples her arms under his nose so that he may see how white they are. She is very demure, her fan comes into play. She glances at him that way and this way over the edge of it, eyebrows lifted, dark eyes smouldering roguishly, the arch coquette. It is easy to see how Damian fell—and the poets and emperors before him.

Her steps grow slower, she sways for her *majo* to catch her, the tired butterfly. She shudders and a strap slips down her arm, down and down, leaving one shoulder bare, pearl-white and seductive. She languishes backwards into his arms—and is away again, he after her, all his defences down. From one side to the other, she darts fluttering into his grasp and out of it, hovering, poising, drooping, darting again. Then, all of a sudden, he has her and the second phrase is finished.

The third phrase—the rapture of love. They fly
to each other's arms, bend to each other, their lips
meet, and drunk with the sweet of it they whirl, leap,
dip and whirl again. No need for guitars, the music
was storming through Bianca's brain, racing through
her veins, her nerves, liquid fire burning and spurring
her. It swept her on, thistle-down swept headlong
on a torrent of melody, whirled her in a cyclone of
sound. She had glimpses of herself in the long mirror,
the milky glimmer of swaying arms, the saffron skirt
billowing out horizontal as she spun and spun, shutting
close about her as she reversed, the enraptured glow
of her cheeks and eyes. The *majo* she could see
also, as plainly as though he actually existed, smiling
through locked teeth, hot colour flooding his dark
face; a tall man, lean and ardent, springing to catch
her.

The imagined music soared to his final crescendo.
She flung out her arms, whirled, whirled, whirled
and collapsed into the shadow embrace. It was all
over. Gasping, burning, she flung her fan on the bed
and tottered out into the cold air of the arch. Unseeing
she blundered into a camellia bush, tripped and fell to
find herself caught in strong arms. The *majo !* She
laid her throbbing head on his breast quite naturally
and the man bent and kissed her on the brow, the cheek,
the pearly shoulder. She did not resist—why should
she? This was a fitting epilogue to the *bolero.* The
majo must be tender to his little *maja ;* she had danced
her best for him and was tired out. She lolled lax and
yielding in the strong arms, saying no word, her brain
clearing slowly.

Presently she looked up. A tall man, darkly handsome, looming above her outlined in stars—bull-curls
powdered with star dust. He took her flushed face
between his hands and kissed her full on the lips. She
laughed softly and nestled closer—it still seemed quite
natural.

There was a knock at the bedroom door and Marta entered unsummoned. "Señora! Señora!"

The stranger sank among the camellia bushes.

"What is it?" Bianca called. "How dare you enter like that? Go back!"

"A thousand pardons, Señora—but it is important. Have you been long on the arch?"

"Why?"

"An English prisoner has been found in the city, close here. They discovered him in a tavern in Peña and pursued him into this Plaza, where he disappeared. Did you see a man run down the passage, not twenty minutes past? A tall dark man?"

Bianca felt her hand drawn in among the camellia leaves, the pressure of lips upon it—strong, sustaining arms; bull-curls powdered with star dust.

"N-o-o," she said, drawing in her breath. "No."

CHAPTER XVI

" London town's a-burning,
    Oh, run with the bullgine run.
    Way yar ! Way yar—— ! "

MACBRIDE, his old slaving mate singing at the
top of his voice, a pewter grog pot in his hand.
The grey African parrot perched on the arms-rack
cursing like a dragoon. A glimpse of a bottle-green
sea rising up as if to smash in the stern-ports; a swoop,
a wild pitch forward and the breaker had gone under.
The picture growing hazy; MacBride's voice fading
in the distance. " Run with the bullgine, run ! "
Ortho woke up. Wind, plenty of it, a two-reef topsail
gale, rattling the window, piping under the eaves.
The west wind too, chanting its familiar burthen :
" Up ! Break your bars and go ! Freedom ! "
None so easy. Iron bars were one thing. You
worked night after night picking the mortar out of
their sockets. Stone walls were simple also, you just
scratched and nibbled and gnawed like a rat; it was
only a question of patience—and being alone. The
prison he was now in—the love prison—was a vastly
more complicated affair.
Little had he guessed what he was running his head
into that night of the pursuit.
He had been twice round Santiago before he came
to the Plaza del Instituto, hunted every step of the way.
Whichever way he turned men seemed to spring up
out of the ground heading him off. The more he
bowled over the more appeared. He was blown to his
last gasp, whereas the pursuers were being continually
strengthened with fresh relays. They were closing

on him, a multitude of them. He dashed into the Plaza, with the lead of a few yards only, and saw the arch with its shrub garden. If he could but get up there ! Could he? His quick eye lit on the heavy iron *reja* of the ground-floor window. The second-storey wondows were also barred. By climbing the first he could reach the second and from there, with a jump, the arch.

He leapt at the *reja*, went up it like a cat, balanced on the top cross-bar and jumped for the second. Not for nothing had he served as upper-yard-man of a crack frigate which expected to be stripped from plain sail to bare poles in less than two minutes.

As the pursuit went under the arch, hallooing and yelping, the quarry was actually dangling over their heads. Had they glanced up they would have seen him, but they did not glance up, they were hunting a man, not a chimpanzee.

Ortho heard them rattle on down the hill and was on the point of hauling himself up, when a door opened and somebody came out on the arch above him. He clung on, jaws locked, every sinew in his arms strained to cracking point. He could not go back, he could not go forward; to drop was to break a leg, probably both. He was in a worse plight than ever.

Just when he was conscious that the strain was no longer bearable, that his fingers were slipping, the unknown retreated. Hauling himself up cost him the bitterest physical effort of his life. He started the pull without any hope of success, but his indomitable body persisted. Slowly he rose, inch by inch, and flopped over the rail among the shrubs, swaying on the brink of a dead faint. He lay motionless for some minutes, battling back the threatening fog, his heart pounding like a sledge-hammer, his empty lungs gasping painfully. He got his breath back with the realization that old age had its chill finger on him at last. Never again would he make royal yard-arm from upper deck in

fifty seconds. He was on the down-grade now. His
splendid body had saved him again, but it had warned
him. There must be no more tricks.

" Time to crawl into the chimney corner," he thought
sourly. " Mittens, gruel and soft tack—my God ! "

It then occurred to him that he was in more immediate
danger of a cold cell than a warm ingle-nook. He
sat up and peered cautiously through the camellia
bushes.

A room blazing with candles and a woman in a
yellow dress, dancing by herself !

He rose to his knees. She danced very well, by
cripes ! Very prettily indeed. The rhythm of her
movements caught hold of him and he began to hum
to himself, some *cancioneta* heard years before from
renegades in Sallee, rocking as he hummed.

He forgot his dread old age even for the moment,
forgot the peril he ran.

" By heck, she dances superbly ! . . . Graceful
creature . . . pretty arms . . lovely slender neck.
. . . My stars, look at her making eyes over her fan !
You'd almost believe there was a man with her," said
Ortho to himself, wishing himself the man.

He crept forward on all-fours, the better to see,
and brought up with only a single bush between himself and the woman.

When she finished he was within an ace of applaud-
ing. The next thing he knew she had stumbled over
the camellia shrub into his arms.

Instantly full realization of his perils returned. One
scream and he was done for. Quick, man, make love
to her ! Strike while the iron was hot. He made
love there and then and made it altogether too well.
The iron was indeed hot—white hot; he struck and
forged shackles for himself.

Three weeks he had been in this house now, well fed,
well wined, waited on hand and foot—an agreeable
contrast to the privations of the past two years. Like

an old war-horse in a clover-patch he rolled neighing in it, for the first week. The second week the novelty began to wear. The third he most heartily wished himself further.

Bianca was in love with him with all the passionate abandon of a woman who after years of severe repression throws down the reins and goes a blind bolt. The trouble was that he was not in love with her.

He had loved one woman in his life, still loved her and would always love her—the one woman Fate had denied him. The rest were but toys, pretty trifles wherewith to pass an idle hour or so. He had read, perhaps, half a dozen books in his life, nautical treatises only, reading with pain and writing with difficulty, spelling his words aloud, like a child. Having no mental resources, when not actively engaged he curled up and went to sleep. He was entirely a creature of rapid, strenuous action. Women had no part in the real heart-stirring problems of life, raids, ship-driving, cavalry charges. They bored him unutterably in an hour or two. When this occurred he embraced them fondly and slipped his moorings. This pretty sport of kiss and run he had played with considerable success half round the world, and experience, combined with a handsome person, had given him an infernal facility, he was a past-master at the game. He had reason now to regret his skill. The woman would not let him go.

Bianca had her charm, he readily admitted, she was very sweet in her way, and there was a marble whiteness about her which had fascinated him at first. Also there was her dancing. When she danced that *bolero* thing she could do what she liked with him—but she could not be always dancing. Twenty minutes in the evening, perhaps—but what of the other fourteen hundred odd minutes that made up the day? He pined for the robuster companionship of men, for the open air. He was sick to death of it, but how to escape he

could not think. He might go to Bianca and say, " See
here, *querida*, you have been very kind to me and we
have had a most enjoyable time together, and so on and
so forth, but though it breaks my heart to go, I really
must be moving on. I will just slip out quietly some
evening—if you don't mind." He might go to her
and say that, but it would be sheer waste of breath.
She had him in her power and she knew it well enough.
He knew that she had known for some time that he
was tired of her, but it had made no difference, beyond
a tightening of his bonds. Bartolomé had taken to
sleeping across the house door of late, the key in his
sash.

They watched him like cats, all three of them—
Bianca, Marta and that hairy little man-of-all-work;
always and everywhere there was an eye on him.

" If you run we will be the first to denounce you
Señor fugitive," the eyes threatened. " You will not
get clear of the Plaza."

He could not escape by day because of the eyes, and
at night he was locked up. The windows, as was
usual in Spanish houses, were barred with heavy iron
rejas, and Bartolomé slept across the door. They had
him trapped all right.

As far as he could see there was nothing for it but to
wait till the husband came home, and goodness alone
knew when that would be. The best of law works
slowly, Spanish law slowest of all. Jeronimo wrote
that he might be another couple of months, possibly
three. Ortho boiled in righteous indignation against
elderly husbands who leave young wives unprotected
and go gallivanting off to places like Toledo for months
on end—scandalous !

Three months more in this house, cooped up in a
few small rooms taking his exercise up and down a
passage, not even daring to look out of the windows for
fear of discovery. Three months more goading and
flogging himself up to respond to Bianca's infatuated

advances. Three months more of billing and cooing
with a woman he had long since tired of and was
beginning to hate—ugh !

He could not do it. He would not do it—not for
another day. There was one way out of this prison
house, over the arch and down the *rejas*, he way the
had come. A hazardous passage; descending is a
vastly more dangerous business than ascending as
any crag-climber will testify, still it was that or nothing,
and ' no gamble no get.'

He rolled over quietly on to his back and gave himself up to the problem. The door to the arch presented
little difficulty, it was bolted from the inside. There
was a chance that in working the bolt back it might
grate and wake Bianca. How to obviate that chance?
Oil, grease. There was olive oil in the kitchen, in a
cow's horn hung by the chimney. Could he risk a
trip to the kitchen? No, the old stairs creaked infernally,
Bartolomé would wake. Stay, there was a pot of
bear's grease on the dressing-table, the stuff Bianca
used to plaster down her side curls when she danced.
That would do. In supposition he had opened the
door and gained the arch without disturbing anybody.
Now the trouble began. The second-storey *reja* was
several feet lower than the arch-top and set to one side.
To get up he had had to balance on the top cross-bar
of the grille and jump obliquely. Could he by swinging
by one arm from the rail reach the window-bar with
the other? Assuredly he could not. He must lengthen
his swing somehow. How? By looping something
round the rail standard and hanging at the end of
that. What? Six feet of rope would do. Might as
well ask for six feet of moon, there was no rope to be
had. A sheet would answer the purpose, two knotted
towels even; only an extra foot or two was needed.
A sheet he could not get without waking Bianca, but
towels were available. So far so good. In supposition he was now clinging to the second-storey *reja*.

From there, by loosening his towels and using them again he could lower himself to the ground-storey *reja*.

What then? Coruña or Vigo? Coruña was slightly the nearer, but he favoured Vigo, knowing the lie of the land. Straight down the Sar valley and then south till he fetched up against the Ria. The Ria de Vigo ! That brought memories back. Three years previously he had landed on one of the bare islets at its mouth, his object being to plunder some goats for fresh meat. The goats led his men a merry dance, and an old woman bobbed out of a hovel in the rocks and cursed them in the name of every saint in the calendar. While his men were goat chasing Ortho climbed the hill, sat down on a boulder and admired the view. The crone accompanied him, squatted on a neighbouring stone and went on with the cursing, never for one instant did she stop—" May the blessed Saint Gonsalves afflict you with pains in the knee and arm ! St. Vincent make you horrible with small-pox, brigand, bandit ! . . ." Ortho waved her off, laughing, and looked up the great inlet. A tongue of placid water with barren mountains hedging it on either hand, the sun lifting over the Sierra del Suido, high peaks touched with fire and smoking with cloud.

" May St. Jerome smite you with a hail of thunderbolts, St. Ovido with deafness, pirate, sea-shark ! . . ."

A gleam of white houses on the left hand—Cangas. More white houses clustered thick about the opposite shore and sprinkled well up the hill-side among vine terraces and pine trees; a swarm of merchant ships huddling for safety under the forts—Vigo. Rooke and Stanhope sailed through the islets in 1702 and plundered the Spanish silver fleet—Vigo Street, London, was built from the proceeds. Vigo had not forgotten the incident, apparently.

> " Con todo el mundo guerra
> Y paz con Inglaterra."

Ortho longed to emulate that raid, his gaze lingered
covetously on the cowering ships. But it was out of
the question. He picked up his meat and went, the
lady accompanying him. "May St. Michael consume
you with cancer and tumours and St. Sebastian burn
you with a wasting fever ! You great goat thief ! . . ."
When last he saw her she was standing on a rock
in the sea wishing him toothache in the name of St.
Apollonia.
That was Vigo Bay, not fifty miles distant. He
should make it in two nights, brisk travelling, three at
the most. Coming down on the north shore at Cangas
he would wait till dark, swim to a fishing skiff and row
out through the isles.
He had heard on the road that English privateers
swarmed off the Ria, waiting for any South American
silver ship that might chance the run in. One of these
would surely pick him up. In imagination he saw her
already, looming through the morning mists, lifting
her copper to the swell, rippling towards him. He was
aboard her—white decks swaying gently, dew dripping
from her rigging, the shrill twee-wheet of the bosun's
call and rosy English faces, English voices, all about.
She would be a West-country ship, perhaps ; he would
hear the good ' down along ' blurr again. " Where
bist from, matey ? P'nzance man, 'scaped all the way
from Valladolid, well, I nevver ! Come along aft
and take a bit o' breakfast to once, dear soul !—take
all 'e do want "—he thought he would cry when he got
aboard that ship.
The west wind, the sea wind, whooped outside,
rattling the window. " Whoo-hoo ! " it shouted.
" Come on, shake a leg ! Only fifty miles more. I'm
covering you, making all the noise I can. Freedom ! "
Ortho loosened the tuck of the sheets, slipped quietly
to the floor and listened. Bianca turned over on the
pillow, sighing. Ortho waited, tense. There was no
further movement from her, her breathing was regular,

all was well. He felt about the room for his clothes, collected them in a pile at his feet and dressed with infinite care. Again he listened. Not a sound beyond the sough of the wind and an occasional creak from the old house.

He fumbled his way across to the dressing-table and laid his hand directly upon the grease-pot. The door next. Dipping his finger in the grease he smeared it all over the bolt and gingerly worked it back, a fraction of an inch at a time. It moved without protest. Splendid ! In a flash he was outside the door and had closed it behind him. His shoes first. Once he was on the ground he would have to make haste, and he could not run bare-footed on those cobbles. He pulled on his shoes, and picking up the towels knotted two ends together.

It was pitch-dark in the Plaza the lamps had been extinguished long since, nobody could see him from below. Everything was in his favour.

Crash !

Ortho jumped half out of his skin, overturning a tub. What was that? The door, without any bolt to hold it, had been blown in. Curse it ! He had forgotten that; should have jammed it somehow. Too late now. The cold air streaming in would wake Bianca in a minute—even if the double crash had not done so already. He had not a second to lose. Bending over the rail he looped his towels round the upright, cocked his left leg over, gripped the towel ends with both hands. A blind swing head downwards into the dark —cobbles below—supposing the towels gave?

" On ! " the wind bellowed. " Quick, man, quick ! "

He hesitated, drew a deep breath, lifted his right leg that was still hooked over the rail and felt a stab of fiery pain shoot right up his thigh. He dragged desperately at the leg, but it would not respond, he seemed to have lost all power in it.

" Knifed," he thought. " Ham-strung ! " and pulled himself wearily back on to the arch. His wounded leg sagged under him and he collapsed at full length among the camellia shrubs, visions of the blue bay of Vigo evaporating in a haze of pain.

"Ten years ago I should not have hesitated," he thought, " I am an old man, an old man."

Two tender bare arms gathered up his head into their trembling embrace. Kisses rained upon his face, kisses and burning tears.

" Love of my life, you cannot leave me *now*."

CHAPTER XVII

PABLO MENDEZ, *escopetero*—or ' armed person '—
strolled along the road to Cangas, his musket on his
shoulder. On his right hand were vineyards, running
in long parallel lines up to the foothills, miles upon
miles of trellises propped on granite posts, five feet high
and split to the thickness of a few inches. Beyond them
the vines grew on transverse terraces scraped out of the
slopes, and over all rose the mountains, olive-coloured
patched with grey stone outcrops. On his left hand
glittered the Ria de Vigo, a sheet of sun-smitten glass,
studded with pine-plumed islets and moored skiffs,
the fishermen in them fast asleep.

It was a warm afternoon. Pablo Mendez took it
easy. There was no call for haste. He could reach
Cangas before sundown and spare time on the way for
a glass of wine and a cigar with his first cousin, Diego
Mendez, and also, perhaps, for another glass and cigar
with Ramon Cana, his second cousin twice removed.
If anybody else invited him in for a third glass, maybe
he could manage that as well. It was of no vital
account if he reached Cangas by sunset, midnight or
next week. There was no lawlessness on his beat,
nothing to report—peace, perfect peace. This state of
utter tranquillity was causing him some uneasiness. If
it continued he might well lose his occupation. In
Eden there is no need for watch-dogs. Pablo did not
want to be turned loose. He enjoyed strolling about
the country, martially equipped, taking glasses of wine
with his numerous relations and their innumerable
ramifications. The thought of exchanging his musket
for a vine hoe caused him acute distress; he was of a

build more suited to strolling than sweating. He wondered if a crime could not be arranged, a small one, a minor robbery. Who could he employ and how much would it cost? That was the rub, the cost. Though his occupation was pleasant the emoluments were slight. He was in debt to at least seven ventas and the cash in hand did not amount to much, about five piastres and a few reals. Antonio Garcia owed him another piastre, but had gone to Cuba. Who among his acquaintances could be beguiled from the path of rectitude for five piastres—with a possibility of six if Antonio Garcia returned solvent from Cuba? Pablo perused a mental list without enlightenment. The country-side was law-abiding to a man. Over on the north of the range they were blessed with a genuine criminal, a one-legged industrialist known as ' El Coco,' who, despite his deficiency, had been very active around Pontevedra of late. He came hopping down from the mountains, stole more or less how and what he liked and hopped back again; the accuracy of his aim, of which he had given many harmless but significant demonstrations, explaining his immunity from arrest. The Pontevedrans accepted this infliction with philosophy. He only stole a few fowls and vegetables here and there, they said. It was cheaper to maintain one brigand than a squad of protective soldiery, who not only stole far more but expected to be paid into the bargain. Pablo Mendez wondered if he could not borrow ' El Coco ' for a day or two, make some honourable arrangement with the thief whereby he might appear in the Cangas neighbourhood, fight a spectacular but innocuous duel with Pablo and retire discomfited. Pablo might then claim to be the saviour of the country and his job would be secure. The difficulty was to get in touch with ' El Coco,' who was not a native of Pontevedra and appeared to have no connections.

Furthermore, would he hop twenty arduous miles for five piastres while there was a fowl left in his own

district? Pablo did not think so, he had no reason to
suppose that ' El Coco ' was a philanthropist. There
seemed to be nothing for it but that he must commit the
crime himself. Turning the pros and cons over in his
mind he came to the *granja* of Diego Mendez. Diego
was out, up in the vineyards, but the Señora was at
home. She furnished Pablo with a glass of wine, and
he in return furnished her with the gossip of the neighbourhood, of which he was the principal carrier.
Since no second glass appeared to be forthcoming, he
took up his musket once more. At the door he halted.

" Oh, by the way, has the happy family event
occurred? "

" What do you mean? " the Señora queried. " Oh !
Enriqueta—not till June."

" I was not referring to your honourable daughter
but to the *puerca?* "

" Her—yes, last night—eight and all well."

" My felicitations. Congratulate Diego for me,
please," said Pablo, and took his leave.

The Mendez sow had eight youngsters. They slept
in a sty behind the granary. He might enter the yard
by night, fire a shot and steal a piglet. The next night
he would repeat the act with Ramon's geese, finishing
up with a raid on the Pascadello goats, one of the latter
had a new-born kid, he knew, a little yellow thing, easily
portable. Three consecutive robberies, accompanied
by gun-shots, would give the impression that there were
lawless spirits abroad and he would retain his musket.
A subtle plan. All three prospective victims were
cousins, he knew his way round their *granjas* blind-
folded. Furthermore, in combining the rôles of thief
and constable he was reducing the chances of arrest to a
minimum.

Approaching the Cana abode, he entered and
whistled. There was no reply. Pablo sat down on a
chair, removed his sombrero, wiped his brow and eyed
the *bota* that hung on the wall. A sultry day, he was

infernally dry. Had Ramon or Elena been in they would not stand by and watch him, a second cousin twice removed, suffering infernal drought. Not they, they would invite him to a glass of wine. In taking it he would only be obeying their unspoken wishes. He took a drink—two—three; one to Ramon's good health, one to Elena's and one to the geese. Then he re-hung the *bota*, lit a cigar and strolled on again. The very next night he would start his depredations—no, not the very next night because there was a wedding at Cangas with a dance to follow; Pablo for all his flesh trod a pretty measure. In imagination he saw himself doing it, with little Faquita, the pilot's daughter—'Tra-la-la, tra-la-lirra.' He hummed merrily, skipped a few paces down the road, then caught himself up. Business first. The great plan. Should he begin with Diego's piglet or Ramon's geese? The old sow might bite him, she had teeth like a shark. Pigs when roused were very treacherous, he had heard. On consideration he thought he would leave the pigs alone. He would raid Hernan Reynosso's fowl-roost instead. Fowls did not bite, and Hernan, the laziest devil in Galicia, would not quit his bed for an earthquake. Fowls be it then, and on the night after next.

" Whist—Pablo ! Pablo Mendez ! "

Pablo whipped round and saw Elena Cana crouched behind a thorn bush, grasping a pitchfork.

" What are you doing there ? " he exclaimed ; then, politely, " Good-afternoon ! "

" To the inferno with your good-afternoons," Elena hissed. " Do not stand there like a fool. Come here, will you ? "

Pablo obeyed. " Well ? "

Elena pointed towards a small hut built of loose stones and thatched with maize leaves that stood a few yards back from the road. " In there."

" What is ? "

" A robber."

Pablo gaped at her. " A real one? You are joking; we haven't any—at least, not at present."

"I tell you we have. I caught this man stealing pumpkins off my wall."

" Who is he? "

" I don't know—a stranger."

" But how do you know he's in that hut? "

" Because I followed him, *bufon !* "

" You did !—alone? "

" Certainly—pumpkins are scarce at this time of the year. Is your gun loaded? "

" No, not yet."

" Then load it at once and fetch him out."

" Hey, wait a bit," said Pablo. " Not so fast. These operations are not as simple as that. One must consider, plan. Your pumpkin thief has the advantage of me in position. He is, as it were, fortified, whereas I am in the open. Strategy is required. What manner of man is he, by the way? "

" I did not see his face," said Elena, " but he is very lame, he hops . . ."

Pablo turned pale to the hair roots. " Hops ! did you say? Elena, be careful how you answer; does this person veritably hop? "

Elena nodded. " Yes, on one leg. What is the matter? "

Pablo waggled a tremulous hand towards the hut. " Matter, *por Dios !* Woman, do you know who we have there? ' El Coco '—no less. A brigand, a bandit, a professional desperado. The ruffian who has been cocking his thumb at all Pontevedra and robbing their pig-pens and fowl-roosts, a very demon ! "

An encounter with ' El Coco ' without any preliminary arrangement was the last thing he desired. The man could shoot through the eye of a needle.

" We are in great luck catching him before he starts any of his demon tricks on our pigs and poultry," said the imperturbable Elena. " Advance, Pablo ! "

Pablo yammered at her, momentarily inarticulate.
"You—you expect me, alone, single-handed, to
beard this assassin who has defied all Pontevedra?
You—you ask that?"

"Why not?" said Elena. "You are an *escopetero*,
aren't you? It is what you are paid for."

"*Por Dios*, I am not paid to commit wanton suicide."

"Very well give me your musket and I will do it
myself."

Pin-heads of perspiration started on Pablo's forehead. This implacable woman would drive him to
his death. Death!—and five minutes before he had
been so cheerful! . . . skipping!

Pablo, for all his fat and futility, was no coward, few
Spaniards are, but he knew that in a shooting match
with an entrenched expert like ' El Coco ' he stood not
a dog's chance. On the other hand, to refuse was to
lose his gun and suffer eternal disgrace.

"But stay, *Elena, alma* ; listen, be reasonable," he
pleaded.

"Give me your musket."

"Halloa, Elena! Hey, Pablo! What is it?"

Pablo turned. More infernal women, three of them,
returning to their farms upon small donkeys. They
would combine to drive him to it now. Death!
Ugh!

"What are you two quarrelling about?" one of the
new-comers inquired.

"There is a notorious character devouring my
pumpkins in that hut and this *probrecito* refuses to arrest
him," Elena explained.

"I did not refuse. I only——"

"He is frightened out of his skin," the pitiless woman
continued, "frightened of a poor, lame, unarmed
ratero."

The three ladies descended as one from their palfreys.
"Then since he is unarmed let us arrest him ourselves,"
said they. "You have your fork and we will throw

stones. Pablo can stay behind the bush till it's over.
Vamos! "

"Halt! Stay where you are!" Pablo advanced,
his hand uplifted. "Who is *escopetero* here, you or me?
Back, Brigida! Back, Juana! and you too, Clara,
do not be so forward! Why did you not tell me before
that he is unarmed?" he demanded of Elena in a
reproachful undertone. "Deceitful baggage!"

He crawled to within a few yards of the door on his
hands and knees, took cover behind a convenient
boulder and brought his musket to the present.

"Hey there, Señor thief! Put your hands above
your head and step out. You are surrounded by the
forces of outraged Justice—stop chattering, Juana!—
do you hear me?"

There was no answer.

"Ahem! You cannot escape, so you may as well
come at once and not keep us waiting here in the hot
sun. Come out!"

No reply.

Pablo raised his voice. "It is useless pretending that
you are not in that hut, Señor Don, because we know
very well that you are—I suppose there is no doubt, is
there?" he asked Elena. "You are certain?"

"Certain," said Elena, firmly. "My eyes do not
lie."

"No, there is no possible doubt about it, Señor,"
Palbo continued. "You know you are in there yourself. Come out like a man."

Still no answer.

"Very well," said Pablo. "I will give you two
minutes' grace and then take drastic action. Two
minutes."

He rested his musket on the rock and waited. The
two minutes dragged by. Clara's donkey strayed
across the line of fire and had to be stoned off. Juana
started chattering again. Pablo admonished her and
hailed once more.

" Your time is up, Señor.   Are you coming out? "

There was no movement from the hut.

" *Bien esta*, I must fetch you out," said Pablo.   " In Heaven's name, Juana, hold your tongue for a moment and go and look for my cigar butt.   It is behind that bush somewhere.   Have you found it? "

" Yes."

" Is it still burning? "

" It is.   What am I to do with it? "

" Circle round behind the hut and throw it into the thatch."

Juana did as bid.   At first the watchers thought the cigar butt had gone out, but presently a wisp of smoke rose up from the dried maize leaves.   The smoke thickened; a thin spit of flame darted like a snake tongue, died down and reappeared jagged and hissing. Another second and the whole roof was one roaring blaze.

Pablo flattened out behind his rock covering the open door with his musket, holding his breath.

Some tense seconds passed.   Pablo released his first breath and took another.

Said Juana, in an awe-stricken whisper, " He is no man, but salamander—such heat ! "

" By the Virgin, I do not like this," said Clara. " This roasting.   It is not as though he were a heretic."

" It is horrible," said Brigida, and began to whimper.

Pablo laid down his musket.   " Compose yourselves, ladies.   There is nobody there.   No living thing could stand that heat.   Elena, for reasons best known to herself, has fooled us all.   Next time you see ' El Coco ' in your yard, Elena, pinch yourself and he will disappear.   I will now proceed to Cangas, where I have business."

" Stay ! " said Elena, her voice coming very strained and queer.   " He comes."

All eyes flashed to the door.   The man was coming, slowly, painfully dragging himself along.   As he passed through the door the blazing thatch fell in behind him.

The man wobbled on for a yard or two, then his leg gave way and he collapsed over a boulder. "Shoot!" he said wearily.

He was haggard and ragged, gristled about the jaws with an ungainly growth of hair, hollowed in at the eyes, tottering. Leaf-ash covered him, a spark smouldered unheeded in his shirt; he was scratched with thorns and cut with stones. This was no devil-may-care mountain brigand, this was tragedy.

Clara uttered a low cry of distress. Brigida let her stone drop. Juana crossed herself. Even Pablo allowed his aim to waver. Elena arose, pitchfork in hand, but it was not the thief she menaced.

"Put down your gun at once, Pablo," she said huskily. "Señor, you are welcome to my pumpkins. I am ashamed of myself. I would have given you bread if you had asked me. The charge is withdrawn, Pablo. Let him go."

Said Brigida, still whimpering, "He is ill and we have half-burnt him. There is a flask of brandy in my saddle-bags. Wait while I fetch it."

"He is starved, poor thing," said Juana. "I have some bread and ham. Pablo, be off!"

Pablo scratched his chin. This was not 'El Coco.' 'El Coco' was short and thick-set, while the man before him was tall and painfully worn. Also he had two legs, though one did not appear to be of much use. Nevertheless the fellow was a suspicious character, and a suspicious character was exactly what he wanted. He bore the man no ill-will, but he had his occupation to think of.

"Put your gun down, Pablo, you fool," Juana repeated. "The poor thing could not hurt a fly. Shame on you!"

Clara brought her tongue to bear. "Let him go, Pablo, or we'll throw stones at *you*."

Pablo shook his head. " That is all very well, but I have my duty to consider. This person was undoubtedly stealing pumpkins. He must come before the authorities and explain himself."

The man looked up. " I have been twelve days crawling from Santiago and can crawl no further, you will have to carry me to your authorities. As for explaining myself, I will do that now. I am an English prisoner of war, escaped from Valladolid three months ago. You will do me a favour by shooting me."

Pablo stared at him in blank amazement. "*Por Dios!* English prisoner of war, did you say? English? "

" That's what I said."

" But—but, Señor Don, where have you been hiding yourself? Surely you know? Peace with England has been declared these last six weeks ! "

BOOK III

CHAPTER XVIII

' JAMES TONKIN, Joseph Battersby and Andrew Lynch, Customs officers from Marazion, being in the neighbourhood of Breage, about midnight, met with seven men on horseback carrying casks, who greeted them with Horrid Oaths and Imprecations. There was a fight with Bludgeons and Battersby was knocked down, a stone hitting him in the chest. He died this day.

' Warned from Head-quarters to look out for a brigantine of 80–90 tons, called the *Naboth's Vineyard*. Griffith Orbin, master. She has remains of a white bottom forward, sides black, gunwales yellow, with a black-and-white scroll, and a flower-pot painted between the cabin windows. Suspected of hovering with twenty butts Brandy and Claret.

' Robert Laity, Custom House officer of St. Michael's Mount, was charged with stealing a silver spoon from one Chastity Proust. On the occasion of the capture of a lot of stuff in her house she slipped the spoon into Laity's pocket and then accused him of theft. The animosities of the smugglers against the Revenue officers are inconceivable.'

Mr. Amelius Bowes, Collector of Customs for the port of Penzance, laid his quill aside, dusted a pinch of sand over the wet ink in his letter-book and, sauntering to the window, peeped through the crack between the curtain and the sash.

From this vantage he could observe, without being observed, the Chapel Street entrance of the ' Ship and Castle Inn.' Not that he expected to see anything sensational, but he found certain comings and

goings of interest. All great deductions are built on
a mass of corroborative detail. Mr. Bowes paid much
attention to apparent trivialities on the principle that
as such they would be neglected by the opposition.
Results had justified this theory. As Collector of
Whitby in Yorkshire he had made the illicit gin traffic
too precarious to be profitable. Moved to another
hotbed, Deal, he had repeated his success. Neither of
these triumphs were bloodless. Within a month of
his arrival at Whitby two of his men were murdered.
At Deal attempts were made on his own life. Mr.
Bowes was a pink and chubby being, with childish
blue eyes that twinkled upon the world through
brass-rimmed spectacles, very nice about his linen
and careful in his dress. An indulgent bachelor uncle,
one would have said, which in fact he was. But he
had his other side. A Yorkshireman himself, there
was a good deal of cold northern iron beneath the
chubbiness. The opposition of Whitby and Deal
served only to whet his temper, with the result that
there was weeping and gnashing in those parts. Now
he was in Cornwall and he found his task more difficult.
In Kent and Yorkshire, near the centre of things, he
could enlist military and naval forces to his aid, but
here in this rugged Ultima Thule, kicked out like a
discarded jack-boot into the wild Atlantic, he was all
alone—except for one Riding Officer, ten men and
an old King's cutter, slow as a hearse. Twelve men
and a hearse to defy a fleet of fast luggers and a population imbued with firm conscientious objections to
the liquor duties. An impossible task it would seem,
but Mr. Bowes did not despair; information was
coming to his hands, thread by thread. Presently he
would have collected enough to plait a rope.

There was nobody of importance at the door of the
' Ship and Castle '; a groom teasing a dog with a
harness cloth and a frizzle-headed chambermaid
watching him from a window above. Presently she

called the groom by name, and as he looked up emptied a basin of slops in his face and retired giggling. The man addressed her by a string of the foulest epithets, but appeared delighted. It occurred to Mr. Bowes that this pair were expressing affection for each other in their own fashion. Queer thing, love. It was a sensation he had never experienced himself, but he was far from deploring it in others. Love and its attendant passions, jealousy and revenge, had brought him invaluable bits of information in his time. He backed away from the curtain, and coming openly up to the window regarded the sky over the roofs opposite. A fair blue sky with a few clouds of the palest crocus drifting idly thereon; wind, what there was of it, east of south. He drew a large silver time-piece from his fob. Ten minutes to nine. By ten o'clock, or half-past at the most, the conference should be over and he would be free to go fishing. He would take one of Mrs. Curnow's pasties, and a bottle of porter, and work up stream from Trevaylor. The trout were small, but they were game and cunning, he would have good sport. He pictured himself crouched among the green fern in delicious solitude, dexterously luring the cunning little trout, the scent of flowering gorse and wet sedge all about.

He was aroused from his day-dreams by a clash of the door-knocker and Mr. Dearborn entered. Mr. Dearborn was the Riding Officer, a ponderous ex-dragoon, with a sour mouth and a large wen on his forehead which caused him to wear his hat tilted more rakishly than his temperament justified. A blunt, blundering person, but incorruptible. Mr. Bowes sometimes wondered why his Riding Officer remained upright; it would have paid him so much better to be otherwise. He concluded that Dearborn could no more help his probity than his wen; God inflicted him with both.

" Morning, Fred," he greeted, with an affable nod.

"Sit you down. Glass of ale? No?" A pause. "Well?"

Frederick breathed heavily through his mottled nose. "Three tubs of gin."

"Ah-ha! Anybody about?"

"Not a soul."

The Collector stepped across to his bureau, unlocked it and, producing a slip of paper, handed it, without comment, to his henchman.

Frederick spelt it aloud. "'Zawn-a-Bal. Wed night, weather suiting. An Honest Man.' It's the same hand as wrote the last," he commented.

Bowes nodded. "Yes, the same hand, and a left hand too if you ask me, from the shakiness."

"How did it come?"

"The same way as the first, pushed in under the door. Lizzie May said she found it when she came down first thing this morning."

Bowes tapped the letter with his forefinger. "The point is that this is from our friend."

Frederick started. "Eh! What! How d'you know?"

"The signature roused my suspicions. I have noted that when a man acclaims his integrity it is time to sew one's pockets up. Secondly, why does he write with his left hand? If he is as honest as he asserts he has nothing to fear from me."

"That's all guess-work, sir," said Frederick, with the proper distrust of brawn for brain. "Moreover, he *was* honest. The first letter said 'Look under the Turtle Rock at Porthguarnon on Thursday night,' and I done so and found three tubs, as I told you. What's wrong with that?"

"Too few," said Bowes. "Who do you suppose would go to the trouble to land three tubs miles from anywhere? They were planted for you to find. And at Zawn-a-Bal on Wednesday next you'll find three more—no, I think, it'll be five this time."

Frederick tweaked his colourful nose. " But whatever for? "

" Because our Honest friend wants to gain our confidence. Every time we obey his instructions we get something. Very well then, one of these fine nights he sends you packing off to, let us say, Sennen to pick up half a dozen tubs, and at the same time lands a couple of hundred casks at Prussia Cove or vice versa. Do you grasp the idea? "

" Guess-work, sir," said Frederick, " guess-work."

" I'll tell you something that is not guess-work," said Mr. Bowes amiably. " Neither of those letters came in under the door."

" Then how——? "

" They came in Lizzie May's pocket. I have suspected the girl for some time and now I know. The letters did not come in under the door for the sufficient reason that they cannot. There is a strip of leather tacked along the bottom to stop draughts. You cannot force a letter through. I have tried with all sorts of letters, limp and stiff. Lizzie May is in their pay— if you will excuse the rhyme."

Frederick scratched his chin. " Come to think of it now, I remember seeing her walking out evening before last in a fine new pair of gilt-buckled shoes. I wondered at the time . . . an ugly slut like that."

" Yes, I noticed them myself," said Mr. Bowes, " and that too set me thinking. Little things, Frederick; little things."

" You'll discharge her at once, sir, of course."

The Collector peered at Mr. Dearborn over his spectacles, his pink forehead netted with amazed wrinkles. " Discharge her! My dear Frederick! Discharge her! On the contrary, I shall cherish her to my bosom. Throughout my career I have prayed for a known spy in the camp, one who would carry to the opposition precisely what information I want them to get, and now I have found this treasure you ask

me to discharge her. Oh, Frederick! Frederick!
My dear Mr. Dearborn!"

He sprang from his chair and, tip-toeing to the
window, looked up-street towards the 'Ship and
Castle.' Mr. Teage was standing under the arch
arguing with Mr. Carclew. Presently they linked
arms and strolled towards the Market House, leaving
the street empty.

"That new cutter commander is coming this
morning," said Mr. Bowes, breaking silence.

"Yes—he's late," Frederick growled, who never
was himself.

"No, he's not, not yet," said the Collector. "If
you're going by that clock it's five minutes fast. I
keep all my clocks fast to keep Mrs. Curnow up to
time."

Again he paced to the window and stood watching
the little crocus clouds drifting over the chimney-pots.
Another two hours and he'd be away in the Trevaylor
Valley . . . birds trilling in the whitethorn breaks and
the sly little trout dozing under ledges. . . .

Mr. Dearborn gave utterance to a labouring mind.
"I believe you're right, sir, about that there 'Honest
Man'; come to think of it, three tubs *was* too few."

"Thank you Frederick! Thank you!" said the
Collector, and began to whistle.

"Rat-ta-tat," went the door-knocker, a brisk tattoo.

"Arrival of the navy," said Bowes. "With one
minute to spare as you'll perceive. A good augury.
Delabere always kept me waiting."

The new commander entered the room. Bowes
was most agreeably surprised. King's cutters were
as a rule officered by men for whom the navy proper
had little use, men who had got themselves into
trouble, or were too old or too slovenly for service
aboard smart frigates and line-of-battleships. Delabere, the previous incumbent, was over sixty and
nearly blind, his predecessor an epileptic who could

not go to sea because he was either expecting a fit or had just had one. Bowes anticipated another of like kidney, some bibulous old salt-horse who had long since bade farewell to ambition and was ' pricking for a soft plank.' Instead here was a young man, a fine young man too, broad-shouldered, deep-chested, upstanding, with frank blue eyes and a most resolute jaw. The Collector, who believed in first impressions, took an immediate liking to him. How had such a one come to the Revenue service? he wondered, and stepped forward, his hand outstretched.

" Mr. Trevaskis, I presume."

" Yes. You are Mr. Bowes, I suppose. Good-morning, sir."

" This is our Riding Officer, Mr. Dearborn."

Trevaskis gave a friendly nod. Frederick grunted, but his eyes glinted approval—and some astonishment.

Bowes indicated a chair, noticing that the sailor's sleeve was pinned to his side, empty. He lacked a left arm. " Poor fellow," he thought, " at his age ! " Aloud he said, " Sit down, sir, pray. You have but lately arrived? "

" Yesterday morning."

" Ah, yes, then you have hardly had time to inspect the *Snapper*. You will find . . ."

" I have inspected her from heel to truck," said Trevaskis. " She is on the mud at this moment."

Collector and Riding Officer exchanged glances. Wonderful ! Delabere was not seen for six weeks after his appointment.

" I trust you find her in good shape? " said Bowes.

" Her carcass appears sound, but her sheathing's in a shocking state."

" Delabere scraped her over the Seven Stones last month," Dearborn explained.

" What was he doing out there? "

" Catching lobsters. He made a tidy penny out of lobsters."

Trevaskis stiffened in his chair. Bowes coughed. "Ahem! Did he indeed? Well, he's dead now. De mortuis, etc. Excuse me, sir, but have you been engaged in Preventive work before?"

"No, sir, never."

Bowes picked up his quill and began idly sketching on the blank sheet of paper before him. "Would you find it tedious if I outlined the salient features?"

"I should be grateful."

"Very well then. To begin at the beginning, the stuff, tea, silk, gin, brandy, claret, etc., comes mainly from the collecting points, the Channel Isles and Roscoff in Brittany. The runners are chiefly Irish wherries and local craft. The Irishmen 'hover' as we call it, lie off the coast and peddle small parcels to fishing boats. Their supply is sporadic and insignificant. Sporadic, Frederick, means haphazard. It is the local wholesalers that do the damage. In the old days, I understand, fishermen used to row across in open gigs and return with twenty tubs or so, also sporadic and insignificant. Then arose one Nicholas Buzza, known as 'King Nick,' who was a personality. He saw the enormous profits to be made out of 'The Trade' and organized it thoroughly.

"His big armed craft ran the goods with the regularity of stage coaches; pack trains drilled to the efficiency of cavalry troops distributed them over the country; as for the Revenue, it was a phantom and a mock. Then the versatile monarch burst a blood-vessel preaching the Gospel at Gwennap and the Trade fell to pieces. Stuff was run here and there, but in no vast quantity, the Preventive kept it in check. Now, after a lapse of twenty-five years, a second Nicholas has arisen and the Trade is once more on the ascendant."

"Big craft engaged?" Trevaskis inquired.

"Yes, big and numerous, but we are principally concerned with three; the *Who's Afraid*, the *Elizabeth and Sarah* and the *Seven Stars*, all of Mount's Bay, cutter and luggers respectively. They are, of course, nominally traders, armed to run."

Trevaskis produced a pad from his pocket and made a note of names and rigs. " Yes? "

" The difficulty is that they can land their goods practically anywhere. To look at this coast you would hardly believe it, but there are half a dozen little coves between here and the Land's End where boats may be launched."

Trevaskis' forehead puckered in thought. " Five, I make it."

" You are a native, a Cornishman? " Bowes inquired. " I take it from your name . . ."

" I know the coast well enough," said Trevaskis, shortly.

Bowes sketched away with his quill, a fanciful outline of the coast in question, then he turned the map into a near-human face with Tol-pedn-Penwith for nose and Penberth Cove for mouth.

" As I was saying, they can land their cargoes anywhere and, what is worse, get help anywhere. When it comes to defrauding the King's revenues, the Cornish, whom otherwise I find a very agreeable people, appear to have no morals whatever. The entire population, gentle and simple, is with the Free Traders."

Mr. Dearborn writhed in indignation. " Only last month the whole congregation of St. Levan, parson leading, broke out of church in the middle of evensong to land a run. Heh ! "

" And dutifully returned to give praise the moment it was disposed of," said Bowes, smiling. " Don't forget the end of that story, Fred; you'll spoil it." He turned on the sailor again. "Now we have ten men only at our disposal, so you see the difficulty. Trying to seal this honeycombed coast with ten men is like trying to plug a sieve with one finger."

"Best cut off the water supply," said Trevaskis. "Catch 'em at sea." The Collector adorned his map-face with curly moustache and beard. "You will not find that so easy, I fear, sir. The three vessels I mentioned to you are no sluggards."

"And mine is?"

"Well—she has not been able to range them, so far."

"Laugh at her," said the blunt Mr. Dearborn.

Trevaskis nodded. "No boat could sail with her copper in that state"—and his blue eyes twinkled—"possibly the lobsters hindered her. I do not pretend that my new command is speedy, gentlemen, but once I get her re-sheathed I'll make her step a lot brisker than she has done. She's stiff at any rate, she'll stand pressing."

"All the pressing in the world won't turn a tortoise into a hare," said Frederick, with unusual brightness. "No offence meant, sir, but you can put the matter o' racing out of your mind. Them luggers are flyers."

"Then exactly what have you gentlemen in mind?" Trevaskis asked. "We can't catch them at sea, you say; we can't catch them ashore—well?"

Mr. Bowes sketched the outline of a trout standing on its tail, added a supporting trout on either side and turned the whole into a fleur-de-lys. "Catch them between the two, sir—landing. That is their weak moment. Ship at anchor, men strung out between ship and beach, pack trains huddled together, darkness, confusion. If we arrive—you from seaward, Mr. Dearborn from inland—at the right moment . . ." He brought his hands together with a suggestion of nut-crackers. "I might be able to borrow a few dragoons from Plymouth for a special occasion . . . I might."

Trevaskis considered. Given the place and the time, his part in the nut-cracking would not be

difficult, closing on a moored lugger under cover of
night. Simple enough, given the place and the time.

"Yes, but—who will find that right moment?"
he asked.

Mr. Bowes sketched a lop-sided anchor, festooned
it with coils of foul cable. "I will. That will be
my share. Information is coming in bit by bit. An
unknown, signing himself 'Honest Man,' appears to
have taken to himself the task of supplying us with
negative information, which once its nature is understood becomes quite as useful as affirmative. The
Government have their agents in Guernsey and Roscoff
who apprise us of what boats are loading there and
whither destined. Also the thirty pieces of silver did
not perish with Judas, they are still in circulation."

"How do you mean?"

"I mean that there is a handsome trollop down on
the quays who was born in the gutter with a taste for
dress. She cast her bright eyes on the mate of the
Susan and Elizabeth and he fell in love with her. When
he comes in from sea she twines her arms about him
and cockers and comforts him and mixes his grog too
strong, with the result that he talks too much. Later
she brings his talk to me and I buy her silk stockings
—there are two pairs in that box at your elbow.
One of these days that boy will swing and she will get
a new dress and be very proud." Idly his pen
sketched a gallows tree with a funny little manikin
dangling therefrom. "Bit by bit it comes in."

Trevaskis' distaste mastered him. "My soul! you
are very heartily welcome to your share!"

Mr. Bowes scribbled on, unmoved—concentric circles.
"The law *shall* run, Mr. Trevaskis. It is the basis of
civilization."

He spoke with a quiet intensity that made the
sailor look at him again. This pink, plump, twinkling
person was a *dévot*. The law was his God, and he
would preserve it by fair means or foul, though he

himself were smirched with filth and stained with blood. Devotion is always worthy of respect. Trevaskis regretted his outburst. "I beg your pardon; yes, the law must run."

There was a pause. Bowes scribbled on, Dearborn tweaked his nose. Trevaskis spoke again.

"You were saying just now that a new personality had arisen. Have you any objection to telling me his name?"

Mr. Bowes arose from his chair and began to pace the room slowly, from sideboard to window, his hands clasped under his coat skirts, causing them to stick out. He looked like a benevolent bullfinch, its tail cocked. "Tell you; why, certainly, Mr. Trevaskis; you are one of us now. Did I not trust you implicitly I should not have told you anything. The personality who controls . . ."

"Hist!"

"What is it, Fred?"

Dearborn was making violent grimaces towards the door. From the passage came the shuffle of feet, softly retreating.

The Collector smiled. "Only Mrs. Curnow, dusting, everlastingly dusting. Lizzie May is out, I sent her down to Russell with a note. Mrs. Curnow is my housekeeper," he explained to the sailor. "Her only virtues are that she can braise a steak and is as deaf as the dead. Lizzie May is the handmaiden. She has no virtues at all and ears like a bat, but I would not part with her for worlds, for what those ears collect she imparts to the opposition, and, as you may imagine, I only let her hear what is good for her. At the present moment she is probably in a crib by the Abbey revealing the contents of a letter I left lying about," he smirked. "Very careless of me."

"And getting more gilt buckles!" Frederick growled.

"Yes," said Mr. Bowes. "Gilt buckles and silk

stockings. Eve! Eve!—and not so long ago you could buy her with an apple!"

He resumed his pacing. "But where were we? Ah, yes, the controlling power. Smuggling, if you will pardon my return to the pedantic, demands too classes of operatives—seamen to run the goods, farmers to distribute them, and that is where the chain breaks, the two can seldom agree. Nicholas Buzza was a plough-boy who ran away to sea, and therefore a bit of both. He held them together. When the Trade again resumed dangerous proportions we looked about for such another, a man who had the trick of command and was equally at home on land and sea. We had not far to look, we found a person who fulfilled all these requirements and who, moreover, had been a lieutenant of the great King Nick."

"Thirty-one years ago, that was, in old Curral's day," Frederick interposed. "I've been reading it up in the books. Curral precious near nabbed him."

"What's he been doing in the meanwhile?" Trevaskis asked. "Preaching the Gospel too?"

Bowes waggled his cherubic head, smiling. "Oh dear, no. To give this rascal his due there is nothing smug about him. He is at least consistent. What has he been doing? Everything. There is hardly a form of bloodthirsty violence that he has not engaged in—barring open piracy. Renegade lancer in the employ of the Sultan of Morocco, blackbirder, master of a privateer—to mention but a few of his sprightly vocations. During the late war he was taken by the Spanish and held two years in prison. When peace was declared he returned, somewhat the worse for wear and with one leg dragging."

"Says a sentry stuck a bayonet through it when he was trying to escape," Frederick testified.

"I regret it was not through his heart," said the Collector, strolling towards the window. "At all events he limped home here and lay low for a while, but not for long. Six months' rest and he is up and busy again, up to his old tricks. There was no good reason for it; the man owns a strong farm away to the westward, he was not in need of money. He has flouted and made mock of the law from sheer love of mischief and taught the whole country-side to do the same, and for that I will surely hang him—when the moment comes."

Mr. Bowes stepped up to the window, and pushing the curtain cautiously aside, peered out.

A horseman was dismounting at the door of the 'Ship and Castle.' He handed over his mare, said some words to the ostler, laughed, showing a splendid flash of teeth, and passed within; a tall man, dressed in a black coat laced with silver, dragging one leg.

"His name," said the Collector, and his round eyes narrowed behind his spectacles, "his name is Ortho Penhale."

CHAPTER XIX

" I'LL take the *Snapper* round to Devonport and get her resheathed at once" said Trevaskis. "And while I'm there I'll try to borrow a long gun . . . got a friend or two in the dockyard."

" How long will you be away? "

Trevaskis considered. " Three weeks at the outside."

" Time enough," said the Collector. " From the signs and portents they will not be bringing off their big run for a month at least. What say you, Frederick? "

Dearborn nodded his grotesque head. " 'Bout a month, sir. The *Seven Stars* is up on the beach at Newlyn, breaming; and I heard that the *Elizabeth and Sarah* is hauling up too."

" There is no immediate hurry, you see, Mr. Trevaskis," said Bowes. " And not too much energy for the moment, if you please. The greater their self-confidence, the harder they will fall. You understand me? "

" Perfectly."

The Collector's gaze wandered away over the chimney-pots, Dearborn fumbled with his hat. The conference was at an end.

Trevaskis shook hands with both of them and took his leave, erect of carriage, wooden of countenance, betraying by no flicker of eyelash or tightening of lip the tumult that was within him.

In the street he hesitated. South or north? South back to his cutter or north to the ' Star Inn ' and the horse he had ordered.

He decided for the north, the ride would be a certain relief. The horse was ready saddled, a chestnut cob with a close-docked tail, a perky little beast for a hireling, pawing the cobbles impatiently.

The ostler had his doubts when he saw Trevaskis—a sailor, and one-armed at that. " P'r'aps you wouldn't care for this little hoss," he brabbled. " I got another little hoss in here would suit you better, maybe; a nice grey hoss. I shan't be a minute changin' . . ."

" What's amiss with this one? "

" Nothin', yer honour. He's a nice little hoss too, but t'other's broader, so to speak; more to sit on."

" I thank you for your solicitude," said Trevaskis. " Nevertheless I'll take this, the narrow one."

" Please yourself, Captain; but t'other little hoss, the grey, ain't hogged like this one. He've got a nice long mane."

" What's the advantage of that? "

" No particular advantage, as it were, your worship; only some gentlemen prefer to have something to place their hand upon going round corners. Some like manes and some martingales."

" I belong to yet another school, I cast myself bodily upon the neck," said Trevaskis, and mounting the cob clattered out of the yard. Whither away now? He might go north over the moors to Castle-an-Dinas, or east towards Marazion—he could get a gallop on the Green, a scamper might clear his brain.

He turned eastwards. The pair proceeded the length of Market Jew Street, the cob stepping briskly, tail in air, Trevaskis sitting like a statue, grim battle raging within him; heart saying ' Go to her ! ' head saying ' How can you? ' Head drove him as far as Ponsandane; there he halted. Jennifer was expecting him and he was riding away from her. Jennifer would be waiting for him out in the Keigwin valley, the girl he loved in the valley he loved. She had been waiting for him for two years and he was riding eastward. She would wait and wait and then go home in tears. Happy little Jennifer in tears! Dear trustful little Jennifer sobbing her heart out. He swung his mount about and rode back again.

The ostler standing at the door of the 'Star' saw him approach and touched his forelock. "Grey hoss, Captain? Shan't be a minute . . ."

"Go to everlasting blazes!" said Trevaskis and rode past.

He had come unscathed through the mauling Riou's division, had been taken from the Trekroner forts at Copenhagen to have his arm shattered in a trifling frigate action. Since then he had been mainly in the hospital hulks and promotion had passed him over. Suppuration had set in, involving two more operations, which reduced his arm, at first shattered below the elbow, to the mere shoulder-joint—it was not completely healed yet. The Grand Fleet or foreign service was out of the question for the time; he could not afford to be idle, so he applied for the *Snapper*, pulled every string he could reach and enlisted Barclay Johns' assistance. Johns had influence, he got the appointment and went bowling westward between vernal hedgerows, song in his heart. 'Jennifer, Jennifer,' hummed the coach-wheels; 'I'm going to Jennifer' rang the flying hooves. He was going to Jennifer and there was all summer before them, glowing blue days and long glamorous twilights, the scent of hay and honeysuckle. What luck! What marvellous good fortune!

And now, within a few hours of his arrival, he was involved in a conspiracy to hang her uncle and bring her family to disgrace! How could he make love to her with that in mind? How could he accept her father's hospitality and at the same time labour to humiliate him? Yet if he cut loose from Jennifer now her heart would break—he took no thought of his own. He was in a cleft stick. That he had schemed and intrigued to get himself into this fix filled him with

bitter mirth. "Damned funny," he muttered.
"Laugh somebody." Was there a way out? He might
apply for a transfer, but he could imagine the reception
it would have. "Here's this Trevaskis fellow bombards
us with petitions for the Penzance station, and having
got it prays for a transfer—throw it in the fire!"

Since Bonaparte had once more torn up his treaties
and turned Europe into a shambles he could not resign
his commission. For an instant he was tempted of
the devil. "Bungle this *grand coup*. Let Penhale slip
through your fingers. Bowes will not suspect, he
trusts you. Quite easy." That *was* a way out. He
could show himself too early, or arrive just too late
pleading wind, tide, unforeseen circumstances.

Trevaskis caught hold of himself, horrified. Lord
God, what black treachery was he considering? Selling
his trust for personal advantage! The thirty pieces of
silver, as Bowes said, were indeed still in circulation;
they assumed subtle and insidious forms. At that
moment Trevaskis saw himself as no better than those
poor drabs who betrayed employers and lovers for
trifles of finery. He put the tempter behind him once
and for all. He would do his duty, come what might—
but at the end he saw Penhale swinging by the neck
and Jennifer stunned, moaning, wild-eyed with grief
. . . such gentle brown eyes!

He drummed the cob's flanks with his heels and sped
across Newlyn Green at a gallop, kicking up clods of
turf. The cob was a frolicsome little beast, it went with
a swing, reaching at the bit, shying at anything that
attracted its attention, pig-jumping occasionally.
Trevaskis, none too robust after his operations, was
hard put to stay in the saddle, but the bucketing did
him good. By the time Jack Lane was reached he
felt hot, shaken and almost cheerful. After all, he
reasoned, the run was not expected for a month or
more, and anything might happen in that time—
storm, fire, plague, accident might change the whole

situation in an hour. The *Elizabeth and Sarah* might wreck herself, Penhale break a leg, catch the small-pox or even reform, there was no saying. It was absurd to fret oneself about what might occur a month hence.

He passed a string of pack-horses toiling up Paul Hill with loads of seaweed for field dressing.

"Day to 'e, zur!" hailed the rustic in charge. "Bra' pretty weather eddn a?"

Three fishermen came lurching down from Tredavoe, bunches of primroses in their red hands. They nodded to Trevaskis in the most genial manner. "Mornin', zur! Mornin' to 'e!" Civil, friendly folk, he thought; why the deuce must they go law-breaking? Like as not those three flowery mariners came from the *Seven Stars*, at present reposing from her labours on Newlyn beach. Probably that whistling farm-hand carried other freight than seaweed on his pack saddles o' nights. Trevaskis hated the idea that these people who greeted him so pleasantly to-day would to-morrow look upon him as an enemy. And it was Ortho Penhale who inspired them in their nefarious practices; Penhale, the arch-mischief-maker who forged rogues from honest men and loomed like a shadow between him and his darling. But retribution was at hand, retri-bution spectacled, pink, cherubic, sitting in a room in Chapel Street plaiting a rope strand by strand. Again he heard the Collector's bland tones: "Smuggling may not be a capital offence, *prima facie*, Mr. Trevaskis; but armed resistance is. Why do you suppose Penhale carried arms if not to use them if necessary? I will force that necessity and hang him for it later."

That was all very well, but was Ortho Penhale the man to have his hand forced so readily, would he not scent the trap? His career was one long chain of alarms and escapes, he must be very sensitive to danger and expert at avoiding it; a daring fellow, quick-witted, with many friends. Again echoes of the

Collector : " From what I hear, not *quite* the man he was, Mr. Trevaskis. He is fifty now, and failure and imprisonment have told. His self-confidence is shaken, and there is that lame leg."

That lame leg. . . . Trevaskis had detested Ortho Penhale ever since he could remember, and the present situation did not tend to modify his dislike, but his sense of sportsmanship was disturbed. A year or two earlier, when the man was in his prime, he would have asked nothing better than a duel *à outrance*. Penhale was still a highly dangerous antagonist, but the salt had gone out of the encounter—the man was lame. Hunting a lame wolf might be a sanitary duty, but there was no honour in it. From every aspect the affair was repugnant to Trevaskis.

Paul church stood on his left hand, grey against the glitter of the sea. Along the hedgerows foxgloves nodded their wands of bells and the campions their ragged pink. Clouds, pure and soft as swan's-down, floated serenely on an azure heaven. Spring in the West Country; the sweet of the year in the sweetest land. Earth flaunting her green and gold, radiant as a girl in new-found beauty. Could tragedy grim and gaunt, lurk behind this smiling scene? Which was real, this gentle loveliness or Bowes with his ' informers ' and greasy hangman's rope? Trevaskis told himself that there was nothing in it, there would be no big run, and if there was, Penhale would not incriminate himself . . . yet all the time he saw a spectre swinging black against the sun, Jennifer crouched, broken, at its feet.

Across Clodgy he rode and over the crest of Trevelloe. Gwithian church tower came in sight, bold on the western skyline. Away to the north-west the lone cairn of Chapel Carn Brea smoked to heaven, a pagan altar, burning its furze in incense to forgotten gods. Trevaskis drew rein for a moment and let his eye rove over the familiar country. Tiny fields, green and

brown, fitted together like patches on a crazy quilt,
strips of moorland yellow with gorse, hedges of bleached
stone and scattered grey farm-houses. A wind-swept,
lonely land, but his heart went out to it. He had been
miserable here—but that was forgotten. He had been
far away—but had now returned. He pricked forward,
feeling that he who had been homeless all his life was
nearing home at last.

Into Lamorna he dipped, waded through yellow
flags and spotted mimulus, drank his cob at the stream
and pushed on over Boleigh hill. A mile of upland
and the Keigwin valley gaped below him, a deep green
river of tree-tops. The pack track split at this point,
one branch curving southwards to where the waters
of Monk's Cove flashed jewel bright between enclosing
headlands; the other plunging straight down-hill
into the trees—the road to the Owls' House. Trevaskis
could see a bit of mossy thatch between the oaks, the
tip of one tall chimney. A queer, rambling old pile
of weathered granite splotched with white and orange
lichen, its upper windows peering under arched eaves,
and two comic little male and female figures carved
on the door-posts. He had been strangely drawn to
it as a child. Times out of number he had crept up to
the gate and peered into the yard. There was seldom
any sign of life about, a lean sow dozing in the midden,
perhaps, some fan-tail pigeons burbling in the sun, but
humans seldom. Ortho Penhale gone overseas; Teresa,
the gypsy woman, away at a cock-fight or a 'feasten,'
Eli wedded to Roswarva—a sad old house, deserted by
all save its singing stream, brooding on past love and
merriment.

A bad old house, so good wives hinted, with a curse
upon it and shadow of wild deeds, but the young
Trevaskis felt nothing sinister in the place. On the
contrary, the old house appeared to assume a most
benign aspect when he drew near, the deep-set windows
twinkled in a friendly fashion, the low door expanded

in a welcoming grin. 'Hello, little son!' it seemed to say. 'Come and talk to me, I'm all alone.' But he never dared go further than the gate, somebody might come home all of a sudden, and that would mean dogs or a thrashing. Nobody had any love for 'those Trevaskis cubs.' He had a good mind to ride through Bosula now, just to pay his respects to the friend of his youth; then he remembered that Ortho Penhale was no longer overseas and turned right-handed through a gap in the hedge.

The track he had taken ran along the hill shoulder for some distance, and descending crossed the stream about a mile above Bosula; it was, in fact, the path he was following the day he broke a girth and first met Jennifer.

Down the steep fields he rode, sitting well back, the cob placing its feet with care, trampled through a patch of young bracken and entered into a fairy forest, white and purple. The may trees looked as if they bowed under a heavy fall of snow. Their heads were crowned with clouds of sunlit blossom, their gnarled and mossy arms were filled with masses of silver froth, and over their roots the bluebells waved a purple sea.

Trevaskis stood still for a moment entranced, and then pushed on. In and out among the glittering trees he wove, and they seemed to play a pretty game with him. Whichever way he turned a tree seemed to spring in his road. Low as he bent, the boughs bent lower, noosing him in tender ivy trailers, loosing showers of petals upon him. They shook as puffs of wind went overhead, but to Trevaskis they rustled with laughter. In and out he wove, between the white and the purple, laughing too; festooned with broken ivy, blossom pelted, a bridegroom running the gauntlet of a hundred merry bridesmaids.

He won through at last, splashed across the stream, sending the little trout darting, climbed the further bank and halted again.

Jennifer! Jennifer in the sprigged dress and cherry ribbons she had worn at the Helston 'Furry,' standing under a thorn bush waiting for him. Jennifer! flushing that wild rose blush of hers, dimpling adorably, her brown eyes lustrous. There was no doubt for whom she was waiting. The hill-side was swept with sunshine, misted with daisies; sweetly blew the scent of the may trees and from the willows came the ripple and purl of the stream. Trevaskis stood transfixed, outwardly stone, inwardly a-tremble. He had a feeling that this could not be real, but a dream only, perfect and fleeting.

It was Jennifer who broke the spell. " I—I thought you would come this way," she said; then her eyes fell on his empty sleeve and she flung out both her hands to him : " Oh, my dearest ! "

Instantly he was off his horse and had gathered her to him; Penhale, Bowes, Dearborn and all that they stood for thrown to the winds, forgotten. " The arm I've got left will hold you tight enough," he laughed. " Kiss me, my sweet."

.   .   .   .   .

" I do hope you'll like mother and father," said Jennifer as they walked towards Roswarva, " but I'm sure you will."

" I'm sure I shall. The question is, how will they like me? "

Jennifer had no doubts about that. " Oh they'll love you I know; only——"

" Only what? "

" Nothing that matters really; but I think they would have been better pleased if you were a farmer—father, that is. He worships the land, would not change his plough for a sceptre."

" Happy man ! "

" Yes . . . but he would be happier if one of us could have contrived to be a boy. You see, Uncle Ortho has no children, so the name will go out, and

that's what frets him. There have been Penhales at
Bosula for three centuries. When father thinks of
somebody else, not a Penhale, farming Penhale land
and possibly neglecting it, his misery is pathetic, poor
lamb."

" Does your mother feel the same way? "

" She feels for him, but for herself I couldn't say.
I always look on father as part of the place, like one of
the Bosula oaks with its roots laced deep into the soil.
He will not leave the farm for a day if he can help it;
but mother is different, though she too was born on a
farm and has not been out of Cornwall in her life."

" How is she different? "

" I don't quite know, but she is. She never says
anything, but she often takes her sewing and goes and
sits on the Luddra Head alone. I have found her there
once or twice, and it is not at her sewing that she is
looking, but out to sea, away past our horizon."

" Dreamer? "

Jennifer smiled. " The farm girls would hardly
tell you that, or the hinds either. They will tell you
she has eyes at the back of her head and second sight.
They may deceive father in small things, but mother
never—nor do they try. She has all our affairs very
firmly in her hands. A dreamer perhaps, but practical.
You'll love her, I believe."

Trevaskis believed he would.

They came to Roswarva gate and passed through. A
bob-tail bitch arose from her siesta on the sunny side
of the yard and rushed forward barking, followed by a
trio of excited puppies. Recognizing Jennifer she
retired, but the puppies remained, three plump little
bundles of brown wool, bouncing round their mistress
in vociferous adoration. A knock-kneed calf wandered
out from behind a haystack and joined the procession,
licking at Jennifer's floating sash ends with a pale
pink tongue.

" Our orphan—but not inconsolable," Jennifer

explained. " You never saw such an appetite. We feed her four times a day and then she's not satisfied. She'll force her way into the house if we aren't careful. Go away, Susan."

" Here's a donkey coming now," said Trevaskis.

" Yes, Mr. Ramsbottom. We called him after the Gwithian clerk; they've both got long, sad faces. He's come to inspect you, Tony. Fall in behind Susan, Mr. Ramsbottom, please. Not too close to the horse or you'll get kicked in the face, and then it'll be longer and sadder."

The procession wound round the corner of a barn and up to the door of the farm-house. There was a man in a snuff-coloured coat standing on the step, looking up at the sky, whistling. His legs in their tight breeches were like tree-stems, massive and sturdy. His shoulders filled the door from side to side.

" The oak tree," Trevaskis thought, " laced into the soil. This is Eli Penhale," and remembered that the farmer had been a great wrestler in his youth, not from any outstanding skill, but because it was next to impossible to throw him.

Jennifer hailed. " Father, stop it at once ! I believe he's whistling for rain ! "

Eli Penhale's gaze descended from heaven to earth, a mild blue gaze. " Eh ! " he said. " Oh, is it you, Jenny? Well, I admit I was, just a small shower, my dear "; then he lumbered forward, his square, corded hand outstretched. " Good-day to you, Mr. Trevaskis."

His smile was winning, his eyes those of a child, at once trustful and trustworthy, his grip that of a gentle bear. A good creature, Trevaskis thought, not over-burdened with brains or humour, but kind and honest. It seemed impossible that this solid, simple yeoman and the flash-jack adventurer were own brothers, but they were and, moreover, reputed firm friends. Trevaskis laid the latter circumstance to Eli's credit and imagined that even his oaken loyalty must have been strained at times.

Eli, feeling conversation needful, picked inevitably on the weather. " Fine day, sir, beautiful. This sun is drawing the crops out nicely. Not but that we could do with a small shower to freshen 'em, just a sprinkle. . . ."

" No sprinkles to-day, father," said Jennifer with decision.

Eli nodded solemnly, " Very well, I'll promise not to whistle again. Reuben, take the gentleman's horse. This is Reuben, Mr. Trevaskis. Been with us twenty years."

" Twenty-one come last 'Tide," Reuben corrected. " Proud to see 'e, Captain. Look, do'e want that there pesky calf in to meat wid 'e, or shall I car' en off? "

" Car' en off, her table manners are shocking," said Jennifer, " and Mr. Ramsbottom."

The faithful Reuben departed, Susan under one arm, the cob's rein under the other, driving Mr. Ramsbottom before him with empty but appalling threats. Trevaskis warmed to Roswarva; his Service eye approved the orderliness of the yard, he liked the easy terms between master and man, the quaint and friendly beasts.

Eli laid a hand on his shoulder. " Step inside, sir."

He entered the farm kitchen, an airy room, bright with whitewash and sunshine, hung with burnished brass and copper pans and long fowling-pieces. On the east side was an open hearth with ingle-nooks—cosy refuge of a winter's night; on the south a broad window staring wide-eyed over the English Channel.

There was a woman standing facing the window. She turned as Trevaskis entered and stepped forward smiling—the mother, who had everybody's affairs in her hands. He took one of them and felt that he might place his own life in it and rest assured. Big, blunted, work-coarsened, a hand that had found no common task beneath it, it was at the same time a hand that could be very tender in time of trouble, he thought. A big woman throughout, a large edition of Jennifer, full-breasted, upstanding, broad of brow, firm of chin, with deep-set dark eyes that were at once humorous and wise. She had her daughter's creamy skin and warm colouring, but she never could have been half as pretty as Jennifer. Middle age was upon her now, the bloom had passed, she was getting creased and heavy, there were glints of silver in her hair's rich brown, but there was a quality in her that time could not destroy. Trevaskis found himself praying that thirty years on might find his flowery girl something like this.

He became aware that Mary Penhale was staring at him, an expression of mingled astonishment and perplexity on her face; her lips were parted, her puzzled eyes swept over him, feature by feature.

Eli, grappling with puppies, uttered a belated introduction.

"Yes, I know," she said, absently, glanced from husband to visitor and again from one to the other. "Trevaskis," she murmured, as one groping among memories. "Trevaskis."

The sailor stirred uncomfortably. Instantly she had recovered herself and was welcoming him to Roswarva, bidding Eli begone with his puppies, twitting Jennifer, ordering her maids, the capable and bustling housewife; but throughout the meal that followed, Trevaskis felt her eyes upon him, no longer puzzled but wide and shining. The memory for which she sought had come to hand.

CHAPTER XX

" As I walked out one sunny morn to view the meadows round,
I saw a pretty primrose lass come tripping o'er the ground,
Singing ' Blow, ye winds in the morning,
Blow, ye winds, Hi ho ! ' "

ANTHONY TREVASKIS came down-hill into Lamorna singing cheerfully. He had been to Devonport and was back again, the *Snapper* re-coppered. At the moment he was returning to Penzance after supper at Roswarva. It was late because he had delayed after Jennifer had been sent to bed, talking stock selection with Eli, who propounded no original ideas but was experienced and logical. It was now past eleven o'clock, starless and still. Up on the high country the track was discernible, but under the valley trees Trevaskis could see nothing, so left the direction to his cob. He was in no hurry, the night was mild and long sea-watches had taught him to make the best of his own company. He would be in Penzance by midnight; three hours' sleep and then away on the turn of the tide. A week's cruise off the Scillies, on the outlook for ' hoverers ' and to practise his new ' long eighteen ' in private; that was his programme. Bowes should have some definite information by then.

A trailing bramble snatched at his hat, a thorn bush scraped his knee. He pressed the cob over to the left and felt the prick of wet holly leaves on his face. The road had grown very narrow all of a sudden ! Standing in his stirrups he looked half left for the lights of old Trewoofe Manor, but could not see them. The Trewoofe folk might have gone to bed, but he thought it more likely that he had taken

the wrong turning. Another fifty yards and he was
sure of it. He was in one of those deep lanes that
split away from the main road and ran south towards
Lamorna Cove. The discovery did not disturb him,
his ride would be prolonged by half a mile perhaps,
not more.

Giving his mount a nudge he pushed on down-hill.
The going was treacherous, seamed with rain courses
and littered with boulders; the cob stumbled and
slipped, yet cleverly kept its feet. Trevaskis, feeling
that he could do nothing to help it and that he had
the valley to himself, opened his chest once more, but
in pastoral vein this time.

> " Near some smooth stream oh, let me keep
> My liberty and feed my sheep.
> A shady nook well lined with trees,
> A garden with a range of bees ;
> An orchard which good apples bears
> Where spring a long green mantle wears."

He caught a glimpse of the sea framed between dark
hills, with a string of fairy lamps strung as it were
across the Cove mouth from headland to headland—
the Mount's Bay fishing fleet far out in the Channel.
A smell of salt and seaweed blew up valley mixed with
the smell of approaching rain. Then the tree-tops
rose up between him and the twinkling lights, and he
was out of the lane and on the Cove road going back
towards Trewoofe.

> " Where winters never are severe,
> Good barley land to make good beer ;
> With entertainment for a friend,
> To spend in peace my latter end
> In honest ease and home-spun grey,
> And let——"

A bit of the hedge detached itself and flung towards
him, an indefinite black smudge on the blurred grey
of the road—the grit of hobnails on stone.

" Stand ! Stand in——"

Trevaskis jabbed both spurs hard into the cob's flanks. It bounded forward. He felt a slight shock as it hit the smudge with its chest, heard a snarl of human pain somewhere underneath him and brought up against a second, larger, smudge with a jar that threw him on to his mount's withers. He realized that he had ridden full tilt into a horseman halted across the road.

" Got you, by Christ ! " said a voice, grimly triumphant, and an iron arm hooked him round the neck. " Quick, Mike ! "

Hands, presumably Mike's, gripped Trevaskis by the leg.

" If you struggle I'll twist your neck," the horseman threatened. " Andrew ! "

" Yessir."

" Where are you? "

" Here on the road. That bloody rascal rode over me, trod on me guts."

" Never mind your guts now. Come here ! "

The down-trodden Andrew arose, groaning.

" Well, now you've got him, what are you going to do with him, sir? " Mike inquired.

The horseman did not appear to know.

Andrew, however, had no doubts on the subject. " Knock him on the head, o' course. Tried to murder me, didn't he? Nobody won't know."

Mike thought this a brilliant idea. " That's the notion. Let's knock his head in and leave him here. When they find him they'll think he fell from his nag."

" Our tracks? " said the horseman, dubiously.

" They'll be washed out," said Mike. " There'll be a scat o' rain before dawn."

" Lookee," said Andrew, inspired. " Let's knock his head in here and then push horse and man over that gully to the right. They'll think he rode over in the dark. We can lay his head on a stone all life-like."

" That'd be murder," said the horseman.

" Murder be damned," said Mike. " If we don't get him he'll get us. What of poor Joe Battersby and Billy Rose, eh? It ain't murder to kill a man before he kills you, it's legal self-defence—moreover, who's to know? Whadyousay, Andrew? "

Andrew was in enthusiastic agreement. " Bloody rascal tried to kill me, didn't he? Stamped on me guts. And think of all the trouble it'd save."

The last commended itself to the leader. " Yes, by cripes, that's true—a power of trouble. Think you could finish him with one clout, Andrew? Wouldn't do to mess him."

Andrew guaranteed satisfaction, provided the others held the head still.

It was time he made an effort, Trevaskis considered. The horseman was on his left with an arm clamped tightly about his head. Being armless himself on that side he could do nothing to him. Mike clung fast to his right leg. Trevaskis gave the problem half a moment's thought and hove suddenly to the left. The horseman shouldered hard against him, Mike dragged with all his might. A violent heave in the opposite direction, and with their joint strength assisting, Trevaskis was out of the saddle and on the ground, clutching Mike by the hair, but with the tenacious horseman on top of him. They rolled together in the mud, tangled up like some dog-fight; the horseman clinging grimly to his hold; Trevaskis kicking, heaving, pommelling with his solitary hand; Mike replying in kind and yelling to Andrew to come quick with his club.

" Hit him, you perishing fool ! "

" How can I when I can't see which is which? "

" Feel for him, blast you ! "

A wet groping hand passed over Trevaskis' face and took him by the scalp. " Got him ! "

" Then *hit*, you fool . . . strong as a bull . . . tear loose in a minute."

Mike's exhortations came gasping, between agonized puffs and groans. The horseman clung on in deadly silence.

" Hit ! " Mike barked.

But no blow fell. Trevaskis felt the grip loosen in his hair, the hand removed altogether.

" Hold on, you," said Mike in awed tones. " My God, there he goes again ! Down there."

The three wrestlers lay still.

Clearly from the gorge below the road came the lilt of a song.

> " Ten busy gaugers watching on the beach,
>   With hangers drawn in readiness and powder in the pan.
>   Up flew a grey gull and let a fearful screech,
>   Off flew the gaugers, sweating every man;
>   Fol de lol de leero,
>   De leero, de leero,
>   Firing as they ran."

Then a loud burst of laughter : " Ha, ha, ha ! "

Mike withdrew his arms from Trevaskis' legs, the horseman from his neck. All three sat up.

" Then who the thunder have we got here? " said the horseman.

" My name is Trevaskis, Mr. Bloody Dearborn."

" Mr.—Mr. Trevaskis ! "

" The same—by your august permission."

" My God ! I . . . I deeply regret . . . but . . . but why didn't you say so at once, sir? "

" Say so ! How the mischief could I with you choking the life out of me? "

" B—but Andrew challenged you before that, sir."

" That's so, sir," Andrew corroborated. " I said ' Stand ! in the King's name,' and you knocked me down and trod on my guts."

" Pardon me, you said nothing of the kind. Those may have been your intentions, but you did not get as far. I see a man jumping out of the hedge at my bridle, yelling 'Stand,' and I acted on a very natural impulse. How was I to know your next words would not be 'and deliver'? that you were not a common footpad; in fact, you acted very like it. Trod on your stomach did I? I wish it had been your face."

"Next time say 'In the King's name' first, and 'Stand' after, Andrew," said Dearborn, and turned to the lieutenant. "Humbly apologize I'm sure, sir; regrettable mistake—but you'll admit you were singing?"

"Certainly I was, and why shouldn't I, egad? Is there a duty on singing? Have His Majesty's Preventive Officers nothing better to do than prowl about the lanes in the dead of night knocking people on the head because they sing?"

"No, no, sir," said Dearborn. "You don't understand, let me explain . . ."

"Explain!" Trevaskis roared. "My oath, I should say you will explain. You fall upon me, a naval officer, do your best to choke me, pommel me, bounce me in the mud, black my eye, tear the coat off my back, and as a finish propose to murder me in the most cold-blooded manner I ever heard of . . ."

He stopped in the middle of his tirade; the voice was singing again.

> " Ten busy gaugers looking for a ' hell ' *
> Came across a deep hole that yawned as black as sin.
> One said ' There's snuff here, or 'baccy by the smell.'
> T'other said 'twas burgundy, another he said gin.
>> Fol de lol de leero,
>> De leero, de leero,
> Then the old mine tumbled in."

"Who the blazes is that?" Trevaskis asked.

"That, sir," said Dearborn, "is what's led to all the trouble."

* Hell—Old Cornish for an underground hiding-place.

" How? "

" We went down to Lamorna Cove to-night following information sent by that there ' Honest Man ' Mr. Bowes spoke about. Sure enough we picked up a nice little drop of goods which have gone on ahead on the horses. Soon as we started back that voice started to sing down in the stream bed, right under our noses, taunting-like. I didn't take any notice at first and we moved back up valley, but the voice came too, keeping pace, and very insulting it was, sir, most provoking. After a bit I felt I'd had enough of it, so I halted the horses and told the lads to stand still and make a bit of a chatter so's to show the singer where they were. Then me and Mike and Andrew slipped ahead and into the woods. Presently we. heard the horses move on and the voice came on too, working up valley alongside 'em—it came to within ten feet of me."

" Well? "

" Andrew trod on a twig, sir," said Dearborn sadly.

" I didn't, I never moved."

" No more did I," said Mike.

" Then the twig snapped itself," said Dearborn with sarcasm. " Anyhow it snapped. I sprang forward to grab the man and went headlong down one of they old prospect pits, and as I fell he jumped past me. I can't understand how you didn't get him, Mike? "

" Nor me either," said that hero. " I heard him laugh right in my face, but when I grasped for him there wasn't nothing there."

" I touched him, I swear I did," said Andrew.

Dearborn sniffed. " Touched him! What's the good o' touching? Anyhow we've been an hour banging for him down in that maze. Times he wasn't more'n a few feet from us. You'd hear him laugh ' Ha, ha ! ' in the darkness right in front of you, and

make a grab and go face-first into a holly bush. Then
you'd hear him singing a hundred yards away. When
you thought he was in front of you he was behind, and
when you were sure he was behind he was in front,
like a blasted will-o'-the-wisp."

"Valley is full of old tinners' tunnels and conduits
that he knows of and we don't," said Andrew, ruefully.
"If I've fallen once this night I've fallen sixty times.
It's a marvel I've a bone left."

"You was complaining of the hurt done to your
coat just now, Mr. Trevaskis, sir," said Mike, "and
I'm sure we're deeply repentful and grieved, but you
ain't the only one. What with those plaguy brambles
and thorns down there I'm torn to rags, breeches,
stockings and all."

Dearborn took up the tale, "After an hour's
scratching and tumbling I called it off and was for
going home quietly, when stap me, if we didn't hear
singing coming down the lane right on top of us,
and if you'll pardon me, sir, *your* singing voice and
his singing voice is so alike you couldn't tell the
difference."

"That's so," said Mike, heartily. "No difference
at all."

"Like as two thrushes," said Andrew.

"The rest you know, sir," said Dearborn. "I'm
sure we're deeply regretful and humbly sorry for any
rough usage . . ."

Trevaskis cut him short. "We'll say no more about
that, but what of this cold-blooded murder you were
contemplating just now? That is a serious matter,
my friend."

Dearborn hesitated. "Yessir, I suppose it is; but
I'll give you my word I had no thought other than the
public interest. The man we thought you were would
be better out of the way, sir. I ain't speaking of the
trouble he puts us to, but the trouble he'll bring all
round. There's many a poor boy will get transported

or hung through the following of him. Believe me, sir, if he was to be put quietly away it'd be better for everybody and there isn't a soul on earth would miss him." He spoke with great earnestness.

Trevaskis relented somewhat. He knew that these Preventive riders had a hard time of it, out at all hours and in all weathers; that, almost invariably outnumbered, they were the butts of much coarse humour and brutal usage. He also believed Dearborn when he said that his motives were not entirely vindictive.

" I am in agreement with you as to the man being better out of the way," he said, " but your methods won't do, Dearborn. The law must take its course, and law officers should be the first to respect it. As for the man not being missed, I have reason to believe that in certain quarters, and innocent quarters, mark you, he will be missed very terribly—strange as it may seem. However, that is beside the point. Give me your word that there shall be no foul play on your part and I will forget this little affair. Will you promise me? "

" I will, sir," said the Riding Officer. " I knew it was wrong at the time, only it did seem . . . well, sensible. I give you my word, sir."

" Very good. The episode is closed. Nothing more to keep us here—eh? "

" No, sir, nothing."

" Then we'll get on for Penzance."

Mike and Andrew produced horses which had been tied up under cover of the bushes; the quartette mounted and rode slowly up valley towards Trewoofe.

" Ten busy gaugers, out to make a kill,
Mounted on their fiery steeds as proudly as a throne.
They pranced through Marazion and might be prancing still,
Had not a jackass chanced to bray in no uncertain tone,
    Fol de lol de leero,
    De leero, de leero.
So the steeds pranced on alone."

The singer accompanied them on their way, mocking and melodious, keeping well down in the gully that ran parallel with the road.

> " Ten busy gaugers prowling on the shore,
>   Saw a barrel floating and straightway put to sea.
>   They hauled at it and hove at it till they could heave no more ;
>   Up sailed an admiral ' Perish you ! ' says he,
>   Fol de lol de leero,
>   De leero, de leero,
>   ' You leave my moorings be ! ' "

The three Preventive men made no comment, but Trevaskis guessed their thoughts and felt for them. " He'll be piping a different tune in a week or so," said he in consolation. A grunt from Frederick answered him.

They turned the corner by Trewoofe and set their faces eastward, riding in gloomy silence. At the foot of Trevelloe hill their feelings seemed to be easier, for all three filled pipes and lit them at the shutter lantern hanging from Andrew's saddle bow—the wild valley and its mocking voice were behind. Three dour, weather-seamed faces they were that bent to the glow. Mike had a jagged scar running from jaw to brow, Andrew's nose was broken almost flush with his cheeks. It was an arduous risky job they plied for no thanks or glory and very little money. Trevaskis felt considerable sympathy for the battered old plugs, out and about all night in the wind and rain at an age when they should have been comfortably in bed. Ex-cavalry troopers, too old for active service and not old enough for almshouses. Another year or two and they would be too old for this work even and would be thrown out to beg round the taverns.

" Guts all right now, Andrew ? " he inquired. " Have some of my 'bacca ?   Navy plug."

" Thank you kindly, sir."

They plodded up Trevelloe hill, puffing comfortably.

Away towards the Glubbens a fox barked to its mate;
rain began to fall, soft as mist.

> " Ten busy gaugers rummaging about,
>   Poking here and prying there and sniffing far and wide,
>   Spied a silken stocking from the bushes sticking out,
>   So they pulled on it and hauled on it—and found a leg inside ;
>   Fol de lol de leero,
>   De leero, de leero,
>   It kicked 'em till they cried."

Dearborn pulled his horse up with a jerk.   " My soul !
If—if he ain't on the road in front of us now ! "

" He cut over the corner of the hill," said Andrew.

They stood still listening; the voice grew clearer.

Mike exclaimed, " Damme if he ain't coming to
meet us ! "

Frederick uttered some appalling curses, *sotto voce.*

" Steady your helm, Dearborn," said Trevaskis.
" The more upset you are the better he'll be pleased.
Let him pass in silence.   You can't touch him."

" Can't touch him !   If 'twern't for my promise I'd
make mince of him ! "

" Not you.   A move on your part and he'd be into
those bushes, leading you another dance.   He knows
his ground.   You don't want to be made a fool of
twice in a night, do you? "

The wisdom of this penetrated Frederick's skull.
" Very good, sir," he growled.   " Shine a light on
him, Andrew, as he passes.   Just to make sure."

" Sure enough now.   It's him right enough.   Going
lame on one leg, ' clip-clop.'   Hear him? "

" Shine that light and shut your mouth."

> " Ten busy gaugers passing Bedlam gate,
>   Prying here and poking there and sniffing low and high,
>   Saw a puzzled lunatic staring through a grate ;
>   ' Glory be to Goodness ! ' they heard the looby cry.
>   Fol de lol de leero,
>   De leero, de leero,
>   ' Have they escaped—or I ? ' "

The singer was within a few yards of them now, advancing down the road. His impudence nettled Trevaskis, though at the same time he admitted some reluctant admiration. A lame man limping boldly up to a party of aggravated hostiles that outnumbered him four to one. Without doubt he was well armed and had his clear line of retreat, nevertheless it was audacious. The singer halted close to the horses.

"Good-night to you, gentlemen," he hailed, his voice shaking with amusement. "A very good night, I say. You are not very responsive. Am I to understand that you have not had a good night? Tut, tut, I am sorry for that, deeply grieved."

He shifted a step nearer and Trevaskis noted that he held a heavy cudgel in his hand.

"Who is this I see?" he went on. "My old friend General Nosey Dearborn as I live! Commander-in-chief of the Rum Sniffing Dragoons, the glorious Gin-Sleuths. Welcome to our wild West, Nosey me lad—but from what I can see it has been somewhat too wild for you. From the state of your uniform you appear to have been in the brambles. Whatever for? Been birds'-nesting have you? Oh, my glittering stars!"

At this point his merriment overcame him and he roared with laughter, shook and rocked with it, holding his sides.

"'*Four* busy gaugers rummaging for kegs,
    Found a dappled mare's nest and sucked the spotted eggs,
            Fol de lol de leero,
            De leero, de leero,
        I hope they liked the dregs.'

Ha, ha, ha!"

His laughter rose up in the still night, blatant and mocking; was echoed by the opposite hill-side to the right and left: 'Ha, ha, ha!' 'Ha, ha, ha!' and again from Trevelloe wood: 'Ha, ha, ha!'

The very country-side seemed to have joined in the scoffing.

Trevaskis' skin tingled. For all his wise counsels it was with difficulty that he kept himself from spurring his mount on top of the man. But he checked himself. It would be futile, he knew. A blow from that cudgel on the nose of his mount would send it over backwards and by the time it recovered the fellow would be among the bushes, laughing still more loudly. Instead he laid a restraining hand on Dearborn's arm. But the Riding Officer had no need of it, he had given his word. " Shine that lantern, Andrew," he said, steadily.

Andrew pulled the shutter up. The beam fell full on Trevaskis for a moment, swept over the wet shrubs and found its mark—a face, insolent, derisive, flushed with malicious triumph?—no, a face aghast, staring out of the surrounding darkness as if it saw a ghost.

" Who is that? You? What are you doing here? —with *them* ? " The voice was no longer mocking, but strained and deadly anxious.

Trevaskis took no notice. " I think that's all, Mr. Dearborn," he said drily. " Shall we move on? "

CHAPTER XXI

"YOU'RE supposed to see to these things. How didn't you know this plaguy cutter had shipped a long gun?" Bosanko demanded, furiously.

"I did," said Ortho.

"You did know it! Then why the thunder didn't you warn Jim? You let my brother get shot. . . !"

Ortho put his hand up. "Don't shout at me. I found out a week ago, but not in time to send word to Guernsey."

"Then why didn't you send to Scilly?"

"I did."

"Then how—why . . . ?"

"What's the trouble?" asked a big, fleshy man who had just entered, Luke Andrawartha, money-lender and tin speculator of Pendeen. "What is it?"

"*Who's Afraid* captured off St. Agnes, Scilly, three days ago," said Bosanko, hoarsely. "My brother . . ."

Andrawartha sat down, the chair creaking under his weight. "Captured! Who by?"

"That King's cutter."

"The *Snapper!* But, damn my blood! she couldn't catch her own breath. How did it happen?"

"She'd shipped a long eighteen. . . Jim didn't know it. . . But "—Bosanko pointed an accusing finger at Ortho—" but *he* did."

"I've told you that I couldn't get word to him, so that's enough of it," said Ortho. "I'm downright sorry for Jim and the others, but they brought it on themselves."

"How?" Andrawartha inquired.

"Playing the fool. 'Stead of legging it when they

spied the cutter they must needs show their tricks off. Tacked about in front of him trailing a tow-rope over the stern and other clownings. When he'd got 'em within range he unmasked this long gun and dismasted 'em."

" How do you know all this? "

" Had it from a St. Agnes crabber who saw the whole thing."

A St. Just innkeeper by the name of Kneebone, part owner of the *Seven Stars* lugger, asked what the damage was.

Ortho told him. " Two men killed, Jim Bosanko hit by a splinter, cutter and cargo confiscated."

" Suppose it'll cost us another fifty pound to buy the survivors off with the jury when they come before the Assize," said Kneebone, ruefully. " Fifty to a hundred."

Ortho shook his head. " They'll come before no Assize. They were taken straight to Falmouth and handed over to the Press-gang."

Bosanko brandished a clenched fist. " Put away to be shot to rags in the bloody navy ! That Trevaskis ! . . . I'll cut his heart out for this one of these dark nights ! "

Ortho slewed round in his chair. " You'll do no such thing."

" I—I won't ! And who'll stop me? "

" I will."

" *You*, i'facks ! What'll you do? By God, you'd be a pretty one to go preaching to the constables, you would ! Ha, ha ! "

" I never said anything about constables," said Ortho. " I can fix you without any outside assistance, and I warn you I'll have no foul play."

Kneebone looked surprised. " Bit of a change, eddn a, Cap'n? Don't remember any such tenderness on your part towards Tresidder and William Rose."

" Nor Battersby," said Andrawartha.

Ortho turned on the pair. " Are you accusing me with their deaths? " he asked with dangerous calm.

Kneebone raised protesting palms. " No, no, Cap'n. I know you weren't there—only they *was* killed and we don't seem to remember you threatenin' anybody for it."

" The men you mention in every case opened hostilities and were killed in open fight, as, I fancy, Bowes himself would admit. That is fair give and take and quite a different thing from cold-blooded murder. Start that sort of thing going and you can measure your necks for a noose—all of you. Have you forgotten the Hawkehurst gang? they that murdered Galley and Chater. What happened to them? The Government followed it up till they'd hung every mother's son. Do you fools want to jerk too? on account of this jibbering lack-skull here who . . ."

Bosanko sprang to his feet. " I've had enough of you, Cap'n Penhale ! My brother's been trapped and pressed and I believe you could have warned him. Top o' that you call me every name you can lay tongue to. Well now, lookee, I aren't afraid of 'e, not by a damsite. You've played the bully about these parts long enough. Stand up, you clopping* old blow-hard and I'll flay the daylights out of 'e ! "

Ortho rose to the challenge, outwardly contemptuous, inwardly cold. Ten years earlier he would have sprung to battle confident of victory. Now he was not so sure. The shipwright was slow-moving, but young and very powerful. Ten years earlier Ortho could have lashed in a decisive blow before the muscle-bound creature had had time to think, but he could not whistle back that lost decade. The electric blaze of speed that had been the main asset of his youth was his no longer—and there was his leg, he never knew when the crippled thing would let him down. He would leave that room a beaten man, the physical authority he had

* Clopping = lame.

maintained over his wild followers gone for ever. Once beaten, every young bruiser, smarting under a reprimand, would be trying his hand with him.

He limped forward sneering : " Stand up ? Why, certainly. I'll gouge your eyes out for this," but his heart was sick with dread.

Bosanko lumbered forward to the attack, head sunk in shoulders, thick arms raised, small eyes sparkling wickedly. With his clumsy body and waddling gait he reminded Ortho of a bear. " My stars ! " he thought, " Ten years ago I could have battered this shambling oaf to ribbons with one hand. Now he'll probably thrash me. Oh, youth ! youth ! "

But there was no thrashing done that night. A hammer-headed crutch whirled between the two men, and after it came Benbow Baragwanath, landlord of the ' Admiral Anson,' knife in hand.

" Stan' back, both of you ! " he ordered, balancing on his one leg. " Zeb Bosanko, you take one step forward and I'll mark you for life. Back, you scum ! " He hopped nearer the shipwright and grasped him by the collar, knife-point at his throat. " Back ! "

Bosanko stepped back.

" Cap'n Penhale, sit down, please ! "

Ortho obeyed with a show of reluctance which he by no means felt. It had been a close call, he hoped no one would notice that his forehead was wet.

Baragwanath poured forth his wrath. " Come here to make all snug for a big run and then fight amongst ourselves ! Andrawartha and Kneebone, you quaking fools ! do 'e want your cargoes landed or do 'e want to see the one man who has all the ropes in his hands laid out and the stuff go where the *Who's Afraid* went— eh ? "

" No," said Andrawartha, alarmed, " no, that wouldn't do."

" No, no, for God's sake ! " said Kneebone, paling.

" Then don't sit there like a pair of mazed dummies and watch these two maul each other. Rise up and push that young snapdragon back in the corner. Shift yourselves ! "

Andrawartha rose. " Stan' back, Zeb. We're powerful sorry Jim and your cutter's been took, an' understand your feelin's. But 'tweren't the Cap'n's fault, as you'll admit yourself when you're cooler."

" He ain't a bird, couldn't fly to Guernsey," said Kneebone, " and Jim brought it on himself by stopping and clownin.' Sit down, boy, and be reasonable."

" The *Who's Afraid* has paid for herself three times over," Baragwanath put in. " And Jim ain't dead, only wounded. There's no sense in carryin' on like a mad dog. Sit down and hold thy tongue or we'll throw you out."

Kneebone and Andrawartha, making soothing noises, took Bosanko by the shoulders and pressed him gently into his seat.

" Well, now," said Andrawartha, genially, rubbing his fat hands together as though washing off all unpleasantness. " Now that we're all good friends again, let's hear what we came to hear."

Ortho drew a scrap of paper from his pocket and made some marks thereon with a pencil. " The *Seven Stars* and *Elizabeth and Sarah* should have left Peter Port last night full, loaded. I gave 'em two days extra in case of accidents. They should be off the Twelve Apostles reef by to-morrow evening. Most likely they'll be there by dawn. One of 'em will lie off and t'other come in near enough to get the signal."

" Which is? " Kneebone inquired.

" A furze fire on the Luddra Head. That'll mean that all is ready and that they're to run in next night, weather serving."

Andrawartha queried, " And if it don't? "

" They're to hover till it does."

"Weather 'll serve right enough," said Baragwanath. "It's set for a week."

"To-night being the twenty-third, they'll hover off to-morrow, the twenty-fourth, and run in at dusk on the twenty-fifth," said Kneebone. "Is that right?"

Ortho nodded. "The twenty-fifth."

"Landing?" Andrawartha inquired.

"We've got every man and woman in Monk's Cove ready and two gigs from Penberth, sixteen boats in all. As for pack-horses, I've got"—he began to count from his list—"four from John Hugh Prowse, three of my own, five from Widow Polgrean, nine mules from the Wheal Fortune mine, three from . . ."

"How about Eli?" said Kneebone. "He've got plenty."

"My brother knows nothing of my connection with the Trade, and would not countenance it if he did," said Ortho. "Agh!" Pressing down on his pencil the point had snapped. "Lend me your knife, Ben."

He sharpened the pencil, laid the knife on the table before him and went on counting to himself. "Fifty-four beasts. They'll come in to-morrow night and be hid away in the farms close at hand. On the night of the twenty-fifth they'll be loaded as fast as the stuff comes ashore and sent off, half to you, Andrawartha, and half to you, Kneebone. The goods that can't be handled at once will be stowed in Monk's Cove and sent you later. Anything else?"

"The Preventive," said Andrawartha. "Supposing they get word of the run?"

"At the first sign of a raid the furze will be lit on Black Carn," said Ortho. "Then the luggers can slip their cables and the rest scatter. But there won't be any raid—that is, not on the south coast. The raid will be on the north coast, on Hayle river."

Kneebone craned forward. "How do 'e know?"

Ortho spun the knife in the air, caught it deftly by

the handle. "Because I've been to some pains and expense to get my esteemed friend Bowes to place his confidence in the writings of a certain 'Honest Man.' 'Honest Man' has written to Mr. Bowes from time to time telling him where certain trifles of contraband might be discovered, and every time Mr. Bowes has found it to be even as written. Mr. Bowes will now dispatch his forces exactly where 'Honest Man' tells him to—and that'll be to Hayle river on the night of the twenty-fifth."

Ortho lounged back in his chair, spinning the knife higher and higher, faster and faster. It glittered viciously in the candle-light. He caught it on his palm, gave it a twitch and it ran up his forearm; jerked his elbow and caught the falling blade in his gold-laced cuff, shook it out again and went on juggling. Four pairs of eyes watched his movements with uneasy fascination.

"A sweet little cut-throat, Ben," he drawled, "nicely balanced. I could do anything with this. Years ago when I was eating time in St. Lucia woods I learnt to throw a knife, Spanish fashion—nothing else to do. At twenty paces I could hit any mark to within an inch. Very useful, quieter 'n a pistol. Strikes like a snake, smooth and deadly."

"Put it away, Cap'n," Andrawartha grumbled.

"Aye," said Kneebone. "Put it up."

"Put it up? Why, certainly," Ortho's eyes, sparkling mischievously, danced round the room and stopped at the door. Some artist had been exercising his talent in chalk on the upper panel, the grotesque figure of a man with a cocked hat on its turnip head, brandishing a sword at the end of an attenuated arm. Underneath, in case there should be no mistake, was scrawled the word "BONEY."

"See that image up there?"

Four pairs of eyes swung towards it.

Ortho spat on the blade, gave his wrist a jerk,

' Thud ! '—the knife was two inches deep in the panel, piercing the chalk figure just above the belt.

" My hand don't appear to have lost much of its cunning," said Ortho. " Well, Andrawartha—anything more on your chest? "

The money-lender wiped his brow with a large, unclean handkerchief.

" Me? . . . Ah, yes, now what was I goin' to say? . . . Ah, yes, have you heard anything about a squadron of dragoons in Camborne? "

" I have. They're not a squadron but a half troop only, and they've been the best part of a fortnight loitering down from Plymouth. They're flying ribbands and banging a drum."

Andrawartha nodded, reassured. " Oh, recruiters are they? That's all right. I thought I'd ask."

" Is there anything more you'd like to ask? The luggers are at sea, the boatmen ready, the horses bespoke, the Preventive accounted for. Have you got that clear in your minds, all of you? "

There was a general mumble of assent.

" Very well then," said Ortho. " Go and run your blasted cargoes yourselves, for I'll have nothing more to do with you."

Amazed silence gripped the room, then Andrawartha blurted, " Hey, what are 'e sayin' of? Have 'e gone mad? What do 'e mean? Damn my blood ! what do 'e mean? "

Kneebone tried to laugh. " Mean—he don't mean nawthin'. He's having his fun—aren't 'e, Cap'n? " His voice implored Ortho to admit it was only a joke. Even Bosanko looked startled; now that he was cooling he remembered that he still had shares in the *Elizabeth and Sarah*.

" Only his fun," Kneebone cackled. " He, he ! "

" Not on this occasion," said Ortho. " Run upon run I've put through for you. Thousands of kegs have been landed on this coast since I've been at the head,

with the loss of what?—not one in thirty. You've
lined your pockets deep through me. Hardly a night
have I been in bed these months past, riding the country
in your business, fooling Bowes and his gaugers, seeing
to the landings, steering the pack-trains through.
Now I'm told that I'm nothing but a clopping old
blow-hard, that I've played the bully too long, that
I . . ."

Kneebone interrupted. "No, no! Listen a
minute. . . ."

"Hold your tongue!" Ortho roared. "I am even
accused of treachery, of being party to the capture of
the *Who's Afraid*, though what my object could have
been God only knows. Howsoever, I'll trouble you
with my blowing and bullying no longer. You can
do the work for yourselves and the devil take you!"

Andrawartha hove his stout carcass out of his chair
and waddled across the room, hands upraised. "Cap'n
Penhale, sir, don't take no notice of what Zeb said in
the heat of the moment. He didn't mean it. Lost
his cutter . . . brother wounded . . . smarting some
'ot. We'd trust you with our lives, wouldn't us,
Isaac?"

Kneebone nodded vehemently.

"Trust you with everything," Andrawartha babbled
on. "I'm sure we're brearly grateful for what you've
done, and you'll do us the justice to say we've paid 'e
well for it. Keep it up, Cap'n, and maybe we could
manage to pay a bit more . . . just a bit. What
d'you say, Isaac?"

"I'm willing," said Kneebone, adding with a groan,
"I *must* have them goods."

"You're a bit late with your offer, you perishing
skinflints," said Ortho. "I'm finished."

Baragwanath arose, propping himself on his crutch.
"Hold on, let me have a word. Zeb here may have
spoke a bit hot just now, but seem me that ain't the
only reason the Cap'n have got for throwing us over so

sudden. I've sailed wid 'e many years and far, and
I never saw you turn tail before, sir—leave alone from
the jealousy of one smarting fool. There's another
reason behind this, sir. What it is I don't know and
don't care. But, with all respect, I tell 'e that thee
canst not throw it up. Andrawartha and Kneebone
and Bosanko here don't matter, they've made plenty
money and it won't hurt 'em to lose some. It's the
men at sea I'm thinking on, the crews of two luggers
running straight for this coast in the certain trust that
you, Cap'n Penhale, are standing by to see 'em through.
Whose word is everybody waiting on? Why, yours.
Do you think a single pack-horse would move at Luke's
orders, or Kneebone's, or mine—at this time o' day?
Do you think the Cove-men would shift an oar? Not
they! ' Where's the Cap'n? ' they'd ask. 'Throwed
it up? Deserted we? My gor! there must be black
doings afoot! Send the horses home quick! Pull
the boats up! Get thee to house, Jan and Tom, home
and lie quiet!'—and what'll happen to they luggers
then? There was speech of treachery just now where
none was, but seem me we were not so far off after all."
He swept a scornful hand over the company. " I'm
not one of these trying only to make money out of 'e.
I'm callin' to 'e as an old shipmate and an old friend,
and I tell 'e that thee canst not do it."

Ortho recognized immediately that he could not.
He must see this run through. He cared little whether
Andrawartha and Kneebone, those fat money-grubbers,
swallowed his pretext or not, but his ex-gunner was
another matter. Ben Baragwanath and the men at
sea, he could not play them false. He could not
honourably withdraw at that time of day.

" You're right, Ben," he said. " I hadn't thought
of that side of it. I'll see this run through—but it's the
last, mind you. After this you'll have to shift for
yourselves."

Andrawartha uttered a long sigh of relief. " Oh,

we'll see about that later on," said he, winking. " A
bit extra on each keg, eh, Cap'n? "

" Aye, we'll persuade him right enough," Kneebone
smirked, trying to look very generous and genial.
" Well, I don't suppose there's anything more to say—
eh? "

" Nothing that I know of."

" The twenty-fifth, then—weather serving. If it
don't, the first night after."

" Correct."

" Well, good-night to 'e, Cap'n."

" 'Night."

Baragwanath hopped out of the room, followed by
Andrawartha and Kneebone. Bosanko slouched after
them. As he reached the door Ortho called to him :

" Hold hard. I want a word with you alone."

The shipwright slewed about, scowling. " What is
it? "

" That knife jiggery just now was for your benefit,"
said Ortho. " If Lieutenant Trevaskis comes by any
foul play I'll knife you. You won't hear it coming
nor see where it comes from. You'll be walking down
some dark lane one of these nights and all of a sudden
you'll feel that knife go home between your shoulder-
blades, and after that I shall come along and rip you
end for end—see? "

" What's Trevaskis to you? "

" I told you I'll have no murder."

" Tell that to the capstan ! There's something
behind this, as Ben Baragwanath says. I believe . . ."

Ortho waved him aside. " Your beliefs are of no
interest to me. But remember, harm one hair of his
head and I'll teach you what pain is. I may be lame
and I may be old, but, as the saw has it, ' A young dog
for running, but an old dog for cunning.' Now go to
hell ! "

He listened to Bosanko's heavy boots clumping down
the stairs and then sat staring at the candle. In three

days' time he would have made his last run—what
then? Farming? Plodding the Bosula acres behind
his sloven oxen, day after day, week after week, year
after year, until one day he could plod no further and
was carried, still more slowly, up to that cold Penhale
vault in Gwithian. Visions of the past swept before
him, days of thrill and wonder. His squadron charging
home at Beni Mezdin; the thunder of four hundred
hooves, black stallion flecked with foam, mad with
excitement, his wild Askar troopers tossing their bloody
lances. The French fleet forming line off Dominica,
the foam sparkling at their cut-waters, their sails like
towers of ivory. The *Charming Helen* running down
the Trade, running like a fallow deer, leaping and
trembling; Barbadoes rising over the sea-line, green
and purple. Great days, high moments—all over now.
Ghosts passed before him, men and women, in silent
procession. Nicholas Buzza, King of the Free Traders,
with his silver hair and clerical black. Pyramus Herne,
the Romany, looking like an Assyrian prince. Osman
Baki, the Turkish adventurer, cynical and true. Oko
Ephraim squatting on his kingly stool, a bronze
Bacchus. Ben MacBride in his blue sea-coat teaching
the parrot to pray. Old ' Parson ' Pentacost in his
wool cap.

And the women, a host of them, bright-eyed and
cherry-lipped, white-skinned and golden. The sweet,
sleek, purring wanton who had been his first love, up
in the April lanes above Bosula. Schems-ed-dah and
Ourida, henna-stained, silken rustling. The Creole
of St. Lucia, ghostly in the blue night, the fireflies
sparkling round her. Bianca dancing among candles
to imagined music. Where were they now? The lusty
men were dead, the fair women dead or withering, the
bright eyes dim, the ripe lips shrunken. So short a
thing is life, beauty but a breath !

It seemed only yesterday that he was a boy, gay and
ardent, with all time before him—now there were but

three days.   He could have gone forth upon the house-tops like some dissolute seer and shrieked across the land, not ' Watch and pray,' but ' Sing, dance, drink, gamble, plunder ! for to-morrow you'll be old, old ! ' . . . Three days more. . . .

He snuffed the candle, limped down the stairs and out into the street.

CHAPTER XXII

" WIND seems to be settling in, sir," said the *Snapper's* mate. " West abouts."

" West sou'-west, and hardening," said Trevaskis. " Have to take in a reef before long. Can you make out the Brisons? "

The man peered into the darkness to port. " No, sir, can't see 'em. But to my belief they're on the quarter. That sprinkle of lights up there are the mine houses on Cape Cornwall, I think."

" Hm-m." Trevaskis stepped up to the helmsman. " Keep her up as close as she'll go . . . That'll do."

The look-out hailed : " Longships light, sir ! "

" Where away? "

" Dead ahead."

" Sure? Sure it's not a vessel."

" No, sir. Too steady."

The lieutenant cursed under his breath. If the Longships really lay dead ahead he would have to tack, and that meant more delay. Going forward he found the look-out was right.

He consoled himself with the thought that it was not yet midnight, and once round the Land's End the fair wind would send him bowling into Monk's Cove. The luggers, deep loaded, could hardly get clear before dawn.

It was the night of June the twenty-fifth. On the morning of the twenty-fourth he had taken the *Snapper* round to the north coast. All day he had been plying off and on, keeping his sail just in sight of any possible watchers. At dusk he had swung his bowsprit westward and piled on all canvas. At dusk that same evening Frederick Dearborn had mounted his roan horse and clattered demonstratively northwards at the head of his riders—northwards as far as Badger's Cross only. There he would be met by the dragoons, their drums and ribbons tossed aside, and the whole party circle back to the Keigwin valley by a system of obscure lanes. Within two hours Trevaskis himself would be anchored between Pedn Boar and Black Carn, blocking Monk's Cove from the sea. The nut-crackers were closing. None of the accidents Trevaskis prayed for had come to pass. Bowes' patience and genius for detail were about to meet their inevitable reward. In two hours' time Ortho Penhale would be either captured or flying for his life; happy Roswarva stricken, humbled to the dust.

Trevaskis conned his vessel onwards skilfully, iron cold. He could not help his sweetheart, his friends or himself. Relentless circumstance was master of them all.

The Longships light showed clearer, he must be close on the Shark's Fin. Dare he attempt to run the passage between the reef and the Land's End? In that darkness, no; clearing the Kettle's Bottom might bring him foul of the Armed Knight, or vice versa, the channel was sown with rocks and ravelled with twisting tide rips. Even with the delay tacking would cause he could still catch the easterly drift.

He put the *Snapper* over on the port tack and went below to look at a chart. Past the Longships, then south-east by the compass for four miles till he had cleared the Runnelstone—then in. He glanced at the clock. Five minutes to twelve. If the wind held steady he could be in position by two o'clock with ease. Bowes had given him till three. He had an hour's margin, everything was working smoothly to the tragic end.

A man brought him a mug of tea. He had to be careful how he drank it, the cutter was plunging so heavily. Her sturdy framework groaned in labour, she was alive with small protesting voices, squeaks, grunts, long-drawn whines, of plank working against plank, beams screwing at their sockets, trennels straining. On a shelf two china cups clicked together as she scended, clicked again as she pitched. The lantern swung forwards and back, drawing steely gleams from the arms-racks. Water burst in dull explosions against her sawing bows, swished and tumbled along her sides, gurgled under her counter.

The sea was rising. Would it interfere with operations at Monk's Cove? Trevaskis thought not, not immediately. The great Twelve Apostles reef and Pedn Boar headland protected the Cove on the westward. The luggers would find safe riding for hours yet. There was no hope to be looked for in that direction, in any direction.

The master's mate hailed him down the companion hatch : " Ship ahead of us, sir."

" Far? "

" No, sir, close aboard. Right athwart our hawse."

" Why didn't you tell me before? "

" Only just seen her, sir."

Trevaskis went on deck and saw the stranger's light close ahead, lifting and drooping.

" Looks to be on the starboard tack, heading south "; then to the steersman he said : " Carry on. We should pass under her stern. Show a light forward ! "

Immediately came a hail from the vessel : " Ahoy . . what ship . . . that? "

" His Majesty's cutter *Snapper* ! "

The voice replied at length. What it said Trevaskis could not distinguish, but it sounded excited.

" What's the matter with him? " he asked his mate.

" Heard something about ' water,' sir. Couldn't get the rest."

The voice broke into fresh howlings, no less unintelligible.

" All I got out of that was ' for Christ's sake,' "
said the mate. " Some perishing coaster lost his way
and wants to know where he is, most like. I've
known 'em hail you off St. Catherine's and ax you if
it's the Eddystone; I have, s'welpm' god ! "

Trevaskis got his speaking trumpet from the companion hatch. " Coming-up-astern-of-you ! " he
shouted.

The strange craft was vaguely discernible now, a
small coasting brig wallowing sluggishly along under
reefed topsails and some rags of headsail.

" Looks very dead," Trevaskis commented.

" Overloaded," said the mate. " Them pinch-
pennys will load a craft till she runs at the hawse-
holes." He evidently had small opinion of the coasting
trade.

The *Snapper* rounded up under the brig's square
stern and hung there shaking. Trevaskis hailed again :
" Now what is it ? "

The voice shrieked in reply : the brig was the
Young Harry, Llanelly to Plymouth. She had sprung
a leak off Pendeen Wra and the water was gaining
on them.

" Very well, get your boat over and come to me,"
Trevaskis shouted. " I'll haul up to wind'ard and
give you a lee. Hurry ! "

But the brig master did not want to abandon ship.
The water was gaining, nevertheless he thought he
could keep his craft afloat until he got round into
Mount's Bay and there beach her. He wanted the
cutter to stand by in case he could not.

This met with a flat refusal. He must abandon
ship or be left to his fate.

The man whined, cursed and implored. The
wretched brig was his property and sole means of
livelihood. What was the blank blank navy for except
to protect merchant-men ? He threatened to report
the lieutenant for neglect of duty, even tried to bribe

him. Trevaskis was adamant. He must come now or never.

The man protested afresh, his boat would not swim.

Trevaskis offered to send his, only he must know immediately. Which was it to be?

The Welshman, after further ravings, decided to take his chance.

From the clamour that arose it seemed that members of his crew were not so hardy. The steady clunk-clunk of the pump stopped, other voices broke out whimpering, scared. But the tenacious master swamped them in a torrent of high-pitched Gaelic, drove them back to their work. The clunk of the pump started again, slowly.

" For the last time, are you coming? " Trevaskis roared.

" No ! " followed by a valedictory stream of abuse.

The cutter filled away.

Twenty minutes later, abreast of the Longships lighthouse, the mate touched Trevaskis on the arm.

" A flare, sir," said he, pointing north. " The water's beat 'em."

" Let 'em sink," said the lieutenant, pacing forward, then back again. The Welshman had had their chance, they had refused to be taken off and must abide by the consequences, damned fools !—He *must* get on. They were probably lying when they said their boat wouldn't swim, let them take it to and get ashore at Sennen. At the back of his mind he knew that no boat could get into Sennen with that westerly sea running. The flare caught his eye, a despairing flicker in the darkness astern. He turned his back on it. They had had their chance—few people got even that—damned fools ! Poor devils !—clinging to the swept poop, praying, whimpering, staring terrified into eternity. Could he leave them on the lurch ? Bowes stood in dire need of him also. Always the cleft stick !

He looked at his watch by the binnacle light,

estimated his distance from the flare. There was still an hour's margin. Could he possibly do both, save those poor fools and get to Bowes in time? An hour . . . the wind was still increasing, backing into the west . . . married men probably, with children.

" Stand by to go about ! " he growled.

When he reached the brig her main-deck was awash, and even then the captain wanted to return for an old sextant. An hour and half's delay the rescue cost him, and he stove his own boat badly into the bargain.

It was ten minutes to three before he saw the Runnelstone breaking close under his port hand and he had still four miles to go.

The *Snapper*, under the big square-sail, was driving dead before the wind, running as she had never run before, but by no possible chance could he be in time. There was the Twelve Apostles to round.

Trevaskis could only pray that Bowes would hold his hand, allow him an extra half-hour—but there was little hope of it, he had had ample allowance already. At three o'clock, perforce, the Collector would pounce and, no matter what happened on shore, the luggers would slip away. Dearborn and his battered old plugs would do their part, the dragoons theirs, only he, Trevaskis, would be lacking. There would be talk after this. ' Could have caught the lot if that Trevaskis had come up in time.' ' Why didn't he? ' ' Says he stopped to assist a Welsh collier, but that's all my eye and Betty Martin—he's engaged to Penhale's niece.'

Heartily did Trevaskis curse the five shivering castaways being coaxed back to animation in the *Snapper's* foc's'le. Why had he been so weak as to return for them? Of what value were their miserable lives compared with the honour of the Service?

He drove the cutter on and on, past black cliffs fringed with booming surf.

Five minutes past three—he must be off Treen

Dinas. Another two miles only. He went forward of the mast and peered ahead. Any sign of alarm? Flare, gun-flash, anything? Nothing; blank darkness transversed by leaping grey ridges of foam. He took the look-out by the shoulder and bawled into his ear : " Keep your eyes skinned for a sudden fire over yonder, on the end of Black Carn—see? " and reeled aft again, white water swirling about his ankles.

" Got about all she'll carry, sir," said the mate, anxiety in his voice. " Pull the backstays out of her."

" Let her pull," said Trevaskis. A quarter past three, off Mertha now, the Twelve Apostles close ahead, he could hear the surf roaring over the reef, it bayed like a great beast, hungry for meat. Another ten minutes and he'd be past it, rounding into the Cove, the luggers under his guns. He launched a dumb prayer to Bowes to hold his hand for another ten minutes, ten minutes only !

Twenty past three. A shout came from forward; the reef was before them, he must yaw seaward a trifle to clear it.

He beckoned the mate. " All hands to quarters, Mister. As soon as I round up, let go the anchor, cast loose your starboard guns, take the tompions out and stand by. I expect. . . ."

" Fire, sir ! "

" Hold hard ! " He sprang forward. Black Carn was afire, a red blaze leaping, gale-fanned against the pale omen of dawn. Bowes had pounced. In a minute or two the luggers would have cut and gone racing like stags to the eastward, he lumbering after them in a hopeless stern chase.

There was but one crazy chance. In an instant he was back at the stern, had thrust the helmsman aside and taken the tiller himself. The cutter swung not seaward but landward.

" Sir ! " the mate sprang towards him, gesticulating

wildly. " For God's safe ! The reef ! We're on top of it. . . . Christ Almighty ! "

" I'm going to cut the corner, run the inside passage," said Trevaskis. " Stand back ! "

The Twelve Apostles lay about a quarter of a mile off Pedn Boar. Inside them was a split rock known as the Minstrel, inside that again lay the Carracks, a half-tide ledge; but between these last and the shore was a deep-water channel, a hundred yards across. The Cove boats used it regularly—in daylight and fair weather.

It was for this Trevaskis headed. If he made it the luggers were his. If he did not—he had no time to think of that.

Landwards he swung, towards the towering cliffs. Breakers thundered and sobbed over the ledges, the cliffs rang with echoed thunder, the flooded caverns gulped and belched and bellowed.

Trevaskis held on and on. The Apostles showed on his starboard quarter, a hill of raving surf, breaker piling upon breaker. On his beam the Minstrel spouted like a whale through its split mouth, whistling as it spouted. Nearer to the cliffs he held, nearer and nearer.

He must have cleared the Carracks by now, but he could not see, could not hear; his eyes were filled with stinging spindrift, his ears with thunder. Nearer and nearer.

The flying mist flawed for a second, he saw the cliffs looming over him immense and imminent.

There was a yell from forward, the mate launched towards him, arms uplifted. " Oh, my God ! *Over !* "

He put the tiller over. The cutter came round on her heel and shot forward, the current thrusting, swirling under her counter. He had found the passage ! The cutter shot through it, tide-borne, sucked like a chip on a gutter—Crash !

The tiller kicked like a horse, Trevaskis went over it,

doubled up, down on his face on deck. He felt the *Snapper* rise under him, lurch forward, free, crash again, grinding and shuddering from stem to stern. A wave bounced over the taffrail, over him, and swept her entire length, rail high, washing men headlong before it.

CHAPTER XXIII

THREE o'clock and all going smoothly. The sudden rise of wind was unlooked for, but, though the increasing sea hampered the boatmen, they were getting the goods ashore. Half an hour and the luggers would be emptied. Ortho glanced to the east. The sky was perceptibly brightening. All the pack trains, with the exception of twelve horses, had long since gone, but there was still a large amount of stuff lying about on the slip-head. He was anxious to get it stowed away before light broke, so that anybody looking down on Monk's Cove from the hills above might see an innocent fisher hamlet arising cheerfully to face the honest toil of day and little guess its labours of the night.

He did not fear any prying eye—were not Frederick Dearborn and his stalwarts crouching among the Hayle sand dunes fifteen miles away in somewhat outworn expectancy? He laughed when he thought of Frederick Dearborn stalking, stealthy as a Cherokee, through the empty sand-hills—but a good general considers all possible contingencies. Now that his smuggling career was over he looked back upon it and congratulated himself on being a very good general. He was afraid that posterity would allot Nicholas Buzza first place, but it could hardly deny him second. He had run enormous quantities of contraband at great local profit and with but a single considerable mishap—the capture of the *Who's Afraid*—for which he was in no wise to blame. Now that he was retiring they would discover his worth. He supposed that clumsy hot-head Bosanko would take his place. Bosanko, i'faith!

He had as much tact as an eighteen-pounder carronade. Ortho could imagine *him* wheedling horses from apprehensive farmers, smoothing over the fisher people's eternal feuds, inventing fresh ruses for the delectation of Bowes and Co. More went to good generalship than the rank and file knew of. But they would know presently, when Bosanko messed things, crews fell out, horses failed to materialize and warring families betrayed each other. His name would be exalted in those days, the minor catastrophe of the *Who's Afraid* forgotten. ' Nick Buzza he lost norra tub, I've heard tell—nor Ortho Penhale. They were the kings of the coast, the old captains. Don't see their like now.'

Bracketed with the great ' King Nick ' he would be, in time. He'd see that he was, even if he had to pay for it. A subsidy to some of those ' droll-tellers,' the strolling bards of the West, and they'd compose a heroic ballad of his exploits and sing it far and wide. He might even have it printed at ' The Temple of the Muses,' Helston, and flood the country with broadsheets.

But light was waxing and the slip-head still covered with goods. The stowers idled, yawning, wearied by the labours of a busy night. Ortho hailed them, dropping into the colloquial " Come on, my busy bees, one more effort ! Hasten thee ! Dawn's blinking yonder. Get this lot stowed and there'll be a drop of hot for one and all up to Kiddlywink. My stars ! Look upon Uncle Zack, eighty-four and slinging three tubs to once ! More power an' might to 'e, my old beauty ! He'd put to shame some o' you younkers. Rozzy boy, that's no way to heft a bale—on to your knee first, then with a twist to your shoulder. That's the sort, Selena May ! good as a couple o' men, you are. Want any help with that barrel ? "

The girl grinned at him. " Lord love 'e, no. I could handle six o' these."

" Believe you could. You're a well-grown 'un, i'
facks ! I wish I were younger—an' free."

" Seem me you're plenty free enough as 'tis, Cap'n."

Ortho laughed, " Ah, ha, smartly said, Miss Sauce ! "
and took her gently by the chin. " You've got bra'
pretty little ears—like sea-shells they are, pink and
pearly. Believe I could find a pair of silver rings that'd
set 'em off very stylish. . . . D'e know I've a good
mind to kiss 'e? "

" Well, I aren't strugglin'."

" Too many folk about now, my jewel. I'd have
John Thomas Kitto dropping his work and racin'
after me with a conger gaff. I'll come and help 'e
stow that barrel in a minute and then we'll see."

A minute later he was assuring another girl that her
neck reminded him of a swan's and promising her a
coral necklace for it.

The ladies shot adoring glances after the raffish
figure in the gold-laced coat and toiled with a will.

Ortho passed on, exhorting, flattering, jesting, and
reached the ' Admiral Anson ' Inn. The last string of
pack-horses stood before it, loaded, ready to go. A
noise of wrangling arose among the leaders.

Ortho broke in upon them. " Here, why haven't
you gone? What's the matter? "

" I demands as how I ought to be cap'n. I was
sixty-six year come Paul feast, while this here forthy
pattick Simon Jago eddn no more'n sixty. I got more
ancient wisdom in my old thumb than . . ."

" Don't care if you're sixty-six nor yet six thousand.
I got five horses here en' you eddn no more'n three,
you old lobba you ! "

" Hold thy clack, both of 'e," said Ortho. " Peter
Trezize goes as cap'n. He's a mere babe of fifty, but
for all that he's a St. Just man and knows the road
better'n both of you. Ahoy, Peter ! It'll be light soon,
so stop at Boquio till to-morrow nigh.. Tell John
Prowse I sent you. Understand? "

" Yezzur."

" Then get along now for mercy's sake ! "

Ortho turned back towards the sea. The last
string of horses had gone, the last boat-loads would be
in before long; his last run was over. Finished the
hazard, the riot and the fun, the high days, the tense-
strung nights, the roaring carousals that celebrated
success. What now? Smuggling was shut to him.
The Guinea traffic wilting under fire of national disgust. Moreover, he had done with the slave trade.
Memories of the *Charming Helen* becalmed in the tropics,
her tween-decks stuffed with dying negroes, haunted
him still. Privateering? More ghastly visions rose;
the *Ghost's* last fight off Finisterre, her decks a shambles,
the dismounted gun lying across its mangled crew—
ugh !

What then? Home to bed. That was the end of
the story. In a few minutes his last run would be over,
dwindling ingloriously out, and he would limp slowly
up valley to the Owls' House—home to bed.

He yawned " Heigho ! " For twenty-four hours he
had not had his boots off or one minute's rest. Some
of his wounds were beginning to twitch, which always
occurred when he was tired. Bed would not be so
distasteful after all—proper place for an old man.
" Heigho ! " Abruptly he halted, his head thrown
back. What was that?

A cavalry trumpet braying clear and shrill, waking
brazen echoes in the hill-side. If he had heard the
whole angelic host in full song with harp accompani-
ment he could not have been more astonished. What
the devil? Who in Monk's Cove had a cavalry
trumpet and why this outburst? As he puzzled he
knew that no rustic lips could blow with such clarity,
it was professional.

His reason said ' Soldiers ! ' His conceit argued,
' How can it be? They're at Camborne—or else
Hayle. Damme ! I've been tricking Bowes, haven't

I? Not Bowes *me*'—refusing to admit that there
could be his superior in chicanery. He stood gaping.

A babel of shouts arose in the direction of the
' Admiral Anson ' and a terrified boy went scuttling
by shrieking, " The Riders—Dragoons ! They got
my Dad. Oh, they got my Daddy ! "

Dragoons ! So Bowes was the cleverer after all.
His last run was not to be uneventful, it was to end in
crushing disaster. The final laugh would be with the
derided Collector.

Ortho woke up, pulled his wits together, determined
to mitigate that merriment as far as possible.

The luggers ! If the Preventive riders had returned
from Hayle, presumably the *Snapper* had also. Bowes
was not the man to bolt the front door and leave the
back open. Probably the cutter was at that moment
anchoring between the headlands. Even so the
luggers must be given their chance, the fire-watcher
on Black Carn signalled. He hurried to the slip-head
as fast as his lame leg would let him, to find the staunch
Selena May atop of a barrel brandishing the red
lantern.

" Good girl, brave lass ! I'll give 'e gold earrings
instead of silver—an' I live !" He cheered, and
whirled on the dazed stowers, waving his arms at them
like a man driving sheep. " Don't stand there gawking !
Scatter, for God's sake ! Get to cliff ! Go home, bar
the door, jump into bed as you stand ! Spring to it !
I'll cover you as long as I can. Hurry ! "

Up the alley towards the inn he hobbled, dragging
his pistols free, cocking them. Of a sudden he was in
the midst of it. A boy cornet dashed round the corner
of a sail-yard, yelping, sword in hand; from the
opposite side came a trooper and an exciseman, the
battered Andrew. Ortho blazed to right and left.
The trio broke back, the trooper wounded in the
shoulder. The cornet gave tongue excitedly : " Here !
An armed fellow here ! Sergeant, cut round to the

left and take him on the flank. To the left, behind
that wall ! "

Then Bowes' high-pitched voice : " Penhale for a
certainty. Five pounds to the man who takes him
alive."

Ortho backed round the corner of the shed. That
would steady the rush, make 'em deploy. Wanted
him alive, did they? Why alive? To hang, of course,
to make an example of. The law liked its meat fresh.
A chill tremor ran through him. Damme he must not
hang ! The idea of having his handsome body dipped
in tar and suspended from a pole beside some main
waterway till it dropped to bits repelled him far more
than the mode of extinction that preceded it. He did
not want to go down in public memory as a ludicrous
piece of offal rotting at the end of a pole. The small
boys would throw stones at the swinging scarecrow,
the quay trollops jeer, the elegant ladies shudder and
hold their noses . . . Ortho Penhale the magnificent,
the erstwhile knave of hearts !

Hang he would not; if the worst occurred he had his
knife, but suicide would not save his body from sub-
sequent defilement.

Standing brooding while the enemy closed about him
would not help matters either. He fired a pistol round
the corner to embarrass any frontal attack and was off
down the alley-way to the left. The alley was a cul-
de-sac terminated by a six-foot wall. The sergeant
with the flanking party must pass on the other side of
that wall, he knew. As he reached it he heard the
jingle of a spur and someone whisper hoarsely, " Come
on ! "

Stones lay at the foot of the wall, heavy round stones
with iron hooks in them, used for pilchard crushing.
Ortho picked up one of these and hove it over the
wall on top of the whisperer, followed quickly by a
second.

A yelp of pain and the clatter of retreating boots

told him that his missile had done good work. Off
he went to the opposite flank.

For ten minutes he was at it, hop-skipping up this
alley way and down that, climbing over walls and
roofs, wriggling through holes and up gutters, appearing where he was least expected, firing, reloading,
thoroughly happy, his fears and anxieties cast aside,
a mischievous and merry boy again, playing a tricksy
game of hide and seek, the more perilous the more
enjoyable. Monk's Cove, cowering in bed with its
boots on, heard the shouts of the troopers outside, the
thud of their sabres on doors, heard their shouts:
" There he goes ! . . . there y' are ! " Spurts of
pistol fire leapt across the dark window-panes; bullets
wailed eerily. Standing astride Zion Kitto's thatch,
Ortho espied three excisemen creeping down the
passage below, and flinging his weight against the
loose stone chimney sent half of it crashing on top of
them. Zion Kitto, feverishly disrobing under the
counterpane, thought the end of the world had come.

Cornered in Seth Treswarna's yard, he seized Seth's
spare mizzen-mast, and using it as a sweep, swept one
dragoon backwards into a brine tub, his companion
into a pilchard well. By the time they had extricated
themselves he was over the wall and gone. When
Dearborn and the cornet crossed the little stone
bridge, Ortho was actually beneath their feet, crouched
double in the conduit, the stream sluicing over him.
The gauger, Mike, smarting from past indignities,
climbed a shed after him. Under their combined
weight the crazy roof collapsed and they were pre-
cipitated into Widow Menhinick's hen-roost. In the
confusion of whirring wings and squawking poultry
Ortho found the door first, kicked it outwards and
escaped. For a merry ten minutes he, single-handed,
kept the raiders diverted, having the advantage of
semi-darkness and an intimate knowledge of his ground.

But light was broadening fast, and despite all delays

the ring was closing. The slip-head was still cluttered
with goods, but the stowers had disappeared. Time
he looked to himself. Ortho fired both his pistols to
his front, saw advancing shadows dodge back among the
houses, then hobbled swiftly westwards for the cliffs as
a sinking fox to its earth.

Too late ! A couple of dragoons sprang in his path,
heading him off.

Both his pistols were empty, remained the knife—
knife against two sabres ! He limped towards the
soldiers, waving excitedly in the direction of a pilchard
press. " Here ! This way ! He's in here—quick ! "
Audacity carried the day, audacity and gold lace.
The smugglers previously encountered by those two
troopers had been common fishermen garbed in tarry
smocks and the roughest homespuns. When this
commanding person in gold lace sprang upon them
they took him to be some superior sort of Excise
officer. They had been trained to obey gold lace. He
ordered them into the pilchard press and they obeyed
automatically. When, a second later, they heard the
door slam on them they realized that they had encountered no less a person than the notorious Penhale.

In the meanwhile the notorious Penhale was
hobbling up the cliff towards Pedn Boar for dear life,
stumbling, tumbling, scrambling along on hands and
knees, wriggling on his stomach from bracken patch to
bracken patch and boulder to boulder. Under Chapel
Rock he fell exhausted, lay tearing at the flowery
thrift with convulsive fingers, his empty lungs gasping
cruelly. He had escaped for the moment, but he had
no illusions about his position. He was a marked
man now. He had been caught red-handed in a penal
offence and had, moreover, resisted the law officers by
force of arms, wounding at least a couple and stunning
as many more.

Henceforward he would be hunted like vermin from
hole to corner and pillar to post. Never again would

he see the Owls' House, Eli, Jennifer or Mary—or Mary. Never again would he ride his jaunty bay mare down Chapel Street, casting bold eyes at the ladies in the bow windows. Never again could he swagger into country taverns, lash the drink about and hear unctuous yokels whisper, " That's Penhale the priva- teersman, that is; him that took the great Dutch Indiaman and was general in Barbary."   He realized that never again could he be what he prized and admired above all else, Ortho Penhale. Even if he escaped he must go for the rest of his life under an assumed name, his flaming past a secret, himself a fugitive, skulking in unpeopled countries, cut off from loved ones and native land. Some words of his old mate, MacBride, returned to him : " Aye, laugh away ! laugh hearty ! Some day your luck 'll turn and you won't laugh so loud. You'll make some little slip and be over a cliff that you can't climb." He was over it now.

Reloading his pistols he crawled on westwards to- wards Pedn Boar. That disused mine adit where he had hidden MacBride, he must reach that somehow. Later he could get in touch with Eli and make plans for escaping abroad. Where? The United States, he thought. They spoke English there, were English stock. But what he would do for a living he did not know. He was over fifty, lame and broken. He had failed in everything—but one; failed in love, neglected his home, lost his ships, his crews, and had now, finally, brought ruin on Monk's Cove and dishonour on his family. For the first time in his career he laid the blame, not on that easy scapegoat, Fate, but on himself. He had lacked mental stamina, the power to endure the irksome task. He had lacked perception, grasping always the glitter for the gold, but beyond everything he had been too clever; the love of trickery, the contempt for more obvious fellow-beings and the passion for outwitting them had been his undoing. In the bitter hour of defeat he realized that in the great things of life he had outwitted nobody but that poor dupe—himself. He was not far from regeneration in that hour—when it was too late. He crawled painfully on, iron in his soul, agony in his leg. The Cove was empty, he noticed, the luggers at least had got clear.

What a crash ! That last pack train was captured, of course, and probably all the loaders in front of the ' Anson '—a dozen at least. There would be further arrests made when Bowes searched the cottages. What a collapse ! There would be no laudatory ballads written about him now; he would go down to posterity as organizer of the greatest disaster the coast had seen. Had not the law desired his destruction he would have hurled himself over the cliff there and then. Perversity kept him going.

Reaching the top of Pedn Boar, he propped himself against a rock and looked back to see if there were any pursuers in view. There were none; Bowes was busy in the cottages, doubtless, thinking to take him at his leisure.

" Hist, Cap'n . . . Cap'n Ortho ! "

Ortho spun about and saw Benbow Baragwanath's rusty head up-thrust between tossing foxglove spires.

Ortho dropped his pistol. " Oh, it's you . . . so you got away."

" 'Es. I was standin' back o' the Kiddlywink when the trumpet blawed, and cleared ovver the wall with Rodney and young Peter Treswarna here. They helped me up the hill."

" What are you going to do ? "

" Slip ovver to Reub Nicholas' place for to fix an alibi—soon as I've got my breath. I'll go back later on. They didn't see me and they won't find nawthin' in the ' Anson.' But what about you, sir ? It's you they're after."

" I'm going into hiding. My brother's in Truro, but 'll be back to-morrow. Get word to him, will you? Just say ' The Old Man ' to him, he'll understand.''

" I'll send word sure 'nough," said Benbow. " Odd rot, but it's a bad business, eh? They must ha' taken the whole passel o' they fellows, outside the Wink, an' it's my opinion they took the other pack trains as well —further out. He's a smart one, that Bowes.''

" He is and he ain't," said Ortho. " He caught us napping ashore I admit, but the luggers got away. He'd forgotten *them*.''

Ben shook his head. " Not he. Go look what the Carracks have caught.''

Ortho shambled to the cliff edge and looked over. He saw great sweeping westerly rollers exploding on the Twelve Apostles in spouts and hillocks of raving surf, stripes of foam writhing to leeward like a tangle of immense serpents, and amidst this boiling turmoil a vessel jammed fast on the inner reef. She was down by the head, bowsprit was gone and topmast, nothing remained but the lower mast, in the shrouds of which men still clung. Seas swept the doomed craft from stern to stem in quick succession, enveloping her, cross-trees high in flying clouds of spray.

Ortho whirled about white in the face, his eyes frantic. " My God ! the King's cutter ! He'll . . . they'll be drowned, drowned ! '' The sentence ended in a cracked wail.

Benbow nodded. " Like rats. Tried to run the passage seemingly. Well, they're gone. She'll smash like an egg when the tide turns.''

Ortho turned upon him. " Hie—give me your crutch.''

" What for ? ''

" I'm going to Monk's Cove to get help. Quick ! ''

" Goin' back to Cove? Are 'e stark mad? If you go back to Monk's Cove, all you get is the gallows. My soul ! are 'e clean off your head? You'll get no crutch of me.''

" Then I'll go on my knees."

Benbow burst through the foxgloves, grabbed him roughly by the coat. " Not while I live. Head 'en off, Roddy ! Peter ! Listen to me; how the hell can you help them? No boat could get near those rocks, if we could launch one, as you well know, and the luggers are gone, half-way to the Lizard by now."

" But he—they *must* be saved I tell you."

" If you can tell me how I'm with you. I wouldn't stand by and see a dog drown if I could help it, leave alone a human being, Preventive or no Preventive." He made a gesture of impatience. " Ach ! but what's the use of this? Nobody can help them now, not God Almighty Himself, and you stand clacking here when thee shouldst be speeding for thy life."

" Let go of my coat ! "

" I'll let go, but if you take one step east'ard I'll trip 'e with my crutch."

Ortho hobbled to the edge and looked over. It was as Benbow said, no boat could approach the rocks, the luggers had gone. If the men jumped overboard they would be beaten to pieces on the ledges.

" Come here," he called.

The gunner obeyed. " Well? "

" If a rope were rigged from that shelf to masthead we could sling 'em ashore clear of the surf."

Benbow spat. " Sure we could. And who's going to fly across with the rope? A sea-gull?—or maybe you've got wings in your pockets."

" Float one end across tied to a barrel."

" A bar'l won't swim across the current, will it? It'd be sucked through that channel like a cork through a drain. What's the use standing here talking nonsense? I tell you there aren't no way. Now get along wid 'e, for mercy's sake ! "

" A bar'l won't swim across the current." The sentence hitched in Ortho's brain, set him feverishly thinking. ' Swim across the current.' The channel

was not above a hundred yards wide, no distance at
all . . . ' *swim* across. . . .'

" Ben," he said slowly, " If a man, supported by a
couple of those little float barrels—or, better still, net
corks—were to jump off that ledge down there and
swim for dear life, do you think he could carry a line
over? "

The gunner shook his head, " Hell, no ! Cross the
channel he might, a strong swimmer, but once those
rollers caught him against the rocks they'd bang him
to jelly."

" Yes—but his body? "

Benbow selected a bit of grass with care and chewed
it, " Oh, they'd toss his body aboard all right."

" How long before the tide turns? "

" 'Bout an hour."

Ortho rose. " Roddy, run like sin down to the Cove
and fetch all the men and tackle you can find. You
know what I want, a stout line, a light messenger,
plenty of corks and a big sheave-block. Hurry ! "

Benbow looked up, puzzled. " Hold on ! What's
the caper? What are you going to do? "

" Swim a line over—or try to."

" You are? "

" I am."

" You mean it? "

" I do."

" You'll never come back."

" What matter? "

Benbow stood up, cursing emotionally. " By the
Lord ! . . . by the Lord God ! I used to be proud
to serve under you, sir. Of late I've had my doubts,
but now . . . by the Lord Almighty . . . your hand,
sir . . . my old Cap'n."

" Oh, tush ! " said Ortho. " I was done for anyhow, may as well finish kicking."

They clasped hands, stood smiling at each other,
tried companions of adventure on the threshold of the

last, Ortho's black eyes sparkling with the old reckless brilliance. Benbow's brown eyes glowing with reborn faith, wet with tears.

"I made a damned mess of most things, Ben," said Ortho, "but now believe I see a clean way out."

"I've heard the Spaniards tell as how King Richard of England won his right to heaven by one great leap," the gunner replied, "but by the holy, he made no better leap 'n you!" He broke away, blinking. "Roddy, blast your soul! you got your orders. Run, you scum! Fetch 'em up! Every man jack!"

His brother hesitated. "Yes, but how can I? Ain't Bowes got 'em all?"

Ben roared at him. "Tell him his crew is drownin' on the Carracks and Cap'n Penhale is up here waitin' to get 'em off. Tell him every seaman and rope is wanted and watch how quick he sets 'em free. If Monk's Cove saves that cutter's people, Bowes 'll wipe the slate, or I'm much mistook. Now gallop, you anointed whelp!"

Ortho turned to the second lad. "Run up to Roswarva and ask Mrs. Penhale to come down here at once. Mrs. Penhale alone."

.   .   .   .   .   .

Benbow lashed a mat of net floats to Ortho's chest, another to his shoulders, made the light line fast. "By coming up here so far to wind'ard you can allow two foot of drift to every foot of headway and still make it." He turned to the group of fishermen behind him. "Got that main-line spliced?"

"Aye."

Bowes stepped on to the shelf; he was bleeding from a cut above the eye, his nice linen was smirched, his coat torn; he blinked short-sightedly, having lost his spectacles. "Mr. Penhale," he said, "an hour ago I thought I had humbled you; now it is I who am humbled. I will do my utmost for your people. I cannot acquit them off-hand, but I will do the next best thing"—his mouth twitched whimsically—"I will send them before a Cornish jury."

Ortho grinned and, on impulse, thrust his hand out. "Thank you! Now that the game is played shall we part friends? Will you shake?"

"Sir," said Bowes, with feeling, "I am honoured."

"All ready," Benbow whispered, hoarsely.

Ortho, stripped to his shirt and trousers, moved to the edge—a fifteen-foot drop. He must wait till a big breaker came in and go off in the back-wash. He looked back and upwards. All Monk's Cove was on the cliff above, men, women and children, tense, silent, overawed. Here and there were dots of scarlet and blue, dragoons and Preventive men. A glow of satisfaction warmed his breast. In the chill face of death his unconquerable conceit returned as a blessing, to comfort and sustain him. He had a good audience and was in the centre of the stage again, with a star part. Down there in the sweeping seas he would not limp or falter. The soldiers would noise his deed over their beer-pots in the taverns that night and for many nights to come; Penzance would ring with him. Sixty years hence, when those children were old, they would still be telling tales of his last swim—God bless their curly heads! Ballad-mongers would hymn his praise without prompting or subsidy. He would not rank second to Nicholas Buzza, he would have a niche all to himself. All was well! The westerly gale had sprung to his rescue, saving him from dishonour and the terrors of old age, the good west wind that had run like a motif through his life. He had come in on the wind and would go out on it, out and out, away, away.

Cloud shadows fleeting purple-winged over meadows of broken jade and emerald; deep-sea breakers roaring home, spray-maned, foam-marbled. Eastwards, over the Lizard, the brave sun up-leaping. Wind and sea, clamour and fury, wonder and majesty . . . and beauty, everlasting beauty! The clouds were ships, bright wraiths of clippers fleeting under kites and stunsails. The breakers were ghostly squadrons thundering at the charge, the flying foam but the spatter of bits, the blown spray but the glimmer of white burnouses, the toss of silver manes. The boom of the surf was the deep roll of drums, the ringing that of ship bells. The wind blew with the sound of trumpets, piercing, exultant. The phantom clippers dipped their gilded beaks, most stately, the ghostly soldiers tossed their lances, " Come on, old comrade," they cried. " Fear not ! Death is but a pang and life immortal. Ride on with us, ride on for ever ! "

A roller surged over the rock ledges, up and up, wrapping white foam arms about Ortho's knees; spume flakes spattered his bared chest, flecked his black bull curls. He flung both hands towards the rising sun as in salute—and plunged.

CHAPTER XXIV

ELI PENHALE, sitting, black-clad and impassive, in Teresa's great oak chair; Mary facing him across the table, holding herself very straight; Jennifer beside her, tragic-eyed, her soft mouth quivering uncontrolled. At Eli's left hand Nicola, smiling with empty sweetness upon everybody, still lovely, still fragrant as on the evening when Ortho first met her, standing in the mire of Kenneggy Downs. Near the door Naomi and Thomas Davy and other Penhale retainers in their best clothes, stiff as wax-works. Somewhere in the background Benbow Baragwanath, tarred hat in hand, pigtail freshly greased, bringing to that inland place an exotic flavour of the sea. Trebilcock the attorney ('young' Trebilcock now) fumbling with his cravat. The brass-faced clock tic-tocking as it had done throughout their grandparents' lives and would through their children's after them. Evening light piercing the shadows of the Owls' House with a shaft of moted gold. Trebilcock stopped fingering his choker and coughed.

"'To my sometime gunner Benbow Baragwanath of Monk's Cove the flag of the French letter of marque *Diable à Quatre* and the sword of her captain, which ship we took off the Birling Isles on the twenty-third of October, 1799, and was the smartest action we fought (being out-gunned and manned), though we got little by it. To Mr. Montague Teage of Carhilly my bay mare 'Ruby.' He never liked me, but he is a pretty shape on a horse and will do her justice. To my natural son Anthony Trevaskis, lieutenant of His Majesty's Navy, all my moneys, investments and ventures, together with my property of Bosula in the parish of Gwithian, Cornwall, with all buildings, furniture and stock appertaining thereto, on the condition that he keep my wife, Nicola Penhale, in comfort (including two new fashionable dresses yearly) for the term of her life, and in the great hopes that he may some day forgive the past and take the name which is rightly his.

"'To my brother Eli Penhale of Roswarva and Mary his wife (who have endured much of me) my dear love. . . .'"

. . . .

Trevaskis walked out of the kitchen and up the western hill path. He wanted air, to be alone, to think. Foxgloves high on the hedge-sides rang their silent chimes, he did not see them. White-flowered brambles clutched at his sleeve, scratched blood from his hand, he did not notice.

Ortho Penhale was his father! The unknown seducer whose fleeting caprice had brought him into the world to suffer miserable childhood and lonely youth. Other boys had had warm homes to go to in the holidays; fathers who wrote long letters (enclosing money-orders) to forlorn midshipmites on foreign service for the first time; mothers, sisters, aunts who sent comforts and much love. Young Trevaskis had none of these things, no home but where he slung his hammock, no friends but what he made himself. Life had been a stern business from the first. This had bred in him a spirit of laudable but bitter independence. For what benefits he had received in this world he had nobody but himself to thank, he told himself, and so would he continue, beholden to nobody. Now the very man he most detested had first saved his life, then left him all his property. Trevaskis grew red with rage . . . an infernal piece of trickery! Getting him into his debt and then presuming on it! Making him heir to dirty money gained in the filthy slave-trade, by

gin-running and dubious privateering, knowing him
to be hard up and out of luck professionally. Trying
to buy his clean independence with tainted money,
that was the idea. No, by God ! a thousand times
no !

Penhale had jumped into the water as much to
save himself as the cutter's crew. It was that or the
gallows. His courage had been that of despair,
nevertheless he had put a fine polish on it. Trevaskis
could see the indomitable head struggling across the
tide-rip, now lost in a trough, now emerging on a
wave-crest, choked spray-lashed but unfaltering; see it
gathered into the sweep of the breakers and come
home with them, swimming boldly, gaily almost, to
its doom.

Brave?—Ah, yes, gallant beyond words, that little
head pitting itself against the huge, maddened forces
of wind and sea.

The fellow—his father—had spirit. He would pay
homage to his courage always and everywhere, but
further he could not go.

He looked out over the Keigwin valley. Below
him the Bosula woods in full leaf, the pale green of ash,
the darker of elm and sycamore, smoke from the Owls'
House rising thin and straight through enfolding oaks.
In the distance the high moors rolling blue and misty
against the sky; Carn Brea like a lion couchant, its
face to the sunset; Bartinny, Sancreed Beacon,
Galva's notched crest and Ding Dong standing bare
and lonely, a watch-tower to the north. A good place,
a dear land, it tore his heart to leave it, yet go he must.
He would be court-martialled for the loss of the
Snapper, reprimanded and returned to the fleet. His
arm-stump had healed and it was war-time, there was
no longer excuse to be idling alongshore. He must go
again, forsake this green and pleasant country for the
barren sea. ' To my natural son Anthony Trevaskis
. . . my property of Bosula in the parish of Gwithian.

. . .' One word and it could all be his, this singing valley, snuggling remote and secret in the bosom of the hills; all his these fat fields, flowering bogs and bird-haunted coppices; his the ugly old house, the friendly old house.

The evening peace soaked into him like a subtle narcotic. He grew quieter, sat down on a stone gap and stared dreamily over the valley. A wheat-field, yellow with charlock, caught his eye. Scandalous !— letting the land get as dirty as that ! The trash was creeping in too, bracken invading the meadows, blackthorns over-running the hedges. The woods wanted attention as well, the old trees were left till they rotted and fell, the young trees grew crooked for want of light and air. Look at that gate yonder !— an old bed-end propped across the opening with two stones and a broken fork-haft, the gaps filled in with gorse bushes. Wicked !

" The place is going to rack and ruin for want of a little care," said a voice beside him.

It so exactly expressed his thoughts that for the moment Trevaskis did not recognize it as not his own.

" You've just come in time."

" I've just come . . . what ? " Trevaskis turned and saw Mary Penhale ; she must have stopped on her way home to Roswarva.

He rose embarrassed. " Oh, it's you ! . . . How do you mean, ' You've just come in time ? ' "

" To save Bosula."

" Supposing I were to tell you that I would not accept it ? "

Mary shrugged her straight shoulders. " I should not be surprised—and I should not despair."

" Why would you not be surprised ? " Trevaskis asked, somewhat surprised himself.

" Because you are a proud man and hated Ortho, and it is very difficult to accept favours from an enemy."

" It is not altogether a question of pride——" He hesitated. " Shall I speak openly? "

Mary smiled. " I cannot imagine you doing anything else. Please."

"Very well then. To put it plainly, Ortho Penhale —er—my father—was respectively slaver, privateersman and smuggler. I maintain that privateersmen are little better than legalized pirates, and Penhale, though he was never actually caught, had some pretty black scores against him. I do not care a damn for the law as law or who breaks it, but swamping the country with cheap liquor and making drunkards wholesale to line one's own pockets strikes me as a dirty game. As for the Guinea traffic, I have seen something of it at both ends, and there is nothing more detestable on the face of the earth. That is my opinion."

" And mine," said Mary, quietly.

" It is? " He looked straight into her steady brown eyes. " Tell me then, would you have me accept money or property gained in the very three trades we most abhor and denounce? You know very well I cannot, it would be shameless. Wouldn't it? "

" It would—if there were any money."

"What ! But the will said ' all my moneys, investments, ventures. . . .' "

Mary laid a hand on his arm. " My dear, that will is years old. Ortho always banked very royally on hope. He always thought he was going to be rich, immensely rich, but it never happened. There isn't a penny."

" But surely . . . all those ventures? "

" Came to nothing. He returned from the East Indies with fourpence in his pocket, his shoes dropping off, from the West with six shillings and another wound. He made a little profit slaving at first, but his agents defrauded him and failed. Then you appeared."

" I."

" Yes, you. He bought you from your step-father, Trevaskis; paid for your schooling and your upkeep; paid your first captain to take you into the navy, paid you an allowance till you stopped it. Furthermore, he bought Trevaskis out of Joppa and paid the whole family to emigrate to America."

" Why did he do that? "

" So that they should not be an embarrassment to you if you returned here. You were the only son he had, the last Penhale. He always hoped he would win you back somehow, to take his place and carry on the family. It cost him the profits of three voyages to get rid of those Trevaskis people. He actually denied himself to scrape money together. Nicola got her silk dresses as usual, but for himself he almost went shabby, no fine new coats or gold lace for two years. If you knew the poor peacock you could guess what that cost him."

Trevaskis thought he could.

" The privateering too, that went wrong," Mary continued. " Plentiful booty at first, but it dribbled away. He lavished money on the *Ghost*, brass carronades for iron carriage guns, paint, gilt and more gilt. If he met the widow of one of his men he emptied his pockets into her apron—especially if she were pretty. As you can imagine, the country immediately swarmed with attractive widows. Smuggling also, expenses cropped up everywhere, bribes, hush-money and so on. He couldn't keep anything."

" So there's nothing left? "

Mary swept her hand over the valley. " Nothing but this, a big farm going to pieces by neglect. Nothing but hard work day in and day out. No golden heritage, my son."

" Your husband? "

" Eli has his hands full with Roswarva and he is not growing younger. It is you—or an end to the Penhales of Bosula."

Trevaskis sat up. He was not afraid of hard work, he was used to it and liked it; it kept a man in trim, body and soul. There were people dependent on him, people he was fond of, looking to him to save the situation. That spelt a finish to his cherished independence, but he did not mind that, coming in this way. An end to the Penhales of Bosula! His heart fluttered queerly.

"How long have we—they been here?" he asked.

"Over three hundred years, I believe."

Three hundred years holding on to this one precious bit of soil! Black bad years many of them. Landings by Algerine and Spanish corsairs; the great Cornish plague of 1578; the Civil War with the Royal Duchy holding out for the King to the last, subsequently ravaged by vengeful Parliamentary horse. Wars, pestilence, drought, flood and fire, and the Penhales clinging on throughout. He could picture them, big, inarticulate, slow-moving men, such as Eli, firing at the invader with their clumsy fowling-pieces out of the top windows of the Owls' House, later rebuilding their burnt barns; existing on snared rabbits and wild-fowl when the murrain had left them no other meat; the father dropping dead of plague at the plough handles, the fourteen-year-old son taking his place, sob-shaken but steadfast. Three hundred years!—a tenacious breed.

Again the queer flutter of heart. "Well, I am one of them, I suppose," he mumbled.

"A Penhale?"

"Yes—in a way. My father was."

"George the Third is King of England for no better reason. You are a Penhale to your bone-marrow; I knew it the moment I saw you."

"Was that the first you knew of it?"

"Yes and no. I had heard gossip, of course, but I was a girl at the time and forgot quickly. When you first came into the kitchen with Jennifer I thought how like Eli you were . . . but I knew all Eli's past. Then you spoke with Ortho's voice and things fitted together —words said by Bohenna when he was dying, the name, Trevaskis; the old gossip—and I knew that John Penhale had returned in his grandson."

" Did Ortho know I was here? "

""Not until he met you that night by Trevelloe Wood. He thought you were with the Grand Fleet. I tried to get word to him, but he was away somewhere on his schemes. After he met you he did his best to leave the Free Traders but he could not, too much was involved, but he made it clear that it was to be his last run."

" How do you know all this? "

" He told me the whole story that last morning on the cliffs while waiting for the men and ropes. ' I have failed in everything but one,' he said, ' been a curse and a deceiver all my time, but by some queer trick of Fate I, a rogue, have brought one fine thing into the world—an honest man. Now even that is threatened. I am going to try and pull that one last thing out of the mess, but whether I am successful or not I shall never know. If I get that boy ashore, ask him to be merciful. Not with me, who deserve no mercy, but with the old place, Bosula.' "

There was a moment's silence, then Trevaskis said, gently, " So he swam off knowing he would not get back? "

" Yes. He knew he would never pass those rocks alive, but hoped the breakers would wash his body on, the body with the rope attached. ' It'll get there,' he said. ' It has never failed yet. It is the best part of me.' I was so glad."

" Glad? "

" That he should finish with honour. All my married life I've been in dread of how Ortho would end. I hated him at first, then I began to understand him and was frightened. He didn't mean badly, could have done great things if there'd been anybody to control him, but there wasn't, and he was his mother's son. I used to dream—oh, horrible dreams ! see him hanging in chains, his head lolling, the crows at his eyes and everyb-body l-laughing. . . ." Her voice shook, her throat worked dangerously.

Trevaskis stared, amazed. Mary Penhale the resolute and serene was breaking down. The erect and omnipotent Mary was going to cry, *cry* like any ordinary woman !

What was the matter? Why on earth . . .?

As he questioned he knew the answer. Light broke on him in a flash, also the knowledge that, next to Jennifer, she was more to him than anyone else in the world.

In an instant his arm was about her, strong, comforting, filial. He patted her shoulder soothingly, cooed at her as though she had been some stricken child. " There, there, my dear, it's all over now; it'll be all right I promise you. I shall have to go away for a bit, only a little while . . . going to be a battle somewhere south . . . must go to it. But I shall come back, I know I shall. Everything 'll be all right. There, there, my very dear ! "

For a minute her head drooped upon his shoulder, the high brown head greying at the temples, the proud brown head that had never bowed before, but he knew it was not his breast she leaned on, not his voice she heard. A minute only, then she recovered herself, the one lapse of her life over. Their eyes met for a second, brimming with mutual trust and understanding, bright with tears, and she drew her blue cloak about her and was gone up the lane, between banks of honeysuckle and trailing dog-rose, Mary Penhale going back to her duty with head erect again and shoulders squared.

Far hills misted with pale golden radiance, high in the west the horned moon, Diana the huntress with slim bow drawn. Down by the Owls' House a cow mooed, a bucket clanked, somebody passed singing across the yard. Ortho's red mare, big-bellied with summer grass, came cropping slowly up the field, fetlock deep in buttercups. A woodpecker tapped among the trees.

Trevaskis sat still as the grey rocks about him, but his heart was trembling. 'Hanging in chains'—how close they had been to it! Mary to her nightmare hauntings, he hounding his father down, unwitting, himself driven. By a hair's breadth, no more, had they escaped, not only the living but the dead. Dead! Was he dead? The broken body, released from its rope, had been swept overboard and they had not recovered it, the sea had taken the sea rover to its keeping. Trevaskis pictured him supernaturally alive, swimming joyously on and on through depths of still green crystal, by fantastic rock-castles and coral grottoes, where great weed-banners streamed, bronze and purple, and rainbow fishes darted—swimming on and on, for ever.

Other wraiths moved in the dusk, dimly in the twilight he saw them, the yeomen farmers of his breed. They rose out of their ancestral earth, generation by generation, passing in shadowy procession, no dolorous ghosts, but cordial and benign. They rose in mist, waved to him as in silent commitment and were gone in mist.

Trevaskis sat on, three centuries of Penhales were rising in his blood, the land was getting its inseverable hold on him, his own land. The light faded, a few timid stars pricked the green east. The red mare cropped her way slowly along the hillside, her feet swishing in the grass. An old badger lumbered across the field, the rabbits scuttering before it. Trevaskis sat on, wrapped in dreams. No golden heritage perhaps, but better than that—home, home!

Hardly waking he sensed that Jennifer was beside him. He put his arm round her and she nestled into his shoulder like a little soft dormouse, sighing contentedly, saying no word, her head against his cheek. From the dusky valley rose the laughter of the moor stream singing to itself and the hoot of the brown owls calling one to another.

EPILOGUE

MARY slowly opened her eyes. The bedroom was dark but for a shaded candle on the table. It was evening evidently, night perhaps, she must have been unconscious for hours. Dimly she made out the familiar furniture. The picture of Christ routing the money-changers on the west wall, 'The Judgment of Solomon' facing it; the tall wardrobe built of mahogany brought by Ortho from Guiana; the lop-sided little ship model her grandson Eli had carved for her; odds and ends hallowed by memories.

Fifty-seven years she had slept in that room, girl, bride, mother, widow. Stout-walled old haven! Staunch maternal old bed! For fifty-seven years she had taken her trials, her pains, her weariness, her tears to its welcoming white bosom and found rest and comfort there. Fifty-seven years, tens of thousands of nights, and now the last had come, she was going.

Now that she knew for certain she felt neither fear nor sorrow, but profound relief. The long watch was over, time to change guard; time for an old woman of seventy to creep quietly away. Mistakes she had made, cruel mistakes, but cruelest to herself. One could not avoid mistakes, being human, the great thing was to cover them up, to bear burden oneself, without murmur. She had done that, at least, been faithful in body and deed. One could not help one's thoughts, not always.

Somebody beside her mumbled incoherently. Mary turned her head. Anthony Penhale drowsing at her bedside, chin on chest. For some minutes she studied him, the firm mouth and jaw, the heavy-boned eyebrows, the long scar furrowing his cheek from end to end—relic of Trafalgar. Not a feature, not a trace of what she sought—except that his hair curled a little. A true Penhale.

Dear Tony! kindest and most understanding of all her good children. They had done well. Polly married to the gay and brilliant Barclay Johns, now rear-admiral, Melinda to a dull but adoring Devonshire baronet, grandchildren galore. The Penhales were in strength again, no alien master would tread the Bosula acres.

Dear Tony! Hard at his work all day and taking his watch at her sick-bed by night.

Should she wake him? He was tired out, but she would not keep him long, and it was for the last time.

"Tony!"

With the instantaneity of all open-air creatures he was wide awake and bending over her. "What is it, mother? Shall I call Jenny? Anything you want?"

"Your hand, my son."

He took her shrunken hand tenderly in his brown fist and kissed it.

"Happy, dear?" she asked.

"Me? Why, of course—but I shall be a lot happier when you're about again, looking after us all. How are you feeling?"

"Better, a great deal better. I shall be quite well soon. Any letters from the boys?"

"Yes, this evening, from both the young devils. They sent their best love to you. Ortho repeats that he is sick of London and the law and wants to come home and teach me to farm. Eli has been posted flag-lieutenant to Barclay and sails for the Cape on Tuesday. He is all agog for foreign service and talks hopefully of war with France."

"There is no chance of it, is there?"

"None whatever, thank God! It's only the young cock crowing in his pride."

" It seems strange to have an Eli pining for adventure
and an Ortho for home," said Mary, smiling. " We
named them wrongly."

Anthony laughed. " True, but how were we to
know? Anyhow there they are."

" Yes, there they are," said Mary, softly, " an Ortho
and an Eli again." She laid her head back, closed her
eyes. " Hold on to me, Tony," she whispered.

" All night if you like, my dear," he said. " Try
to go to sleep. Pillows comfortable? "

" Quite, thank you . . . Tony ! "

" Yes? "

" How do the West Indies appear, coming in from
the eastward? "

The West Indies ! Why was she interested in
those remote islands she had never seen and would
never see? " 'Fraid I can't remember much. Years
since I last saw 'em, forty or so. I could tell you
better how the Lizard looks homebound from the
south'ard—the fairest sight on earth. The West
Indies? Depends where you're bound for. Barbadoes
now. . . ."

He did his best, gave various dry geological details,
sailing marks, etc., but he had no gift of description, no
enthusiasm for the subject. England, as he said, was
the fairest land he knew. His account trailed lamely
on for a while, then stopped. The grip on his fingers
had relaxed. She was asleep, praise be !

Settling in his chair once more he pulled out his
watch. Nearly eleven o'clock. Another hour and
Jenny would relieve him. Thank heaven, Melinda
was coming on Saturday, that would take some of the
strain of nursing off them. He was on the bench at
the Penwith Petty Sessions on the morrow, and had a
board meeting of the Wheal Melody mine in the
afternoon—a busy day. Some time or other he must
get over to Treganhoe and see Philip Cara about that
bull. Other pressing affairs crossed his mind, details

of thatching, firewood to be sawn and hauled, a wheel
to bush, a plough to mend—all hazily intermingled.
His head drooped again, he drowsed. The candle
burnt lower and lower. . . .

" Tony ! "

He started. " Eh ! I thought you were asleep."

" Is the wind rising? "

Anthony listened, heard a long-drawn sigh in the
night outside, a lifting whimper, saw a curtain stir.
" Yes," he said, " coming in from the sea." His
first thought was for his ricks.

" The west wind? " There was a queer tremor in
Mary's voice.

" The west wind."

" Ah !—will you draw the curtains, please? "

" Certainly, if you wish it—but you can't see anything, blank dark outside."

" Please ! "

He did as he was bid, wondering. There was nothing
visible through the window, no star or ship-light, blank
squares of glass smeared with rain-drops.

" Now lift me up a little."

" But, my dear, is it wise? Hadn't you better
lie . . .? "

" Please, Tony ! " The voice implored, there was
no gain-saying it. Gently he lifted her, noting with
astonishment that the colour was running to her
cheeks, that her eyes were burning bright, fixed on
the dark window in a glow of rapt expectation.

Where had he seen that same look before? In
Jennifer's eyes thirty years ago when he had found her
waiting for him under the Keigwin may-trees, that day
he came home from sea.

Anthony was startled. What could Mary be expecting in the dark window? There was something
uncanny abroad, he could feel it coming, closer, closer.
In a minute, in a second, something would have
happened, something he could neither fathom nor avoid.

His impulse was to shout for Jennifer, but he stifled it. Whatever occurred must be between Mary and himself. He bent forward, his eyes drawn to the dribbling panes as to a magnet, sweat on his forehead.

The voice of the wind rose to a long-drawn moan, the rain pattered loudly, the candle guttered.

Mary drew herself erect. He was coming ! Her first love, her true love, the faithful Wind-Man. Presently she would hear the creak of the old sycamore tree as he swung himself aloft, the tap on the window and the low voice whispering, " Mary ! Mary ! "

He was coming, in a moment, in an instant she would see him again, swinging among the boughs, tall, dark, stripped to his shirt and breeches, dripping with salt water. But this time he would not call in vain, her earthly bonds were slipping from her. She would slough off her painful, wrinkled old body and go forth with him, freely, gladly, over the seas and far away to the isles of sunset and the gates of morning.

He was coming ! He was coming ! She could hear him ! Her heart raced unbearably, the choke in her throat was strangling her. But he was coming, her first love, her only love ! She heard the creak of the boughs, the tap at the pane, the gay voice calling, then clearly through the dark window she saw his face at last, spume in his bull locks, his eyes like stars.

She toppled forward into the shadow arms— " Ortho ! Ortho ! "

. . . . . .

Anthony Penhale sat motionless for a long while in thought. Then, rising, he kissed the happy face and went downstairs to tell his wife that all was over—or all beginning.